# Storm Rising

## by

## Rachael Richey

*The NightHawk Series, Book One*

**Storm Rising**

Cover Art by *Tina Lynn Stout*

The Wild Rose Press, Inc.
PO Box 708
Adams Basin, NY 14410-0708
Visit us at www.thewildrosepress.com

Publishing History
First Historical Fiction Edition, 2015
Print ISBN 978-1-62830-766-5
Digital ISBN 978-1-62830-767-2

*The NightHawk Series, Book One*
Published in the United States of America

## Dedication

To my wonderful family,
David, Francesca, and Ben,
who were there to support me all the way through,
and to my sister Julie,
who was my first critic and proofreader

Chapter 1

*Tuesday, 15th November 2005*

Abigail Thomson stood beside her father at the graveside, her dark grey coat pulled tightly around her, her mouth set in a thin line. The wind whirled the fallen leaves around her feet in a golden flurry, and the first drops of rain began to fall as the minister finished his last few words and gently closed his prayer book. Abi turned away to start off across the dismal churchyard towards her car, but her father's hand on her arm halted her progress. She looked over her shoulder.

"What?" she demanded shortly, her face hiding none of the dislike she felt for the man at her side.

He recoiled momentarily, then, visibly plucking up courage, reached out his hand to her again.

"Abi, please, come back to the house."

Abi turned to face him. She saw a broken man. Never very tall, he seemed to have shrunk to a caricature of his former self, his shoulders turning inwards, his worn hands clenched, his face showing all the tightly controlled emotions of the last forty years. She sighed.

"Why, Dad? Why should I? You and—that woman tried to ruin my life and treated me so badly, you're lucky I even came today. Why should I care for you now? You don't need me any more than I need you."

Her words were hostile, and she stood poised for flight as soon as he gave the word. He stared at her, mute in his appeal, his haggard face white with stress, his trembling hands clutched together. Abi sucked in her breath and closed her eyes. "Okay, you win. I'll come back to the house for the wake—but I'm not staying. I've got my own life now, and you're nothing to do with it." She turned away from him and strode off towards her car.

She sat for a good five minutes before starting the engine. Anyone seeing her probably thought she was grieving for her mother, but Abi's thoughts were far from that. As she finally turned the key, she glanced in the mirror. God, she looked awful! Her face was pale to the point of whiteness, and all her makeup did was enhance the black rings under her eyes. Even her hair appeared limp and lifeless. She scowled and mentally blamed her mother for her loss of looks. She was glad the woman was dead; maybe her own life would look up now. Angrily she put the car in gear and shot out of the churchyard towards her father's house.

Abi hadn't been near the place since she left home more than eight years earlier, and her heart beat faster as she turned the familiar corner into the street of her childhood. The row of 1930s semidetached houses stared blankly back at her. They were neat and tidy, their gardens highly regimented, their paths newly swept. Her father's house was no different. No different from the other houses; no different than it had been ten and twenty years earlier. The houses were—Abi searched for the right word—inoffensive. And that had been her problem; she had caused offence.

Her father's old Saab stood in the driveway. It annoyed Abi that he hadn't even changed his car in all the years she'd been away. She was sure the house would be the same inside, as well—the same wallpaper, the same stained carpets and smoke-smelling curtains, the same old photographs on the mantelpiece. She wondered if they'd removed the pictures of her after she left, or if they'd kept them as a shrine to what she used to be. Before she'd met him. Before her life had begun and ended so quickly.

Abi parked carefully behind a blue Mini she was rather afraid belonged to her Aunt Margaret, then picked up her bag, gave her hair a quick brush, and made her way slowly up the path to the front door. She felt so alienated from the house and its occupants that she could no more have opened the door and gone in uninvited than gone to the moon, so taking a deep breath, she rang the bell and waited. After a moment the door creaked open and a large, overweight lady hove into view.

"Abigail, why on earth are you using the bell, child?" cried Aunt Margaret, noisily ushering Abi in through the door. "It is your home, after all."

Briefly wondering how on earth someone could have her head buried so deeply in the sand as her aunt appeared to, Abi gave her a look of intense dislike and followed her into the dining room. To her dismay the room was full of relatives, all wearing the look of those who were glad it was someone else's funeral, casting furtive looks around to see who was going to be next. As Abi entered and stood awkwardly in the doorway, her father came over to her. He smiled slightly and drew her towards the kitchen door.

"Thanks, love," he said simply, taking her hand and giving it a squeeze.

Abi accepted a glass of sherry from a passing cousin before retiring to a corner to sip it. She was prepared to give her father her support for the duration of the wake, but as soon as the last mourner was away she was off, back to her own life, and she would not be returning again. As her eyes flitted around the room, she noticed the pictures on the mantelpiece. There were some of her, but all taken before she was fourteen. They were happy family pictures. It was amazing how a photograph could lie, she thought to herself, shaking her head slightly.

****

"For Crissakes, Gideon, you can't do it!" Simon roared, his face suffused with anger towards the man striding ahead of him.

They reached the door almost simultaneously, and Gideon swung round to face him. He thrust his face close to the other man's, his angular features dark with fury.

"I fucking well can, and I fucking well have!" he hissed, his piercing eyes narrowed dangerously. Simon almost stepped back and gave up the chase, but for the sake of a twenty-year friendship he had one last try. He put out a hand and grasped the sleeve of Gideon's sweat-drenched white shirt.

"Gid, please, for the sake of us, for our friendship at least. Sod everyone else, just do it for me," he pleaded, running a chubby hand through his damp fair curls. Gideon's eyes flicked momentarily to Simon's hand, then back to his face. His long dark hair swung round over his shoulders as he leaned towards his best friend. There was a slight pause, and Simon held his breath. Then Gideon smiled his sardonic smile.

"Get stuffed," he spat out and slammed the bedroom door behind him. Simon stared in disbelief after his friend, then with a sigh, turned and faced the swarm of reporters rushing towards him like a tidal wave, cameras flashing and tape recorders hissing.

****

On the other side of the door Gideon stood with his eyes shut, hardly breathing. The room was dark. A slight stale smell, reminiscent of tobacco, old clothes, and coffee, assailed his nostrils. Silently he flung himself down on the bed, his left hand groping on the bedside table for his tobacco pouch. Finding it, he leaned over, switched on the television, and rolled himself a joint. As he expected, he was the first item on the news. He lay back in the darkness and listened to his life story.

"The main news story today is a real shock to everyone. At his concert in Central Park this afternoon, Gideon Hawk, founder, lead guitarist, and vocalist of the grunge rock band Nighthawk, announced he was leaving the band, taking a year off, and then beginning a solo career. The announcement came as a shock to the band as well as to the rest of the world. Gideon started the band back in 1992 when he was still at school in England, and one of the founder members, his best friend of twenty years, Simon Dean, is here with us now."

Gideon closed his eyes as Simon's florid face appeared on the screen, sweat rolling down his neck and soaking his shirt.

"So, Simon, tell us everything. When did you first

suspect that something was wrong?"

Simon ran his hand through his curls again and faced the camera.

"I didn't," he stated bleakly, his voice aggrieved. "Gideon has always been close with his feelings, but if anyone should have known something was wrong, it was me. We've been friends for over twenty years—ever since junior school…"

Gideon flicked the remote control and the picture fizzled.

"You're waffling, Simon," he muttered, taking a long toke on his joint.

****

As her father closed the front door after the last guest, Abi picked up her coat and began to shrug it on. Arthur took a deep breath and turned to face her. She tensed, turning away to pick up her bag.

"Abi," he began tentatively, "could you consider doing me a favour?"

Slowly she turned towards him, her face set and hard, her eyes like flint.

"What?" she asked shortly.

He swallowed and took a step towards her.

"Would you help me sort out her stuff? I just can't face it on my own. I know how you feel…felt about her—and me—so maybe it wouldn't be so hard for you…" He tailed off under the scrutiny of his daughter and stood, small and cowed, an awkward figure, out of place even in his own home.

Abi sighed. Slinging her bag over her shoulder, she placed her hand on the doorknob.

"Goodbye, Dad," she said, turning the handle slightly. "I'll come back tomorrow at eleven. I can give you a couple of hours, but that's all. Then…that's it." She opened the door and stepped out into the cold November air. "I've got a life to live, Dad, and I suggest you start trying to do that too." Then she strode down the path and climbed into her car.

As she reversed out into the silent road, Abi was acutely aware not only of her father standing on the doorstep forlornly watching her go but also of the row of twitching curtains that followed her as she drove away.

"Fuck the lot of them," she said out loud as she accelerated out onto the main road.

Driving fast, Abi headed out of Newbury and booked into the local motel for the night. She was cold, tired, and very angry, and wanted nothing more than a long soak in the bath followed by an early night of alcohol-induced sleep. She let herself into her room and flung her bag onto the bed. Then, kicking off her shoes, she padded into the bathroom and began to run a bath. A long soak beneath a sea of bubbles would go some of the way towards relaxing her, and as the bath slowly filled up, she opened the bottle of Muscadet she had picked up at the local Spar shop. Pouring herself a large cupful, she grinned wryly at the limited choice of drinking vessels. She pulled her dress over her head and slithered out of her underwear before carrying her wine to the bathroom and adding some bubbles to her bath. The room had filled with steam, and the gentle warmth had Abi relaxing even before she stepped into the hot fragrant water. With a long sigh, she leaned back and closed her eyes, letting her body slide beneath the hot foam, wiggling her toes and fingers as she unwound.

Half an hour later she was warm, dry, curled up on

the bed dressed only in an oversized T-shirt, and making good inroads on her bottle of wine. A large bar of nut chocolate lay open beside her, and she was casually flicking through the channels on the TV. Suddenly a familiar face caught her eye, and she sat bolt upright, her finger urgently turning the sound up. Simon, his anxious face red and sweaty, filled the screen. He was standing outside a hotel in Manhattan, surrounded by reporters. Abi wriggled forward to the end of the bed and peered intently at the TV screen.

"God, Simon, you look dreadful," she muttered as her brain tuned in to what he was saying.

"Yes, it's true. I don't know what else to tell you—Gideon has left the band." He leaned towards the flocking reporters to catch a question, then shaking his head he took a step backwards and held up his hands. "Look, I don't know any more than you do. He didn't tell me anything. He announced it on stage, and that was the first I heard about it. I tried to talk to him, but, well, he was tired and wanted to be on his own."

"I bet he bloody did," murmured Abi as she watched in amazement, her thoughts racing. Apart from photos of the band on stage, Abi hadn't seen Simon for more than ten years, and she was shocked by his appearance. He had put on several stone in weight and looked ten years older than his twenty-nine years. Naturally her thoughts strayed to Gideon—surely he would look the same as he ever did? Mentally shaking herself, she flicked through the channels again to see if there was any more about the band, then pressed the Text button on the remote control to see if it was reported on any of the pages there. She found only one small section, repeating the conversation with Simon she had just seen and giving a short biography of Nighthawk.

With a sudden movement she leapt up from the bed, turned the television off, then picked up the wine bottle and took a long swig. This was all she needed after the day she'd just had. Being at her father's house had already brought back memories she'd tried to bury—and now this. She sat down abruptly on the bed and picked up the chocolate. Then she put it down again and got to her feet. Wrapping her arms around her thin body, she began to pace the room, her mind vividly reliving events of ten years before. Eventually she sat back down on the bed and reached for the phone, her hand hovering uncertainly over the receiver for a moment, then dropping back onto the quilt beside her. She sat for a moment in silence on the side of the bed before picking up the wine bottle and finishing it in a single gulp. Then she slid under the covers and turned off the light.

\*\*\*\*

Three thousand miles away, in a smoky hotel bedroom, Gideon Hawk was lying in the dark watching TV. An open can of beer was in his right hand and an unlit joint in his left. He hadn't changed his clothes since the gig ended, and he was beginning to smell bad. His once white shirt was stained under the arms, and his fashionably ripped designer jeans were covered in unidentifiable and very questionable stains. He was twenty-nine years old and at that moment felt about a hundred. He was tired. Very, very tired. And full of hatred and unfulfilled dreams. And...her. Why had she suddenly come back into his mind? Why could he not rid himself of the image? The image of the child she had been and the woman she must surely have become. What did she have to do with his decision to leave the band? Had he gone mad? Had the legacy of the last ten years of hard living finally taken its toll? Gideon lay back and closed his eyes. He would probably feel different in the morning. Then he would make his decisions. That would be time enough.

## Chapter 2

*Wednesday, 16th November 2005*

At eleven the following morning, Abi got slowly out of her car, which she had parked a hundred yards down the road from her father's house. She couldn't bring herself to pull into the drive—to be seen by all the neighbours peering speculatively out from behind their net curtains. She couldn't even bring herself to park right outside the house. She locked the car and, slipping the keys into her bag, made the seemingly endless walk along the tree-lined road. She took a deep breath. The sights and smells were bringing it all back to her. That and the astonishing news she had seen on the television the previous night. What timing, she thought wryly, her lips twisting tightly together.

Pausing fractionally, she pulled her bag more securely onto her shoulder before turning up the drive. She squeezed between the Saab and the gatepost, snagged the bottom of her jumper on the hedge, and marched up to the front door, taking care not to look at either of the neighbouring houses. She rang the bell and took a step backwards. Within seconds her father had opened the door and stood back to usher her in. He looked even worse than the day before, thought Abi sadly, wondering how the death of such an evil person could have so devastating an effect on those who had lived with her. But that was the really sad thing—her father had loved the evil person. He had spent well over half his life with her, and he knew no better. A tiny part of Abi felt momentarily sorry for him, but she immediately pushed down the sympathy and forced herself to remember his behaviour all those years ago when he could have helped her but instead had just stood by and let that woman control her.

She walked past him into the dark hallway.

"Morning, Dad," she said as she dumped her bag on the telephone table, thinking how antiquated the house was. She shrugged off her jacket and flung it onto the newel post. "What d'you want me to do?"

Arthur Thomson stared at his daughter mutely. It was as if he had ceased to function as a member of the human race since the death of his wife. He couldn't seem to form the words needed. His shoulders sagged, and he leaned back against the wall, giving the slightest hint of a shrug and dropping his gaze to the worn, dark-red, patterned carpet beneath his feet.

Abi sighed. "Right," she said, taking his elbow and leading him down the passage towards the kitchen. "A cup of tea, to start, I think. Then we can decide what needs doing."

The kitchen was cold and smelled of rotting vegetables. Half a dozen mugs and some sticky sherry glasses lay in the sink waiting to be washed, and the table was covered by piles of unopened post. Abi pulled out a chair and pushed her father down into it, then filled the kettle and set about making some tea. The milk in the fridge had gone off, so she poured it down the sink and went in search of the powdered milk she knew would be a staple in her mother's food cupboard.

Her assumption proved correct, and five minutes later she and her father were both seated at the circular kitchen table sipping from mugs of hot sweet tea. Abi hadn't taken milk or sugar in her tea for years, but somehow the effect of being back in her parents' house had forced her to regress, and she had added them without thinking.

"There are some biscuits in the tin," said Arthur suddenly, gesturing vaguely in the direction of the sink. Abi glanced up and located an old-fashioned biscuit barrel parked next to the drainer. She retrieved it and plonked it on the table in front of her father. He didn't look up. "I just thought you might like one," he said. "You used to like biscuits. They're chocolate ones."

Abi cleared her throat. "No, thanks. I'm okay. Got to watch my weight," she said, her mind immediately remembering the large bar of chocolate in her room the night before. Why had she said she needed to watch her weight? That was the sort of thing her mother used to say. God, she had to get out of here, and fast. She drained her cup and stood up. "Right. Let's get started," she said, standing back to allow her father to pass.

He got slowly to his feet and led the way silently up the steep staircase and into the bedroom. The unmade bed was strewn with clothes, and the drawers of the dressing table were all half open. It looked as though someone were in the middle of packing and had had to abandon their task. Abi glanced at her father. He coughed slightly.

"I started to take out her clothes," he explained, "but I just didn't know what to throw away and what to keep. Should I send them to the charity shop, d'you think? Would anyone want them?" He gestured pathetically to the piles around the room.

Abi picked up a dress distastefully with her finger and thumb and held it at arm's length.

"Well, I s'pose some poor soul might want them," she remarked disparagingly, "but personally I'd just chuck the lot." Her father made no response, and she turned to see he had sunk down on the edge of the bed with his head in his hands. Abi sighed and sat down beside him. "Sorry, Dad," she said bleakly. "I'm not taking your feelings into consideration at all. Just because I hated her doesn't mean you did too. You can't have done. You stayed with her for forty years." She paused and tentatively put a hand over his. "But I'm sure we can sort this out together."

After a moment, Arthur raised his head and stared at the wall directly in front of him. It had a damp patch that looked like a small sheep, and the rose-patterned wallpaper was beginning to peel around it. When he spoke, it was very quietly, and Abi had to lean towards him to catch his words.

"I hated her too," he whispered softly. "I hated her for what she did to you, the way she treated you. I hated her for the fact that you left home and never came back. I hated her for the way she treated me." He paused and looked directly at Abi. "But she needed me, and I needed her. I couldn't leave her. I can't really explain why, but I had to stay. I think I always hoped you'd come home, so I needed to be here to wait for you." He paused again and tentatively reached out a hand to his daughter. "Maybe one day you'll understand. I realise you can't forgive me, but maybe you can learn not to hate me."

With only a moment's hesitation, Abi took his

hand and squeezed tightly. "Oh, Dad." Her eyes filled with tears. "Oh, Dad, I'm so sorry."

He patted her hand and then, rising to his feet, pulled her gently up.

"Let's do this, then, shall we?" he said with the ghost of a smile.

Abi pulled a tissue from the pocket of her jeans and blew her nose hard. Then she smiled at her father and nodded.

"I suggest we bin all the clothes, and then we can go through her other stuff, and you can see what you want to keep," she said, her eyes quickly scanning round the room. "Is there a lot of stuff other than clothes to go through?"

Arthur nodded and handed her a black bin bag. "Loads of paperwork, photos, books, and stuff," he said. "I really don't care to keep any of it, apart from some photos, but I just can't bring myself to throw it all out. I just wondered if you could have a quick squint through it all and see if there's anything you want, or think I might want." He paused. "I suppose we should maybe offer some things to your Aunt Margaret…" He tailed off when he saw the look on his daughter's face, and gave a small smile and shrug. "Oh, well, at least I never need to socialise with her again," he said and began to help Abi pile the clothes into bags.

\*\*\*\*

Simon Dean leaned in towards the mirror and stuck out his tongue. It was pale and blotchy and covered with a type of fur. With a shudder, he quickly put it away again, then splashed his face with tepid water and picked up his toothbrush. He wasn't sure how he was going to face the day, but trying to do so without cleaning his teeth was out of the question. He reached for the toothpaste and discovered it was empty. Really empty. It had been squeezed and rolled and folded to within an inch of its life and had not an iota of toothpaste left to offer. He swore loudly and flung the offending tube into the bin. Then he strode over to the phone and called for room service.

"I need toothpaste!" he barked into the receiver. "Right now, Room 917." Then he slammed it back down into its cradle.

While he waited for the toothpaste to arrive, Simon lay back on the bed and closed his eyes. After the media attention had finally subsided the previous night, he had proceeded to get ridiculously drunk with bass player Charles Bond, in the privacy of his own room. Gideon had refused to see either of them and, to the best of Simon's knowledge, had admitted no one to his room at all. A muffled groan from the floor beside his bed alerted Simon to the continued presence of Charles, and he peered over at him. The bassist was lying flat on his stomach, his head cushioned on Simon's discarded shoes. Simon leaned down and hit his friend on the shoulder with a nearby book.

"Ow!" came the response, and a tousled head was raised slowly, accompanied by more groaning. Despite his own diabolical hangover, Simon grinned evilly and swung his legs off the bed.

"Come on, Chas," he said, bending down and retrieving his shoes from beneath his friend. "Time to meet your fans. There's a queue of girls at the door."

Charles's head shot up, and he began to scramble to his feet, pausing half way in an attempt to stop his head from spinning.

"God, Si, right now? Can't you stall 'em while I clean my teeth?" and he began to stagger unsteadily towards the bathroom.

"No toothpaste." Simon leaned back against the wall, crossing his arms, and Charles shot a suspicious glance at his friend.

"There're no girls, either, are there?" he said finally, allowing himself to fall backwards onto Simon's bed and cover his eyes against the morning sun streaming through the floor-to-ceiling window.

Simon gave a snort of mirthless laughter. "No girls," he admitted. "I suspect they're all outside Gideon's door. No one will be interested in us today." He sat down on the edge of the bed to put his shoes on. Charles opened a bloodshot eye and peered at him.

"You goin' out?" he asked.

Simon nodded. "As soon as the toothpaste arrives, I am," he said. "Got to get some fresh air and see what the world is saying this morning."

He paused at a short knock on the door, followed by a shout of, "Room Service!" and strode over to open it. He took the proffered toothpaste, nodded his thanks, and closed the door on the inquisitive and expectant face of the bellboy. He went straight to the bathroom, cleaned his teeth, ran his fingers through his still rather greasy hair, and turned back to his friend.

"I'll see if Gideon'll see us, too," he said with a grimace, adding, "Wish I knew what the fuck he was thinking," then snatched up his jacket and headed out into the nearly deserted corridor. He closed the door behind him and set off towards the elevator, ignoring Charles's feeble cries of, "Wait for me, you sod!"

His hangover was not even considering abatement,

and Simon found his mood getting progressively worse as the elevator made its descent to the foyer. He was mildly annoyed when the Americans sharing the elevator insisted on calling it the first floor when in fact it was, as everyone knew, the ground floor. It was in this mood that he stepped out into the foyer—to be immediately engulfed in a sea of flashing cameras and thrusting microphones. As he tried to push his way through them towards the huge glass revolving doors, one particularly tenacious reporter leapt in front of him and stuck her microphone so close it hit him on the nose. He sneezed violently, swore as his head throbbed, and thrust his face right up close to hers.

"If you were a man," he hissed at her, "you wouldn't be leaving here on your feet. Now get the fuck out of my way!" He pushed her to one side, forced his way through the rest of the crowd, and exploded out onto the pavement.

The Western International Hotel on Central Park West was situated just on the edge of the park itself, and as Simon dodged across the road, he was aware of several groups of people attempting to attract his attention. He jumped sideways to avoid being flattened by a yellow cab and scooted into the park, losing himself momentarily amongst the trees before jogging very slowly towards the Central Park Loop. He then headed along West Drive towards Sheep Meadow, the venue for the previous day's concert. His steps slowed as he approached the open space, and he found himself watching from a safe distance as the huge stage was dismantled by a swarming crew. He wasn't sure what had brought him back there, except maybe the desire to look for answers to the shocking events of the day before. What he would be able to find out there he had no idea. The only person who could shed any light on the revelations had locked himself in his room and was refusing to speak to anyone.

The effects of the night before were beginning to take their toll, and Simon suddenly felt extraordinarily hungry. He hesitated a moment, wondering whether to return to the hotel, then decided to head across the grass towards Le Pain Quotidien, where he ordered a cheese-almond Danish and a cappuccino. He carried them to a secluded corner of the park, out of sight of any inquisitive fans, and sat down on the grass. Despite it being mid November, the day was unseasonably warm, the temperature peaking at a balmy twenty degrees Celsius, and Simon began to relax in the warming sun.

By the time he had eaten his pastry and downed his coffee, he felt a lot better and decided he was ready to attempt to face Gideon again. Taking a deep breath, he struggled to his feet and set off towards the towering hotel.

****

The bedroom was beginning to look a little more orderly. Half a dozen black bin liners crammed with clothes were piled near the door, and the now empty wardrobe and chest of drawers had been closed and dusted. Arthur had decided he no longer wished to sleep in the room, so Abi set about stripping the two single beds that had stood side by side ever since she could remember. Her parents had never shared a bed, in her memory, and she understood that in the final months they had not shared a room, either. A lot had happened in the eight years she had been away. Things had not been as she'd imagined.

After hauling the soiled linen off the beds, she gathered it all up and lugged it downstairs to the washing machine. She loaded it in, added the powder, turned it on, then set about tidying the sadly neglected kitchen. Her father was nowhere to be seen, and she refilled the kettle, then ran a bowl full of soapy water and quickly washed the waiting cups and glasses. It did not escape her notice that there were no plates or cutlery awaiting washing, a clear sign that her father was existing on either coffee and biscuits or takeaways. She finished drying the crockery, then investigated the contents of the kitchen bin. She nodded to herself. A large quantity of crumpled paper and a few polystyrene cartons. Fish and chips, and Chinese takeaway. Well, at least he was eating something, and she proceeded to empty the bin and then wiped down the surfaces.

Eventually she stood back to review her work with satisfaction, made another pot of tea, and went in search of her father. She finally found him in the shed. To all intents and purposes he was cleaning his gardening tools, but Abi noticed that nothing was really getting done. He was standing staring out of the small window onto the pocket handkerchief of lawn that Abi had grown up with as her childhood garden. It was edged with neat but neglected flowerbeds containing a large quantity of shrubs and a number of rosebushes. All were in need of a good pruning, quite different from the way Abi remembered them from her childhood. The back of the house looked forlorn and desperately in need of a coat of paint, and the windows all needed cleaning. Abi's heart lurched as she realised just how bad her father's life must have been lately.

She put her arm around his bowed shoulders and

gave him a squeeze.

"Another cup of tea, Dad?" she asked gently.

He turned and looked at her, his eyes sorrowful.

"Okay, love. I'll be in directly." He turned back to his tools and lined a few of them up along the workbench under the window. Then he turned and slowly followed his daughter across the damp lawn. It had begun to drizzle, and Abi irrelevantly thought how she was going to need a session with her hair straighteners when this was all over. Once in the kitchen, she poured them both a tea and sat down at the table. Arthur joined her and ladled far too much sugar into his cup. He looked up to catch Abi staring at him in disbelief, and grinned sheepishly.

"I think I need a bit of sweetening," he muttered, stirring rapidly.

Abi laughed. "Why not!" she said with a grin.

They sat in a companionable silence for a few minutes, sipping their tea, each lost in their own thoughts, until Arthur looked over at Abi.

"I think we need to start on the attic next, love," he began, delving his hand into the biscuit barrel and coming out with a bourbon. "That's where all the papers and stuff are. You can probably chuck most of it, apart from the photos, of course, but I'd really appreciate it if you could go through it first, just in case there's something we might like to keep."

Abi looked at him over the rim of her mug. He was beginning to shed the totally lost and hopeless look he'd worn when she arrived. Maybe her being there was helping him. He had a hell of a life change to cope with, after all. She was beginning to realise she would need to be involved in his life from now on, something she hadn't even considered until today. She took a deep breath and stood up.

"Okay, then, let's get to it, Dad. Show me where it all is."

Together they left the room and headed towards the stairs.

On the landing, Arthur reached up to the hatch in the ceiling with a long metal pole, unhooked it, and pulled it down towards him, revealing an extending ladder. Cautiously Abi climbed up, reaching her hand through the hole above her head to find the light switch. She flicked it on, and a dim bulb illuminated the shadowy, low-ceilinged loft space. The space extended the whole length of the house and rose to a height of just under six feet at the centre, sloping away to almost nothing at the sides. Abi peered around her before heaving herself off the ladder and into the loft. As was to be expected of her parents' house, everything had been packed neatly and tidily in boxes and cartons; her task was probably going to be much easier than she'd anticipated.

Large sheets of chipboard had been placed across the joists to provide a safe walking area, and she crawled towards a large pile of cardboard boxes in the far corner, where she knelt up and peered into the top one. Finding it full of neatly folded bedding, she pushed it back into place and leaned round to the next stack. The first one of these contained a selection of old kitchen implements, mostly from the 1960s by the look of them, and Abi abandoned them and crawled across the makeshift floor towards a rather more haphazard pile on the other side of the loft. On investigation, the top one of these proved to be full of old photograph albums, so Abi heaved it down beside her and began to go through them. The first few albums she pulled out proved to be the oldest, containing numerous black-and-white photos of her paternal grandparents' wedding. She smiled to herself as she peered at a very stilted and formally posed pre-war photo. Her grandmother, always a rather scary woman, had even looked fierce on her own wedding day, and her grandfather, struggling to match his new wife in height, was smiling nervously at the camera. Abi flicked quickly through the book, then put it carefully to one side and delved deeper into the box.

Right at the bottom she came upon a couple of albums from her childhood. There she was, a smiling, chubby, blue-eyed baby, dressed up in a flouncy white dress, a ribbon in her very sparse hair. The photo was obviously posed and taken by a professional photographer. She turned the pages and watched as she grew from baby to toddler, from toddler to child, and finally to lanky teenager. The last photo in the book was of her at age fifteen, dressed for her school Christmas dance. It had been 1994, and she was going through her grunge phase. Her dark auburn hair had been very long and left to curl naturally, and she was wearing a short droopy khaki skirt, a tummy revealing (in December!) white top, and an oversized plaid shirt. She had on thick black tights, Doc Martens on her feet, and a very moody expression on her face. Abi studied the photo intently, her face solemn. That was the day it had all changed. Carefully she removed the photograph from the album and slipped it into the breast pocket of her shirt.

She sat back on the floor and rested her chin on her

knees. The photo, combined with recent events, brought out feelings that were never far from the surface and memories of things she had hoped were buried. She tossed the photograph album aside and pulled the next box towards her.

This one seemed to contain a multitude of papers and correspondence, and Abi's heart sank as she realised this was probably the sort of thing her father was hoping she would go through. She took a deep breath and sat up onto her heels in front of the rather tattered box. The first bundle of letters she retrieved turned out to be old utility bills, as did the next half dozen.

She was just about to abandon that box when her eye fell upon a much larger bundle of what looked like more personal letters. In the unlikely event these were love letters her mother had been keeping for sentimental reasons, Abi pulled them out and held them under the light. To her surprise, the top letter was addressed to her. The postmark was dated June 1995, and the name and address was handwritten in faded blue biro. The handwriting was untidy and sprawling, resembling a spider crawling across the paper. Her heart gave a tiny lurch as a half-forgotten memory tugged urgently at it. The bundle was secured by a thick rubber band, which fell apart as Abi eased it off. The first letter had been neatly slit open at the top, but a quick glance at the others told her they were all unopened. She thumbed through them and saw they were all addressed to her.

Numbly her hands fell onto her lap and she stared down at the letters, her head spinning, her heart beating wildly. A huge pile of at least fifty letters, all addressed to her and all—she quickly checked—dated between June '95 and May '96. Someone had read the first one, then kept them all, unopened, and never told her anything about them. She knew without looking who they were from and what they were about, and that knowledge fuelled her hatred of her mother still further. She pushed to the back of her mind the thought that her father had had anything to do with the deception. That was not for now. She took a very deep, shaky breath, carefully placed the bundle to one side, and delved into the box again. This time she came up with some picture postcards, all showing scenes from the USA, Canada, and New Zealand. Cautiously she turned one over. It was addressed to her and again dated sometime in 1995. This time she allowed her eyes to stray to the few words written on the back.

*"Darling Abi, I miss you so much. Please answer my letters. You can still come and join me. You'll love it here. Please come."*

She caught her breath and sank back on her heels, her head whirling with emotion. She stared back at the card with its simple signature at the bottom—*"Love, Gideon."*

Slowly Abi reached into her pocket and pulled out the photograph she had removed from the album earlier. She stared down at her fifteen-year-old self, all dressed and ready to go out on an evening that would change her life forever.

Chapter 3

*Friday, 16th December 1994*

Abi took a step back and surveyed herself in the long mirror on the inside of her wardrobe door. She shook her head and her long dark auburn hair fell in a tangled mess over her shoulders. Grinning at her reflection, she shoved her hands into the pockets of her oversized shirt. She looked good and felt ready for anything. The evening was going to be epic. She glanced over at her bedside clock. Nearly seven thirty, almost time to leave. Snatching up her bag from the bed, she flung out of the bedroom and slammed the door behind her, ran downstairs, the impact of her heavy footwear shaking the pictures on the walls, and jumped the last four steps to land on the hall carpet just as her father appeared in the living room doorway. He frowned slightly.

"Quietly please, Abigail," he said. "Your mother's watching her programme." Their eyes met and, for a second, a look of understanding flashed between them. Abi twirled around in front of her father.

"Do I look okay, Dad?" she asked with a grin, already knowing the answer. Arthur Thomson sighed and shook his head slowly.

"Not in my book, love," he said, his eyes moving over her figure. "In my day, no self-respecting young lady would have left the house looking like a ragamuffin."

Abi tossed her head back and laughed out loud.

" 'In my day,' " she mimicked. "It's not your day now, Dad. It's mine. And I intend to enjoy it!" And with that she moved past her father and stuck her head around the living room door. Her mother was installed in her chair, directly in front of the large television set. She had her feet up on a tapestry-covered footstool and was rapidly knitting some nondescript item in beige.

"I'm off now, Mum," announced Abi loudly, above the noise of the television. Joan Thomson looked briefly at her daughter over the top of her glasses, then returned her gaze to the screen in front of her.

"Behave yourself," she ordered in her strident voice, "and make sure you're back by eleven."

Abi rolled her eyes. "Judy's Dad's bringing me home," she said with the air of one who has already explained this a dozen times before, "so I don't have any control over the time."

"Well, all right," Joan conceded, her eyes not leaving the screen, "but I don't want to hear any reports of bad behaviour."

Abi went back out into the hall and slammed the door behind her, ignoring the annoyed tutting of her father. Her parents had both been well into their forties when she was born, and she suspected they hadn't intended to have any children at all. Now they were both over sixty, and she found herself beset with problems stemming from their post-war mentality. Until she was about twelve Abi had not really noticed that her parents were any different from anyone else's. Her mother was fairly strict; Abi was not alone in that, but once she started to seek a social life outside the home she really noticed the difference. Her mother was strict to the point of sadism, in Abi's eyes, and her father just meekly went along with everything his wife said. Abi had little respect left for her father. She loved him, but she had recently begun to see just how much he was dominated by his spouse. She would never admit it to herself, but it was mainly a desire to fight back against their attitudes that had turned Abi into a rebel. She deliberately chose to wear clothes she knew they wouldn't like, and she frequently stayed out much later than she should have done. So far she hadn't had a boyfriend, but she was fairly sure that was another area in which there would be conflict, and she was secretly rather looking forward to it.

With a flick of her hair over her shoulder she headed for the front door, calling to her father as she went, "C'mon, Dad. We've got to pick up Judy and Sammy. Mustn't be late."

She skipped out into the cold December evening and climbed into the front seat of her father's old Saab. Arthur followed his daughter more sedately and eased his spare frame into the driver's seat with a sigh. Abi immediately felt annoyed with him. Why did he have to sigh at everything? Why couldn't he be happy and smile sometimes? She took a deep breath and grinned at him.

"This evening's going to be so cool, Dad," she said, fastening her seat belt. "Everyone is going to be there. All the Year Tens, Elevens, and Sixth Form have been invited, *and* all the boys from King Edward's, too." She twisted round, to check that the back seat was clear for her two best friends, and continued, "*And* we've got a live band who used to be at King Edward's. They all left last year and are doing really well. One of them is Simon Dean—you know, Mrs Dean from number seventy-eight's son?"

Arthur nodded his head as he pulled out of the drive, turned down the quiet suburban road, and headed towards Judy's house, in the next road.

"I remember Simon," he said. "Slightly chubby boy, came to one of your birthday parties when you were tiny."

"He's not really chubby anymore," said Abi with a giggle. "He dieted all through Sixth Form, so he looks pretty good now. The other band members are Charles Bond and Gideon Hawk. I don't know them so well. Gideon has always seemed a bit standoffish." She paused thoughtfully before adding, "I think he thinks rather a lot of himself, actually."

The car pulled up outside a neat semi-detached red brick house, not dissimilar to the Thomsons' own, and a face peered out from an upstairs window. A few moments later the front door was flung open, flooding the garden with warm yellow light, and two teenage girls came running down the drive, giggling loudly. With a lot of noise and bouncing they climbed into the back of the Saab and strapped themselves in.

"Hi, Mr. Thomson," shrieked the smaller of the two, her huge brown eyes heavily rimmed with kohl and her dark hair gelled into spikes at the front. The taller girl, her long blonde hair tied back into a high ponytail and her pale, lightly freckled face surprisingly free of makeup, leaned forward and grabbed Abi's shoulders.

"It's going to be brilliant!" she cried, shaking her

friend and bouncing up and down on her seat. Then she glanced over at Arthur. "Oh, thanks for the lift, Mr. Thomson. Dad will pick us up later. Can Abi stay at my house? Sammy's going to, and Mum says it'll be okay."

Abi glanced at her father. "Can I, Dad? It'd be such fun," she pleaded, looking up at him under her heavily mascaraed lashes and adding temptingly, "Then you and Mum can go to bed and not wait up for me."

Arthur sighed in his normal manner and, after a brief hesitation, nodded without taking his eyes off the road.

"All right. I suppose it makes sense," he said, carefully pulling out onto the dual carriageway that led to the outskirts of the town, where Queen Mary's Grammar School for Girls was situated. Abi squeaked and reached out to squeeze his arm.

"Thanks, Dad," she said, adding nervously, "You'll clear it with Mum?"

Arthur glanced briefly at his daughter, then nodded with a slight smile.

Five minutes later the car pulled up in the huge car park behind the school and the three girls piled out, chattering loudly to each other. With hasty shouted goodbyes to their chauffeur, they set off in the direction of the school hall, from whence issued the sound of East 17's "Stay Another Day," accompanied by rhythmically flashing lights. As they approached the hall entrance, the three girls linked arms and looked at each other. They paused for a second to assess the situation, then all together they passed through the wide-open double doors and joined the fray. The hall was teeming with excited teenagers of both sexes, and Abi, Judy, and Sammy stood for a moment attempting to locate the rest of their friends. Eventually Judy spotted a small group of girls at the far side of the hall, clustering around a couple of rather nervous-looking gangly boys. They made their way through the flailing arms of the dancers in the middle of the floor and joined the group, were welcomed warmly by the others, and spent the following hour alternating between chatting (or rather shouting above the volume of the music) to each other and expending a great deal of energy on the dance floor.

By nine o'clock, Abi had danced with three Year Eleven boys whose names she had failed to hear and been asked out by one very overconfident Year Ten who was at least three inches shorter than she was. She let him down as gently as she could and rejoined her friends, who were leaning against the far wall attempting to look nonchalant. The band, whose name Sammy had discovered was NightHawk, were to do their first spot at nine thirty, and the girls strained their necks in an attempt to watch them setting up their equipment. Abi put her mouth close to Judy's ear and shouted, "So they're called after that Gideon Hawk, then? I've always thought he seemed a bit above himself," she said with a grimace, standing on tiptoe to see if she could glimpse them near the stage.

Judy shook her arm. "He's okay, actually," she said seriously. "I met him a month or so back, when my Mum had a coffee morning in aid of the hospital. His mum came, and Gideon came to pick her up. He seems more grown up than Simon or Charles." Pulling Abi closer, she giggled a bit. "He's very good looking—you must agree there."

Abi snorted and raised her eyebrows at her friend.

"Honestly, Judy, you always get swayed by a pretty face," she said with a chuckle, "but I'll check him out anyway."

Sammy came bounding up to the other two, her small face bright red and dripping with sweat. Her black eyeliner had begun to run slightly, and her hair had lost most of its gel and was drooping badly. Abi giggled and fished in her bag to bring out a tiny mirror she held up in front of Sammy's face. The shorter girl squeaked, and the three of them headed off in the direction of the toilets to repair the damage.

Away from the intense noise of the disco, all three girls relaxed, and Abi and Judy perched on the work surfaces between the hand basins while Sammy rummaged in her bag and retrieved her makeup. Abi leant back against the mirror and closed her eyes.

"I'm bored," she stated.

Judy and Sammy looked at her in surprise.

"Thought you were having a great time." Judy turned to face her. "What's up?"

Abi shook her head. "No, not bored tonight," she said, "bored in life. I want excitement. Nothing ever happens in this place. I mean, how much more middle class and suburban can you get than here?" She gestured vaguely around her, a look of mild dissatisfaction on her face.

Sammy, peering into the mirror, kohl pencil in hand, murmured, "You need a boyfriend," as she carried on serenely applying her makeup.

Judy giggled, and Abi heaved a sigh. "No, I don't," she pronounced. "All the boys are boring, too. I mean those ones I danced with—it wasn't even worth asking their names. They're just kids. No excitement there."

And she slumped back against the mirror again.

The door to the girls' toilets suddenly opened and a couple of sixth formers came in, laughing loudly. They saw the little group of Year Elevens and stopped short.

"The band's about to start," one of them said. "You don't want to miss that, do you?" and they both disappeared into the cubicles.

Judy jumped down from her perch. "C'mon, guys, let's go back in. Maybe this'll be more exciting for you, Abs," and she pulled her friend off the counter and dragged her towards the door.

Reluctantly Abi followed her friends, and the three of them re-entered the hall and made their way down towards the front, ready to listen to the band.

The boys were assembling on the stage, and Abi managed to get her first really good look at Gideon and Charles. Simon was busily doing a sound check, his slightly too-long fair curly hair already shiny with sweat and his round, rather baby-like face rosy with the heat, but Abi had to admit his recent diet had worked well, for his body looked lean and well exercised. His fellow band members were busy setting up their instruments. Charles, short, dark, and moody, was tuning his bass, and Gideon—okay, Abi had to agree he was pretty good looking—was setting up his microphone. All three boys were obviously attempting to copy the dress style of Nirvana and managing to pull it off fairly well. Especially Gideon. She found herself watching him as he moved about the stage. He was tall, probably well over six foot, and very lean, yet muscular. His dark hair was thick and messy and, falling to the bottom of his collar, just the right length. At that moment he turned on the stage and stared straight into Abi's face. His dark blue eyes were moody and piercing and seemed to be holding some strong emotion in check. Abi drew in her breath and stared back at him. Their gazes locked for just a second before he went back to his task. Abi took a shaky breath and dragged her eyes away from him. She turned to Judy at her side. "Okay, you're right," she whispered in her friend's ear. "He's gorgeous. Looks loads older than eighteen, though."

Judy grinned and whispered back, "Thought you'd like him. He's just your type." She grabbed Abi's hand and gave it a squeeze, adding, "Maybe he can be your excitement?"

Abi slapped her friend's hand and gave a short laugh. "Hmm…we'll see," was all she said.

Just then Miss Ferguson, the deputy headteacher of the school, stepped up onto the stage in front of the band and tapped the microphone.

"Girls and boys, I have great pleasure now in introducing tonight's special guests, NightHawk. All the boys are probably known to you, so I hope you'll give them a really warm welcome!"

She led the applause and cheering as she left the stage and moved to the side of the hall to observe the proceedings.

As the band began to play, Abi, Judy, and Sammy managed to edge their way forward until they could lean against the front of the stage and look directly up at the boys as they played. Gideon, his guitar slung around him, stood at the front, leaning towards the microphone, his lips almost touching it as he sang. Simon, drumming violently at the back, was sweating even more profusely as he played, and Charles hung at

Gideon's side, plucking morosely at his bass.

Abi found she couldn't tear her eyes away from Gideon as he threw himself wholeheartedly into his performance. After three classic grunge covers, (one by Alice in Chains, and two by Nirvana) the band paused and Gideon leant forward to his microphone.

"Thank you," he muttered nodding at the audience. "Now for one of our own numbers, 'Storm Rising.' "

He stepped back, turned, nodded to Simon, and they started to play the opening notes of the song Abi would remember for the rest of her life. As the music swelled and Gideon started to sing, he turned until he was facing directly towards Abi, his penetrating eyes locking onto hers. Throughout the four minutes of the song his eyes kept straying back to her, and by the end of the piece Abi found she was holding her breath, her head spinning, quite unable to tear her eyes away from him. She felt he could see right into her soul, could read her thoughts and feelings. She had never met someone like that before. As the closing bars of the song faded out, Gideon held her gaze once more, and Abi was sure she detected the hint of a smile. The band then performed two more of their own works before eventually ending up with another Nirvana cover.

As the music finally died away, the entire hall erupted into a torrent of cheering, whistling, and clapping, Abi and her friends leading the way in front of the stage.

Gideon unplugged his guitar and, with a quickly murmured comment in Simon's ear, he vaulted down from the stage and landed beside Abi.

"Hi," he said staring her in the eyes. "You look cool."

Abi grinned slightly. "Ta," she said, staring back at him, her heart beginning to pound in her ribcage. She licked her lips and shifted her stance in an attempt to look even more cool. "That was brilliant," she went on. "Are you playing again later?"

Gideon shook his head, his thick dark hair swinging forward and brushing over his shoulders. "No, not this time. Think they only let us play 'cause we went to King Edward's." He paused and glanced away for a second before returning his gaze to Abi's face. "We've got a gig in Reading next week. Hoping we might get spotted," he said, his eyes sliding away from hers awkwardly.

Abi grinned and nodded, attempting to appear knowledgeable. "That sounds great," she said, flicking her hair back in as casual a manner as she could manage.

Gideon shifted his position and leaned back against the stage. He looked at her under his lashes. "D'you wanna come and watch us?" he asked with a shrug, then grinned. "It'll be spectacular."

Abi blushed, despite her attempt to remain cool, and nodded her head vigorously.

"I'd love to! When is it?"

Gideon grinned at her. "Next Tuesday. It's in a pub, but apparently scouts from the record companies hang out there looking for talent."

Abi's face fell. "I can't come. I'm only…sixteen. I'll never be allowed in."

Gideon raised his eyebrows. "'Course you will. You can come in the van with us. I'll tell 'em you're a roadie." He chuckled. "Can I get your phone number, so then we can arrange it?"

Abi sucked in her breath. There was no way on earth her mother would allow her to go to a pub in Reading. On a school night. To listen to a band. In the company of three eighteen-year-old boys. In fact, she had to admit that maybe just for once she could see her mother's point of view. However, she was going to go, so she needed to think quickly.

"Our phone's not working properly at the moment," she said. "P'raps you could ring Judy and leave a message? Simon has her number. He lives just down my street."

Gideon gave the tiniest of frowns, then shrugged and nodded. "Okay, whatever," he agreed. "I'll call her with the time, and maybe you could walk round to Simon's and I'll pick you up with him?" He glanced back at the stage where his friends were busily packing up the equipment and shooting him dangerous looks. He grimaced at Abi. "Okay, I'd better go and help the guys. See you on Tuesday." He vaulted back up onto the stage and prowled away towards the others.

Abi exhaled and leaned back against the stage, her eyes shut. She couldn't really believe what had just happened. She had been craving excitement, and now it seemed she'd found some. Tuesday night was going to need some planning, and she needed to speak to Judy and Sammy and enlist their help. She couldn't help having just a bit of a wobbly feeling in her tummy about the whole thing. Especially the fact that she'd lied about her age. She wasn't even sure why she'd done that. It just felt right at the time. She hadn't wanted him to think she was too young. Anyway, she would be sixteen in four months. She opened her eyes to find herself being confronted by two very expectant faces.

"Well?" asked Judy impatiently. "What happened? Did he ask you out? Is he going to be your excitement?"

Abi tried to keep a nonchalant look on her face but failed and broke into a huge grin. She grabbed both girls by the hands. "Toilets," she ordered, and they weaved their way through the milling dancers and burst back into the toilets again. As the door slammed behind them, Sammy did a quick check to make sure they were alone before all three girls clambered up onto the worktop.

Abi grinned at them again. "He's gorgeous!" she exclaimed. "You were dead right, Jude…and I think he likes me. He asked me to go to a gig they're doing in Reading next Tuesday, and I said yes."

Sammy squeaked and clapped her hands, and Judy looked smug. "I knew you'd hit it off," she said, with a toss of her ponytail. "So how're you gonna work Tuesday? Your mum'll never go for it."

Abi nodded. "I know. I told Gideon to call you and tell you the time, and then I'm going to get picked up at Simon's." She paused, adding with a frown, "I thought maybe I could tell Mum and Dad that I'm staying at your house that night or something."

Sammy widened her eyes. "Are you staying out all night, then?" she asked in awe.

Abi grimaced. "Well, no, I guess not, but I can't just turn up back home at some unearthly hour, can I? What should I do, d'you think?"

Judy surveyed her friend thoughtfully. "This needs some serious thinking," she said with a giggle. "I'm sure between us we can come up with something."

Abi glanced at her two friends under her lashes. "I

also"—she paused and cleared her throat—"I also told him I was sixteen."

Chapter 4

*2005*

"Another cuppa, love?" Her father's voice jolted Abi out of her reverie and returned her to the present. All the memories that had come flooding back when she discovered the letters were pushed to the back of her mind as she turned to face him, forcing her mouth into a smile.

"Sure, why not?" She leaned forward to take the proffered cup from his hand. She had already noticed his hands had a slight shake to them, and as he passed the tea to her, a small amount slopped over the edge and dripped onto the photo in her hand. With a stifled oath, Abi snatched the photo to her and pressed it against her jeans to wipe off the tea before it stained.

Arthur stared at it anxiously. "Oh, no! I'm sorry, love. My hands are so shaky these days. I hope it wasn't anything important." He watched as she studied the picture.

She shook her head. "No harm done," she muttered, managing a slight smile to reassure him. She slid the photo back into her pocket before lifting the tea to her lips and taking a sip. "Lovely tea, Dad. Thanks. I'll be down soon. A lot of this stuff is my old things, so I'll pack them up and take them away with me." She paused and looked him straight in the eye, adding significantly, "A lot of letters I didn't even know I had."

Arthur shrugged. "Oh, well, your mother kept all sorts of junk," he said, dismissing her comment. "You take whatever you want, pet." and his greying head disappeared once more down the ladder.

Abi sank back onto her heels and sighed. It would seem that maybe her father hadn't been a party to the deception orchestrated by her mother more than a decade ago. Although she felt some relief that only one of her parents had betrayed her, she nonetheless felt a little cheated at having no one on whom to vent her anger. She slowly sipped her cooling tea and couldn't help wishing it were something a little stronger. The emotions that had surfaced when she made her discovery were never far away, but for the past ten years she'd managed to suppress them in order to function as a normal human being. Otherwise, she doubted she could have carried on. Now they were all back. Coupled with the news she'd seen on the television the night before, they gave her an overwhelming sense of drowning, with nothing to catch hold of to save herself. She really needed to talk to someone. Someone who knew what had happened all those years ago. Someone who understood.

With a sigh, Abi piled everything back into the box and heaved it across the floor towards the loft hatch. She wriggled around until she could lower her legs onto the ladder, turned off the light, and made her way down onto the landing. Balancing the box on her hip, she pushed the ladder back up into the loft and closed the hatch with the pole before heading downstairs.

Arthur was pottering in the kitchen, making some

sandwiches, and Abi paused in the doorway, her arms clasped around the precious box.

"Dad."

He turned at the sound of her voice, butter knife in hand.

"You finished, love? Would you like a sandwich?" He waved towards the kitchen table, which held a clutter of jars and packets.

Abi shook her head. "Can't stop now, Dad. Got to go and see someone." She paused, wincing at the lost look on his face. "I'll come back tomorrow to help you finish off. If you want."

Arthur put down the knife and came to her.

"That would be lovely, Abi," he said quietly. "I've really missed you these last few years, you know. Maybe now…" The wistfulness of his expression said it all as his arm fell to his side.

Abi nodded and smiled at him.

"Yes, Dad, maybe now. Maybe now we can spend time together again, but right now I have to go. Do the Cromwells still live in the same house?" she asked over her shoulder as she headed down the hall.

Arthur squeezed past her and opened the door. He nodded. "Yes, they do. Creatures of habit, just like your mother and me." Abi could think of no two sets of parents more different than hers and Judy's, but she nodded again, smiling her thanks.

Once back in the car—her father had insisted on carrying the box for her and putting it in the boot—Abi sat for a moment to take stock. She needed to see Judy. She really couldn't think of anyone else she could talk to about this, but there was a problem. When Abi first left home and went to college, she and Judy had kept in constant touch and met up frequently, but in the last couple of years they had drifted apart. Abi found it hard to believe it could have happened; they used to be inseparable, but four years ago Judy got married. Her husband was lovely, Abi was the first to admit that, but she had always felt slightly awkward visiting them, almost as if she were an intruder. So she began to see Judy less often. She would still phone and they would chat, but she was always aware of Robert in the background, and later on baby Thomas (who must be at least two by now, she calculated), and eventually their contact had dwindled to Christmas and birthday cards. Now Abi desperately wanted to see her friend but was too embarrassed to simply arrive on her doorstep after so long. The only other thing she could do was to make her approach through Judy's mother.

Taking a deep breath, she fastened her seatbelt and started the car. As she left, she could see her father's silhouette in the living room window, and she felt a wave of sorrow. She still couldn't forgive him for his part in her life all those years ago, but she did love him, and she needed to be there for him now. The revelation that he too had hated her mother warmed her heart, and she had begun to understand the way he'd acted ten years earlier.

She swung the car around the corner and turned into the road that Judy's parents had lived in since before the girls first became friends at the age of four. She pulled up alongside the kerb just outside the house and turned off the engine. Pulling down her sun visor, she quickly checked her hair and makeup. Considering the way the day had gone so far, she didn't look too bad. She grabbed her bag and, opening the door, stepped out into the familiar street. As she stared up at the blank windows, Abi realised that most likely Mrs. Cromwell would be at work. She used to be a midwife at the local hospital, and as far as Abi knew she still worked there. She gave a little shiver, then tentatively opened the gate and walked slowly up the path to the front door. She rang the bell and within a couple of seconds the door was pulled open by a tall, slightly plump middle-aged woman wearing jeans and a pink jumper. Her faded blonde hair was caught into an untidy bun at the back of her head, and she was wiping her hands on a tea towel. She started in surprise when she saw Abi on the doorstep and took a step backwards.

"Oh, I wasn't expecting—I mean, I thought you were the postman!" With a throaty laugh, she peered more closely at her visitor. "Surely that's not Abi, is it?" Her eyes widened. "It is! Come on in, love. I heard about your mother." She stopped there, knowing any form of condolence was inappropriate, and ushered her guest into the hallway.

Abi stared around her, bemused. Just like her parents' house, Judy's house had not changed at all since she was last there. The same wallpaper, the same carpet, the same rather old-fashioned furniture— probably the same photos on the mantelpiece. She followed Mary Cromwell into the kitchen and was waved into a seat at the cluttered table. Abi perched on a pine chair, one of a set that actually was new since her last visit, and clutched her handbag nervously on her knee. Mary smiled encouragement at her.

"So, to what do I owe this pleasure?" she asked as she filled the kettle. "I take it you're here for your mother's funeral?"

Abi nodded curtly and licked her lips. "Yeah. And now I'm helping my dad sort out some stuff."

Mary pulled out a chair and sat facing Abi across the table. After a moment she reached out and caught one of Abi's hands in hers. "It must be very hard for you to come back," she said, her voice gentle. "The memories must be dreadful." She paused and scanned Abi's face. "I guess you want to see Judy?"

Abi swallowed and raised eyes filled with unshed tears. She nodded, then pulled her hand away and delved into her pocket for a tissue. After noisily blowing her nose, she wiped her eyes and sat back in her chair with a sigh.

"I'm so sorry, Aunty Mary," she said, regressing to her childhood name for her friend's mother. "It's been an emotional couple of days"—she paused, a slightly sardonic smile playing about her lips—"not for the traditional reasons, as I'm sure you understand, but a lot of unexpected stuff has happened, and it's thrown me. I really need to see Judy if I can, but I feel dreadful just turning up, when we've rather lost touch over the last couple of years." She paused again and looked appealingly at Judy's mother. "It's all my fault. I kept feeling I was in the way after she got married. Then they had Thomas and were a real little family, and, well, it made me feel..." In her misery she halted and rubbed an impatient hand over her eyes.

With a sigh, Mary Cromwell got to her feet and moved around the table to put her arm comfortingly around Abi's shoulders.

"There, there, love," she soothed, handing her a box of tissues. "I understand. I understand more than you can imagine." She stared over Abi's head into the distance, a slight frown creasing her brow. Then she gently shook Abi's shoulder and looked her in the eye. "And of course you can go and see Judy. She'll be delighted. I know she understands how you've been feeling." She glanced up at the clock above the cooker. "If you go now, she'll be home, probably about to bathe the kids. Shall I call to tell her you're coming?"

Abi looked up in surprise. "Kids?" she asked. "She has two now?"

Mary smiled. "Yes, she had a little girl in April. She's six…no, seven months now. She's called Sabrina. Judy's been dying to show her to you. Shall I call her?"

Abi nodded, attempting to take in this new information. Her best friend had a new baby, and she'd known nothing about it! That was outrageous. She mentally chastised herself and realised she needed to get her act together and stop being so selfish. She had thought only of her own feelings when she stopped contacting Judy. She had not considered how her friend might feel. How she might have needed a friend to help her through her pregnancy, someone to gossip with, someone to shop with…someone to be there for her. Abi felt like such a jerk. Just because of what had happened to her all those years ago, she had abandoned her best friend. The friend who had stuck with her through all her bad times. She slowly got to her feet. Mary had disappeared off into the living room and was speaking quietly to someone on the telephone. Abi held her breath—suppose Judy didn't want to see her? Suppose she had really upset her friend? She didn't think she could bear that, and she edged closer to the kitchen door in an effort to eavesdrop on the conversation. Mary gave a short laugh, and then Abi heard the ping of the receiver being replaced in its cradle. She was standing nervously in the kitchen doorway when Mary reappeared, smiling.

"Don't look so worried, pet," Mary said. "She'd love to see you, but not tonight, unfortunately. She has the kids in the bath just now, and then she and Robert are going out for dinner as soon as the babysitter arrives. It's an early celebration for her birthday." After a pause and a glance at Abi, she continued, "But she'd love to see you tomorrow morning. She said to drop in around eleven, and you can have coffee and a real catch-up."

Abi's shoulders sagged, and with a sigh she turned back into the kitchen again. "Okay, it was probably asking too much to expect to see her tonight." She glanced up at Mary. "I'll just go back to the hotel and get an early night."

Mary tutted loudly. "Nonsense," she said briskly. "You're not going anywhere until you've had a nice cup of tea and a natter." She indicated that Abi should sit at the table again, then turned away and flicked the kettle back on. A couple of minutes later she plonked two steaming cups on the table, along with a large box of assorted chocolate biscuits. Abi absently reached out and took one. She dunked it in her tea and glanced over at Mary.

"Thanks," she said simply. "You're being very nice to me."

Mary gave her head an impatient shake. "And why shouldn't I be?" she demanded, raising her eyebrows. "You're my daughter's oldest friend."

Abi sniffed. "Not a very good friend, the last couple of years. I'm really surprised she wants to see me at all. Or that you would, either, after what happened ten years ago." She stared down into her cup, where tiny particles of biscuit were floating in the tea.

Mary surveyed her cautiously. "That's all in the past," she said at last, "and anyway, it was you that was the victim then."

Abi looked up at her. "That's not what my parents thought." She managed a wry grin. "To them I was the devil incarnate."

Mary thought for a moment. "Your mother had a…a rather blinkered view of life," she began. "She had her ideas, and she wouldn't be moved from them. She couldn't help how she felt. What she could help was her treatment of you. That was inexcusable."

Abi managed a watery smile. "Thanks for that, Aunty Mary. I'm glad you didn't all think of me so badly."

Mary leaned forward and patted Abi's hand. "Of course we didn't, child. Now let's put all that out of our minds for now. Tell me what you've been up to." And she sat back in her chair and looked expectantly at her guest.

****

Gideon stepped out of the shower and rubbed his body vigorously with a huge white hotel towel. Then, with his hair still dripping down his back, he walked into the bedroom and pulled on a pair of clean jeans before going over to the window and opening the blinds. The surprisingly strong November sunshine flooded into the room, and he moved back with a muttered oath. His head was still pounding after last night's battering with alcohol and cigarettes, and his eyes were overly sensitive to the light. He picked up the towel from the unmade bed and gave his hair a quick rub, removing the worst of the water, before going to the window again to peer outside. His room looked directly out onto Central Park, and as he watched he saw Simon emerge from the trees and pause on the pavement opposite the hotel. Gideon kept watching as his friend dodged across the road and disappeared from view beneath him. He took a deep breath and turned away from the window. In a couple of minutes Simon would be pounding on his door again, demanding answers. He slumped down on the edge of the bed. Well, he didn't have any answers. None that made sense, anyway. At least not to anyone else.

He picked up the remote control and flicked on the television. A second later NY1 News blared out into the room, a picture of the band filling the screen. Gideon swore and muted the sound. God, couldn't they let it go? Surely there must be more interesting news happening in New York than the breakup of a band. He flicked through the channels for a moment. Finding nothing that caught his attention, he flung the remote down on the bed and leapt to his feet, opened the closet, and pulled out his rather battered leather suitcase. He heaved it onto the bed, began to toss items into it with no thought of method or order, and was just emptying the drawers next to his bed when he was interrupted by a loud knock at the door, followed by, "Gid? Are you in there? Please let me in," from a very aggrieved-sounding Simon. Despite his mood, Gideon grinned slightly and, with a sigh, moved across the room and flung open the door.

"At last!" Simon erupted into the room, round face red and sweaty, clothes crumpled. "Honestly, Gideon, what the hell are you playing at? We need to talk." He crossed the room and stood in front of the window, his arms folded.

Gideon closed the door quietly and turned back to his packing. "Morning, Simon," he said easily. "Nothing to talk about. Said it all yesterday."

Simon snorted and leaned towards his friend. "Firstly, it's afternoon, and secondly, there's a helluva lot to talk about! You casually make this announcement, but had you thought to tell the rest of the band? Had you even intimated you might be thinking along those lines? Had you…" He paused, then threw his hands in the air and crossed the room to stand directly next to Gideon. "Had you given a single thought to your friends, not to mention the fans who are expecting a new album?" he yelled, his face suffused with rage.

Gideon stopped packing and sighed. He glanced at Simon, then slumped onto the bed, indicating for his friend to sit, as well. Simon shook his head and remained standing stiffly in the middle of the room.

"Okay, Si, I've been out of order," conceded Gideon slowly. "I've been totally selfish and didn't consider your feelings or Chas's at all, or the knock-on effect on the band." He looked up at Simon with the glimmer of a smile. "Will that do, or do you want more?"

Simon gritted his teeth. "More," he muttered.

Gideon shrugged. "Okay. Well, it was kind of a sudden decision, actually; you may have noticed that I've been a bit down lately." He raised an eyebrow at his friend, who gave a curt nod. "Well, I couldn't really put my finger on it, but yesterday morning, as we were getting ready for the gig, I had a bit of a revelation." He paused again and, shifting his position on the bed, reached for his cigarettes and lit up, without offering one to Simon. "I shall be thirty in a few months, and I'm not ready. So much has happened to me…to us…in the last ten years that I feel like I've lived a hundred lifetimes, but in reality I'm only twenty-nine. I need to do other things, and I need to do them now. There are things in my past that I want to revisit." He paused as he heard Simon catch his breath. "I haven't properly been home to England for years, apart from touring. I need a break from all this"—he swept his arm around the room—"from the hotels, the groupies, the parties…everything." He took a drag on his cigarette and looked over at Simon. "D'you understand, Si? I've had enough of this life. I want a rest." He paused again and leaned back against his pillows with a wry grin. "Chances are I'll be bored stiff in a week and be back to join you, but I need to know, and since that was the last gig of this tour, it seemed like the best time. It'll probably send album sales through the roof, too, so you'll not be out of pocket."

Simon sighed and pushed himself upright from where he'd been leaning against the door frame. After a long moment, he said, "Yeah, I get you. I feel like that sometimes, but to be honest, I don't have the courage to do anything about it. Still, now we have an enforced holiday, thanks to you. Maybe I'll go for a wander around America. Fucking hope the sales go up. We can hardly start the new album now."

Gideon looked sadly at his friend. "I'm sorry, I didn't really think this through. I kinda thought you and Chas would carry on without me, but I s'pose you can't, really." He made a face. "Maybe you could get a session guitarist for the album?"

Simon snorted. "No, I don't think so, do you? The band is named after you, for fuck's sake. How can we have NightHawk without a Hawk?" He sat down on the end of the bed, fished in his pocket for his tobacco pouch, expertly rolled himself a cigarette, and accepted the proffered light from Gideon. "The only thing that worries me," he went on, glancing sideways at his friend, "is the 'things from your past' that you 'want to revisit.' If you mean what I think you mean, then don't go there. Leave well alone."

Gideon shifted on the bed and shook back his long hair. "Butt out, Simon. I know what I'm doing. That last time when I went back…all those years ago…something didn't feel right. I think I was lied to. There's more to the story than there seems, and I really need to find out. Then maybe I can move on." He leaned forward and gently shook Simon's chubby arm. "Let me go, Si, I need to do this."

Simon ran a hand through his damp curls and sighed again. "Well, okay, then, but Gideon—please be careful. You have no idea what you might be doing." With those words he leaned forward, gave his friend a quick hug, then left the room without a backward glance.

Gideon watched him go, his mind in a whirl. Talking about his feelings had left him curiously disturbed, and he realised just how much he'd been thinking about her recently. If he didn't sort this soon, it was going to drive him mad.

\*\*\*\*

By eight o'clock that night Abi was once more in

her room at the hotel, a large paper bag from the nearby fast food place by the side of the bed and a bottle of Pinot Grigio chilling in the wash basin. She had a quick shower "to wash the bad faeries down the plug-hole" as Judy had always said, then changed into her nightwear, rescued the wine, and curled up on the bed. The box she'd taken from her parents' loft sat on the floor just beside her, screaming to be explored. Abi poured herself a cup of wine, delved her hand into the bag, and flicked on the television. She skimmed quickly through the channels, pausing on a news programme showing pictures of NightHawk in concert in Central Park the previous day. She leaned back against the pillows and turned up the sound.

"And our New York correspondent, Maria Gillespie, finally managed to get a glimpse of the elusive Gideon Hawk as he left his hotel this afternoon. Maria, how did he seem?"

The voice of the newsreader seemed overloud and indifferent, but Abi watched the screen, transfixed, as they showed a shot of a very sombre-looking Gideon leaving the hotel via a side door, clutching a large battered suitcase, a guitar case slung over his shoulder. He was accompanied by an extremely harassed Simon, in a sweat-drenched shirt, carrying no luggage. Abi watched as Maria Gillespie almost threw herself in front of the two as they crossed the pavement towards a waiting limousine, thrusting her microphone at Gideon's face.

"Are you leaving, Gideon? Have you anything to say to your fans?" she called loudly as he passed her. Gideon briefly turned his head, put his lips close to her microphone and said distinctly, "No comment." Then, ducking his head, he tossed his luggage into the limo and clambered in after it. Simon slammed the door behind him, pausing to mutter a few words through the half-open car window before the limo moved off and got lost in the throng of Manhattan traffic.

Simon turned back towards the hotel and came face to face with the insistent reporter. "So, Simon, do you have anything to add? Where's Gideon going?" she demanded. He scowled at her, then pushed past and hurried back into the hotel.

Abi muted the sound and watched as the rather annoyed reporter attempted to follow Simon into the hotel but was foiled by security. Shaking her head, she flicked through the channels again until she found a re-run of *Frasier* to keep her amused for half an hour while she finished her take-away.

When the food was all gone and the wine level had dropped considerably, Abi took a deep breath and lifted the large cardboard box onto the bed beside her. Cautiously she opened it and gazed again on the piles of mostly unopened letters that lay therein. On top of them all lay the photo of her fifteen-year-old self glowering moodily up at her. She picked up the photo and gently leant it up against her alarm clock. Then she lifted out the pile of correspondence and leafed through the letters, scanning for the earliest date. To her shock that proved to be June 19th, 1995, just one week after she had last seen Gideon. Predictably, this one had been opened. Abi's eyes narrowed as she visualised her mother carefully slitting open the envelope with her mother-of-pearl letter opener, then holding the letter by finger and thumb while she read it, a look of distaste on her face.

Abi unfolded the single sheet of hotel notepaper and began to read.

*My dearest darling Abi, I miss you so much already. We've played our first gig over here and it was terrifying! America is so big and so very different from Berkshire— thankfully! Please write back soon, you can contact me at the hotel above. We'll be here for a couple of weeks, then I'll write again and let you know the next address. There's no point writing to the record company 'cos I know they probably won't bother to pass anything on. Oh, I do miss you so much, I can't wait to see you. Not sure I'll be able to get any money to you just yet, so maybe you could get saving as well, then you can come and join me.*

Abi stopped reading for a moment, her head spinning. He had sent her his address within a week of leaving England! All that time she had thought he'd abandoned her, and he had contacted her within a week of leaving. She glanced down at the letter again.

*I was a bit worried about you when I saw you last, I felt there was something on your mind that you weren't telling me. Please let me know if something's worrying you. And please don't let it be that you've gone off me. I couldn't bear that. I want to spend my life with you, Abi. I love you. Keep safe, Gideon.*

He had ended the letter with six kisses, and as Abi finished reading, a single tear dropped from her eye and fell onto the page, causing a smudge just above his signature.

With a long shuddering breath, she picked up the remote control again, unable to face any more of her past. She changed the channel to Sky News, just in time to see the same shot of Gideon leaving the hotel. Could this tall, dark, haggard-looking man be the same insecure, gentle, and caring boy who wrote that letter so long ago? As he bent to get into the limo, he turned momentarily and stared directly at the camera, and Abi couldn't help a slight intake of breath at the sight of the obvious pain in his piercing eyes. That was not a happy man, and she wondered sadly who had made him that way. She had taken care not to follow the well-publicised accounts of his love life over the past few years, but she felt sure some woman was the cause of his present mood and the reason for his sudden momentous decision to leave the band.

Glancing at her watch, she noticed it had just gone ten o'clock, and she reached for her mobile. She speedily dialled a number and held the phone to her ear as she leaned back against her pillows.

"Hi, it's me," she said quickly when her call was answered. "Yeah, I'm okay, sort of. Listen, I'm going to have to stay up here for a couple more days. Are Lilt and Flora okay?" She paused, listening for a minute. "Oh, I know you have, but I really meant to come back today, and I know it's a lot to ask, but…" Another pause to listen. "Thanks. You're the best. I owe you. See you in a day or so."

She ended the call and laid her phone back on the bedside table, then wriggled into a more comfortable position and realised how much she was missing her home. The quiet dark nights, the constant sound of the sea, catching the rays from the warming sun in her little garden, running down to the beach for a quick surf before dinner. She needed to get back soon. Once she'd seen Judy and had a really good heart-to-heart, everything would be easier. Judy would know what to do. She always did.

Chapter 5

*Thursday, 17th November 2005*

When Abi woke the next morning, she pulled back
the curtains and peered out into the gloom of a heavy
dark sky threatening rain. She had promised to drop
back in to see her father, but then she was going to
make her way to Judy's house. After a quick shower
and teeth cleaning she grabbed the box she had found in
the attic and headed down to her car. She paused at the
hotel desk to confirm she wanted to stay another night,
then stepped out into the dismal November day. A
biting wind whipped around the side of the building,
catching Abi's long hair and blowing it in front of her
eyes. She swore under her breath and pushed against
the wind to reach her car.

As she sped along the dual carriageway towards
her father's house, she wondered how she was going to
approach the subject of the hidden correspondence. She
had to know for sure if her father had been a part of the
deception or whether it had all been her mother's evil
plan. Her stomach turned over at the possibility that
they had been in it together. That they had both lied to
her all those months and watched her life disintegrate
while knowing they could do something to stop it. She
could believe that of her mother, but surely not her
father, too? It was bad enough he had done nothing to

stop her mother's later actions, but this would be just too much to bear.

She pulled up in the drive behind the ancient Saab, not caring now if anyone saw her, and got out of the car, slamming the door behind her. With the box tucked securely under her arm, she marched up the drive and rang the doorbell. Her father had tried to give her a key the day before, but Abi hadn't felt ready then to have that sort of connection to the house. After a few moments, Arthur opened the door and smiled at his daughter.

"Hello, love, the kettle's on," he said, ushering her in and closing the door behind her. "You're earlier than I was expecting."

He moved down the passageway to the kitchen and busied himself making a pot of very strong tea.

Abi followed him and sat down at the table, placing the box carefully on the chair next to her. She cleared her throat. "Dad," she began, "I've got something to ask you."

"What's that, love?" he asked without turning around. "You'll need to speak up. I'm getting a bit deaf these days." He carried the teapot and a couple of flowered mugs over to the table and put them in front of Abi while he turned back to the fridge to fetch the milk. Then he sat down opposite his daughter and waited. Abi gave a short laugh, shrugged, and carefully poured out two cups of tea. When they were both cradling the warming drinks in their hands, she began again.

"I've got something to ask you," she said loudly. Arthur nodded expectantly, sipping his tea. "I found something in the loft yesterday." She paused and swallowed. "Something that has really, really upset me."

Arthur looked up in consternation. "Abi, what on earth was it?"

"A box containing a lot of letters," she said, watching him. "Letters addressed to me—that I never received." A look of non-comprehension passed over his face.

"What d'you mean?" he asked, puzzled. "Letters that were delivered here, but you never got?"

Abi nodded. "Yes. Someone kept them from me. The first one was opened, but the other forty-odd hadn't been." She paused, still watching his face intently. "There were postcards, too. All to me. All from the same person." She continued to watch him as realisation dawned and his face drained of all colour.

"Abi," he gasped, "you mean from…all those years ago? You mean there really were some letters? He really did contact you?"

Abi nodded, her face stony, still watching for any hint that her father had been complicit in the plot.

"Oh, my poor girl! I'm so sorry. I knew nothing about this. This is all your mother's doing." His sorrowful look underlined his words. "I'm sure that's what you're asking, isn't it? Did I know what she was doing?"

"Yes." Abi gave an abrupt nod. "I don't think I could have borne it if you'd been involved too. I expected that sort of thing from her, but although you've almost always let her have her way, I couldn't bring myself to believe you would have let her get away with that." A tear trickled unheeded down her cheek.

Arthur got to his feet and moved around the table to put his arm around his daughter. "Oh, Abi, love!"

60

His voice cracked with emotion. "I would never have done that! I am so sorry for all the hurt I did cause you, but I had nothing to do with the letters."

Abi leaned her head against his arm and sniffed.

"Thanks, Dad," she whispered. "Thanks." After a few moments, she pulled away, rubbed her hand impatiently across her wet eyes, and looked up at her father. "Sorry, Dad, got to go now. I'm going to see Judy. I'm a bit nervous about that too, actually. I haven't seen her for a couple of years. We've lost touch a bit, and it's all my fault."

Arthur patted her shoulder. "If I know Judy," he said, "she'll be delighted to see you and won't mind at all. Now off you go, and have fun." He glanced down at her. "When are you going back to Cornwall? Will I see you later, or tomorrow?" He sounded so dejected Abi felt a flash of guilt at her immense desire to get out of the confines of Berkshire and back home to her beautiful adopted county.

"I'll go back tomorrow," she said, "but I'll come and see you again in the morning before I leave." She pushed back her chair and stood to face him. After a moment she put out her arms, and they clung together for a second before she picked up her box and headed towards the front door.

Arthur put out a hand and touched her on the arm. "Will you take this now?" he asked holding out the key to a Yale lock on the palm of his hand.

Abi paused, then shook her head. "Not yet, Dad," she said. "Maybe next time." Then she flashed him a quick smile and made her way down the drive to her car, leaving him with a bright face at her words indicating there would be a next time.

Before she set off for Judy's house, Abi spent a moment consulting her map. Since Abi had visited her last, Judy and her husband Robert Jameson had moved to the tiny hamlet of Lower Padworth, about half an hour's journey away. Within a couple of minutes she was out of the claustrophobic suburban atmosphere and into the countryside. Not, she had to admit, the real open, wild country she was used to these days, but country, nonetheless, albeit rather tame. As she drew nearer to Judy's house, the roads got narrower and more winding, and she began to realise why she'd been told it would take half an hour.

Abi had seen pictures of the cottage when Judy first moved there, and it had looked idyllic. She could imagine Judy, surrounded by small children, relaxing in a leafy garden bordered by a stream, while Robert chopped wood by the back door. She giggled to herself at the thought of Robert chopping wood. He was an estate agent, and she had very rarely seen him in anything other than his dark suit. He had always looked immaculate. Quite unlike his wife, who with the best will in the world could only at best be described as untidy.

Abi shivered a little when she realised it was two years since she'd had any real contact with her best friend—apart from Christmas cards. And now she had another baby. Suppose Judy had changed? Suppose they didn't get on any more? Abi gripped the steering wheel tightly as she negotiated a particularly tight bend, and chewed on her bottom lip. She realised just how much she was relying on Judy's help today. She needed to talk to someone who understood. Someone who had been there at the time and who knew everything. Even

Sammy had not known everything. She and her family had moved away as soon as their exams were over, and Abi and Judy had lost contact with her almost immediately. Now Abi couldn't help wondering if Sammy had written to her, as well, and her mother had concealed those letters too.

Suddenly, as she reached the brow of a steep hill, Abi found herself looking down onto what must surely be Judy's cottage. It lay nestled at the bottom of the hill, a little white square topped with a moss-spotted slate roof and surrounded by a box hedge. Abi coasted down the hill and drew up in front of the wooden gate. She peered around her and saw that just past the house was a brick garage with a concrete parking area in front of it. She pulled forward and eased her car into the small space next to a red Fiat equipped with two child seats in the back. She hopped out of the car and, after hesitating for a moment, locked it and dropped the key into her bag. She took a deep breath and walked the few yards along the road to the little wooden front gate. It opened with a creak, and Abi took a tentative step onto the overgrown gravel path leading up to the brightly painted red front door. As she approached the door, her hand poised to ring the bell, a small boy erupted around the side of the house, yelling loudly and banging a toy drum. He was dressed in a puffy quilted anorak, jeans, and blue wellington boots. He stopped short when he saw Abi, and for a moment they stared at each other in silence.

Then he turned and ran back the way he'd come, calling loudly, "Mummy! Mummy! Strange lady!"

Abi grinned to herself. So that was Thomas. She calculated he must be nearly three years old; the last time she had seen him he'd been less than one. She hesitated for a moment, wondering whether to follow the child around to the back of the house, but the front door was flung open and a smiling woman launched herself onto Abi and gave her an enormous bear hug.

"Abs!" she screamed, clutching her friend as if her life depended on it. "Oh, god, I've missed you! Come in, come in!" and Judy caught Abi by the hand and pulled her into the cottage, shoving the door shut behind them with her foot. Abi followed Judy through the dark hallway and into a large low-ceilinged kitchen. The floor was covered by a dark brown, rather worn carpet, and the pine cupboards all appeared to be full to bursting. There was a huge rectangular pine table along one wall, covered by a mound of papers, toys, and dirty breakfast dishes. Judy hadn't changed.

"Sit down, sit down!" ordered Judy, propelling Abi into a chair at the end of the table. "I'll just get rid of these." And she swept most of the dirty dishes up in one go and deposited them on the draining board. The dishwasher was already running, and there appeared to be more than enough to refill it already. Having cleared a fair amount of the table, Judy wiped her hands on a tea towel and turned to face her friend. She pushed a strand of straying blonde hair out of her eyes and grinned widely. "Abi. I've missed you sooo much! When Mum called yesterday, I was over the moon. How could you ever imagine I wouldn't want to see you? Of course I understand why you stopped coming. I probably would've done the same in your place." She paused to draw a breath, then laughed out loud, adding with a grin, "But it's brilliant to see you! I've dreamt of the day when I could show you my castle."

Abi smiled back at her friend. She was the same old Judy. Her blonde hair, now shoulder length, was caught back from her face in a large tortoiseshell clip, and her still model-slim body was dressed in jeans, a stripy T-shirt, and a long black cardigan. She had big fluffy slippers on her feet and a large number of gold and silver bangles around her wrists.

Abi laughed. "Oh, Judy, it's so good to see you! You haven't changed a bit. I've been so worried you might be mad at me, but you don't seem to be."

Judy frowned and shook her head. "Of course not, you doofus. I'll always love you. You're still my best friend, you know." She paused, a twinkle in her eye. "Now come and meet the new addition to the family." She beckoned to Abi to follow her.

Leaving the kitchen, they walked through into a big sunny conservatory furnished with a motley collection of wicker chairs and tables. In the middle of the room sat an old-fashioned wooden playpen. The current incumbent of the playpen was lying face down in the middle, fast asleep, her thumb stuck firmly in her milk-encrusted mouth.

"Meet Sabrina Abigail Mary Jameson," said Judy proudly, watching Abi's face.

Abi stared at her. "You called her after me?" she whispered in disbelief. "Why? I've been such a bad friend."

Judy stepped forward and lifted her sleeping daughter out of the playpen.

"Don't be daft," she chided. "I knew you'd be back. I knew you only needed time. Now have a hold—she's really cuddly," and she thrust the sleepy baby into Abi's arms. "There you go, enjoy. I'll put the kettle on." She slipped out of the room, leaving Abi with an armful of sleepy, chubby, baby girl.

Abi gazed down at the little bundle with her mouth open. She was holding a baby. She, Abigail Thomson, was actually holding a baby, and it didn't seem to mind. She smiled down at the tiny girl who lay in her arms, her chubby little hands clenched into fists, her sleepy blue eyes flickering open as she became aware of her surroundings. Awkwardly Abi hoisted Sabrina into a more comfortable position and gently stroked her cheek with a finger. Sabrina's eyes opened properly, and she stared at the stranger who was holding her. Abi held her breath, waiting for the expected scream, but none came. Instead, Sabrina reached out her hand and grabbed Abi's finger. Then she pulled it towards her mouth and gave an angelic smile before closing her teeth around it.

"Ow!" Abi snatched her finger back and grinned down at her tiny charge. Sabrina chuckled, and Abi found herself joining in. When Judy returned with two steaming mugs of coffee, she found her best friend sitting cross-legged on the floor with Sabrina perched on her knee playing with her necklace.

Abi looked up and smiled. "She's gorgeous," she said simply, "just like her mum."

Judy grimaced and carefully placed the mugs on the table, out of reach of tiny hands.

"You wouldn't say that at three in the morning," she said with a laugh, reaching out her arms to her daughter. Sabrina looked up at her mother and chuckled, bouncing up and down on Abi's knee. Judy grinned and, bending down, scooped her daughter up and tucked her under her arm. "Come and have a seat, Abs," she said, dumping Sabrina unceremoniously back into her playpen. "It's lovely and warm in here when the sun's out." She slumped down into a well-cushioned wicker chair with a sigh.

Abi picked up her coffee and sat in the chair next to her. She took a sip and watched Judy over the rim of her mug. "It's so cool to see you, Jude." The tone of her voice gave away exactly how much the meeting meant to her.

Judy leant back in her chair and tucked her legs up underneath her, then raised an eyebrow at her friend. "So what gives?" she asked. "I take it you've seen the news?" Abi nodded, and Judy went on, "So it still bothers you, then? It's been ten years, Abi. You need to move on." She gently reached out and touched Abi's arm.

"I had, or at least I thought I had. More or less-ish." Abi gave a wry smile. "The news brought it all back. But it's not really that, Judy. Something else has happened." She took a deep breath and glanced at her friend. "I found something when I was clearing out Dad's loft. Some letters—to me."

Judy was watching her, a slight frown on her face. "To you? So? Who from?"

"From Gideon."

"But you said he never wrote to you. You never heard from him…" Judy clapped a hand over her mouth. "Oh, god, d'you mean she hid them from you?" Abi nodded, mute. Judy's already pale face whitened still further. "Had she read them?" she asked slowly.

"Only the first one, and probably the postcards," said Abi, taking a long slurp of coffee. "There are loads of them, dated from June '95 to about May '96. Judy, he didn't abandon me. He thought I abandoned him. He still wanted me." Her voice cracked as she finished speaking.

Judy took a deep breath. "Have you read them all?" she asked quietly.

Abi shook her head. "Just a few. I only found them yesterday. I've brought them with me. But do you see what this means? I should have tried harder to find him. I needed to find him, but I gave up."

"You only gave up 'cause you thought he didn't want you. You thought he was having fun with those girls we kept seeing in the photos and on the telly. You never heard from him, and, well—the evidence seemed to be there that he'd moved on." Judy paused and grabbed Abi's hand. "It's not your fault. As usual, it's all your bloody mother's fault." Judy didn't even bother to apologise for speaking ill of the dead. There had never been any love lost between her and Abi's mother, and she wasn't pretending there had been. "After all, Abs, we all felt the relationship was doomed from the start. Remember how hard it was for you to get to see him, especially that first time?"

Chapter 6

*Tuesday, 20<sup>th</sup> December 1994*

"Okay, so how're we gonna manage this?" Judy stood with her hands on her hips, facing her friend. "You really haven't thought it through at all, have you?"

Abi tossed back her hair and scowled. "Of course I have," she muttered crossly. "I'm gonna tell Mum and Dad that I'm staying at your house. They'll never bother to phone to check. You can come over and invite me, in a bit. Then we can go to school tomorrow together and no one will be any the wiser."

Judy snorted. "As I said, you haven't thought it through. You'll be arriving at my house in the middle of the night. Okay, so I could manage to let you in secretly, but how do we explain your presence in the morning? Don't you think my parents might notice an extra person at breakfast?"

Abi screwed up her nose. "Okay," she conceded, "I hadn't thought of that, but I'm sure we can get round it." She paused and thought for a moment. "I know— I'll sleep in your summerhouse!"

Judy clapped her hands to her head and stamped her foot in frustration. "Oooh," she said through gritted teeth. "It's December, Abi! It was trying to snow earlier. You're not sleeping in the summerhouse. I don't want to have to explain to my parents why the frozen dead body of my friend is languishing in their gazebo. Now think sensibly, woman! We need a proper plan." She picked up her school bag and slung it over her shoulder.

Abi sighed and followed suit, trailing in her friend's wake as they made their way to where the school buses waited. At a faint cry to their left, they turned to see Sammy waving energetically as she boarded her bus. They waved back and climbed the steps onto their own, where they made their way to the back—a privilege of being Year 11—and shoved their bags under the seat. Abi, in the corner seat, twisted round and leant back against the window. Judy perched cross-legged on the seat beside her.

She grinned at Abi. "You wanted excitement," she said, giggling. "Excitement is never uncomplicated."

Abi grinned back. "Fair enough." She brushed her hair out of her eyes. "But how are we gonna work tonight?"

Judy bit her lip. "There is one way, but we'd have to be very careful—and it does involve the summerhouse." She giggled again. "You tell them you're staying with me, I'll confirm it, and then when you arrive back, you get Gideon to drop you at the end of the road. Walk up to my house, and I'll let you in the back way. Mum and Dad both have early starts tomorrow, so hopefully they'll be in bed by about eleven. You can sleep in my room, but then around six-ish you'll need to get up and go out to the summerhouse and wait till it's time for school. Then you can arrive at the door to pick me up, ready to walk to the bus," she finished triumphantly. "How does that sound?"

Abi was dubious, but she shrugged. "Okay, I guess. I'll need to stay in the summerhouse till eight. I'll freeze!"

"Considering you were suggesting you sleep there, I think you can survive a couple of hours. Anyway, you could always call for me at seven-thirty. That wouldn't be suspicious. They may even offer you a cup of tea." Another giggle.

"Okay, we'll do it." Abi nodded, wriggling with excitement. "Oh, god, I hope it works!"

"What are you two plotting?" asked an inquisitive voice from just in front of them. They looked up to see a girl from their class peering over the seat in front with a calculating glint in her eye.

"None of your business, Collette," said Judy shortly.

Collette sneered. "Oh, yeah? We'll see about that." She turned back to her companion and whispered something that was inaudible to the girls behind her. Her friend laughed and glanced round at Abi and Judy for a moment. Abi stuck her tongue out at her before turning back to Judy. "Problem?" she asked quietly.

Judy shook her head. "Don't think they heard anything important. Last thing we need is Collette and her cronies dobbing us in."

****

Three hours later, Abi was ready to go. She was sitting on her bed, dressed in pretty much the same clothes she'd worn for the school dance, with the addition of a tatty combat jacket and a long knitted scarf, waiting for Judy to arrive at the door to "call for her." Impatiently she drummed her feet on the floor, her hands picking at the loose threads at the end of her

scarf. Her stomach was churning with excitement and—
if she was honest—absolute terror, and her mind was
constantly going over the plans for the evening. Gideon
had phoned Judy as arranged and said he would pick
her up with Simon at seven. Abi glanced at her watch:
Six thirty. Judy should be arriving right now. She stood
up and moved over to the window, peering out into the
street, lit now only by a dull yellow streetlight. As she
watched, Judy came into view, trotting along the road,
her breath puffing out like smoke as she ran. She turned
into Abi's driveway, squeezed past the Saab, and
arrived on the doorstep. As the bell pealed, Abi started
down the stairs, arriving at the bottom just as her
mother opened the door.

"Judith," said Joan Thomson formally, "come in. I
believe Abigail's ready for you." She turned and
ushered Judy through into the hall just as Abi's booted
feet jumped off the last stair. "Now, remind me, what is
it you're doing tonight?" she continued, directing her
piercing stare at the two girls.

Judy smiled encouragingly. "Oh we're going to
meet up with Sammy, go to a film, then go back to
Sammy's house to sleep." She paused and looked up at
Abi's mother with an innocent gaze.

Joan inclined her head slightly. "That sounds
acceptable," she conceded. "Then you'll all go to
school together tomorrow?"

Judy nodded. "Yeah, it's the last day of term
tomorrow. Don't wanna miss that," she said with a grin.

Joan turned to her daughter. "Behave yourself,
Abi," she said firmly, "and make sure you thank Mr.
and Mrs. Lucas for having you. I'm trusting you girls
not to be too late to bed. It is a school night." She

nodded to them before she turned and went back into the living room and closed the door.

Abi looked at Judy and rolled her eyes. Giggling, the two girls left the house and set off down the road together, whispering as they went.

"Okay, you remember the plan?" asked Judy breathlessly as they sped along the icy pavement, gloved hands clasped together to keep each other from slipping.

Abi nodded. "Yep. When I get back to your house, I pull on the string that'll be hanging from your window. That'll make a noise, and you'll then let me in the back door. In the morning, I'll go out to the summerhouse at six and wait there until seven-thirty, when I can come and knock at the door." She paused. "In theory, it should work brilliantly. And since my mother doesn't know Sammy's parents, she won't be likely to phone them to check I'm there. That was a stroke of genius to say we were going there."

Judy grinned and inclined her head. "Well, thank you," she said. "I think so. Now, look, here's Simon's house. Are you going in or meeting them out here?"

"I daren't go in 'cause his mum knows me and my mum, and might tell her. I'll wait out here." Abi stopped jogging and leant forward to get her breath, and with a hiss Judy pulled her into the shadows.

"Don't stand under the lamppost, you moron! The whole street'll see you. Come back here by the wall."

Abi leaned back against the high brick wall that bordered Simon's front garden, and waited impatiently. Her heart was pounding, partly due to their hasty trip along the road, but more because of nerves. She was going on a date with someone she hardly knew, to a place she'd never heard of, and she'd lied to her parents about where she was staying. Maybe she had found the excitement she craved. She shivered and wrapped her arms around herself. Judy caught her hand and squeezed.

"You okay?" she asked, her teeth chattering. "Are you excited?"

Abi nodded silently, her eyes fixed on the end of the road, waiting for the first sign of the van approaching. Suddenly the door of Simon's house opened, and he appeared on the doorstep, clutching a large bag and calling to someone over his shoulder.

"Okay, see you later." He slammed the door behind him and strode down the path to the pavement, starting in surprise when he saw the two girls standing against the wall. "What are you doing here?" he demanded with a scowl.

Abi grinned at him. "Gideon invited me," she said watching him. "Just me, not Judy. Didn't he tell you?"

Simon snorted. "No, he bloody didn't," he said crossly. "Since when did we include girls? This is not on." He moved about twenty feet away and leaned against the wall.

At that moment, a very noisy, tatty transit van appeared around the corner and shuddered to a halt in front of Simon's house. Simon strode over, pulled open the passenger door, and began a heated discussion with someone inside. After a minute he shrugged, tossed his bag in the front, and climbed in after it.

Abi was approaching the van tentatively when a grinning Gideon appeared from the driver's side.

"Hi. You'll have to sit in the back with the gear, I'm afraid. Only three seats in the front, and the guys have them." He gave a wry laugh. "I seem to have upset the applecart a bit by bringing you along. They may be rude to you. Sorry." He pulled open the back door of the van and indicated to Abi that she should get in.

With a quick, agonized glance over her shoulder at Judy, Abi climbed up into the van and clambered over some boxes. She found a space on the floor between a couple of speakers and, curling her legs under her, sat down. Gideon nodded briefly and slammed the door shut, leaving her in complete darkness. She leaned against the speaker on her right and clutched her jacket tightly around her. So far the evening was not going the way she had imagined. Could she have made a dreadful mistake?

****

After what seemed like an eternity, the van shuddered to a halt again, and Abi heard the sound of the front doors being opened and voices coming nearer. She got up onto her knees and braced herself for the ordeal to come. The side door of the van suddenly slid open, flooding the interior with bright light, and Simon's curly head appeared. He totally ignored Abi, grabbed hold of a couple of guitar cases, and swung them out of the vehicle. Abi was wondering if she should exit through the side door when the double back doors were both flung open and she found herself face to face with Charles. He winked at her and pulled the nearest speaker towards him. Abi crawled over to the door and lowered herself out onto the road. Simon reappeared and hauled the other speaker out without a word, a very moody expression on his face. Abi moved onto the pavement outside the pub and hovered uncertainly. Tonight wasn't going according to plan, and she was desperately wishing she were back at Judy's house getting cosy with a film and loads of sweets. She edged towards the open door of the pub and peered inside.

As she did so, Gideon appeared in the doorway and stepped out onto the pavement. He grinned at Abi. "Okay, come with me," he said catching her hand in his and pulling her around to a door in the side of the building. "Go down that corridor, and it'll bring you out into the room we're performing in. Stay at the back, out of sight if you can. They have a strict no-under-eighteens policy, especially on music nights, and I don't think we could pass you off for eighteen. I'll bring you a drink as soon as I can." He appeared to be about to leave, but he turned back to her with a crooked smile. "Glad you came. Don't worry about Simon. He'll get over it." And with a wave, he disappeared back outside to unload the equipment.

Abi took a deep breath and walked down the corridor towards a slightly open door. She pushed it and found herself at the back of a small room leading off the lounge bar. Simon and Charles were busy setting up the equipment, and she went and found herself a stool to perch on in the back corner, behind their makeshift stage area. Charles glanced over at her and grinned, but Simon studiously continued to ignore her. She watched in awe as the boys set up their equipment with the ease of the well practised, then tuned their instruments and did the sound checks. Eventually Gideon hurried over to where she was lurking in the shadows.

"You okay?" he asked with a smile. "Funny first date, this, isn't it? Not what you had in mind, I'm sure." He handed her a can of Coke, winked, and returned to his place on the stage.

Abi watched the performance, her head spinning. When Gideon had invited her along, she had hoped he meant it as a date, but she'd had a sneaking suspicion he might just be being nice. Now to have it confirmed that she was on a date was mind blowing. She sipped her Coke and grinned to herself as she watched from the safety of her invisible seat.

The band played a mixed set of covers and original material, ending with "Storm Rising." Abi felt a little thrill of pleasure as she heard the opening chords and saw Gideon turn momentarily to face her before turning back to the audience and belting out his amazing composition. The final number, and the whole set, were extremely well received, and Abi joined in the tumultuous applause when the boys played the final note. She kept well back in the shadows while they were chatting to the pub clientele, and she watched with interest when a tall thin man with a receding hairline and a large nose had a long conversation with Gideon. As they carried the last of the equipment out to the van, Abi followed and waited quietly on the pavement.

Eventually Simon saw her and rolled his eyes. "Gid, what are you going to do with her? She can't stay while we have a few beers. They don't let fifteen-year-olds in the bar. She'll have to sit in the van." He scowled at Abi and stalked back towards the bar.

Gideon slammed the back doors of the van and sighed. "God, Simon, don't make such a fuss! She's not causing you any harm. Anyway, I'm going to take her home now and come back for you two later." He turned to Abi and nodded his head towards the van. "Get in," he said, and pulled the door open for her.

Silently she climbed into the cab and belted herself in. Gideon got into the driver's seat and started the engine, which reluctantly spluttered into life. Abi stared straight ahead, her mind in a whirl since Simon's revelation about her age. She sneaked a sideways glance at Gideon. Perhaps he hadn't noticed.

They didn't speak until they were on the A4 heading for Newbury, and then Gideon glanced over at Abi.

"I already knew you were fifteen," he said with a grin, "and kind of wondered why you lied, though…"

Abi felt her face turn a fiery red and leaned forward so her hair swung to cover it. She cleared her throat and moistened her lips. "I…um…I thought you'd think I was too young for you. And I am nearly sixteen," she added in defense.

Gideon laughed. "S'all right. I don't care how old you are. I like you for who you are. It doesn't make any difference to me."

Abi flicked her hair back over her shoulder and sat back with a sigh. The implied question still hung between them, and she hoped it would remain unasked, because she couldn't have truthfully answered it. She was shocked at herself when she considered why she might have told him she was sixteen, and gave a little shiver of fear. What was she becoming? Was she, Abigail Thomson, actually considering the idea of losing her virginity to a boy she barely knew, just—and she had to admit this—to get back at her mother? Abi pulled her jacket more tightly around her and leaned her head against the cold glass of the window.

After a few more minutes Gideon turned off the main road towards Aldermaston Wharf and pulled up in a lay-by overlooking the water. He turned off the engine and sat for a moment staring out into the darkness. Then he swivelled round in his seat to face Abi.

"Bit early to take you home yet," he remarked. "It's only eleven fifteen. I guess you need to wait until Judy's parents are in bed, don't you?"

Abi gasped. "How d'you know I'm staying there?" she demanded, sitting up and facing him.

Gideon raised an eyebrow at her. "You wouldn't give me your phone number—some cock-and-bull story about it being out of order—you get picked up at Simon's house, accompanied by Judy. I worked the rest out." He shrugged. "If I was the parent of a fifteen-year-old girl, I wouldn't want her going to a bar with some strange men on a school night."

Abi stifled a snort. "You know my mother, then," she said. "I wouldn't be here at all if she knew anything about it." She paused. "I'm glad I am here, though, even if Simon clearly objected."

Gideon sighed. "Bloody Simon, he's got this thing about girlfriends. Thinks they're bad luck." He grinned at her. "Maybe I'm being presumptuous about the girlfriend bit…?"

Abi grinned back and shook her head. "No, not at all," she said shyly.

Gideon undid his seatbelt and slid over on the passenger seat beside her. He put his arm around her shoulders and pulled her close to him.

"My god, you're freezing!" he chided, taking one of her hands in his and rubbing it vigorously. Abi chuckled and, looking up at him, snuggled into the curve of his arm. He took her other hand in his, then bent his head to hers and gently pressed his warm lips on her cold ones. Immediately a warm glow flowed through her body, and she pressed herself closer to him, her mouth hungrily accepting his. They clung together, their lips locked and their tongues gently probing each other's mouths until they both needed to breathe. Then they pulled apart, panting heavily, their eyes glazed. Abi leaned back and took a shuddering breath. It wasn't her first kiss, but it was by far the best kiss she had ever had. Gideon put his hand on the back of her head and gently twisted it round to face him,

"And here endeth the first lesson," he said with a grin. "Time for little girls to go home to bed." He lightly brushed the top of her head with his lips, then slid back over into the driver's seat and started the engine.

They didn't speak again until Gideon pulled the van up alongside the pavement a few hundred yards down the road from Judy's house. Abi glanced at her watch. It was nearly midnight. Hopefully Mr. and Mrs. Cromwell would be safely tucked up in bed by now. She undid her seatbelt and turned to Gideon.

"Thanks for tonight," she said. "Sorry it's all been a bit cloak and dagger."

Gideon leaned over and kissed her briefly on the lips. "Don't worry. It'll get easier." He paused. "I may not take you to all the gigs, though—got to let Simon win some. He is my best friend, after all." He looked her straight in the eye. "I'll come and pick you up at your house next time. Your parents can see I'm okay then."

Abi looked doubtfully at him, secretly thinking he had a lot to learn about her mother. Then suddenly she remembered something. "Oh, yes, who was that man you were talking to after the gig? You looked so serious."

Gideon shrugged. "Oh, he was just a scout from a record company," he said, watching her from under his lashes. "He liked what he heard. He wants to meet with us all after Christmas."

Abi gasped, her eyes wide. "You mean you've been discovered?" she squeaked in excitement.

Gideon gave a short bark of laughter. "It's early days to say that." He was unable to keep the glint of excitement out of his eyes. "But maybe. Let's wait and see." And with a quick wink at Abi, he got out of the van and ran round to the passenger side to open her door.

Abi jumped down onto the icy pavement and bit her lip. It was only a few days till Christmas, and she realised how unlikely it was she would be able to see Gideon again beforehand. She thought quickly.

"Judy's parents are having a New Year's Eve party," she began hesitantly. "Would you like to come with me?"

"'Course I would," said Gideon, grinning at her. "I was already planning to. Simon mentioned it earlier; I can meet your parents then, too."

Abi forbore to say that she felt it unlikely her parents would venture out to something that interesting, and instead she nodded and pulled her jacket tight against the cold air.

Gideon caught her by the hand. "Come on, I'll walk you back to Judy's house. Remind me which one it is?" And they set off along the deserted road, past the rows of identical houses with their tightly drawn curtains and almost uniformly darkened windows. "Does everyone go to bed early around here?" asked Gideon in a loud whisper as they passed yet another completely silent residence.

Abi giggled. "Only on a school night," she said, grinning up at him.

At Judy's gate they parted, clinging together for a moment, their breath thick and white in the freezing air. Then Gideon gave her a quick kiss and set off back along the road to the distant van.

Abi took a deep breath and made her way very quietly up Judy's path and around the side of the house to carry out their plan.

## Chapter 7

*2005*

It was late afternoon, and the two friends had chatted about nearly everything under the sun. Abi sat back in her chair and watched as Thomas systematically began to throw all his toy cars into the playpen, where his sister was happily chewing on whatever came her way, her chubby hands reaching out in delight as yet another small object invaded her space. Abi was just beginning to wonder whether she should remove the smaller cars when Judy reappeared in the conservatory and quickly set down a bottle of baby milk and a red plastic bowl of creamy-coloured mush.

"Tommy!" she said, sounding slightly harassed, "don't give Sabrina the tiny ones. She could swallow them." She leant into the playpen and retrieved a tiny model car just as it was entering her daughter's glistening mouth. Sabrina looked most taken aback and was just opening her mouth to bellow her annoyance when Judy scooped her up in her spare arm and collapsed into the chair next to Abi with a sigh. She stuck the bottle in the baby's mouth and leaned back against the cushions.

"They're bloody hard work sometimes," she said with a grin. "My friend has four, all under five—no idea how she copes." She shook her head slightly, and a strand of blonde hair escaped from its clip and fell over her face. She blew ineffectually at it, and Abi caught a glimpse of the teenager she used to be. She grinned affectionately at her friend, and Judy grinned back. "This is nice, Abs. I'm so glad you came. It's fun reminiscing." She paused and screwed up her nose. "Mostly, anyway."

"Yeah. Those early days were quite a laugh. Trying to hide from my mum how often I saw him. Making up more and more weird stories to cover where I was."

Judy glanced at her from behind her daughter's silky head.

"You know, I reckon my mum knew what we were up to that very first time," she said thoughtfully. "I thought she was smiling rather too much when you turned up for breakfast."

Abi gasped. "Really? Oh, I wish I'd known. I wouldn't have had to freeze in that summerhouse for so long," she said with a giggle. "It was worth it, though."

She fell silent as she remembered the unopened letters lying in the box in the boot of her car. She was still finding it hard to comprehend what her mother had done. All this time she had thought she knew just how evil her mother could be, hence the years of estrangement, but now—now she was beginning to get the hollow feeling inside just as she had so long ago. With something akin to panic, she turned to Judy.

"Judy, can I show you the letters?" she asked urgently. "I can't get my head round this. What with the news, as well. It's all too weird."

Judy nodded. "Go and get them. I'll get these two off to sleep in a bit, and then we can have a look together." She paused for a glance at the clock. "Rob has to work late tonight, so we can natter as long as we like."

An hour later, curled up on the sofa in the cosy living room, in front of a roaring log fire, the two girls sipped large glasses of Pinot Grigio, with the box from the attic between them. Judy had hurried the children into bed while Abi lit the fire. She wanted to do her bit in return for the hospitality. Judy had invited her to stay the night, so she had telephoned the hotel to let them know she'd be back in the morning to collect her luggage. A whole evening and night with her best friend was just what Abi needed. Judy was the only person she could discuss this matter with—she was the only one who knew all the details, and she was probably the only one who would ever understand how she felt.

Wearing a pair of borrowed snuggly tracksuit trousers and a baggy sweatshirt, and with the heat of the fire and the warming effect of the wine flowing through her bloodstream, Abi at last began to relax. Judy pulled out her hair clip and shook her blonde hair out onto her shoulders.

"That's better," she said with a sigh. "I need to keep it up during the day so little hands don't keep pulling it, but it's a real relief to let it out at night." She glanced over at Abi in the light of the fire, adding enviously, "Your hair's as gorgeous as ever."

Abi smiled and subconsciously put a hand up to her head and pushed a strand of auburn hair behind her ear.

"Ta. I like it," she said with a childish giggle. She stared into the fire for a moment, then turned to Judy. "Shall we?" She pulled out the first bundle of letters.

Judy gasped when she saw how many there were,

and leaned forward for a better look.

"Oh, my god," she whispered. "He wrote all those to you? Oh, Abi, this is so sad! You poor thing." She gently picked up one of the envelopes and peered at it. "This one's open," she observed, frowning.

Abi nodded and reached over to take it.

"Yes. Apparently that bitch read the first one, then just kept the rest, unopened." She grimaced. "I guess it's better that she didn't open them all. That would have been even worse." She reached down into the box again and pulled out a pile of picture postcards. "She must have read these, I s'pose. That sucks, too." Abi handed the postcards to Judy, who flicked through them in amazement.

"Abs, he must have sent one from each place he visited. And they all say pretty much the same thing, *'Come and join me, you'd love it here.'* Oh, Abi, how could she?"

Abi shrugged and tossed the bundle of letters back into the box.

"Because that's who she was," she said flatly. "She was a total bitch who for some reason hated her only daughter. She was a control freak whose only mission in life was to make things difficult for her husband and child." She paused and looked at Judy, her eyes sorrowful. "And she certainly managed to do that really well." She stuck her hand back into the box again, "There are some photos, too," she said, pulling out a paper wallet. "I suspect these are the ones we took at that New Year's Eve party your parents had. I always wondered what happened to them. She must have taken them when they arrived in the post, too." She hesitated for a moment with the photos in her hand before thrusting them at Judy. "You look. I don't think I can bear to."

Judy took them and tipped them out into her lap. She quickly flicked through them all, nodding.

"Yep," she said, "loads of the party. Lots of you and me, and several of Gideon. There's a lovely one of the two of you…" She paused as she saw Abi's face. "But let's not look at that now." She replaced the pictures in their wallet and put them aside onto the coffee table, then picked up the bottle of wine and leaned over to top up Abi's glass. "You can look at them later, when you feel more like it," she said calmly, leaning back against the cushions.

Abi picked up the box and gently placed it on the floor to the side of the sofa.

"Okay," she said with a sigh. "I really can't do this just now. Why am I feeling quite so bad, Jude? I really thought I'd put all this behind me. Almost."

"Oh, god, Abi, what d'you expect? Not only have you made this awful discovery about your mother doing something horrible that helped to ruin your life, but the news of Gideon's split from the band coming at the same time… It's a wonder you're even upright!"

Abi gave her a watery grin. "That's why I need the help of my best friend." She raised her wine glass and took a long swig, adding cheekily, "And you, of course!"

****

Gideon stretched his long legs out and luxuriated in the warmth from the huge log fire that crackled just a few feet in front of him. He took a long swig from the bottle of beer in his hand and closed his eyes with a sigh.

"Thanks for this, guys," he said. "You have no idea just how good this feels, to be away from…everything. I've just had enough of everything and everyone to do with the music business—and the media!" He opened his eyes and raised his glass to his hosts.

"You're more than welcome, Gideon." The slim, dark-haired woman curled up on the hearth rug at the feet of her lanky husband smiled. "You should always know you can use us as a bolt hole. Have some more clams?" She held out a loaded plate towards Gideon. He shook his head slightly and adjusted his position on the deep-cushioned sofa.

He had fled Manhattan the day before and headed straight for Martha's Vineyard, where he knew he would find a welcome with his old friends. He had first met Kurt and Sonia van Dieman when he came to America on tour nearly ten years before, and they had taken pity on the raw young musician, so far from home and clearly in mourning for the loss of a love. They had taken him under their wing, and over the years a relationship formed between the three of them that Gideon had to admit was far stronger than any other he'd ever experienced. They were the only people he felt comfortable talking to about Abi, and as he leaned back against their welcoming cushions, he found himself spilling out his heart to them yet again. Over the years, whenever something was not right in his life, he had escaped to Martha's Vineyard and the sanctuary of their home to sort himself out. Right now his plan was to go back to England, but before he embarked on his mission he needed the energy boost that the Vineyard and the company of his friends always gave him.

He had arrived the previous evening and spent the day relaxing around the island and enjoying the unseasonably warm temperatures. Now the evening was drawing in, the temperature had dropped, and Gideon was very glad of the warmth of the log fire. By the morning he might feel ready to take on the next stage of his journey.

His main aim was to return to England, avoiding the media attention that seemed to follow him everywhere. Luckily Kurt had his own Lear jet, kept on the Vineyard, and had offered Gideon safe passage to a location close to where his parents resided in the South of England. Gideon stretched and sat up.

"I know it's early, but I think I'll hit the sack, guys. Got a long day tomorrow. Are you sure you don't mind flying me, Kurt? It's really good of you."

Kurt, a tall, spare, balding man in his early forties, waved a hand at Gideon.

"'Course not, man, no problem. Sonia and I fancy a trip to England anyway. Been a while since we visited," he said, ruffling his wife's hair as he spoke.

Sonia slapped his hand away and stood up.

"D'you need anything else in your room, Gideon?" She gathered up the empty plates they had left around the fire. He shook his head, so she went on. "I'll wake you at five thirty. Kurt says we need to leave early." She paused and laid a hand on Gideon's arm as he passed by. "It'll be fine, Gid. I'm sure you'll be able to lay all your ghosts to rest." And she stood on tiptoe and kissed him lightly on the cheek.

He patted her on the shoulder, waved a hand to Kurt, and made his way up the open wooden staircase to the guest bedroom overlooking the sea. He stood for a moment at the window, gazing down on the lights of the town and the boats bobbing out in the bay, before pulling off his clothes and sliding between the sheets. He checked his mobile before he turned out the light and found thirty-seven missed calls and seventeen text messages. He rolled his eyes and checked the first few. A large number were from Simon, a few from Chas, and most of the rest from the band's manager—almost certainly irate. With a quick movement of his finger he deleted them all and turned his phone off. He flicked off the bedside light and lay in the semi-darkness staring at the shadows playing on the ceiling above his head. The full moon shone directly into his room and cast an eerie glow over everything. As he drifted off to sleep, he found himself wondering if the moon was shining down on Abi, as well.

****

Abi sat up in bed and hugged her knees. She was cosily tucked into the single bed of the tiny guest room that nestled in the converted attic of Judy and Robert's cottage. The roof sloped so steeply she couldn't sit upright in bed without danger of a headache, and the only window was a tiny Velux affair in the ceiling. It sported a gaily striped red-and-white roller blind, but Abi had left it open so she could see the stars in the clear winter sky. She glanced at her watch. It was well past midnight. Robert had returned home at half past eleven, and Abi had felt she should give them some time together, so she had excused herself and scurried up to her room laden with an assortment of towels and toiletries Judy had pressed onto her. She peered over into the shadowy far corner of the room where her precious box was tucked under the only chair. She sighed. Sleep was an age away, and she felt her gaze drawn, tantalized, towards the box. She was feeling stronger now, after her day with Judy, and she wondered if she was ready to take a look through the photographs.

She took a deep breath, then slid out of bed and padded barefoot across the wooden floor to the corner of the room. As she passed under the skylight, the light from the full moon caught her attention, and she stared up at the beautiful sight in the night sky. A small shiver passed through her, and she bent down, retrieved her box, and scampered back to bed.

She had no bedside light, so she decided to use the torch built into her phone rather than put on the overhead light. Delving into the box, she pulled out the wallet of photographs, then slithered back down under the covers, rolled onto her stomach, and switched on the torch. Biting her lip in anticipation, Abi gently drew the pile of glossy prints out of the wallet and laid them on the pillow. The top one was of her and Judy dressed up ready for the New Year's Eve party. She couldn't help grinning to see the large quantities of glittery eye makeup they both sported, and the curious coloured streaks that adorned their hair. They were both wearing flowered dresses but had managed to make them look disreputable with the addition of some tatty accessories and the fact they were both wearing Doc Martens on their feet. Abi grinned and put the photo at the bottom of the pile.

The next few proved to be general pictures of the decorations and the food, and Judy's mum icing a cake, wearing a party hat. She turned over the next one, and there was Simon, a sulky look on his round face, leaning nonchalantly against the mantelpiece. If ever anyone looked like they'd rather be anywhere else but there, that was Simon. Abi shook her head. He had really had issues at that time. He'd been nearly as much of a problem as her mother. The next photo showed Judy hiding in the cupboard under the stairs with a half-drunk bottle of wine and a very red face, and the next one was, surprisingly, of Abi's parents. They were very conservatively dressed, her father in grey trousers with a sports jacket and tie and her mother in a severe purple belted dress and sensible black shoes. Neither looked happy, and her mother looked decidedly disapproving. Abi couldn't help wondering again why they had actually gone to the party. She paused her search and reached out from under her quilt to have a quick swig from the glass of water by the bed. Then she pulled the quilt right up over her head and turned over the next picture.

For a moment the world disappeared. There was a rushing sound in her ears, and her head spun. This was the picture she'd been awaiting with both trepidation and anticipation, and her fingers tightened, badly creasing the edges. There they were. Eighteen-year-old Gideon and fifteen-year-old Abi. They were both smiling widely, and Gideon had his arm around her. Her head was resting on his shoulder, and her hair was falling across her face. Her mind raced back to the very second the picture had been taken, and a sob caught in her throat. How different things should have been! If only she'd been just a bit older and wiser. If only her mother hadn't been such an evil bitch. And now Gideon had left the band. For all she knew, he could be on his way back to England; and for all these years he'd thought she had abandoned him. He knew nothing of what had happened after he left, nothing of the hell her mother had put her through and the agony she had suffered for years afterwards. Her head shot up, and she stared at the wall behind the bed. The agony she was still suffering. What had happened to her in the months following Gideon's departure had left her scarred for life, and he knew nothing of it.

Chapter 8

*Saturday, 31<sup>st</sup> December 1994*

"Judy, come and finish setting out the food, please. You can have fun later!" The sound of her mother's voice brought Judy's head round the kitchen door.

"What, now, Mum? Abi's just arrived. We were going to do our makeup."

Mary Cromwell looked at her daughter over her glasses.

"Yes, now, Judy. Plenty of time for makeup later. Abi can help," she said firmly, nodding at Abi as she sidled into the room in the wake of her friend.

"Hi, Aunty Mary. Thanks for inviting me," she said politely, adding, "I actually think Mum and Dad are coming later, too." Her voice showed her surprise and displeasure.

Mary Cromwell nodded briefly. "Yes, I think they are. I saw your father the other day, and he mentioned they might." She paused and looked quizzically at Abi. "I must say, I was rather surprised. They don't normally join in any social activities."

Abi grimaced. "I think they're coming to keep an eye on me," she said with a sigh. "I know they've heard about Gideon, and they probably want to make sure I behave myself."

Mary raised her eyebrows. "I hope you will while

you're in my house!" She chuckled and applied herself once more to her cooking.

Judy caught Abi by the hand and dragged her into the dining room.

"Is he definitely coming?" she asked in a loud whisper. "Simon wouldn't tell me."

Abi snorted. "Simon's probably trying to put him off," she said crossly. "You know what he's like about girlfriends."

Judy giggled. "Don't worry. I'll keep him busy so you two can get some time together," she said serenely, moving to the dining table and starting to lay out some placemats. Abi grabbed a pile of paper napkins and began to fold them into triangles.

"I don't think Simon's the main problem tonight," she said. "How are you going to keep my parents occupied?"

Judy grinned at her over her shoulder.

"All sorted," she said. "Dad's going to show all the oldies his holiday slides. That should keep 'em busy for hours."

Abi's eyes widened in surprise.

"What a curious thing to do at a New Year's Eve party." She giggled. "That doesn't sound much fun."

Judy shrugged. "Well, it is their party, I s'pose," she conceded, "and since there's no way either of us would be allowed to go to a proper party anywhere, we'll have to make do. We're very lucky Gideon and Simon are coming. I'm sure they could be somewhere much more fun if they wanted to."

By seven o'clock the girls had finished laying out the food, done their makeup, streaked each other's hair with spray-on colour, and were sitting on the stairs waiting impatiently for something to happen. Gideon had told Abi he would be arriving with Simon's family at about eight, and she was seriously wondering how she was going to get through the next hour. Judy nudged her friend.

"Let's get some wine," she suggested with a grin. "We can hide a bottle just for us. No one'll notice. Dad bought up most of the supermarket."

She pulled Abi to her feet, and they jumped down the stairs and went into the kitchen. Judy's mother was upstairs getting dressed, and her father was setting up his slide show in the living room, so the girls were able to raid the fridge with no risk of discovery. Judy pulled out a bottle of Muscadet and peered at the label.

"Dry white," she muttered to herself. She looked back at Abi. "Is dry white okay, d'you think?"

Abi shrugged; her experience of wine was limited to a glass with Christmas dinner, and she had no idea what it might have been.

"Probably," she said. "Is it nice and cold?"

Judy held the bottle against her cheek and nodded.

"Yeah, really cold. Let's hide it somewhere." She looked furtively around the room.

Abi shook her head. "Not in here, you twit. How can we ever get to it when your mum'll be in and out of the kitchen all night?" She stepped out into the hall. "How about in the cupboard under the stairs?" She opened the door and peered in. The space was dark and cobwebby and partially filled with coats and boots, but it seemed like a safe place to secrete their bottle, and Judy hid it in the far corner along with a couple of glasses. She crawled out backwards and grinned at Abi.

"There, we can get to that easily. Better not start it

yet. Mum might notice, this early in the evening."

Giggling together, they made their way back upstairs to Judy's bedroom and positioned themselves at the window, to be best placed to see the guests arriving. Abi picked up the large panda that lived on Judy's bed and cuddled it to her.

"How many people are coming?" she asked burying her face in the toy's fur.

"Oh, god, hundreds!" Judy said, rolling her eyes. "Mum's invited the whole of our street and most of yours, plus her colleagues from the hospital, and most of Dad's friends from work, too." She paused, and then added morosely, "All old and decrepit, of course, except us."

Abi sat down on the window seat and held the panda tighter.

"Not quite all," she said, her eyes shining. "I'm really worried he's going to get bored and want to go somewhere else. What should I do if he does?"

Judy frowned at her. "He won't," she said firmly. "If he's agreed to come at all, it's only because of you, and so he won't go anywhere without you. And he must know you won't be allowed to go to a proper party."

Abi stared at her. "I wasn't allowed to go to the gig with him," she pointed out. "But I still went."

Judy was peering down into the street below and answered without looking at her friend.

"Well, you can't this time," she said decisively. "Your parents'll be here. I s'pect you'll have to go home with them." She leaned forward and pressed her face against the window. "Ooh, look, guests arriving! Now, who is it?" She opened the window to get a better look, letting in a blast of icy air.

Abi shivered and moved away. "Who is it?" she asked nervously.

Judy brought her head back in and closed the window.

"Couple of Mum's work people," she said with a shrug. "Shall we go downstairs and be sociable?"

It was another half an hour before Simon, his parents, and Gideon arrived, and Abi was beginning to think they'd changed their minds. She and Judy had made their first visit to the understairs cupboard, and amidst much hilarity had managed to get the cork out of the bottle and pour themselves a glass each. They both found the wine rather too dry, but neither was prepared to admit it, so they downed it as fast as they could manage, then hid the bottle again and re-joined the guests just as Mary was greeting Gideon and the Deans at the door.

Abi shoved Judy in front of her as they emerged into the hallway. Gideon was being introduced to Judy's parents and was shaking hands politely. He was very tidily dressed in clean jeans, a gleaming white shirt open at the neck to reveal a black T-shirt, and a khaki combat jacket. As he shook Mr. Cromwell's hand, his eyes met Abi's, and she detected the slightest hint of a wink.

"Hi," he said strolling over to where the two girls waited by the kitchen door. He leaned casually against the doorframe, his hands in his pockets. "You okay?"

Abi nodded and felt herself blushing warmly. She dipped her head to cast her hair over her face and shifted her position so she was more in the shadows. Judy glanced at her and tutted.

"Right, you two, now go somewhere and talk," she

ordered, catching both their wrists and propelling them into the dining room. "I'll look after Simon." She vanished in a swirl of skirt and left them alone.

The dining room was deserted, due to the fact most of the guests were being ushered directly into the living room to see the slide show, and Abi found herself standing facing Gideon less than a foot away. She smiled nervously.

"Did you have a good Christmas?" she asked, trying to be polite.

He nodded. "Yeah. Not bad. Bit boring." He paused. "We had another gig on Boxing Day."

Abi grinned. "I bet Simon was glad I wasn't there."

Gideon gave a short laugh. "Yes, he did seem in a better mood. The gig went well. We've got a meeting with that scout next week. In London."

Abi gazed up at him in awe. "Wow, that all sounds so…" She searched for the right word, came up with, "grown-up," and immediately bit her tongue. How incredibly childish she must sound. She blushed again and looked down at her feet. Oh, why did she have to open her mouth? If she just stood there and kept quiet he would like her much better… His hand touched her shoulder, and she looked up to find him smiling broadly down at her, his lips just inches from her own.

"Abi, stop worrying," he said quietly. "I like you." His mouth came down on hers as his arms slid around her body and pulled her to him. She snaked her arms up around his neck and pressed closer, her lips responding to his kiss. When they finally pulled apart, Gideon grinned down at her.

"That's better," he said. "You look much more like yourself. Now I want to meet your parents. Are they here?" He started to move towards the door.

Abi grabbed his arm. "I don't think they're here yet," she said, panic in her voice. "Gideon, they won't like you." He glanced round at her and raised his eyebrows. "No, no, it's not you. They don't like anyone. Especially me," she ended sadly.

Gideon looked at her in surprise, then threw back his head and roared with laughter.

"Abi, you kill me!" he spluttered. "Of course they like you. They're your parents." He paused and nodded. "You're right that they probably won't like me, but that's fairly normal. Still want to meet them, though," he added firmly.

Abi sighed and, moving away from him, began to pick at the food on the dining table. She turned back to face him, a sausage on a stick in her hand.

"Dad's okay, I s'pose," she conceded. "But Mum's a bully. She bullies Dad, and she bullies me, and she hates everyone. She'll do all she can to prevent us from seeing each other, mark my words," she finished darkly, and popped the sausage into her mouth.

At that moment Judy's head appeared around the door.

"Your parents are here, Abs," she said. "They're asking for you, and I think you'd better come *now*." She grimaced as she disappeared from view again.

Abi took a deep breath and started towards the door.

"C'mon then," she said resignedly. "Let's get it over with. Oh, yes, they're very old, too. Don't be surprised."

Gideon chuckled. "S'okay, mine are pretty old too. I know what it's like." He gave her a push towards the door, leaving her realising she knew next to nothing about his family—and she hadn't even asked.

Joan Thomson was standing at the bottom of the stairs with her husband, in stilted conversation with Judy's father, when Abi and Gideon appeared. She fixed her daughter with a stern gaze.

"There you are, Abigail," she said, frowning slightly. "I hope you haven't been making a nuisance of yourself."

Abi bit back a retort and took a deep breath. "Hello, Mum. No, I've been helping get the party ready." She added nervously, "This is Gideon."

Joan narrowed her eyes and surveyed Gideon.

"How old are you?" she asked abruptly.

Gideon stepped forward and held out his hand to her. She took it reluctantly and gave it a peremptory shake.

"Hello, Mrs Thomson. Pleased to meet you. I'm eighteen and a half," he said with a smile.

Joan's eyebrows shot up as she pulled her hand away.

"And how do you know my daughter? I hope you're not making her neglect her studies. She's only fifteen, as I'm sure you're aware, and she's far too busy at school studying for her GCSEs to be bothering with a social life." She fixed Gideon with a withering glare.

He smiled engagingly at her. "Of course I wouldn't let her neglect her studies," he said calmly. "I was at King Edward's until last summer. I met Abi when my band played at her school dance. "

Arthur leaned forward. "So, you're a musician then?" he asked politely. "What do you play?"

"Lead guitar, mostly," replied Gideon, smiling at

him.

Arthur nodded. "Ah," he said. "Very loudly, I expect."

Gideon laughed and nodded his head. "Yes, sir, I guess it is usually pretty loud." He paused and addressed both of Abi's parents. "Don't worry. I won't keep Abi from her studies, but I would like to have your permission to take her to the cinema sometimes."

Joan bristled slightly and glanced at Arthur, who put his hand on her arm.

"I'm sure that would be all right," he said. "So long as you don't keep her out on a school night, and we always know where you're going."

Gideon nodded energetically. "Of course you will, and I'll look after her very well." He smiled at Joan again.

Reluctantly she inclined her head. Then, taking Arthur by the arm, she marched him into the living room.

Gideon looked at Abi and grinned. "That wasn't so bad," he remarked.

Abi snorted. "You don't know her," she said scowling after the retreating back of her mother. "She won't let this go. She doesn't trust me at all, and now she'll be watching me like a hawk." Suddenly aware of what she had said, Abi giggled and looked up at Gideon under her lashes. She had to admit he fitted his name, with his dark complexion and chiselled features so reminiscent of a bird of prey. "If I'm so much as one minute late back from a date, she'll probably ground me."

Gideon leaned down suddenly and dropped a light kiss on her lips. Then, putting an arm around her shoulders, he drew her away from the hall and into the dining room.

"Well, I thought that was a pretty good result," he said with a shrug. "They agreed I could take you out, didn't they? Where we go is something they don't need to know." He grinned mischievously at her as he picked up a sausage roll and popped it in his mouth.

Abi gave a reluctant smile. "Yeah, I guess that's okay," she conceded. "I thought she was going to forbid me from seeing you at all." She grinned up at him more widely. "Actually, yes, you're right. That *was* quite a result. When can we go somewhere?"

Gideon shrugged. "Let's meet up the day after tomorrow. I'll pick you up at, say, eleven o'clock, and we can go somewhere for the day." He thought for a moment. "We'd better tell your parents we are going to the cinema, though, and I promise to get you back at a decent time."

Abi made a face and, wandering over to the table, began to fill a paper plate with a selection of buffet food.

"Okay." She glanced shyly at him, then added in a rush, "Any chance I can come when you go to London?"

Gideon pursed his lips. "Well, your mum would never go for that, so if you do we might have to make up a story. Leave it with me," he said with a grin. "I'll see what I can do. Although I'm not making any promises. This has to get past Simon and Chas, too."

Chapter 9

*Friday, 18th November 2005*

Abi awoke the next morning to the sound of footsteps thundering up the stairs to her attic room. It was still dark outside, and she reached for her phone to check the time. It was seven thirty, so she hoisted herself into a sitting position just in time for Thomas to throw open the door and jump on to the bed beside her. He was wearing Thomas the Tank Engine pyjamas and had jam around his mouth. He bounced onto the bed and grinned at her.

"Bekfas?" he asked, spraying toast crumbs all over the bed.

Abi laughed and nodded. "Yes, please," she said, smiling at him. "Tell Mummy I'll be down in a few minutes."

Thomas jumped off the bed again and ran back down the stairs, leaving the door to slam shut behind him. Abi lay down again and, shivering, pulled the covers up to her chin. A few more minutes wouldn't hurt. Her very vivid dreams were still with her, and she needed a few minutes to adjust. The events of the last couple of days had been momentous, and her gaze strayed across the room to her box. Part of her wanted to dive back into it again to see what other memories would resurface, but another part was tempted to get rid of the lot and never look at it again. Feelings she thought she had successfully suppressed for many years had come flooding to the surface, and she was floundering a bit about how best to deal with them. Her evening with Judy had both helped and worsened the situation. They had had a wonderful time rekindling their friendship. She had hardly dared hope that was possible, but seeing her friend again had also brought back even more memories she would rather have left hidden. She pulled the covers right over her head for a moment, revelling in the feeling of security it gave her before she took a deep breath, threw them off, and jumped out of bed. Once her morning ablutions were finished, Abi dressed in the only clothes she had with her, ran a brush through her hair, and made her way down to the kitchen.

Judy was standing at the cooker, gently shaking a large frying pan full of sizzling bacon, and she grinned widely at her friend as she entered.

"Take a seat if you can find one," she called gaily, waving her arm in the direction of the table.

Abi cleared a pile of clothes off the one remaining vacant chair and sat down. Thomas was sitting at one end of the table, a large mug of milk in his hands, and Sabrina was securely strapped into her high chair at the other end. An empty coffee cup and the remains of a slice of toast indicated that Robert had already left for work. Judy came up behind her and placed a large plate of crispy bacon on the table.

"Hope you still like it like that," she remarked. "Tea or coffee?"

"Tea, please, and yes, I do. Thanks." Abi grinned up at her friend. She started on the bacon, and a few moments later Judy joined her at the table and plonked two cups of steaming tea in front of them. She stretched across Abi and placed a sippy cup of milk in front of Sabrina, then leaned back in her chair and surveyed her friend.

"Well, did you sleep okay?" she asked, looking at her closely. Abi, her mouth full of bacon, nodded. Judy narrowed her eyes. "No bad dreams, then?"

Abi glanced at her. "Mmmmm…" she muttered. "Maybe one or two. Not so much bad as disturbing."

Judy nodded sagely. "Not surprised," she said, taking a sip of her tea. "You can't discuss what we were talking about last night without dragging up some unwanted memories." She looked closely at Abi. "And I can bet you looked at those photos in bed, didn't you?"

Abi looked at her in surprise. "Am I so transparent?" she asked with a sigh.

Judy laughed. "No, but I would have done the same," she said, giving her a grin. "How did they make you feel?"

"Like I'd been kicked in the stomach, actually," admitted Abi with a shiver. "It's brought everything right to the forefront of my mind again. I actually thought I'd almost dealt with it all, especially now that woman's dead, but with finding this stuff, and all the stuff on the news…well, I quite clearly have a lot more to deal with." She pushed her empty plate away and picked up her tea.

"Can you stay another night?" asked Judy hopefully.

Abi shook her head with regret. "Wish I could, Jude, but no. I really should have been back for today, but I can't leave it any longer. Chris has been looking after Lilt and Flora, but I can't ask him to do any more." She finished her tea and placed the mug back on the table. "Thank you so much for having me last night, and for the breakfast. It's been amazing to see you again. Will you come down and stay soon? There's still lots I'd like to talk about," she implored her friend. "Should I try to contact Gideon, d'you think?"

Judy pursed her lips. "I knew you'd ask that," she said slowly, "and to be honest, I don't really know. It's all a bit weird, since he's just left the band. Maybe he's coming to look for you," she added with a laugh.

Abi shook her head. "Why would he?" she asked sadly. "He thinks I abandoned him. I doubt he's just found a box of unopened letters that I sent to him."

Judy frowned. "Where did you send your letters?"

"To the record company. Remember in that first letter he said not to do that? They probably never got to him." She stared down at her hands in her lap. "I always wondered if he didn't reply because..." She tailed off and glanced up at Judy. "But now I know that isn't the case. He never received my letters, just like I never received his. He knows nothing about what happened after he left."

Judy stood up and started clearing the table.

"It's really hard to know what to do. If he comes to England, maybe you should call him and see if he wants to see you. Tell him about the letters?" She stopped as she saw her friend's face.

"Oh, Judy, how can I tell him? Then I'd have to tell him everything. I don't think I can bear to." She pushed her chair back sharply and stood up. "I really need to think about this." She shrugged apologetically and made her way back up to the attic bedroom.

Closing the door behind her, she sat down on the bed, taking care not to bump her head. Her stomach was churning, and she was beginning to feel sick. Her hatred for her mother flared, and she thumped her fist into the pillow. This was all wrong. This was not how her life had been meant to be. This was not how she and Gideon had planned it.

****

Gideon undid his seat belt and sat forward to look out the window of Kurt's Lear jet. They had left Martha's Vineyard at six a.m. Eastern Standard Time, and their ETA at Southampton Airport was seven p.m. GMT. Because his friend was on board, Kurt had delegated the flying to his co-pilot, Brett, and was taking a bit of time to socialise in the cabin. Sonia appeared from the galley, carrying a small tray, and handed them two steaming cappuccinos before she slid down into the seat next to Gideon, cradling her own coffee. She curled her feet up under her and leaned back against the cream-coloured upholstery.

"So, Gideon," she said, smiling at their guest, "where are you planning to go first?"

Gideon turned to face her and took a sip of his coffee.

"I shall go to see my parents first," he said. "They've got a house in the New Forest—it's quite secluded, so hopefully I won't get bombarded by the paparazzi too much. I've warned Mum I'm on the way, and Dad's coming to fetch me from the airport." He paused and closed his eyes for a moment. When he opened them again, Sonia could detect the anguish in his soul. "Then I shall go to Newbury. I need to see her.

To lay the ghosts." He looked at his friends for support. "You do see why, don't you? I've got to stop the dreams."

Sonia reached over and patted his hand. "Of course we do, Gideon. I really think this is something you need to do." She glanced at her husband, who was nodding in agreement. "Unless you can find out why she left you, you'll never be able to get on with your life. You shouldn't really have left it ten years, you know," she added gently.

Gideon flicked back his hair and scowled. "Oh, god, don't I know it!" He slapped his hand on his leg in frustration. "But I got so caught up in things, and I was hurting so much to start with, that I found it impossible." With a glance at Kurt and Sonia, he continued, "But I have to do something now. I'm not sure why, but something's pulling me to her again."

Kurt stood up and put his hand on Gideon's shoulder. "You're doing the right thing," he said in his Southern drawl. "Now I'm gonna take over from Brett for a bit. See you later." And he sloped off towards the cockpit, coffee cup in hand.

Sonia moved over to the seat opposite Gideon and once more curled her feet up under her. She smiled her wide, engaging smile and brushed her hair back from her face. "I've got a good feeling about this, Gid," she said with a decisive nod. "I reckon things'll turn out well for you."

Gideon raised an eyebrow. "Maybe," he said bleakly, leaning back in his seat and closing his eyes. "We'll see."

****

By the time Abi finally set off for home, it was

109

nearly two o'clock. She had dawdled at Judy's until eleven, not able to tear herself away, and then, having collected her luggage from the hotel, she popped in to see her father. This proved a rather more lengthy business than she'd anticipated, because he insisted she stay for lunch, and foisted some more boxes on her to take home and sort out for him. Abi had protested mildly, but Arthur had been insistent, suggesting that bringing them back when she had been through them would give her an excuse to visit him. She didn't have the heart to deny him, but she still refused his offer of a front door key, and she still couldn't bring herself to offer him the hospitality of her own home. He'd never been to her cottage, and for the time being she wanted to keep it as her safe haven, away from all reminders of her past.

She glanced wryly at the box on the seat beside her, realising she was in fact taking much of her past back home with her. The rest of the stuff her father had given her consisted of another cardboard box, apparently full of photograph albums and old newspapers, and a locked black metal tin, about the size of a box file, for which there was no key. Abi had remonstrated with her father over the wisdom of her taking the locked tin home, but he was firm about not wanting to prise it open himself and most insistent that Abi should take it. She couldn't help wondering why. Did he know what was in it?

As she approached Bristol on the M4, Abi encountered the first of the Friday night rush-hour traffic, and by the time she finally made it onto the M5 heading south towards Exeter, it was almost four o'clock, and the sun had sunk nearly down to the horizon. As she sped down the motorway, Abi watched as the golden orb disappeared from sight and the darkness began to creep in.

By Exeter it was completely dark, and her eyes were beginning to get tired. She pulled into the services and stopped just long enough to grab a burger and a Coke to keep herself awake, then got back onto the road again, joining the A30 just past Exeter, the road which would take her all the way home. She was excited to be going back to her cottage by the sea, but at the same time she felt much more vulnerable than usual and really wished Judy had been able to come back with her. With a little persuasion she had managed to get her friend to agree to come down the next weekend, when they would be able to have a really good chat. Shell-shocked by the events of the past couple of days, she still badly needed someone to talk to.

The stars were beginning to come out in the clear night sky as she crossed Dartmoor, and by the time she reached Bodmin Moor, the moon had risen behind her and was shining directly in through her rear window. The lights from Jamaica Inn looked welcoming as Abi sped past, but she resisted the temptation to stop for a drink and carried on towards her destination. She had texted her neighbour Chris earlier in the day and was hoping he would have been able to pop in and put the heating on for her. The thought of the cosy little cottage awaiting her return spurred her on for the final leg of her journey, and soon she was passing through Penzance and on the road to Sennen.

As Abi approached the little village and saw the sign for the primary school at the top of the hill, she got a little tingle of excitement in her stomach. She could just make out the shape of the little row of four cottages on the cliff top overlooking the bay, and even though she had lived in the tiny cottage on the end of the terrace for over four years now, it still had the same effect on her. A light was shining from a downstairs window, a sure sign that Chris had been in to put on the heating. Abi grinned. She could already taste the toastie she was going to make, and the wine she was hoping she'd left in the fridge.

As she turned into the narrow driveway at the front of the cottage, the clock on the dashboard clicked onto seven o'clock, and she was greeted by the excited barking of her two rough collies, Lilt and Flora.

****

At the same moment Abi arrived home, Gideon's plane touched down on the tarmac at Southampton Airport. He stretched his long legs out in front of him and yawned. The flight had been uneventful and rather boring despite the company of his friends, and he was glad to have arrived. He was hoping his father was already there to meet him so he didn't have to hang around avoiding the press. He stood up and heaved his luggage down from the overhead locker. He had invited Kurt and Sonia to stay at his parents' place for the night, but they had politely declined, saying they had booked into the Harbour Hotel on Southampton waterfront. He thanked them profusely for their help, then walked down the steps and headed for customs.

As he approached the long low building, he saw a familiar figure, tall and thin, silhouetted in the window. Gideon raised his hand to his father and received an acknowledging wave. He smiled to himself. It was good to be home.

\*\*\*\*

Simon lay on the bed in his hotel room with the blinds lowered against the afternoon sun. He had spent the day alternating between avoiding the paparazzi and attempting to contact Gideon. He had left dozens of messages, both voice and text, but had had no reply. He strongly suspected his friend was on his way to England, and he had kept a close eye on the news in case Gideon was spotted arriving at an airport in Britain. Simon sat up and ran a hand through his hair. He was wearing the same clothes as the day before, and he hadn't had a proper night's sleep since Gideon's shocking announcement.

He got off the bed and went into the bathroom to get a glass of water. Throwing two Advil into his mouth in the hope of banishing his thunderous headache, he swallowed them down with the tepid water, then walked over to the closet and pulled out his well-travelled canvas sports bag. He heaved it onto the bed and carefully unzipped a pocket on the inside. Thrusting in his hand, he drew out a small bundle of letters, then tossed the bag onto the floor, sat back on the bed, and picked up the first envelope.

It was addressed to Gideon in a childish hand, with an English stamp and a postmark of July 1995. Simon's hand tightened on the envelope, and he closed his eyes. This was the reason why Gideon must not meet up with Abi again. She had written him ten letters in all, over the six-month period from July '95 to January '96, via the record company. They had eventually been passed on to the band, albeit somewhat tardily, and Simon had concealed their existence from Gideon.

He knew Gideon had written dozens of letters to

Abi, so he assumed these had been sent in reply, but he had always balked at actually reading them, feeling the extent of his deceit had gone far enough. Now Gideon planned to seek her out, and Simon realised he was about to be found out. The only thing that had always puzzled him was the fact that Abi had stopped sending the letters when she did, when he knew Gideon continued to write to her until the summer of '96. For the first time, he wondered if perhaps she had not received Gideon's letters.

He held the earliest letter up to the light. The envelope was a thick vellum and completely opaque. Impatiently he tapped it on his hand, his mind in a whirl. Surely if he opened just one, to see if she'd been receiving Gideon's letters, he would not be making things any worse? He had already committed the sin of withholding them from Gideon and therefore being the cause of his break-up with Abi. All for the good of the band, he continued to tell himself, although now, ten years on, he wasn't sure his motives had been quite so altruistic as he had thought at the time.

With a sudden decisive movement, Simon slid his chubby finger under the flap of the envelope and peeled it open. He slipped out the single sheet of good quality notepaper and unfolded it carefully. He began to read and discovered in the first sentence that Abi had not received any correspondence from Gideon at that time. He narrowed his eyes speculatively and looked down at the page again. As he read, his eyes widened and his tongue slipped out and hastily moistened his lips. Tiny beads of sweat began to appear on his forehead, and he leaned back heavily on the pillows.

He sat up again and dropped the letter on the bed,

scrabbling through the small pile for the last one Abi had sent. This was dated mid-January '96, and he took a deep breath before he tore it open. Once again the envelope contained only a single sheet of paper, this time roughly torn from a reporter's notepad. It had just a few words scrawled on it, ending with *"...so this will be the last time I write to you. I think I know now that you've moved on and I must learn to do the same. All my love for ever, Abi."*

Simon screwed the page into a tiny ball and clutched it tightly in his hand. The sweat was now pouring down his face, and he was breathing heavily. He finally realised the enormity of what he'd done, and that there was nothing he could do that would right that wrong. He had to stop Gideon from meeting Abi again, at all costs.

Chapter 10

*Saturday, 19<sup>th</sup> November 2005*

The following morning Abi awoke to the sound of the dogs barking and someone hammering on her back door. Muttering an oath under her breath, she rolled out of bed and staggered over to the window. As usual, the spectacular view made her catch her breath, even on such an overcast and gloomy day. She opened the small leaded window with a loud creak and peered down into the back yard. A young man dressed in tight faded jeans, a gleaming white T-shirt, and a black denim jacket was standing at the door looking back up at her. He grinned and pushed his floppy blond hair out of his eyes.

"Morning, darlin'," he said, stepping backwards so as not to crane his neck too much. "What you doing still in bed?"

Abi leaned dangerously far out of the window.

"What time is it, then?" she asked sleepily, rubbing her hand across her eyes.

"Half past nine, you sleepyhead," came the reply. "Now, let me in, and I'll make you some breakfast."

Unable to resist the offer, Abi slammed the window shut, shrugged on her dressing-gown, and padded barefoot down the stairs. The tiny living room still held the remains of her last night's supper, and the dogs appeared to have made a good job of licking the last of the toast crumbs off her abandoned plate.

"Bad Lilt, naughty Flora!" she scolded mildly as she drew back the bolts on the heavy wooden door. "Come on in then, Chris," she said standing back to admit her young neighbour.

He ducked his head to avoid the low beams and gave her a quick hug.

"Glad you're back, Abs." He squeezed past her and made himself at home in her tiny kitchen. "Place has seemed very quiet without you."

While she watched, he filled the kettle, assembled the wherewithal to make tea, and popped some bread into the toaster. Abi wandered into the living room, curled up on the nearest chair, and tucked her chilly feet beneath her.

"To what do I owe this pleasure?" she asked, stroking her two dogs. "I assume you've got news, if you've got me out of bed this early on a Saturday."

Chris looked pained and carried on with his culinary efforts.

"Abi, you malign me," he said in an aggrieved tone. "Perhaps I just want to spend some time with my best friend."

Abi raised an eyebrow and looked unconvinced. The living room was beginning to smell badly of dog, so she struggled to her feet and padded across to the back door to let the animals out into her tiny garden. They bounded out into the dreary early morning and began chasing each other around the muddy lawn. Abi grinned at them and closed the door, then gazed around the room and sighed. God, she was messy! Reluctantly she bent to gather up the various items of clothing she had left scattered the night before, drew back the curtains, and finally plumped up the cushions. She had just flopped back down into a deep, well-stuffed armchair when Chris appeared from the kitchen and plonked a steaming cup of tea and a plate of golden toast dripping with melted butter on the coffee table in front of her.

She smiled up at him. "Thanks, you're a gem," she said and blew him a kiss.

He winked at her and, taking his own tea and toast, sat down in the chair opposite.

"So, what gives?" he asked between munches. "How was the funeral? As awful as you thought?"

Abi shrugged. "Pretty shitty," she replied with a nod. "I kinda made up with my dad a bit, though." She paused and bit her lip, thoughtful for a moment.

Chris glanced over at her. "Something happen?" he asked perceptively.

Abi screwed up her nose and wriggled a bit in her chair.

"Yeah, something," she said. "Something to do with my past, that's all. I helped Dad clear out the attic a bit"—she hesitated—"and I found some old photos. Brought back a lot of memories, actually, not all of them good."

Chris watched her from under his long lashes.

"Can I see the photos?" he asked. "I bet you were sweet as a kid."

Abi snorted. "Probably, but these were just from ten years ago. I certainly wasn't very sweet then! At least that's what everyone told me. I suspect I was a nightmare, to tell you the truth." She fell silent and bit savagely into a piece of toast.

Chris watched her for a moment, then finished his tea, sat back in his chair, and crossed his legs.

"You're right, of course, I have got news," he said with a small smile. "George is back."

Abi looked up in surprise. "What, your George?" she asked.

Chris nodded. "Yeah. Not back with me, but back in the village. He came up to see me two days ago." He watched Abi's reaction, his eyes gleaming.

She wiped some butter off her chin and surveyed him closely.

"Well, don't you go and do anything silly, like letting him back to live with you," she warned in a big-sisterly way. "You know he can't be trusted."

Chris grinned at her. "I know." He sighed, adding with satisfaction, "In fact, I've been teasing him that I've got someone else. He didn't like that."

"Be careful." Abi frowned at him. "He'll have you wrapped around his little finger again. He's not good for you." She finished her tea and replaced the mug on the table, adding with a wry chuckle, "Not that I've any right to give relationship advice."

Chris looked at her affectionately and began to clear up the dishes.

"What are you up to today?" he asked, dumping all the crockery in the sink.

Abi followed him into the kitchen.

"Just enjoying being back home," she said with a small smile. "And going through some more of the stuff from my dad's attic."

Chris looked at her over his shoulder. "Can I see it, or is it all secret?"

Abi grimaced. "I guess you can see the photos. But

there's some other stuff that's a bit private. Sorry."

He shook his head. "No problem. I don't want to pry," he said comfortably, piling the dripping dishes on the draining board, where Abi studiously ignored them.

"I saw Judy," she said, after a moment's silence.

Chris grinned in delight. "'Bout time," he said. "How is she?"

Abi grimaced. "She's had another baby, and I didn't know. She's called it after me—as her middle name." She grinned at Chris. "And she's coming to visit next weekend!"

He grinned back and nodded in satisfaction.

"About time, too," he said. "I can't wait to meet her. Is she bringing her husband?"

Abi shook her head. "No, just her. She's leaving the kids with him. And anyway, Robert's not your type, besides being married to Judy."

Chris laughed and finished tidying the kitchen.

"Only joking, sweetie," he said with a wink.

After Chris had gone back home, Abi got dressed in her warmest combat trousers, a stripy jumper, a waterproof jacket, and welly boots, called to the dogs, and set off down to the beach. The wide sweep of Sennen Cove below the village was one of the most beautiful beaches in the country, and as usual Abi got a little thrill of disbelief that she was lucky enough to live there. They scrambled down the steep grassy hill to arrive panting onto the sand dunes.

The tide was almost fully out, and Abi and the dogs raced down to the water's edge, splashing through the numerous little pools that had remained on the sand when the tide receded. Abi waded out to ankle depth and stood lost in thought, the icy water lapping around her boots. The events of the last few days had left her confused and feeling vulnerable, and she was glad to be back in her own familiar surroundings where she could attempt to come to terms with what had happened. Everywhere she looked she fancied she saw Gideon's face, sometimes as the fresh-faced teenager she'd fallen in love with and sometimes as the moody, slightly haggard man he'd become. She'd studied his pictures in the papers since the band split and could sense a haunted look in his piercing eyes that tore at her heart.

She realised she'd been kidding herself all these years, thinking she was over him.

****

"I'm just off to Lyndhurst for a bit. Would you like to come?" Caroline Hawk addressed her son as she pulled on her gloves and picked up her bag.

Gideon looked up at her from his seat by the fire.

"Not this time, Mum. I think I'll just chill out here for a bit," he said with a smile. "Anyway, I'm trying not to be seen, remember?"

Caroline snorted. "Yes, and we're talking about Lyndhurst in November," she said. "Do you really think anyone there will recognise you? They're mostly older than your father and I." And with a brisk wave of her gloved hand, she left the room and headed out to her car.

Gideon leaned back in his chair and stretched his long legs out in front of him, causing Berwick, the chocolate Labrador who'd been dozing in front of the fire, to shift slightly and whine in his sleep. As he heard his mother's Range Rover shoot off down the drive, Gideon sighed and leaned forward to toss another log onto the already roaring fire.

"Don't waste it, son. It doesn't grow on trees," came his father's voice from the doorway. Used to the corny wit, Gideon groaned and grinned at him over his shoulder.

"Dad, your jokes get worse," he stated firmly, reaching down to stroke the sleeping dog.

Roger Hawk folded his lanky body into the chair opposite his son and smiled at him. "It's good to have you home, Gideon. But I can't help thinking there's more to this than just a social visit." He raised his dark eyebrows enquiringly. Gideon shrugged, then stared into the glowing embers. Part of him wanted to pour his heart out to his father, but a larger, stronger part insisted he keep it all to himself. Roger watched his son. "You know, her mother died a couple of weeks back," he said suddenly.

Gideon's head shot up, and he turned startled eyes on his father.

"What?" he said sharply, his brows coming together.

Roger cocked his head to one side. "Young Abi. Her mother died. Your mother heard it from one of her old friends in Newbury." He paused. "I'm fairly sure she won't be shedding many tears." He glanced at Gideon. "I know your arrival has something to do with Abi. If you don't want to tell me, then so be it, but I'm here if you want to talk." He continued to watch his son, his balding head tilted.

Gideon's shoulders slumped. "I want to see her, Dad," he said quietly, his eyes never leaving the fire. "I know it's mad, I know it's been ten years, but I can't stop thinking about her." He paused for a long moment, almost hypnotised by the flickering flames. "I told myself I'd got over her. For years I told myself that, but underneath, something always niggled at me. I had a feeling right from the start that something was wrong." He turned anguished eyes on his father. "I don't believe she would've deliberately left me like that. No letter, no card, nothing?" He leant forward and put his head in his hands. "We were in love, Dad. Really in love. I was going to marry her when she was older. I know we were both far too young then, but I knew, and I thought…well, I thought she did too." He paused again and looked up. "No, I know she felt the same. Something must have happened after I left, and I'm sure it was to do with her mother."

Roger sat quietly while Gideon spoke, his dark eyes sombre. Only when his son had fallen silent did he speak again. "Your mother tried to see her before we moved, but she was refused admittance."

Gideon looked up in surprise. "Mum went to see her? Why would she do that? She barely knew her."

Roger smiled a rueful smile. "No, but she liked her, and she knew how much she meant to you. She was surprised when you told us she hadn't replied to your letters, so she went to see if she'd received them okay." He shook his head. "Mrs Thomson was extremely rude to her and told her Abi was away. Your mother left our new address with her, but I rather suspect it never reached Abi." He paused again and chewed on his lip. "Your mother also felt something wasn't quite right. She couldn't put her finger on it, but she just had a feeling."

Gideon got to his feet and began pacing the room.

"Dad, that's exactly how I felt when I tried to see her in '97. You remember on that brief trip home I made that November?" His father nodded. "I was sent away and told she didn't live there any more. But something else was going on, I'm sure." He stopped and stared imploringly at his father. "Or is that just wishful thinking on my part? Is it really that she forgot me as soon as I went away and really didn't want anything to do with me?"

Roger looked his son in the eye. "Only one way to find out."

****

Judy was humming to herself as she loaded the dishwasher. She had really enjoyed her time with Abi and was busy planning what she would take with her at the weekend. The revelation that Abi's mother had concealed the letters from Gideon had actually not been that much of a shock to Judy. In the years since he went away, she had often found herself wondering why he hadn't written. She was the only one who knew how strong the feelings had been between the two teenagers, and she had been very taken aback when he had failed to contact Abi.

She paused as she was heaving a large saucepan into the machine. This new information also brought up another issue. In the letters she had read, it was quite clear Gideon had not been receiving letters from Abi, either. Judy knew she had sent at least half a dozen; the first about a month after he left, when she started to worry about not hearing, and the last…the last one had been in January '96.

She closed the door of the dishwasher and turned it on. Then she picked up her coffee and carried it into the conservatory, where Sabrina was happily cooing to herself in the playpen and Tommy was building a train track. She curled up in one of the chairs and gazed at them fondly. She was so lucky.

Before long, her mind went back to the puzzle it had been mulling in the kitchen. She leaned back in the chair and frowned in concentration. So if Gideon had not received Abi's letters, what did that mean? Could her mother somehow have prevented them from being sent? She dismissed this thought almost as soon as it came into her head. She had watched Abi post those letters herself. Unless Joan Thomson had mugged the postman who emptied the box—and done it each time a letter was sent—then that idea didn't work.

She knew Abi had sent the letters to the record company because she didn't have any other address, but she felt sure they would have passed them on to the band, even if it took a while. She must ask Abi if Gideon mentioned her letters in any of his. Maybe he got them all together much later. She shook her head impatiently. But if he had received them at all he would have realised Abi had not received his letters, and he would have taken action. Judy could remember the content of Abi's letters like the back of her hand, and there was no way Gideon could, or would, have ignored them.

So, she thought to herself slowly, if Gideon didn't receive the letters, there were only two options. One, they were never passed on by the record company, or two, someone else concealed them from him. She was just mulling this information over in her head when the phone rang. She jumped to her feet and sped back into the kitchen to answer it.

"Hello," she chirped. "Oh, hi, Mum, you okay?" She carried the receiver back into the conservatory and curled up again in the chair. "Really, that's nice…Yes, we had a lovely time, thanks, and guess what? I'm going down to Cornwall to stay with her next weekend!" She took a swig of her coffee and a slight frown crossed her face. "What d'you mean? What information? Mum, what are you talking about?" She listened intently for a moment, incredulous. "Are you sure? Mum that's almost too incredible to take in…Why don't you come over, and you can tell me more?" She paused again. "Yeah, okay, I'll see you about one. Love you." She disconnected the call and thought. If what her mother had just told her turned out to be true… She shook her head in disbelief. How on earth could she tell Abi?

****

Abi had spent the day just relaxing with the dogs, doing a minimum of housework and washing, and checking her work schedule for the coming week. She was a commercial artist and provided the art work for the advertising of a number of local—and national—companies, as well as teaching twice a week at a local primary school and running a night class once a week in Penzance. All these jobs, with the addition of the occasional landscape she sold to tourists in the summer, provided her with a comfortable income and meant she could live her secluded existence with a feeling of security.

By five o'clock she had done everything she felt she ought to do, and decided to run herself a bubble bath, then settle down for a cosy evening perusing her way through the rest of the letters and photos. She thought she felt strong enough to read them all now, and hoped that after that she would have a better idea of what she should do next. As she started up the stairs to the little bathroom, she passed the strange tin box she'd brought back from her father's house. She paused for a moment and stared at it, eyes narrowed. She had a very vague feeling she remembered the box from some time in her childhood. After a moment, she shook her head and continued upstairs. Maybe it would come back to her later.

An hour later, warm, clean, relaxed, and dressed in cosy pyjama bottoms and a bright red sweatshirt, Abi padded downstairs and busied herself lighting the fire. The tiny low-ceilinged living room heated up quickly, and by the time she had the fire roaring the whole house was feeling cosy. She wandered into the kitchen, turned on the oven, and raided the freezer. After a moment she found what she was looking for and pulled out a large cheese-and-tomato pizza.

Ten minutes later, with a variety of toppings added, it was in the oven, and she had poured herself a glass of wine and was sitting by the fire straightening her hair. The prospect of a lovely comfortable evening in her own home, with good food, good drink, and a lot of memories, was getting more appealing by the minute, so she was slightly annoyed when she heard a sharp tap on her door. Muttering to herself, she struggled to her feet, balanced the straighteners on the hearth, and padded over to the door. She opened it cautiously, prepared to turn away the unexpected visitors, only to discover Chris standing on the doorstep, a hopeful grin on his face and his arms full of goodies.

Abi rolled her eyes and laughed. "Come on in, then," she said, opening the door fully. "What's all this in aid of?"

He ducked into the room and deposited his armful on the kitchen counter.

"Thought you needed company tonight," he said. "We could have a bit of a girly night. I brought wine and pudding."

Abi laughed. "You're incorrigible," she said. "I've got a pizza in the oven. I guess it could serve two, if we have pudding, as well."

He grinned at her and poured himself a glass of wine from her open bottle.

"Help yourself, why don't you?" she said, raising her eyebrows.

Chris smirked at her. "You love me, really," he said squeezing past her and going over to the fire. Abi joined him and continued to straighten her hair.

They sat together in a companionable silence until the timer on the oven buzzed to say the pizza was ready. Abi went to serve it up while Chris rearranged the furniture to allow them both to sit by the fire and have a table to use.

By the time they had both had enough to eat and were making good inroads on the wine, it was nearly eight o'clock. Chris glanced over at Abi, who sat on the hearth rug, directly in front of the fire, her arms clasped around her legs and her chin resting on her knees. Her long hair hung forward, concealing her face. He spoke quietly. "Any chance I could look at some of those photos you brought back?" he asked tentatively.

Abi looked up, considered for a moment, then nodded. "Okay," she conceded. "Just the photos, though. Not the other stuff."

She scrambled to her feet and fetched the two boxes from under the stairs, leaving the metal box where it was for the time being. Dropping them unceremoniously on the hearth rug, she sat down cross-legged beside them, then delved into the original box, felt around under the bundles of letters, and pulled out a photograph album.

"These are mostly holiday snaps from about fifteen or sixteen years ago," she said flicking through it before handing it over. "We all look very happy. It's amazing how a photo can lie."

Chris winced at the bitterness in her tone, and began to flick through the album.

"You were sweet," he commented, indicating an out-of-focus shot of her riding a fat little pony when she was about ten.

Abi crawled over to have a look. "Oh, yeah. That was a fun day, actually. I loved that pony," she said with a slight grin. Suddenly she thrust a slightly wrinkled photo under his nose. "This is me aged fifteen, on my way to our school Christmas dance."

Chris sneaked a look at her under his lashes, interested in the alteration in her voice. Her face looked slightly flushed, and she was definitely showing some strong emotion. He held up his hand.

"If you'd rather I didn't see these, I don't mind."

She shook her head and rifled through the box again. This time she pulled out the photos from the New Year's Eve party.

"There's Judy, New Year's Eve '94. And me and Judy. And me and…my boyfriend." She looked away and pulled the other box to her.

Chris studied the photos and frowned.

"Abi," he began, "isn't that Gideon Hawk?" There was no reply, so he looked over at her. She was sitting very still with another pile of loose photos in her hand. Chris crawled across the floor towards her. "Abi?" he asked, stopping next to her.

She looked up at him, her eyes glistening with tears. "Yes," she whispered. "It's Gideon. Here he is again. On my sixteenth birthday."

She held out a photo of her and Gideon sitting on top of a five-barred gate. The wind was blowing their hair, and they were both laughing. "We fell off the gate the moment after Judy took that," she said with a tearful giggle. "He landed in a huge cow pat!" Pulling a tissue from her sleeve, she blew her nose. "Sorry, Chris. Just caught me unawares, that one," she said after a moment. "I'd forgotten about that. Not forgotten my birthday, just forgotten the photo. The birthday was great." She gave a whimsical smile.

Chapter 11

*Wednesday, 19<sup>th</sup> April 1995*

"Happy birthday, Abs!" shrieked Sammy down the phone.

Abi grinned. "Thanks. Are you coming over later?"

"I can't," moaned her friend. "We're still in Swanage with Granny and Granddad. Won't be back till Friday. You shouldn't have your birthday in the Easter hols. We always go away."

She sounded so downcast that Abi laughed. "Well, I like the fact that I don't have to go to school on my sixteenth birthday!" she retorted. "But don't worry. We can have another celebration when you get back. Thanks for the card. See you at the weekend."

She replaced the receiver and went back into the kitchen, where Judy was sitting at the table reading through Abi's cards.

"Who on earth is Katerina?" she asked, peering at a signature.

Abi grimaced. "Oh, some cousin or other. I think she might be Russian," she said dismissively.

Judy stared. "You've got Russian cousins?" she said in amazement. "You never told me before."

Abi shrugged. "Well…I think they're Russian. Or Polish, or Welsh or something."

"Welsh!" shrieked Judy. "Abi, are you crazy?

Russia and Wales are nothing alike!" She stared at her friend in astonishment.

Abi had the grace to giggle. "Oh, I know. I've no idea where they're from. I don't know why she sends me a card. We've never met." She took the card out of Judy's hand and put it on the pile. "Now, come on, we need to go. Gideon's picking us up in ten minutes." She caught Judy's hand and pulled her to her feet.

As the girls sped down the road towards the junction where Gideon had arranged to meet them, Judy gasped, "Are you sure you don't mind me coming?" as she struggled to keep up.

Abi shook her head. "'Course not. Got to spend my birthday with my best friend," she managed between puffs. "Anyway, I told Mum I was going out to lunch with you."

Judy snorted. "So I'm just a smokescreen, then?" she said, as they came to a halt at the pre-arranged meeting place. "I thought your mum was okay with you going out with Gideon now?"

Abi made a face. "She is…sort of. But we've seen each other three times this week already, and I was afraid she'd make a fuss. Then we would have had a row, and I would have gone anyway and then got grounded…so I thought it easier to tell her I was going out with you."

Judy nodded. "I can see the logic," she conceded, "but why am I actually here? You only had to tell her I was."

Abi looked shocked. "But I wanted you here too," she said in surprise. "I always spend my birthday with you. This one's no different."

Judy looked at her doubtfully but kept her thoughts to herself.

At that moment Gideon's old van appeared around the corner and ground to a juddering halt beside them. Abi ran round to the passenger side and clambered in, Judy just behind her. Abi grinned at Gideon, and he leaned over and kissed her firmly on the lips.

"Happy birthday, Abs," he said with a smile. "Hi, Judy. Is the door shut? Okay, then let's get going."

He set off again and headed out of town in the direction of the A34 towards Winchester.

Abi fastened her seatbelt and peered out of the window.

"Where're we going, then?" she asked.

Gideon pulled out onto the dual carriageway and increased his speed accordingly.

"To the New Forest."

Judy bent forward to see around Abi. "Oh, it's nice there," she said with a smile. "Lots of horses."

"Ponies," corrected Gideon absently, his concentration on keeping the van moving. "My parents are thinking of moving there. Thought we should go and see it too."

Abi looked at him in surprise. "They're selling that gorgeous house?" she asked, raising her eyebrows. When she'd first seen Gideon's parents' house she'd been quite shocked. Unlike her parents' little three-bedroom semi in a suburban road, they lived out of town in a large ivy-covered detached house set in large grounds. They even had a paddock and stables. "Why are they moving?"

Gideon shrugged. "Want to move further from London, I think. Dad can work from anywhere, really, and they loved the Forest when they went there to visit some friends. They've seen a house they like already."

If Abi thought it a little strange to be spending her

sixteenth birthday looking at prospective houses for her boyfriend's parents, she kept it to herself. She was just glad they were able to spend the day together.

After about an hour they crossed the cattle grid that marked the border to the New Forest, just outside Lyndhurst. They drove slowly as they approached, and Gideon found a parking space near Bolton's Bench on the edge of the village. The girls squealed in delight when they saw all the ponies and foals grazing around them, and they both scrambled out and immediately began to search their pockets for any food to give them.

"You shouldn't really feed them," called Gideon from where he was trying to make the van door lock. "At least, don't give them sweets or anything silly."

Guiltily Judy thrust her packet of Chewits back into her pocket and contented herself with stroking the mane of the nearest pony. Gideon joined them, carrying a small rucksack, and they spent a happy couple of hours wandering around the environs of Bolton's Bench, with its large expanses of grass and a small hill rising in the centre, crowned by a magnificent yew tree. Eventually they climbed to the top and flopped down on the grass beneath the tree, surveying their surroundings. Abi lay flat on her back and stared up at the clear blue sky. Gideon's face appeared above her, and he bent down and gently kissed her on the lips. She responded, putting her arms around his neck and pulling him down on top of her.

Judy laughed. "Shall I leave you two alone?" she asked, smiling.

Gideon raised his head and grinned. "Nope. Sit down. I've got stuff in my bag for us all." And disentangled himself from Abi's arms and pulled his rucksack towards him.

Abi leaned up on her elbows. "Presents?" she asked, her eyes shining.

Gideon shook his head. "Wait and see."

Judy squatted down on the grass next to Abi, and they watched as Gideon unloaded his bag. First he produced a large tin, then a pack of six colas, then finally a very tiny present wrapped in stripy paper.

He placed the tin in front of Abi and said, "Close your eyes."

He proceeded to reveal a large chocolate cake with Abi's name written in Smarties on the top. He pulled a packet of candles out of the bag and stuck them all around the edge of the cake. Then he produced a cigarette lighter and, with Judy shielding them from the breeze, lit the candles.

"Come on, you guys," pleaded Abi, her hands clasped firmly over her eyes. "What's going on?"

"Okay, you can look now," said Gideon finally, sitting back on his heels and watching her face. Abi slowly lowered her hands and found herself staring straight at what she thought was the most beautiful birthday cake she had ever seen.

"Oh, Gid," she breathed. "It's lovely! Did you make it?" She crawled closer to get a better look.

Gideon laughed. "Well, sort of," he said. "Mum made the actual cake, but I did the decorating. That's why it's a bit messy."

Abi shook her head. "No, it's not. It's beautiful," she whispered, tears pricking the backs of her eyes. She couldn't believe he'd taken so much trouble just for her. She leant towards him and kissed his nose. "Thank you so much. It's perfect." Then she turned and, with one huge breath, blew out all the candles.

Judy laughed and clapped her hands. "Well done! Hope you made a wish."

Abi nodded. "Oh, yes, of course I did. Not telling you, though." She grinned at them both. "This is the best birthday ever," she stated simply, positioning herself cross-legged beneath the huge tree. "Is there more?"

Gideon snorted. "Never satisfied!" he said with a laugh, then held out the tiny present to her. She took it from him tentatively. This was the first present she had ever had from a boyfriend, and her heart was pounding in her ribcage as she began to unwrap it. Inside the stripy paper was a tiny tissue-paper parcel. She carefully unfolded it and revealed a solid silver ring embossed on the inside with both their names, Abi and Gideon, with a tiny heart between them. She caught her breath and held the ring tightly in her hand.

"Do you like it?" he asked anxiously. "I know it's the right size. Try it on."

Abi glanced up at him, her eyes shining.

"It's gorgeous," she murmured. "I love it. And I love you."

The moment the words were out of her mouth she regretted saying them. Just because he'd given her a ring didn't mean he loved her. It was the sort of thing a boyfriend did. It didn't necessarily mean anything. She flushed and bent her head, her hair falling over her face. Gideon reached forward and put a finger under her chin to raise it up.

"I love you too," he said, staring into her eyes. He took her right hand in his and gently slid the ring onto her third finger. It fitted perfectly. "Has to be that hand for now," he said. "But one day I'll get you one for the other hand." He paused and considered. "Call it an engaged-to-be-engaged ring."

Abi gave a tearful giggle and flung her arms around his neck.

"Is that a proposal, then?" she asked, her voice muffled by his neck.

He squeezed her tightly. "I guess it is," he said, his mouth pressed into her hair.

Judy got to her feet. "I'm just going to go and have an explore," she said tactfully. "Back in a bit." She set off in the direction of the village, her hands in her pockets and her long ponytail swinging.

"It's okay, Judy," began Abi, turning to watch her friend walk away, then Gideon's lips on her neck made her forget everything else. She moved her head and latched her lips onto his, at the same time pulling him down onto the grass beside her. "I love you," she repeated, liking the way the words sounded on her tongue. "I...love...you."

Gideon responded by running his hands gently down her body, caressing her firm round breasts through her thin T-shirt, then further down to knead her curvy buttocks. She moaned in pleasure as his hands moved over her body, and responded by arching her back and pressing closer to him. Their lips locked, and they clung together hungrily, devouring each other, until Gideon finally pulled away and held Abi at arm's length.

"Not here, Abs," he said, breathing heavily. "Too many people. We should find somewhere secluded." He got to his feet and gazed around them. Everywhere he looked there were people or ponies. Or people and ponies. He sighed and ran a hand through his hair. "Not anywhere here, actually." He glanced down at Abi and raised his eyebrows. "That is, if you want to…" He looked suddenly very vulnerable.

Abi looked up at him and smiled. "Of course I want to," she said in surprise. "I've been waiting for this day since we first met." She found herself blushing and let her hair swing forward to cover her face. "Where can we go?"

Gideon sat down on the grass beside her and opened a can of cola. He shrugged. "Not here. We'll think of something after we take Judy home. You know I have to go to London tomorrow. I'd love this last night to be special."

Abi's head shot up, and she stared at him in dismay. In the excitement of the day she had totally forgotten he was due to leave for London the next day. The band had secured a recording deal the previous month and were due to begin recording their first album. That meant Gideon would be in London for the next couple of months, and Abi would be able to see him only occasionally. She felt a lump forming in her throat and scrambled to her feet.

"I'm really going to miss you." Her voice broke on the last words.

Gideon caught her in his arms. "I know," he said, stroking her hair. "I shall miss you dreadfully. But it won't be for long, and you've got your exams coming up. Your mum probably won't let you out during those, will she? I'll be back before you know it." He tilted her head up to face him and smiled down at her. Abi managed a watery smile in return, then pulled away and sat down on the grass in front of her cake.

"Let's have cake," she said decisively. "Look, there's Judy coming back. I'll cut it. Did you bring a knife?"

Having established that Gideon had failed to bring anything to cut the cake with, the three of them picked it up and broke it into pieces by hand.

They spent the rest of the day exploring the Forest, and, to the girls' amusement, having a quick look at the house Gideon's parents were planning to buy. Then they headed back in time to get Abi home for her birthday tea.

"I've had such a brilliant day." She sighed. "I really don't want to go home yet."

Judy grinned. "I know what you mean, but your mum'll freak out if you don't get back for tea." She wrinkled her nose. "Maybe we could all meet up again this evening?"

Gideon and Abi were silent, and Judy eyed them suspiciously.

"Oh," she said at last, grinning. "You *are* planning to meet up tonight. That's fine. I've been enough of a gooseberry today anyway. Thanks for letting me come with you, though."

Abi grabbed her friend's hand and gave it a squeeze. "Oh, I'm sorry, Jude. I feel really guilty now, but Gideon leaves for London tomorrow, and we just wanted a wee bit of time on our own." Her brow furrowed anxiously. "D'you understand? And we're so glad you came with us today, aren't we, Gid?"

Gideon nodded his head vigorously. "Wouldn't have been the same without you," he stated as he pulled out into the rush-hour traffic on the A34.

Judy laughed. "It's fine. D'you need an alibi for this evening?"

Abi bit her lip. Neither she nor Gideon had actually thought about where they were going that evening.

She shrugged. "No, don't worry. I'll tell them we're going to the cinema. They're usually cool about that," she said, and exchanged a secretive smile with Gideon.

They arrived back in Judy's road at five o'clock, and the two girls jumped down from the cab.

Abi turned, smiled at Gideon, and said, "Okay, pick me up at seven, and I'll tell them we're going to the pictures. It should be all right." She blew him a kiss, then slammed the door of the van shut. As he drove off, Judy gave Abi a quick hug.

"Happy birthday, Abs. Thanks for letting me come with you today, and have a brilliant evening." She paused and squeezed her friend's hand, a look of concern on her face. "And Abi, please be careful."

Abi squeezed back. "I will," she said, with a self-conscious grin. "Don't worry." With a wave she skipped off down the road in the direction of her own house.

****

By seven o'clock Abi was dressed, made up, and raring to go. She had had a birthday tea with her parents and her aunt and uncle, and they had reluctantly agreed she could go out to the cinema with Gideon. She had explained he was going to be away in London for several weeks and this was her last chance to see him, and her father had actually appeared sympathetic. Her mother's eyes had gleamed, and she remarked that maybe Abi would finally get around to doing some revision for exams.

As she sat waiting on the stairs for the doorbell to ring, Abi's heart was racing. Ever since she'd met Gideon she'd known this day would come. She knew he was the one for her. She was in love, and everything was wonderful. She leant back against the banisters and smiled to herself. She just had to get these ridiculous exams out of the way, and then they could be together all the time. Her thoughts raced on to the amazing summer they would be able to have together. The buzz of the doorbell jolted her out of her reverie, and she jumped down the last few steps and ran to let him in. He stood on the doorstep grinning at her. He looked amazing, in ripped jeans, a black T-shirt, and a distressed leather jacket. His dark hair was dishevelled and had got tucked inside his collar.

"Ready?" he asked.

Abi nodded silently and turned to shout to her parents, "We're off now. Won't be too late."

As they were closing the door behind them, she heard the faint voice of her mother following them, "Be back by eleven."

"Okay," Abi called back, rolling her eyes at Gideon, then laughing quietly as they ran down the path and out to the van. As she belted herself in, Abi glanced up. "So where're we going?" she asked breathlessly.

Gideon started the van with a loud roar and answered without looking at her, "My house."

Abi's eyes widened in surprise. "Your house? But won't your parents be there?" she asked with a frown.

Gideon shook his head. "Nope. They've gone to a party in Winchester. They won't be back till the early hours. We'll have the house to ourselves."

Abi leaned back and digested this information. Not only did she find it hard to comprehend the idea of parents who had a social life, but the thought of having that amazing house all to themselves all evening was mind blowing. She grinned to herself. This was going to be even better than she had imagined.

The drive out into the country took about twenty minutes, and Abi watched in excitement as they turned up the long drive towards the Hawks' beautiful home. Gideon parked the van in front of the garage and jumped out, striding over to the front door, calling as he went, "Mum, Dad, are you there?" He unlocked the door, beckoned to Abi to follow him, then stepped into the hallway, calling again. "It's only me. Are you still here?"

There was no response, so he caught Abi by the hand and led her into the huge farmhouse kitchen. He tossed his keys onto the aged pine table and walked over to the fridge. Abi hung back in the doorway.

"What d'you want to drink?" asked Gideon without looking round.

Abi edged a little further into the room.

"Erm…don't mind," she said. "Whatever you're having."

Gideon pulled two cans of lager out of the fridge and handed one to Abi. She took it gingerly. She hated lager, but there was no way she could admit this to Gideon, so she followed his suit and snapped it open. She took a tentative sip and just managed to stop herself from shuddering. Gideon didn't notice, and nodded to the door.

"C'mon, then. Come and see the rest of the house."

Abi had only seen the house from the outside before, so she was curious enough to follow him as he gave her a whistle-stop tour, ending outside a pale blue door on the first floor. He paused with his hand on the doorknob. "And this is my room. S'cuse the mess."

He flung open the door of a large, high-ceilinged room filled to bursting with musical instruments of all kinds, piles of clothes, both clean and dirty, an assortment of books, games, and childhood toys (including a large teddy bear), and somewhere beneath everything else, a wood-framed bed.

Abi laughed. "Don't you get lost in here?" she asked, grinning at him.

Gideon shrugged. "Don't spend much time in here these days," he said, walking over to the bed and sweeping the piles of clothes onto the floor.

Abi gasped and put out a hand. "Oh, no, I think those are clean..." Her voice dwindled as she saw his face. "Never mind."

He turned and walked over to where she stood awkwardly clutching her jacket around her. He took her hands in his and gently pulled her towards him. Slowly she began to relax and raised her face to his as his arms snaked around her and held her tight. When his lips met hers, Abi felt all her fears drain away, and she responded with a depth of passion that surprised them both.

Chapter 12

*Sunday, 20<sup>th</sup> November 2005*

Gideon awoke on Sunday morning to the sound of church bells pealing just outside his window. He grinned to himself. How beautifully English they sounded! He realised how much he'd missed the traditional things he grew up with. It had been a great adventure, travelling the world for the last few years, but he had to admit it was lovely to be back in England where he could relax and be out of the public eye. He realised his mother would be getting ready for church just now, and any minute would probably knock on his door to ask if he'd like to accompany her. For a moment he wondered if perhaps he would, then shook his head and pulled the covers up to his chin. He had come here to escape and wasn't yet ready to go and be sociable with the "country set." He still hadn't decided what to do about Abi, and he felt that another day or two of relaxing at home with just his parents was exactly what he needed. Luckily, they both seemed to understand his needs and so far had not attempted to pressure him into doing anything he didn't want to. Predictably there came a knock at his door.

He grinned. "Come in, Mum."

Caroline Hawk popped her head around the door in surprise.

"How did you know it was me?" she asked, smiling at her son.

Gideon laughed. "Intuition," he remarked, "and no thanks, I don't think I'll come to church today."

Caroline raised her eyebrows and walked over to open the curtains.

"Okay, darling. Don't stay in here all day, though. You look as if you could do with some fresh air and exercise. Why don't you go riding with Dad?"

Gideon propped himself up on his elbow. "Fresh air and exercise?" he exclaimed. "Do you know how energetic one of our gigs is? I'm on the move for a solid two and a half hours. Each night."

Caroline surveyed him with her arms folded.

"And then go back to your hotel room and drink and smoke too much, no doubt, thereby undoing all the good you may have done." She looked at him sternly. "And I'm quite sure you've been existing on junk food, too. Crisps and chocolate, knowing you. So, none of that here. You can help your father get the roast started while I'm at church."

Gideon rolled his eyes at her. "I thought you wanted me to go riding." He grinned.

She straightened his jacket on the back of the chair.

"You'll have plenty of time for both," she said serenely, then blew him a kiss and left the room.

Gideon grinned to himself. His mother was in her element. She had someone to organise. He stretched his long limbs, then threw back the covers and jumped out of bed. The morning was overcast again, and the clouds seemed to be threatening rain, so he hoped his father might abandon the idea of riding and just stick to the cookery. He rifled in his bag for some clean clothes before padding down the passage to the bathroom. He had a quick shower and a shave, then dressed in jeans and a dark green hooded sweatshirt. As he made his way downstairs, the enticing smell of slightly burnt toast wafted up to him, taking him back to his childhood.

He found his father in the kitchen, seated at the table, with his glasses perched on the end of his nose, deeply engrossed in the *Sunday Times*.

"Morning, Dad," he said as he squeezed past him and flicked the kettle back on. Roger raised a hand to his son and carried on reading. When Gideon joined him at the table with a cup of coffee and some of the burnt toast, he folded his paper and surveyed him over his glasses.

"Jet lag all gone?" he asked, not waiting for a reply. "Your mother thinks I should take you riding this morning." Gideon said nothing. "Personally, I don't really want to, so unless you're very keen…?"

"Not at all, Dad." Gideon grinned. "She also told me we're to cook the lunch. That actually sounds more appealing this morning."

Roger nodded in agreement. "Right, that's settled. She gets these ideas about fresh air and exercise." He shook his head. "We'll tell her we went for a walk." He picked up his paper again and resumed reading.

Gideon smiled to himself. His parents never changed. For a couple of minutes the two men sat in a companionable silence, the one reading and drinking tea, the other munching contemplatively on some toast. Then Roger looked up again.

"Have you decided what to do about Abi?" he asked directly.

Gideon put down his toast and considered the question.

"No. Not really. I guess I shall have to go and see her sometime, but I'm not sure I'm quite ready yet." He leaned back in his chair with a sigh.

Roger sat back and crossed his legs.

"So if it wasn't a sudden desire to seek out Abi, then what prompted your precipitous departure from the band?" he asked curiously.

Gideon ran a hand through his long hair.

"It was Abi," he said abruptly. "I think. I keep dreaming about her, and it's driving me crazy. But also things were just getting on top of me. I felt I was going mad. I had no privacy, no life outside the band, and to be perfectly honest, I don't think I really like Simon and Chas as much as I used to." He paused and looked at his father with a shrug. "Not sure I like Simon at all, actually. He's very controlling, and it really gets me down. And then I remember what he was like when I first started going out with Abi. He never accepted her, even though he'd known her for years. I did wonder if he liked her himself, but I don't think that was it. Having seen his more recent taste in women, it doesn't seem likely." He paused again, with a frown. "He even tried to warn me off seeking her out again. That's not really the way a proper friend should behave." He got to his feet and began to pace around the room, "Dad, d'you think I behaved badly? Was it really wrong of me to leave the band with no warning?"

Roger gave a wry smile. "Well, in an ideal world you could have done it more gently, I suppose," he conceded. "I suspect you may have to put up with some backlash from various quarters, but if your state of mind was such as you have described, then you really shouldn't beat yourself up over it. You're famous enough to weather the storm, even if it means some financial penalties," he added with a twinkle in his eye.

Gideon sighed. "I think that's part of the problem," he admitted. "I'm fed up with being famous. I want to be normal."

\*\*\*\*

As Simon's plane touched down at Heathrow Airport, he considered his options. His sole aim was to prevent a reconciliation between Gideon and Abi, but he had absolutely no idea how to achieve that. He pulled his hand luggage from the overhead locker and joined the queue of travellers leaving the plane. Predictably, the press had got wind he was arriving that morning, and as he made his way down the steps and onto the concourse, he was immediately aware of the flashing cameras and thrusting microphones, all pointed at him from behind the barriers.

"Over here, Simon!"

"Have you come home to find Gideon?"

"Do you know where Gideon's hiding?"

"What happened, did you have a fight?"

"Have NightHawk split up for good?"

The questions came thick and fast, firing at him from all directions, and he did what he did best: he turned on them, stuck two fingers in the air, and swore loudly. He carried on into Arrivals and passed through customs with no problems. Then, having collected his bags from the carousel, he took a deep breath and walked out into the damp, dreary, November day. At once he was surrounded again by thronging reporters, but he pushed his way through them and forced his way into the nearest taxi.

"Where to, mate?" asked the driver cheerfully over his shoulder, as he pulled away from the kerb and negotiated his way through the persistent media personnel who were edging out into the road.

"Any fucking where but here," snapped Simon rudely, running a hand through his sweat-drenched hair.

The driver looked at him in the mirror.

"Bit of a pain that lot," he remarked. "You famous, then?"

Simon gave an incredulous snort. "Ya think?" he said. "Yeah, but it's not me they're interested in. They only want Gideon."

"Gideon?" The driver raised his eyebrows. "Who's that, then?"

Simon sighed and rolled his eyes. "Lead singer of NightHawk," he said impatiently. "He left the band suddenly last week in New York and has now vanished god knows where. I'm the drummer," he added.

The driver shook his head, "Oh, yeah, think I may have seen something about that on the news. Can't say I'd really heard of them before. Probably not my type of music. I'm more of a country-and-western man meself. What sort of music do you do?" he asked curiously.

Simon scowled at him. "Grunge," he snapped. "Now take me to Newbury."

The driver raised his eyebrows. "That'll cost you, mate. Close on a ton, that'll be."

Simon sighed. "Just drive. I'm famous, remember? I can afford it." And he sat back in the corner of the cab and closed his eyes. The decision to go to Newbury was probably fairly sound. His mother still lived there and, as far as he knew, so did Abi's parents. He had no idea what he was actually going to do, but at least if he was back in his home town maybe something would come to him. Also, he could hide out at his mother's house for a bit until all the media attention died down. He guessed Gideon had probably headed for his parents' house, as well, and he decided that a little trip to the New Forest might have to be the order of the day, too, although he didn't know exactly where they lived. He pulled out his phone and quickly tapped in a number.

"Hello, Mum," he said. "I'm on my way home. Be about an hour." He paused and took a deep breath. "No, everything's okay. I'll explain all when I get home. Bye." He hung up before his mother could ask him any more questions.

****

Judy bit her lip. Since her mother's visit the day before, she'd been in a state of turmoil. She could hardly believe what she'd heard, and if it turned out to be true, she had no idea what she should tell Abi. She was supposed to be going to visit her at the weekend. Could she manage two whole days with her friend without mentioning something? Her mother had been quite clear that she must not do that until they knew for sure.

She gathered up a pile of dirty washing and absently pushed it into the washing machine. She and Abi had always told each other everything, and she knew she wouldn't be able to keep her mouth shut, but she did agree with her mother that nothing should be said. She nodded to herself. The only way round this was for her to postpone her visit to Cornwall until later. Then she could either legitimately tell Abi what they'd

150

found out, or, if it turned out not to be true, she need never mention it at all. That was the answer. She would make up some excuse as to why she couldn't go next weekend. Maybe leave it until later in the week and say the children were ill? No one ever doubted the validity of an excuse like that.

She turned on the washing machine, then made herself a cup of tea. Robert was playing with the children in the conservatory, and she stood in the doorway watching them unobserved for several minutes. She couldn't help comparing her life to Abi's and feeling rather smug. She mentally chastised herself and went and joined the rest of the family, ready to enjoy her birthday.

****

Abi slept late on Sunday morning. She and Chris had sat up talking until nearly two, and she finally crawled out of bed at ten thirty the next morning. The emotions that had been stirred up by the photo of her sixteenth birthday had led to a very disturbed night, punctuated by bad dreams and moments of waking sadness, and she was determined not to let it influence her day. She dressed quickly and ran downstairs for her first cup of tea of the morning. Accompanied by a slice of hot buttered toast, it hit the spot, and she began to feel a little more human. She curled her feet under her, leaned back in her chair, and flicked the remote to turn on the television. As she scanned through the channels, her attention was immediately caught by pictures of someone arriving at Heathrow, surrounded by reporters. Her first thought was that it might be Gideon, so she turned up the volume.

"The drummer of the band NightHawk made short

shrift of waiting reporters when he touched down at Heathrow earlier this morning. Simon Dean refused to comment about the whereabouts of his former band member, Gideon Hawk, and was then seen to board a taxi and head out of the airport. His current whereabouts are unknown." The announcer paused and smiled conspiratorially. "So too are the whereabouts of Gideon Hawk, who hasn't been seen since Wednesday of last week when he left his Manhattan hotel in a limousine. Hawk announced his sudden retirement at a concert in Central Park on Tuesday afternoon, much to the consternation of his fans and other band members. It's suspected that he's staying with friends in Martha's Vineyard."

Abi muted the sound and gazed thoughtfully at the picture on the screen. It showed the band in Central Park earlier in the week, signing autographs among throngs of adoring fans. Gideon stood out, towering over the others, his dark hair swinging over his shoulders, his face moody. As he turned towards the camera, Abi gasped as she gazed into his piercing eyes. The pain she could see there was almost tangible, and her heart went out to him. Wherever he was now, she wished so much she could be there to comfort him. Someone had hurt him badly, and her whole instinct was to dive in and make him better. She turned off the television and got to her feet. She needed some fresh air to clear her head, so she called to the dogs, donned her jacket and wellies, and set off for the beach.

The day was grey—damp, dreary, and typically Novemberish. Not at all the sort of day to raise one's spirits, and by the time she'd clambered down to the shore, thrown a few sticks for the dogs, and made her way slowly back to the cottage, Abi felt no better. She kicked her boots across the room, stomped into the kitchen, and made another cup of tea. Even that didn't seem to help, so she fetched a large bar of nut chocolate from the cupboard and started on that. As she ate, her eyes fell on the boxes from the attic, in their resting place under the stairs. Reluctantly she found herself pulling them towards her and starting to rummage. Carefully she laid out all the loose photos in— roughly—date order, cataloguing her relationship with Gideon from the day they met until the day he left to go on tour. The last time she had seen him in person. The last time she had spoken to him. Then she lifted out the pile of letters and laid them out in date order, too. She had been working her way through them from the earliest one but hadn't yet plucked up the courage to read them all, particularly the very last one, dated in May '96. That was four months after her last letter to Gideon had been posted. It was becoming very clear to her that he'd not received any of her correspondence either, and her head was spinning with the possibilities as to why that was. She felt she really couldn't blame her mother for that one, but it seemed very unlikely that all her letters had gone astray. Maybe they were all still sitting in the office of the record company, never delivered. She thought that was unlikely, too. Cautiously she picked up a letter dated $12^{th}$ January, 1996. She caught her breath, and tears pricked the back of her eyes. That date, so very nearly ten years ago, was etched firmly in her mind forever. It was just after that she had written her very last letter to Gideon. The one in which she finally accepted she must move on since he clearly didn't love her any more. Gently she slit open the letter and unfolded the single sheet of hotel notepaper. Something fell out, as she did so, and fluttered to the floor. Slowly she bent to pick it up. It was a snowdrop, her favourite flower, pressed flat and preserved in its long sojourn in the envelope. Abi swallowed and bit her lip. Gideon had sent her a snowdrop on the very day… She sat down heavily on the nearest chair, her legs refusing to hold her up any longer. Her head was spinning, and memories came flooding into her mind with almost physical pain.

She leant forward and picked up the last photograph in her timeline. It showed Gideon just about to climb into his van. He had paused with his hand on the door handle and turned to face her, the look on his face so loving and tender that she almost cried out. That had been the day he left to go on tour, the last time she'd seen him. Slowly and silently, tears began to fall unheeded down her cheeks.

Chapter 13

*Friday, 9<sup>th</sup> June 1995*

"Abi, come on!" called Judy as she made her way across the playground towards the waiting bus. "You're going to miss the bus. Hurry up!" She beckoned violently to her friend as she finally appeared, running, round the corner of the school building.

"Sorry, Jude, sorry! I needed the loo. Couldn't wait." Abi grinned. "Must be the strain of sitting for three hours in an exam. Let's go."

The two girls climbed onto the bus and wended their way to the back seat. Judy slid into the corner and shoved her bulging bag to the floor. Abi flopped down beside her and fanned herself with her hand.

"Phew," she said, pushing her hair out of her eyes. "Is it usually this hot in June?"

Judy shrugged. "Probably," she said vaguely. "Always seems to be when we're stuck indoors." The GCSEs had begun that week, and the two girls had been subjected to a particularly hard day with Maths in the morning and English Literature in the afternoon. "What did you think of the English?"

Abi screwed up her nose. "Hmm, not bad, I s'pose. Couldn't really concentrate, though," she added with a grin.

Judy rolled her eyes. "Abs, you can't go on like

this. You mustn't let Gideon ruin your exams. Maybe it's no bad thing he's going away on Monday. You need to concentrate."

Abi scowled at her. "How can you say that?" she demanded. "You do realise he's going on an open-ended tour, don't you? He could be away for years!" Her eyes began to fill.

Judy stroked her arm sympathetically. "It won't be that long," she reassured her. "Anyway, aren't you planning to go and join him in the holidays?" Abi nodded and blew her nose. "There you are, then. Just get saving, and you'll see him before you know it."

"Can you honestly see my mother agreeing to me going to America on my own?" Abi mourned.

Judy considered. "It does seem unlikely," she conceded. "But when have you ever done as she said?"

Abi grinned and nodded. "Yeah, you're right. Anyway, I'm sixteen, so can she actually stop me?"

"Not sure." Judy looked doubtful. "Maybe you could find someone to go with. Someone a bit older."

Abi snorted. "Yeah, right. She'd probably suggest Auntie Margaret or something," she said with a shudder.

Judy giggled, and the two of them continued to chat quietly until the bus reached their stop.

Gideon was waiting at the bus stop when the girls arrived. Abi jumped down the steps and flung herself into his arms. He'd been away in London rehearsing, and she hadn't seen him for nearly two weeks. He swung her round, laughing.

"Hey, careful! Don't damage me, I'm potentially worth a lot now," he exclaimed, dropping a kiss on her nose.

Judy heaved Abi's bag up from the ground where it had landed, and Abi took it and slung it over her shoulder.

"Where're we going, Gid?" she asked, grabbing his hand.

He looked down at her. "Well, I think you'd better go home and change first, don't you?" he remarked, glancing at her school uniform. "Then we'll go to the cinema."

Judy chuckled. She was well aware that Abi told her parents she and Gideon were going to the cinema whenever they went out, yet she was fairly sure they hadn't seen a film for many a month.

Gideon grinned at her, then turned to Abi. "Thought we might drive out to Donnington Castle. It's lovely there in the evening."

Abi nodded and squeezed his hand.

"Oh, Gideon, I'm really going to miss you. D'you think the tour will last for ages?" she asked plaintively.

Gideon shrugged. "Dunno," he said. "Could do. Depends if they like us. But don't worry. As soon as you finish school and I get some of the advance they promised us, I'll send you the money for your ticket, and you can come out to join me." She grinned, and he went on. "I'll write and let you know all the details as soon as I know where we'll be, and I'll suss out how easy it'll be to accommodate you." He grinned down at her. "I mean, it's not like you need a room of your own or anything, is it?" he added with a twinkle in his eyes.

Judy groaned. "Too much information, guys!" she complained, wrinkling her nose. "Come on, Abs, let's get you home so you can get changed and enjoy Gideon while he's still here." She grabbed Abi's hand and pulled her towards her house.

Abi let go of Gideon, waved her free hand, and called, "See you in a bit. Don't be too long," before following Judy and turning into her driveway. "What's Dad doing home?" she wondered out loud as they squeezed past the Saab. "Oh, I suppose it is Friday. He does sometimes finish early at the end of the week."

The girls opened the side gate and made their way round to the kitchen door, letting themselves in quietly in an attempt to avoid a confrontation with Abi's mother. As they entered the hall, they could hear the television in the living room, and the low sound of her parents talking. They crept upstairs and scurried into Abi's bedroom. The huge poster of Kurt Cobain that Abi had drawn for her mock GCSE Art exam dominated the room, and Judy looked up at it.

"You'll have to replace that with one of Gideon when he gets famous," she remarked with a grin.

Abi glanced up. "Yeah. Good idea. I'll keep Kurt, though. He's been good inspiration for me," she said with a grin.

Abi was by far the best art student in the school and was planning to make it her career. Her chosen A Level subjects were Art and Design, Textiles, and Photography, and she was tipped to continue on to Art College after Sixth Form. As Judy watched her friend rip off her school uniform and rapidly search through her chest of drawers for something more exciting to wear, she couldn't help wondering if she would ever make it to college or would spend her life following Gideon around the world. She sat cross-legged on the bed and narrowed her eyes.

"Abs," she started carefully. "You are still planning

to do your A Levels, aren't you?"

Abi turned to face her in surprise. "Of course I am," she said, startled, her eyes suddenly wary. "Why wouldn't I?"

Judy shrugged. "I just thought you might go and visit Gideon and never come back," she said bleakly. "I think that would be a shame, 'cause you're really talented."

Abi went to sit next to her friend.

"If I'm going to marry Gideon," she began, "which I am, I need to have my own career. Rock stars have a shelf life, you know. He'll need me to support him when he's washed up."

Judy chuckled. "Cheeky besom," she said. "Well, at least you're still thinking straight." She reached out and squeezed her friend's hand. Abi squeezed back and stood up again.

"However," she added with a crooked grin, "maybe when I get to America I won't be able to leave him. You'll have to wait and see. Who knows what the future holds." She abruptly turned away from her friend, pulled out a pair of faded jeans, thought for a moment, and then discarded them on the floor. "Too hot for jeans," she muttered. "I need a dress, or skirt."

She proceeded to pull clothes out of the drawers, tossing them anywhere around the room as she decided against each one. Judy sighed and moved over to help her.

"How about this one?" she asked, holding up a pretty, flowery cotton dress that Abi had found in a local charity shop.

Abi shrugged. "Yeah, I guess that'll do. I can wear it over my favourite T-shirt, too."

She quickly pulled them on and surveyed herself in her long mirror. Letting her hair out of its restraining elastic band, she messed it up with her hands, then pouted at herself and posed provocatively.

"You look fine," Judy giggled. "Gideon won't be able to keep his hands off you."

Abi spun round and grinned. "No, he won't, will he?" she said rather cockily, diving under her bed and pulling out a pair of tatty black baseball boots. She sat down on the floor and quickly laced them up, leaving the overlong laces trailing, then jumped to her feet and snatched up a knobbly brown cardigan from her bed and grinned at Judy.

"Okay, I'm ready. Shall we go over to your house while I wait for him?" she asked. The sudden sound of footsteps on the stairs heralded the arrival of Abi's mother at the bedroom door.

"Abigail, please unlock your door. I need to speak to you," she ordered, rattling the handle. Abi rolled her eyes and stomped over to pull the bolt back. She opened the door as slowly as possible.

"What?" she demanded. "We're just going out."

Judy got to her feet and smiled nervously at Joan.

"Hi, Mrs. Thomson," she said politely.

Joan nodded to her, then turned back to her daughter.

"I hope you haven't forgotten we're going to Uncle Martin's for the weekend," she said with a frown. "We'll be leaving very early tomorrow morning, so I want you back home early tonight."

As Abi opened her mouth to shout at her mother, Judy leapt forward.

"Oh, Mrs. Thomson, does Abi have to go? We've

got exams on Monday, and she and I were going to revise together this weekend. She could come and stay at my house. My parents won't mind." She surreptitiously grasped Abi's hand in hers to prevent her from joining in the conversation. Joan Thomson looked doubtfully at Judy for a moment, then turned to Abi.

"Is this true? Were you planning to revise with Judy?"

Abi nodded mutely, gripping tightly to Judy's hand and rubbing her right foot up and down her left leg.

"Well, I certainly don't want to stand in the way of your revision," continued Joan. "I shall speak to your father, and if he agrees, then you may stay at Judy's house. So long as it really is all right with her parents."

Judy nodded vigorously and squeezed Abi's hand. Joan turned and started back down the stairs to consult with Arthur, and the two girls held their breath until she was out of sight. Then Abi slammed the door shut and flung her arms around her friend.

"Oh, Judy, thank you!" she squeaked. "You saved my life there. I couldn't possibly miss this weekend with him. Not only is he going away, but do you realise it's his birthday tomorrow? I was just about to shout at her and end up having a huge row, and you saved the day. You're totally brilliant!"

Judy hugged her back and giggled. "You need to think quickly when it comes to parents," she said rather smugly. "D'you think your dad'll agree?"

Abi snorted. "He'll do whatever she tells him. D'you need to phone your mum?"

Judy shook her head. "No, she's still at work, and anyway, she says you can stay any time." She grinned at Abi. "This makes it much easier for you to see Gideon over the weekend. You won't need to keep making up excuses." She looked around the messy room. "You'd better get a bag packed. Bring loads of clothes. You never know where you might end up going."

She reached into Abi's wardrobe and pulled out a large canvas tote bag with Friends of the Earth printed on it. Between them they managed to stuff it full of most of Abi's more summery clothes, and were just cramming her makeup bag on the top when there came a quiet knock at the door. Abi jumped up and pulled it open. Her father looked at her seriously.

"I gather you're staying at Judy's this weekend," he said. Abi nodded. "Well, it certainly wouldn't be much fun for you at Uncle Martin's." He had the grace to smile slightly. "So as long as you really do spend the time revising, then that's all right with me."

Abi leaned forward and gave him a quick peck on the cheek.

"Thanks, Dad," she said. "We've got History and Biology on Monday. We really do have to revise."

Arthur nodded and started back down the stairs, turning half way to look back at her.

"We still want you back early this evening," he said. "Your mother and I are going to bed at ten, ready for our early start, and I want you home before that."

Abi opened her mouth to protest, but Judy appeared beside her.

"She's going to stay with me tonight, as well, Mr. Thomson," she said, smiling winningly at him. He paused for a moment, then nodded at her.

"All right, then, that's probably more sensible. Let

us know when you leave, Abi," he said and continued down the stairs.

Judy shut the door. "God's sake, Abi," she said with a sigh. "You were going to argue with him then, weren't you? You really are your own worst enemy when it comes to your parents. You have no idea how to deal with them. Now come on, let's get going." And she scooped up Abi's school bag and headed for the door.

Abi grabbed the bag of clothes and followed her friend rather sulkily. Judy was quite right. She was far too quick to anger when her parents spoke to her, and she only ever managed to make things worse and end up getting grounded. If it weren't for Judy's intervention she probably wouldn't have been able to see Gideon half as much as she had over the last few months. As they passed the living room door, she opened it and popped her head in.

"We're off now. Give my love to Uncle Martin," she said. "And thanks for letting me stay at Judy's."

The words seemed to mollify her mother, who glanced up from her knitting and inclined her head at her daughter.

"That's fine. Now make sure you thank Mrs. Cromwell for having you, and behave yourself. We'll be back at around six on Sunday. Please make sure you're home by then. Have you got your key?" Abi nodded mutely, biting her tongue to prevent herself from arguing about the Sunday curfew. She closed the door behind her, and she and Judy stepped out into the hot June sunshine.

As they wandered down the road towards Judy's house, Abi was deep in thought. "I really do make things worse for myself, don't I?"

Judy grinned. "Yep," she said simply and giggled. Abi glanced at her and couldn't help joining in, and by the time they arrived at Judy's front gate they were collapsing in hysterical laughter. Judy opened the door with her key, and they carried Abi's luggage upstairs.

"Where're you meeting Gideon?" she asked as they dumped the bags on her bed.

Abi grinned. "On the junction of our roads, as usual," she said, her eyes shining at the sound of his name. She reached inside the neck of her dress and pulled out a thin silver chain on which dangled the ring Gideon had given her on her birthday. She unclasped the chain, then unthreaded the ring and placed it on her finger. "I hate not being able to wear it at school," she said with a pout, gently caressing it.

Judy glanced over at it. "It's a lovely ring," she said enviously. "I wish I had someone to give me one like that."

Abi looked up at her. "I'm sorry," she said contritely. "I keep going on about him, and it must be hard for you. I'm sorry."

Judy grinned. "Don't be daft," she said. "I love that you have him. I just hope someday I can meet someone who loves me that much."

Abi's eyes shone. "He really does, doesn't he?" she said. "I really wish he didn't have to go away, but I know we can still make it work. We love each other so much that it has to."

Judy grinned at her. "What have you got him for his birthday?" she asked suddenly.

Abi smiled a self-satisfied smile. "A really nice leather wrist band with his name on it." she said proudly. "I'm going to make him wear it forever."

****

"I can't believe they're making me be home by six," Abi complained as she and Gideon wandered hand in hand by the river on Sunday afternoon. Abi was carrying her shoes in one hand and the bottom of her skirt was damp from paddling. Gideon, in ripped jeans and a black T-shirt, grinned down at her affectionately.

"Don't worry," he soothed. "You need to keep them on side just now if you're going to persuade them to let you come out to America. It won't hurt you to be home early for once."

Abi scowled at him. "When did you get so sensible?" she demanded. "You sound like Judy. Can we sit down for a bit? I'm tired." She slumped down on the grass at the edge of the river.

Gideon sat down beside her and glanced curiously at her.

"Are you okay, Abs?" he asked with a slight frown. "You seem a bit distracted. And you seem to get tired very easily."

Abi shook her head impatiently. "I'm fine," she said. "Just late nights catching up with me, I guess. I'm distracted because you're leaving tomorrow and I've got to say goodbye to you tonight and won't see you for months…" She turned tear-filled eyes to him, "That's why I'm distracted. And I think I'm going down with a cold."

Gideon put his arm around her shoulders. "I understand. But don't worry. I'll let you know my address as soon as I arrive. I'm not going to try and phone, 'cause it's so expensive, and with the time difference and stuff I think it would just get too frustrating." He grinned at her. "Imagine your mother's face if you started having long phone calls in the middle of the night! It'll be fun to write to each other anyway. You can say more in a letter. And I shall never take this wrist band off, and you can wear your ring, so we'll always have something of each other."

Abi leaned against him and nodded. "I know," she said with a sigh. "Oh, bugger, I need the loo again. Shall I go behind a bush?"

Gideon laughed, so they sought around for a suitable place, and he stood guard while Abi disappeared to do the necessary. When she reappeared, he grabbed her hand and pulled her further into the bushes. His strong arms came round her and held her close, and his firm lips came down on hers. Her arms went around his neck, and she gently slipped her tongue into his waiting mouth. Together they sank to the ground amongst the concealing undergrowth and let their passion consume them.

****

"That was probably the worst Biology exam I've ever taken!" exclaimed Judy as she and Abi took their places on the bus on Monday afternoon.

Abi lay back with a sigh and closed her eyes.

"Definitely," she agreed. "But just think… We never have to do another one. Biology is now a thing of the past."

She shifted her position and sat cross-legged on the seat. Judy watched her closely.

"You okay?" she asked quietly. "Did you have a good last day with him?"

Abi opened her eyes and glanced at her friend.

"Every day is good with him," she said simply. "It

was awful when we had to part." She stopped and looked down at her hands resting on her lap. She seemed about to say more, then changed her mind and closed her eyes again. They sat in a companionable silence until the bus reached their stop, where they got off into the hot June sunshine and began to saunter along the road.

"Abi," Judy asked suddenly, gently touching her friend on the arm. "Are you okay? Is something bothering you, or is it just Gideon going?"

Abi stopped walking and dropped her bag on the ground. She turned to face Judy, her eyes haunted. She swallowed audibly and bit her lip. "Ummm..." She hesitated. "I have got something bothering me, actually." She paused again and stared at Judy, fear in her eyes. "I think I'm pregnant."

Chapter 14

*Monday, 21ˢᵗ November 2005*

Gideon stood on the pavement opposite Abi's childhood home and stared up at what had been her bedroom window. The day was bleak and windy, with a touch of rain in the air, and he pulled the collar of his leather jacket up against the elements. He had left his parents' home early that morning before he could lose his nerve and arrived in Newbury just after ten. His mother had lent him her car for the day, and he had parked it some hundred yards along the road. He had attempted to hide his identity as much as possible, with the help of a baseball cap and dark glasses, but the overcast day had forced him to remove the latter within minutes. He was still not sure what he was going to say when he saw Abi's father. He hadn't seen him since his brief visit in late '97, and they had never really talked. How could he now knock at the door and ask the newly bereaved man why his daughter had dumped him so unceremoniously ten years earlier?

He took a deep breath and crossed the road. The house loomed tantalizingly in front of him, and he squeezed past the ancient Saab, astonished to see it was the same one Abi's father had owned ten years before, and walked up to the front door. With a tremendous effort he raised his hand and rang the bell. Nothing happened at first, and he wasn't sure if he was feeling relief or frustration, but then he heard footsteps coming nearer inside. A shadowy figure loomed on the other side of the frosted glass, and the door finally opened with a creak. Gideon found himself face to face with Arthur Thomson for the first time in eight years, and he was shocked at the change in the man's appearance. Always a small man, he seemed to have shrunk still further, and his skin had an unhealthy yellowish tinge. He had lost most of his hair, and his hands were shaking.

"Good morning, Mr. Thomson," Gideon began with a slight shake in his voice. "I don't know if you remember me…"

Arthur peered at him and took a step backwards.

"Yes, I remember you. You're the boy who ruined my daughter's life." He stared at Gideon, an inscrutable look on his face.

Gideon swallowed nervously. "I wrote to Abi," he said, and was unable to keep the pain out of his voice. "I wrote to her every week…but she didn't reply. Why did she abandon me? I just came here to ask her. I just need to have closure."

Arthur surveyed him cautiously, then his shoulders sagged, and he sighed.

"She doesn't live here anymore," he said finally. "I don't know if she'd want to see you. I can't help you any more." He stepped back and started to close the door. Just before it finally clicked shut, he opened it a crack and peered out at Gideon. "She never got your letters," he said. "She didn't abandon you." Then with a sad look he closed the door and went back into the house.

Gideon stared after him, his mind in a whirl. She never got his letters? How could she not have got his letters? He sucked in his breath in sudden anger. The only possible answer must be that her parents had concealed them from her. Maybe she still didn't know he'd written. She must have believed he'd abandoned her. But why did her father say he'd ruined her life? With his mind in torment, he turned and walked back down the road to where he'd left his mother's Range Rover. As he reached the car, he suddenly realised he'd parked on the corner of the road Judy had lived in. Maybe her parents still lived there. Maybe they could shed more light on what had happened. He pulled his collar up a little further, shoved his hands into his pockets, and walked towards the Cromwells' house. He fully expected to find no one home, so when the door opened at the first ring, he stepped back in surprise. Mary Cromwell stared in amazement at the visitor on her doorstep.

For a moment neither of them spoke, then Gideon cleared his throat. "Hello, Mrs. Cromwell. I don't know if you'll remember me—"

Mary gave a short laugh. "Gideon, you're famous, love! If I hadn't recognised you from ten years ago anyway, I think I'd know who you are. Come in." She stood aside to allow him to enter the house.

He followed her into the kitchen and took the seat she indicated at the table, where he remained silent while she filled the kettle and got some mugs from the dishwasher.

"Tea or coffee?" she inquired, raising her eyebrows.

Gideon licked his lips. Was he losing all control

over his life?

"Ummm, coffee, please. Thank you," he muttered, attempting a smile, which failed dismally and made him appear to be grimacing in pain. Mary smiled slightly and turned back to the job in hand.

"I saw all the hoo-ha about you on the telly last week," she remarked calmly. "I did wonder if you might turn up here again." She paused as she poured the hot water into the mugs and placed them on the table along with a jug of milk and a bowl of sugar. "Abi was here last week. Sat exactly where you are now. Her mother died, you know." She added milk to her tea and watched his dark face intently, noting how his hand clutched the handle of his mug. "She was quite distressed," Mary went on. "Not about her mother, I hasten to add, but something had really upset her. She went to talk to Judy." She leant across the table and patted Gideon's hand.

"D'you know what was wrong?" he asked, his mouth dry and his hands beginning to sweat.

Mary sat back in her chair and pursed her lips. "I really don't think that's for me to say," she said eventually. "I suggest you go and see Judy. She can tell you what's going on." She paused, watching him. "Judy's married now. She has two children."

Gideon nodded his acknowledgment and took a sip of his coffee. After a moment or two of silence he looked at her guardedly.

"Is…is Abi married too?" he asked tightly.

Mary shook her head. "No. No, Abi isn't married," she replied gently.

Gideon found himself relaxing slightly, and took a longer drink from his mug. Mary reached behind her and produced a packet of chocolate digestives. She offered one to Gideon.

"You look like you've had a bit of a hard time lately," she remarked, taking in the dark shadows under his eyes, and his excessive thinness. "I suspect you've been surviving on alcohol, cigarettes, and junk food," she added, quoting his mother almost word for word.

He grinned slightly and nodded his head.

"Yeah. That's right. The life of a rock star, eh? Not that good for you, really," he said, looking up at her. "I've had enough, actually. I just had to get away before it drove me over the edge." He paused again and ran a hand through his long hair. "And I had to know."

He didn't elaborate, but Mary knew exactly what he meant. She pulled a piece of paper towards her, scribbled an address, and pushed it across the table towards him.

"That's my Judy's address," she said. "I'll call and tell her you're coming."

Gideon took a deep breath and got to his feet. "Thank you," he said. "Thank you for not condemning me."

Mary smiled. "I don't think you did anything that deserved condemnation," she reassured him. "Go and talk to Judy before you do anything else." She ushered him to the front door. "I'll call her now; she's bound to be in. It'll take you about half an hour to get there. Give me your mobile number, just in case." She quickly made a note of it, then waved him off down the drive.

Back in the car, Gideon sat motionless for a while, staring out at the familiar suburban street. He remembered back to the summer of '95 when he had left to go on tour and Abi had been in the middle of her exams. They had had such plans. He had written to her within a week of arriving in the States and had heard nothing. He had written again, week after week, month after month, each time getting more and more despondent and confused. Looking back, he realised he probably should have done more to contact her, but he had been nineteen, on his first tour with his own band, and pretty much under the control of the tour manager. He had had no time to call his own.

With a deep sigh, he started the car and set off out of town in the direction of Judy's cottage. He hadn't bothered to programme it into the SatNav and decided to rely on his memory of the area.

This proved fairly reliable, and less than half an hour later he drew up outside the little cottage and parked exactly where Abi had parked just a few days earlier. He locked the car and approached the front door nervously. He had no idea of the reception he was going to get and steeled himself for the wrath of a best friend. He couldn't help thinking that meeting Judy was even more scary than meeting Abi would be. He knocked at the door, stepped back a little, and waited. A few moments later he heard a key being turned, and the door slowly opened. He caught his breath. Judy stood there, slightly older but otherwise identical to the Judy of ten years ago, with a smiling baby balanced on her hip. She surveyed him solemnly for a moment, then grinned broadly and stepped back to let him in.

"My god, Gideon, you look dreadful!" she said bluntly, shutting the door behind him. "Come on in. I've got the kettle on."

She led the way through the cluttered kitchen and into the conservatory. A small boy with blond hair was sitting on the floor doing a large jigsaw, and an empty playpen was in the centre of the room. Judy dumped the baby into the playpen, indicated to Gideon to take a seat, then disappeared into the kitchen to make some tea. Gideon shifted uncomfortably in his chair and looked around him, suddenly becoming aware that the small boy was watching him solemnly.

He smiled at him. "Hello, I'm Gideon. What's your name?"

The child stared at him for a moment, then said, "Tommy," and went back to his puzzle.

Judy appeared in the doorway, carrying a loaded tray she set down on the table.

"He's a man of few words," she said with a laugh, looking fondly at her son. She handed Gideon a cup and curled up in the chair next to him. They stared at each other for a moment in silence, then Judy shook her head. "Until last week, I never thought this moment would come," she said with a grin. "I never expected to see you again—in person, that is."

Gideon smiled back. "Why last week?"

Judy cocked her head on one side. "Well, first you left the band and disappeared," she said. "Then Abi turned up and told me something rather shocking…" She paused and watched him closely. "Something that upset her a lot."

Gideon shifted uncomfortably again. "I tried to talk to her father," he said, "but he sent me away. Told me she didn't live here any more." He paused for a long moment. "Then, just as I was leaving, he said Abi hadn't received my letters…and then he shut the door."

Judy sighed. "She didn't get them," she said sadly. "She thought you'd abandoned her. She was completely distraught. I watched her turn from the slightly cocky, over-confident wild child you knew into a pale, insecure, and broken woman." She paused again. "Then last week, just after her mother's funeral, she found a box full of letters from you, letters her mother had concealed from her. Dozens of them, and postcards too."

Gideon turned towards her, his face anguished.

"She never got any of them?" he whispered. "So she never knew where to write to me. No wonder I got nothing from her."

Judy sat forward abruptly. "She *did* write to you. When she didn't hear from you she wrote to you care of the record company. She wrote about ten letters, right up to January '96. Did they not pass them on?"

Gideon looked confused. "Actually, they did pass on mail to us. Fairly regularly. Why did I not get hers?" He frowned. "How could they all have gone astray, when I got other mail?" He stared at her, his pain-filled thoughts working overtime. "Does she hate me?" he asked at last.

Judy gave a slight laugh. "She never hated you, even when she thought you'd abandoned her." She paused at Gideon's wince. "And now she knows you wrote to her, she's in a state of turmoil." She paused again and looked him in the eye. "But she doesn't know for sure that you didn't get her letters—although that must be pretty obvious by now, if she's read all yours to her—and there are things in her letters you really need to know about." She fell silent, and Gideon gave her an intent look.

"What things?" he demanded.

Judy shook her head. "Nothing I can tell you," she

said firmly. "You must see Abi for that." She chewed her bottom lip. "I'll give you her address. I won't tell her you're coming—she'll probably hate me for that, but so be it—because I think it would be better if she wasn't expecting you." She handed him a piece of paper that was in the pocket of her jeans, and he raised his eyebrows at her. "Yes, okay, I'd already decided to give it to you. Now, go—now. You need to see her. Maybe leave it till tomorrow, if you want. It's a long way." She stood up from her chair and gazed down at him. "And if I were you, I'd have a bit of a think about what could have happened to the letters she wrote to you."

He got to his feet and gave her a quick hug. "Thanks, Judy. You always were the sensible one. You saved Abi from a lot of scrapes in the past. I'll go and see her and try to make peace." He made his way down the path towards his waiting car without a backward glance.

****

After Gideon left, Arthur went out to his shed and spent a couple of hours re-potting his geraniums. Then he went back into the dark, cold, empty house, boiled the kettle, and made a sandwich. As he sat at the kitchen table slowly sipping his tea, his sandwich lying untouched beside him, he reflected on his actions of earlier that day.

Why had he sent Gideon away without telling him where Abi was? Why at the last moment did he relent just that little bit and tell him about the hidden letters? He knew if Gideon really wanted to find Abi he would do so one way or another, so his actions had not prevented them from meeting, however much he really desired that. So why tell him about the letters?

Arthur concluded it must have been guilt. Although he had not known about the concealment of the letters, he had plenty of other worse things to feel guilty about from that time. He nodded to himself. It must be the guilt. He took another sip of tea and wondered sadly if Abi had opened the tin box yet.

****

Abi spent Monday morning in the garden shed she had recently converted into a studio. She was working hard to prepare a portfolio of landscapes to sell throughout the tourist season from the various outlets who agreed to stock her work. On dry days she worked out in the garden or on the cliffs, painting numerous views of the bay, but on dreary, wet winter days such as this, she worked in the studio copying from photographs she had taken. She was presently working on a view of Land's End in a violent storm, and was beginning to be quite pleased with the progress she was making.

She kept working right through until her hunger finally drove her indoors and she discovered it was nearly three o'clock. Surprised she had painted for so long, she decided to call it a day and go for a nice long walk with the dogs, so she cleaned her brushes, tidied the studio, and locked it securely. Then she donned her boots and waterproof jacket and called to the dogs, who had spent the morning dozing in front of the fire.

The trek down to the beach proved to be very cold, wet, and windy, and Abi and the dogs didn't hang about. Their proposed long walk took only twenty minutes. As Abi paddled in the swiftly moving water, Lilt and Flora splashing around her feet, she tried to make some sense of the last week. Her emotions, held in check now for so many years, had all suddenly been hauled unceremoniously to the surface from all directions. The death of her mother—she didn't miss her, but it was an emotional upheaval, nonetheless. The news of Gideon leaving the band and then the incredible discovery in the attic of the stolen letters—those things had changed her life completely. Abi was in an emotional turmoil and badly needed someone to talk to. It had been wonderful spending time with Judy, but it hadn't been enough. She really needed her best friend with her now, to help her sort her head out. The sight of Gideon getting into the limo in New York was haunting her, too. Since that day, he seemed to have disappeared off the face of the earth. The press had been unable to track him down, and no one so far had given away his whereabouts. Not even Simon, who Abi had seen footage of on the news as he arrived at Heathrow, seemed to know where he was.

Abi wondered if Gideon ever thought of her. If he hadn't received her letters either, then he must have thought she'd abandoned him. He would have known none of the things she wrote to him about. He would know nothing of what she went through after he left. He would never have known she was pregnant. As she stood ankle deep in the cold sea, Abi stared into the distance and felt overwhelmed, as all the buried memories of ten years ago came flooding to the surface. She shivered suddenly, thrust her hands deep into her pockets, and whistled for the dogs to follow her home. She needed the security of her safe, warm, little cottage, with all its familiarity. More practically, she needed a shower, a cup of hot chocolate, and a large piece of cake.

Half an hour later, tucked up on the sofa, hot chocolate in hand, Abi was plucking up the courage to rummage through the boxes again. She had the two cardboard ones on the floor at her feet, but the enigmatic tin one remained in its shadowy hiding place under the stairs. Abi glanced over at it. For some reason she couldn't bring herself to prise it open yet. She felt sure her father had wanted her to have it for a reason, and she was convinced he knew what was in it. She gave her head a slight shake. That one was for another day. Maybe when Judy was with her.

She turned her attention to the boxes at her feet. The first one contained all the letters and cards from Gideon, and a large number of photographs, both loose and in albums. She had pretty much looked at all of them. The second box, however, seemed to contain a number of old newspapers, and newspaper cuttings bundled together with a large elastic band. She picked them up, and as she did so noticed a CD case glinting at the bottom of the box. Curiously, she fished it out and dusted it off. It was her copy of NightHawk's first album, called simply *NightHawk*. The album they'd been recording in London in the spring of '95. The album that contained the track "Storm Rising," that Abi had first heard the night she and Gideon met. She smiled slightly, carefully removed the CD from the case, and inserted it into her CD player. She selected the track she wanted, then pressed play.

As the first notes of "Storm Rising" echoed around the room, Abi curled up on the sofa and removed the bundle of newspaper cuttings from the box. Carefully she slid the elastic band off and smoothed them out.

Having braced herself to expect anything, Abi wasn't shocked to see that the first one had a picture of NightHawk performing at their first concert in the States, just a week after her last meeting with Gideon. She remembered cutting the picture out of the paper herself. She had felt so proud to be able to say, "That's my boyfriend. He's famous," to anyone who would listen. She remembered how she'd also been so nervous. She'd been waiting to hear from Gideon before she wrote to him, so she hadn't at that point written the letter telling him she was pregnant. The letter she had believed, for the last ten years, had been the thing that had led him to desert her.

Taking a deep breath, she picked up the next cutting, and bit her lip so hard it almost made her cry out. Dated in August '95, it was again a picture of Gideon, but this time he was with a skinny blonde girl who hung possessively onto his arm and gazed adoringly up at him. Gideon himself was snarling at the camera, his hand outstretched in a attempt to prevent them from being photographed. Abi remembered how she had kept that picture to torture herself. She lay back against the cushions, the cutting clutched in her hand, and remembered the day she had first seen him on the news with another girl.

She thought that was the day her heart finally broke.

Chapter 15

*Wednesday, 23$^{rd}$ August 1995*

"Abi turn on the news!" yelled Judy down the phone. "Quickly! Channel 4! It's Gideon!"

Abi squeaked, "I'll call you back!" and flung the receiver back onto its cradle. She raced into the living room, where her father was watching a gardening programme, and snatched up the remote control. "Sorry, Dad, need to see something," she gasped, pressing the button for Channel 4 and completely disregarding his mild remonstrations. The picture flashed up on the screen just in time for Abi to see Gideon and the rest of the band standing outside a large hotel in the middle of some American city. She thought it might be Seattle.

She perched on the edge of a chair and peered at the screen. The band were surrounded by reporters and photographers, and a number of security men were attempting to clear a path through the throng for the boys to get to their waiting limousine. Abi caught her breath. She could hardly believe these were the same boys who had left England two months earlier as total unknowns. She dropped to her knees in front of the television in an attempt to get a closer look at Gideon, just as he appeared out of the throng of fans and reporters and reached the waiting car. She stared in disbelief when she realised he was accompanied by a very thin, very glamorous blonde girl who was hanging on to his arm. She shook her head violently; it couldn't be true. Gideon wouldn't do that to her. He wouldn't go with another girl. He was hers. She was his. She stared at the screen as the picture faded and the news reader went on to the next subject.

"I knew he couldn't be trusted," said her mother from behind her, satisfaction in her voice. "Now will you forget about him and get on with your life?"

Abi looked up at her, her eyes shining with unshed tears.

"There must be some mistake," she almost whispered. "He wouldn't do that. He loves me." She struggled to her feet and began to stumble from the room.

"I think we now have the reason why he hasn't written to you, anyway." Her mother's voice followed her as she let herself out the front door and walked rapidly to the street.

She had to get to Judy as soon as she could and found herself almost running down the road towards her friend's house. She met the other girl running to meet her just as she rounded the corner. Judy held out her arms and they clung together, Abi finally letting the sobs come flooding out.

****

"Gideon! Gideon! Over here! How're you liking Seattle? Were you pleased with last night's concert?"

"Where are you off to next?"

"How d'you spend your time off? What d'you think of Seattle nightlife?"

The questions came thick and fast, firing at the

boys as they attempted to leave the hotel, shielding their eyes from the sea of flashing cameras.

Their rise to stardom had been meteoric, starting at their very first concert in New York back in June. Their reception had been unexpectedly tumultuous, and they hadn't had a moment's peace ever since. The fact that they were all so young seemed to be in their favour, and they had amassed an enormous, mostly very young, fan base within about a week. Consequently they were now being mobbed by a throng of young teenage girls all clamouring for their autographs or trying to pull off items of their clothing. As Gideon finally reached the limousine, he ducked inside with a sigh of relief, sliding over into the far corner to allow his companions some space. The girl accompanying him slid in next and attempted to snuggle up to him. He glanced down at her, contempt in his eyes.

"How many times do I have to tell you," he said harshly, "I'm *not* fucking interested. Now get off me, and leave me alone." He pushed her along the seat towards Simon, who greeted her with open arms and a large grin. She scowled at him and sank back in her seat with her arms folded and a sulky expression on her painted face.

Gideon stared out the window as they sped through the streets and out onto Interstate 5, northbound towards Vancouver for their next gig. He was enjoying the concerts and the sudden stardom, but he was hating the unwanted attention from the girls, and he was missing Abi so much he could hardly sleep. He had written to her every week since he'd left England and so far not had a single reply. To begin with he'd not been too worried—they had moved around so much he could understand it if her letters had been one step behind him, but he'd been gone for over two months now, and he was getting really worried. He had tried to phone her on a couple of occasions, but getting the times right and actually getting through proved far too difficult, so he'd doubled his efforts with the letters, and started sending a postcard from each location, as well. Every night he went to sleep picturing her face and having imaginary conversations with her. He couldn't even bring himself to contemplate the possibility she no longer felt the same way he did. They had promised to be together forever, and to him that really meant forever. The fact they had to be apart for a while shouldn't matter if they both felt the same. He clung to the thought that her letters had got held up as he rested his head against the window and bleakly watched the countryside fly by.

****

Abi sat cross-legged on Judy's bed, her face mottled from crying and her hair falling in a tangle across her eyes. Judy stared at her in frustration. There was nothing she could say or do that would make her friend feel any better, and she was at a complete loss what to do next.

It was the day their GCSE results were due, and the two girls were planning to go up to the school in a while to see how they'd done. Since the news report the previous day, Abi couldn't have cared less, but Judy was going to force her to go with her.

"Abs, can we try and tidy you up a bit?" she said gently, sitting down beside her. "We have to go up to school very soon. Mum says she'll take us."

Abi stared at her soulfully. "None of that means

184

anything anymore," she stated dramatically, tears beginning to run down her cheeks again. Judy sighed. She totally understood her friend's despair, but she also knew that life had to go on, and that in fact Abi had a much bigger problem to deal with than just the loss of a boyfriend.

"Abi," she said tentatively. "I think you're going to need to tell someone about the baby soon. You're beginning to show," she patted Abi's stomach, concealed by a baggy cotton top.

Abi rubbed her eyes and pushed her hair back.

"I can't," she said decisively. "I know what'll happen. My mother'll want me to get rid of it, and I'm never going to do that." She paused and fixed Judy with a steely stare. "I'm going to America and have my baby there with Gideon."

Judy jumped up and stamped her foot.

"Abi, you can't!" she almost yelled. "You have no money, you don't know where he is, and you don't even know if he…" She was unable to utter the damning words.

"I don't even know if he still wants me," Abi finished for her bleakly. "But I really can't tell my parents. They'll kill me."

There was a tap at the door, and Judy's mother popped her head in.

"Nearly time to go, girls," she said, taking in the situation at a glance. "Judy, could I just have a quick word with you downstairs?" She disappeared again.

Judy rolled her eyes at Abi. "Won't be a sec. You wash your face and tidy yourself up." And with that she followed her mother down the stairs.

Mary Cromwell stood leaning against the kitchen

table with her arms folded when Judy walked in.

"What's up?" asked Judy, stopping in front of her.

Mary surveyed her sternly. "Has Abi seen a doctor yet?" she asked.

Judy started, and stared at her in surprise. "What?" she gasped. "Why should she see a doctor? She's not ill."

Mary sighed. "Judy, what job do I do?" she asked patiently.

"Midwife," muttered Judy, feeling her face begin to flush.

"Exactly, and I know a pregnant teenager when I see one. How many weeks is she?" she asked with a frown.

Judy shrugged. "Not sure," she said. "She told me at the beginning of June. The day after Gideon left."

Mary did a quick calculation. "Good grief," she exclaimed. "She must be at least sixteen weeks, if not more! She really needs to see someone." She looked closely at her daughter. "Don't worry. You haven't broken her trust. I guessed, remember. She can't keep it a secret forever. I take it she doesn't want her parents to know?"

Judy nodded. "She thinks her mother will make her have an abortion," she said quietly.

Mary sucked in her breath. "She can't force her," she said. "But I agree she could make things very hard for her. Nonetheless, she will need to tell them. She must be beginning to show by now."

Judy nodded. "She is. She just keeps wearing baggy tops." She paused and thought for a moment. "She wants to go to America and have it with Gideon," she said at last.

Mary shook her head. "Oh, dear. And I suppose she still hasn't heard from him? Has she told him about the baby?"

Judy shrugged. "Well she wrote to him about it, but we don't know if he got it."

Or if he got it and it scared him off, thought Mary to herself.

"If she'd agree to it, I could check her over, just to make sure everything's going okay so far. D'you think she'd let me?"

Judy considered, then shrugged. "Worth a try, I s'pose," she said. "Shall I ask her?"

Mary nodded. "Yes, but let's wait until you've got your results. It's time to leave now, so go and fetch her."

The drive to the school was taken in silence. Abi and Judy sat in the back, and Mary kept an eye on them in the mirror. Abi's face was still a bit red, and her eyelids were slightly swollen, but she'd brushed her hair, touched up her makeup, and managed to make herself look reasonably presentable. She was showing no interest whatsoever in the results of her exams, and Judy had given up trying to talk about them.

When they arrived at the school, Mary dropped them off and moved into the car park to wait for them. As the girls approached the school hall, the door was flung open and a number of laughing students ran out, waving pieces of paper in the air. They squealed their results to Abi and Judy, then ran off to their respective cars.

Abi gave a wan smile. "Oh, well, at least someone did well," she said. "Come on, then. Let's get it over with." She quickened her pace and walked into the hall.

The place was thronged with girls, some excited, some looking depressed, and some trying to pretend it didn't matter. Abi and Judy went to the table where their Form Tutor, Mrs. Leadbetter, was handing out the envelopes. She glanced up as the girls approached.

"Ummm…Cromwell, Judith," she said, handing a sealed white envelope to Judy, "and Thomson, Abigail. Good luck, girls," and she turned to the next arrivals.

Judy and Abi carried their envelopes over to the side of the hall and slit them open with their fingers. As she unfolded the sheet of paper within, Abi felt the first hint of interest. Despite all that was going on in her life, she found she did still care to see if she had managed to get an A for Art. She took a deep breath and scanned down the rest of the page. She grimaced at the two Cs for Geography and Maths, but sighed with relief when she saw the Art result: A, as expected. She finished reading them. In all she had got three As, four Bs, and two Cs. Not bad, considering she hadn't really bothered with her revision.

Judy looked over her shoulder. "Oh, you did it!" she exclaimed with delight. "I knew you could. And I got As for French and Spanish!"

Abi gave her friend a hug, and they started to make their way to the door. Suddenly someone stepped in front of them, blocking their way.

"Move, Collette," said Judy with a sigh. "I can't be bothered with your nonsense today."

The other girl gave a malicious smile and spoke to Abi. "Saw your boyfriend on the telly yesterday." She laughed unpleasantly, her eyes gleaming. "Got a new slut in tow now, has he? Has all this fame gone to his head, then?"

Abi raised her hand to slap the other girl's face, and as she stretched up, her top clung to her body and for just a second revealed her pregnant belly. With a swift movement she lowered her arm again and began to walk rapidly towards the door, but not before Judy had had time to see the look of realisation on the other girl's face. She thrust her face close to Collette's.

"You keep your nasty little nose out of our business," she hissed menacingly, then turned and ran after her friend. Collette watched them go, a sneaky little smile playing on her lips.

Judy caught up with Abi in the car park, and grabbed her arm.

"Don't worry, Abs, she can't hurt you," she said breathlessly.

Abi turned on her. "Yes, she can. She can tell everyone, and then my mother will find out. Then it's all over." She walked towards the gate.

Judy jumped in front of her. "Abi, come on. We've got to go back to the car. Mum's waiting." She caught Abi's hands. "And Abs, your mum's going to find out sooner or later. You know she is." She paused and licked her lips. "My Mum has already guessed." Abi stopped walking and stared at Judy in horror. Judy shook her arm. "Abi, she's a midwife; it's her job to notice. Don't worry. She wants to help."

She pulled Abi towards the car where her mother was waiting. They climbed into the back seat, and Abi sat silent, staring straight ahead. Mary turned to face them.

"Well?" she asked. "How did you do?"

Judy thrust her results letter at her mother and said, "Fine, and Abi got A for Art, so that's fine, too."

Mary raised her eyebrows at her daughter. "Has something happened?"

Judy nodded. "Collette saw Abi's belly. Abi thinks she'll tell everyone."

Mary sighed. "Oh, dear. This was bound to happen sooner or later. Come on. Let's get you two home. We'll talk then." She started the car and headed back towards their house.

Once back inside, Mary made them all cold drinks and they carried them out into the garden and sat in the summerhouse. Abi gazed around her, remembering the morning she'd spent an hour and a half hiding in there on a cold December day, following her first date with Gideon. Her eyes began to fill with tears, and she leaned forward to let her hair conceal her face. Mary sat back in her deckchair and surveyed Abi shrewdly.

"So, young lady, how many weeks pregnant are you?" she asked in a matter-of-fact tone. "When was your last period?"

Abi looked up, peering through her hair. "The fifth of April," she whispered.

Mary did a quick calculation and looked shocked. "Good grief, girl! You're nearly half way. And you haven't seen a doctor or midwife at all?"

Abi shook her head. She felt so vulnerable and lost that she wished she could just disappear until it was all over.

Mary smiled encouragingly at her. "Don't worry, love. I'm sure everything's okay, but if you don't mind, I'd like to give you a quick examination." She saw Abi's face and laughed. "Nothing intrusive. I just want to take your blood pressure, listen to the heartbeat, that sort of thing."

Abi pushed her hair off her face. "The heartbeat?" she asked. "D'you mean my baby's heartbeat?"

Mary nodded. "Yes. Just to check it's doing okay. Is that all right?"

Abi nodded and managed a small smile. "I'd love to hear her heartbeat," she said shyly. "It'll make her even more real."

Judy glanced at her. "How d'you know it's a her?"

Abi shrugged and smiled. "Dunno. Just do."

Mary stood and held out her hand to Abi. "Right. Come along, then, and let's do this." She paused and fixed Abi with a stern gaze. "But you really must see your doctor, too, and you will have to tell your mother."

Abi nodded slowly and followed her back into the house.

****

"Abigail Thomson, get out of bed immediately!"

Abi awoke to hear the thunderous tones of her mother standing over her. She opened her eyes and pulled the quilt up to her chin.

"What's up?" she asked nervously.

Joan Thomson grabbed the quilt in her left hand and pulled it off her daughter. Her sudden intake of breath told Abi her mother had seen her distended belly. She rolled onto her side in an attempt to conceal it, but Joan caught her by the wrist and pulled her out of bed.

"Mum! No, leave me alone!" Abi cried as she pulled herself upright and stood facing her mother.

"So it's true," Joan said flatly. "You little slut! How dare you disgrace the family like this! Get dressed." She turned to leave the room.

Abi stood staring after her, transfixed, her mind in turmoil. She sat back down on the bed and found she was shaking all over.

Joan turned just before she left the room. "Get dressed," she repeated. "We're going to sort this out, once and for all." She closed the door behind her, and Abi heard her steps disappearing downstairs.

Abi wriggled backwards on the bed and huddled up against the wall. her arms wrapped protectively around her stomach. She knew what her mother meant. She was going to take her somewhere to get rid of the baby. Abi looked around her in a panic. What could she do? Where could she go? Apart from leaving through the window—a drop of at least fifteen feet—there was no other means of escape. She would have to try and make a break for it when they were out. She would go to Judy's and throw herself on Judy's parents' mercy. Judy's mother would never countenance an abortion.

She dressed quickly in baggy shorts and a long loose flowery top, and pushed her feet into her baseball boots. She stuffed a few essentials into a canvas shoulder bag and ran a quick brush through her hair. Then she made her bed and went downstairs. Her mother was waiting for her in the hall, impatiently drumming her fingers on the banister.

"Right. Come along. I've arranged an appointment with Dr. Slater at the Merrilees Clinic in half an hour. She'll sort you out."

Abi's eyes widened in surprise. The Merrilees Clinic was a private nursing home about five miles away and was well known for being overpriced and oversubscribed.

"Why aren't we going to Dr. Ford?" she asked, thinking quite fondly of her family GP. She'd known him since she was tiny.

Joan looked her up and down. "If you think I am going to let our own doctor know the shame you've brought on this family, you have another think coming," she said brusquely. "We're going where no one knows us. Now, come on. I've ordered a taxi, and it should be here any minute."

Abi followed her mother out onto the drive, and they waited for a moment until the black cab drew up outside. As Abi climbed into the back, she was reminded of the sight of Gideon getting into the limo with a girl on his arm, and she suddenly wondered if anything really mattered any more.

The clinic proved to be a twenty-minute drive away, and when Abi and Joan arrived they were shown into a very comfortable and beautifully decorated waiting room. Joan had a quiet word with the receptionist, filled in a couple of forms, and then took the seat next to Abi. They sat in tense silence until a door in the corner of the room opened and a tall slim lady with short blonde hair peered out.

"Abigail Thomson?" she asked with a smile. Abi nodded, and she and her mother entered the doctor's consulting room. Dr. Slater gestured for them to sit on the comfy sofa that faced her desk, and then she sat down and picked up her pen. "So, what can I do for you, Abigail?" she asked pleasantly.

Abi cleared her throat. "I'm pregnant," she said in little more than a whisper.

The doctor nodded. "A lot of girls who come here are," she reassured her, with a smile. "How many weeks are you?"

"About twenty," Abi said with a quick glance at her mother.

Joan frowned, and spoke to the doctor. "I didn't realise she was that far advanced," she said apologetically. "Can anything still be done?"

Dr. Slater looked from mother to daughter.

"I take it you are seeking a termination?" she asked, laying down her pen and focusing on Abi's face.

Joan nodded and began to speak, but Abi got to her feet and faced her mother.

"No, I'm not! I want to have this baby, and you can't make me get rid of it. I'm sixteen. I'm not a child." Her voice was shrill until it broke, and tears began to run down her cheeks.

Dr. Slater stood up and raised a calming hand. "It's all right, Abigail. No one can force you to do anything you don't want to do. Now, would you just let me examine you? Just to check your dates are correct."

She led Abi over to the examination table and helped her up onto it. She warmed her hands for a moment before she gently lifted Abi's top and pressed lightly on her belly. Then she applied her stethoscope and asked Abi a few questions regarding her last period. After a few minutes she indicated that she could go back to her seat.

"Well, I think we're correct about the dates; twenty weeks seems to be about right," she said, sitting back down behind her desk. She leant forward and spoke to Abi's mother. "Under the circumstances, I wouldn't advise a termination. At this stage it's a very traumatic event, and I don't think it would do Abigail any good at all." She paused and looked from one to the other of them. "Is there no way you could keep the baby?"

Abi sucked in her breath. "Yes. I want to keep the baby," she repeated emphatically. "She's mine, and I'm going to keep her."

Joan gave her a look of dislike. "And how do you propose to look after a baby?" she asked, her voice shaking. "You're a child. You know nothing of what having a small baby means. The crying, the endless, endless crying…the sleepless nights, the constant feeling of tiredness… You wouldn't be able to cope on your own, and you can forget any idea of me looking after it."

Dr. Slater looked slightly taken aback, but waited while Abi composed herself.

"I wouldn't *let* you look after her," Abi spat out eventually. "I shall leave school and take her to be with her father."

Joan gave a bark of mirthless laughter and gestured to the doctor.

"See what I'm up against, Dr. Slater? The girl lives in cloud cuckoo land. The father is in America and wants nothing to do with her." She turned to Abi. "We'll abandon the idea of an abortion," she conceded, "but when the child is born we'll have it adopted immediately. I'm sure Dr. Slater could advise on that. I should also like to book Abigail in here for the birth."

Dr. Slater looked from mother to daughter again, and a slight frown creased her forehead.

"I will happily book her in for the delivery," she said. "But I must point out that we don't countenance forcing anyone to give up her baby unless it's threatening to the well-being of either baby or mother, so it must be Abigail's decision."

Joan inclined her head slightly, then shook hands with the doctor before they made their way back outside.

As they stood in the shade of a large chestnut tree waiting for a return taxi, Joan spoke quietly to Abi. "You will give that baby up. Make no mistake—there's no way on earth I'm letting you keep it." Her voice was icy.

Abi glanced at her. "Over my dead body," she said calmly.

Chapter 16

*Tuesday, 22nd November 2005*

Simon awoke on Tuesday morning having finally shaken off his jet lag and his hangover. He rolled out of bed, marvelling that his bedroom still looked the same as it had ten years before when he'd left home, and dived into the bathroom for a quick shower. His headache might have gone, but his mood was little better than it had been when he'd arrived at Heathrow two days earlier. His mother had been very patient with him, allowing him to rant on about Gideon's behaviour and the horrors of the paparazzi, and leaving him to his own devices as much as possible, which mainly meant letting him sleep all day, but Simon was beginning to realise that he wasn't being a very good son.

He dressed rapidly in jeans and a faded NightHawk T-shirt, then ran down the stairs and into the kitchen. His mother was sitting at the table eating toast and reading the paper, and she glanced up as her son came in. From the resigned look in her eye, Simon realised he had probably tried her patience rather too far, so he summoned up a cheerful smile and dropped a kiss on her curly head.

"Feeling better today, love?" she asked with a smile, the relief sounding in her voice. Simon nodded, poured himself a cup of tea, and sat down opposite her at the table.

"Yes, thanks. Sorry I've been such a bear. Bit of a culture shock being home, actually."

Josephine Dean surveyed her son speculatively. "I don't think you really want to be here, do you?" she said with a slightly quizzical smile. "I assume you came over to England to look for Gideon."

Simon's face darkened, and he ran a hand through his hair. "Partly," he said at last. "I also want to find Abi."

His mother looked at him in surprise. "Well, that's a name I haven't heard for many years. She left home the minute she finished school and hasn't been back since, as far as I know." She paused in thought. "Well, her mother died a couple of weeks ago. She may have been here for the funeral—I don't know. I couldn't stand the woman. Didn't go near the place."

Simon took a long slurp of tea, then wiped his mouth with the back of his hand.

"Where does she live now, then?" he asked casually.

Josephine shook her head. "No idea, love. As I said, I haven't even heard her name for years. You could try asking Mary Cromwell. I'm sure Abi kept in touch with her girl. You remember Judy?"

Simon nodded morosely. "Yeah. Pair of bloody interlopers," he muttered, mostly to himself.

Josephine frowned. "They were both nice girls," she said reprovingly. "It was a shame Abi and Gideon lost touch. They made a lovely couple."

Simon stared at his mother in horror. How could she talk like that? Abi could have completely ruined everything for the band if he hadn't stepped in. But he hadn't known everything. And now he had to stop Gideon finding out what had happened after he left. If Gideon ever knew that Simon had kept Abi's letters from him, that would be the end of their friendship, and he didn't think he could bear that. He had only been acting for the good of the band—he had to keep reminding himself of that.

"Where do you think Gideon has gone?" asked his mother suddenly.

Simon shrugged. "Dunno. Wish I did," he murmured.

Josephine frowned. "Maybe he's gone to his parents' house," she said brightly. "They moved to the New Forest somewhere, I believe. We lost touch after that. Lovely couple."

Was there a couple she didn't think were "lovely"? Simon wondered. He sighed and pushed his empty cup away.

"Best way to find him is probably to watch the news," he said bleakly. "The press are bound to find him eventually. I'm expecting them here any day now." He peered out of the kitchen window as if expecting to see a cameraman concealed in the shrubbery.

Josephine shook her head. "Well, I hope they don't come here," she said shortly. "I can do without that again. We were mobbed when you started to get famous. No idea what they hoped to get from taking pictures of your father and me doing the garden." She pushed back her chair and carried the cups to the dishwasher. "I suggest you go and see Mary Cromwell if you want to find Abi."

Simon sat for a moment, contemplating his movements, before he got to his feet and left the room without a word. Five minutes later Josephine heard the front door slam as he left the house. She shook her head sadly. Stardom didn't really suit her son, she thought to herself.

****

The phone rang just as Judy had got Sabrina off to sleep for her morning nap. She swore under her breath and snatched it up as fast as she could.

"Hello," she said quietly. "Oh, hi, Mum. You okay?" She carried the phone into the living room and curled up on the sofa. "What…really? You are getting a lot of visitors this week, aren't you?" She laughed out loud. "What'd you tell him?...Oh, good. I was going to say, please don't give him her address. I've sent Gideon off down there, and I don't think they should be in the same place at the moment." She listened again, chewing on a chipped nail. "Okay, glad you did that. I really don't want him coming here. We never got on, and I don't trust him." She paused. "Oh, I don't know for sure, but I've been thinking, and I reckon it may have been Simon who stopped Abi's letters getting to Gideon…yes, I think so, too. By the way any more news on…" She listened intently. "Right, well, I think I will have to go and see Abi at the weekend whatever. I had an e-mail on Sunday saying happy birthday, and I could tell from it that she really needs someone to talk to. Of course, now I've sent Gideon down to see her without telling her, she may not want to see me," she added with a laugh. She stretched her legs out in front of her in an attempt to warm her feet by the fire. "I know, maybe I should have told her, but I didn't want to scare her off. I think they just need to be thrust together. Hope so, anyway." She grimaced. "So let me know if there's any more news...Bye for now." She switched the phone off thoughtfully.

If Simon did turn up at Abi's house, she could foresee disaster. If she was correct about him having kept Abi's letters from Gideon, then at the moment he was probably intent on keeping the two of them apart so there was no danger of him being found out. She got to her feet and walked over to the computer to check her e-mail. She'd better reply to Abi's message and reassure her that she would be down on Friday.

****

Gideon had borrowed his mother's car again, this time for an unspecified time, and he was speeding along the westbound carriageway of the A30 between Exeter and Launceston. He was extremely nervous about turning up uninvited at Abi's house, but he had to admit that if she knew he was coming she might have fled by the time he got there. He had no idea what she felt about him now. So much time had gone by since they'd last seen each other, they would be bound to have changed immeasurably. And she had spent the last ten years thinking he'd abandoned her, while he had thought the same about her. He gave a rather sardonic smile. They would either have lots to talk about—or nothing at all. He was fascinated to find out which.

As he drove, his mind went racing back through the years to his relationship with Abi. They had been so young but had both been so sure they were meant to be together. He had planned to marry her as soon as his tour was over—the tour that ended up lasting for two years. But in that time he never heard from her, and now he'd discovered she had never received his letters either. He began to feel a great overwhelming anger at the circumstances that had torn them apart. Something, or someone, had been against them. He realised he wasn't particularly surprised at Joan Thomson's betrayal, but recalling Judy's words to him, he couldn't for the life of him find any reason why he'd not received Abi's letters to him. The thought that someone in his life had betrayed him in the same way left him feeling cold and deeply angry. He put his foot to the floor and increased his speed, hoping he could in some way outrun his feelings.

At around two thirty, Gideon arrived in the little village of Sennen and dug Judy's scrap of paper out of his jacket pocket. He located the little cottage fairly easily, and could see immediately there was no car parked outside. He knew from Judy that Abi had a variety of jobs she did on different days of the week, so he assumed she must be at one of them at the moment. He decided to park up where he could see the cottage, and wait for her to return home.

He found a large lay-by on the main road into the village. It commanded a perfect view of the row of cottages, and he settled down for an extended stay. His mind was racing with thoughts and memories, and still struggling with the idea that someone had betrayed him. He needed something to help him relax. Since a beer was clearly out of the question, he delved into his pocket and brought out his tobacco pouch and cigarette papers. He proceeded to roll himself a joint, thinking it perhaps unwise since he was parked on a main road. Then he sat back and enjoyed its relaxing qualities while he waited. Luckily for Gideon, no one passed for at least an hour, by which time the joint was long finished, and he was beginning to doze off.

Finally the sound of a car approaching caused him to sit up and take notice. It came up behind him fairly fast, then slowed suddenly and turned down the track towards the cottages. Gideon had only managed to catch a slight glimpse of the driver, as the car passed, just enough to see it was a female with long hair. He sat up and peered down at the cottages. The little car pulled up outside the one Gideon had identified as Abi's, and shuddered to a halt. After a moment or two the car door opened and a girl got out, a girl wearing a sheepskin jacket and jeans, and with a long scarf wound round her neck. She didn't bother to lock the car but walked straight up to the front door and let herself in. As she turned to close the door behind her, Gideon fancied she paused for a moment and stared straight up at his car. Then she went inside and closed the door.

****

Abi saw the car as she came along the main road. There were never many tourists around in November, and to see a strange car parked in the lay-by was worthy of a second glance. Probably someone who got lost, she thought to herself as she turned down her track.

She had spent the day with one of her clients in Penzance, sorting out the artwork for their new marketing campaign, and she was very glad to be home. She had lit the fire before she left the house that morning, and the chimney was smoking cheerily as she got out of the car and headed for the front door. As she turned to close it behind her, she once again noticed the strange Range Rover parked on the main road. She paused for a second, then shivered and closed the door. For some reason the sight of it had given her a little chill in her heart. She shook her head in exasperation.

What was she turning into? The events of the past week must really be taking their toll.

She tossed her jacket down on the sofa and went into the kitchen to put the kettle on. As anticipated, the little cottage was very warm and cosy, and Abi anticipated a lovely warm relaxing evening. Although she was very fond of her friend and neighbour, she couldn't help hoping that Chris wouldn't pop over. She really fancied a night to herself.

She made a cup of tea, cut herself a slice of cake, carried them both over to the fire, and sat down on the hearth rug. A basket of logs stood to one side of the woodburner, and Abi opened the doors and tossed another log onto the already roaring fire. She gave a little shiver of pleasure. She really liked to be warm. She was going to enjoy the evening.

She leant back against the sofa, extended her legs in front of her, and took a large bite of cake. No sooner had she done that than the doorbell rang. Abi rolled her eyes and tried to swallow her cake.

"Come in, Chris, the door's open!" she called, spraying crumbs in all directions.

After a moment the door slowly opened and a deep voice said, "I'm not Chris. Can I still come in?"

Abi leapt to her feet and swung round to face the door. For the last ten years she had dreamt of the moment when Gideon Hawk would appear on her doorstep, and now it had finally happened she had no idea what to do. For a few long seconds they stared at each other, neither daring to speak. Then Abi took a tentative step forward and nodded her head jerkily.

"Yes. Come in," she croaked, her mouth suddenly dry, adding automatically, "Mind your head."

Gideon ducked into the room and squeezed past the two dogs who came bounding up to greet him. Abi remained rooted to the spot, totally unable to think what to say. Eventually she waved her hand vaguely towards the sofa and waited for Gideon to sit down. He lowered himself onto the soft cushions, looking ridiculously big in her tiny living room. She had almost forgotten just how tall he was. At five foot seven, she was fairly tall, but Gideon had always towered above her. Cautiously she sat down at the other end of the sofa, and turned to face him.

He glanced at her. "Sorry. Hope you don't mind me just turning up," he said inadequately. Abi shook her head and tried to speak, but this time no words came. Gideon cleared his throat. "If you're expecting someone, I can go," he said politely.

Abi shook her head. "No, not at all," she managed.

Gideon watched her closely. "What about Chris? Is he your boyfriend?"

It was that question that broke the tension for Abi. She smiled, then started to laugh, and found she couldn't stop until the tears were pouring down her cheeks. Gideon thought Chris was her boyfriend. Wait until she told him. He'd love that. She wiped her eyes and blew her nose, then grinned shyly at Gideon.

"No. He's not my boyfriend, and I'm not even expecting him," she said at last. "He's my neighbour, and he often just drops in." She gave another little giggle but didn't bother to explain it, adding politely, "Would you like some tea?"

Gideon paused for a moment, then nodded his thanks. He would much have preferred a beer, but he didn't like to ask.

He watched as she went into the kitchen, and suddenly felt completely out of his depth. He was in the house of the girl he had loved for the last eleven years, and she was a stranger. He stared around the room trying to find signs of the Abi he had fallen in love with—the rebellious teenager he had planned to marry—and could find none.

From the kitchen, Abi could just see into the living room and found herself watching Gideon as she waited for the kettle to boil. He looked so different—and yet the same. He seemed much more than ten years older, his face was haggard and shadowed, and he was much too thin. She put her head on one side and watched as he flicked his hair back over his shoulder impatiently. She smiled—maybe he hadn't changed completely. She made the tea and carried the mugs into the living room. She handed one to Gideon, then sat down cross-legged on the hearth rug again. He took a sip and gave a slight smile.

"Milk and one sugar," he said. "You remembered."

Abi shrugged. "Took a chance." She bent her head forward and let her hair hide her face. Gideon smiled again and sat back in his seat.

Abi peered up at him through her hair.

"What?" she demanded suspiciously. He shook his head and took another sip of tea. Abi pushed her hair out of her eyes and surveyed him sternly. "Why are you smiling?" she persisted.

"Because you did that thing with your hair," he said. "Hiding behind it. You always did that." To her dismay she felt herself beginning to flush, and in her confusion she turned away from him and pretended to tend to the fire. Gideon grinned to himself and began to relax slightly. "How long have you lived here? It's lovely."

"Just over four years." She didn't turn round. "I like it. So do the dogs." She pulled her knees up to her chin and linked her arms around them. Her mind was in complete turmoil, and she had no idea how to deal with the situation. Until the previous week she'd believed Gideon had abandoned her after she told him about the baby. Now she knew that wasn't true. She wondered how on earth one told a complete stranger they had fathered a child with you... She ran a hand through her hair in frustration and spun to face him. She found he was watching her intently, his still-piercing blue eyes boring right into her soul. She shivered and looked back at the fire.

"Who told you where I was?" she asked eventually.

"Judy," he said carefully. "But don't be cross with her. I think she understood why I had to see you." He paused and waited, but she gave no response. "She told me you never got my letters." He paused again and corrected himself. "Well, actually, your father told me that, and Judy confirmed it." He saw then that he had got her full attention and carried on. "Judy said you wrote to me. I never got those letters, either."

Abi finally looked round at him, her eyes anguished.

"None of them?" she whispered.

Gideon shook his head. "None of them. She said there was something in them that you needed to tell me."

"You saw my father?" Abi said finally, staring at him.

Gideon gave a crooked smile. "Well, sort of. He

pretty much sent me away. Same as he did when I tried to see you in '97." He saw her whole face change. "When I was briefly back in England, I went to your house to find out why you'd left me. Your father told me you'd gone to college and that you never wanted to see me again."

There was a very long silence while Abi digested this latest piece of information. That her father could have betrayed her like that after all she'd been through… It was beyond her understanding. She still believed he hadn't known about the concealed letters, but clearly he wasn't as innocent as she'd thought. Gideon was still watching her.

"So what is it you need to tell me?" he asked again, his long fingers nervously drumming on the arm of the sofa.

Abi took a deep breath and got to her feet. She pulled a chair closer to the fire and curled herself into it, facing Gideon.

"A lot happened to me after you'd gone," she began, winding a strand of hair around her finger as she spoke. "A lot of really rather dreadful things." She paused for a long time. "When I didn't hear from you, I realised I couldn't wait any longer, so I wrote to you via the record company." Her voice wavered slightly, and she took a deep breath. "Let me show you something." She got to her feet and pulled a large cardboard box out from under the stairs. She heaved it over to the sofa and sat down next to Gideon with the box at her feet. She pulled out a photograph and held it out to him. "Remember that?" she said with a lopsided grin. "That's the day you left."

He slowly took the picture in his hand and stared at

the sight of his younger self—so raw, inexperienced, and confident. However sad he'd been feeling about leaving Abi, he couldn't deny the excitement he'd been struggling to hold in check. He thought back to that day and frowned slightly.

"I always thought there was something wrong that day," he admitted slowly. "You seemed very distracted." He grinned and looked a bit sheepish. "I always put it down to the fact that you didn't want me to go, but then when I never heard from you I assumed you'd been wondering how to tell me it was over." He watched her face. "Was it something else?"

Abi was searching through the box again. She brought out another photograph and held it pressed to her chest.

"This was taken at Christmas of that year," she said quietly and held it out to him. He turned it over and found himself staring at the young Abi, her face serious and her eyes haunted. She was standing in front of the Christmas tree and was quite clearly pregnant. Gideon felt his whole world beginning to slip away from him. He had spent the last ten years torturing himself over what had gone wrong between them, and never once had he even considered this as a possibility. He raised shadowed eyes to hers.

"You had a baby," he managed at last. "I'm a father?"

Abi's anguished, tear-filled eyes met his sadly.

## Chapter 17

*Thursday, 11<sup>th</sup> January 1996*

"Abi! Calm down. You're only a week late. It's not the end of the world." Judy attempted to mollify her friend as they sat in Abi's bedroom on a cold January afternoon, playing Connect 4 to try and take their minds off the impending birth. Abi scowled at Judy and impatiently pushed her hair back off her face.

"Until you've had one of these inside you," she growled, "you don't pass comment. I feel like a balloon that's about to burst, and there's absolutely no single position I can get comfortable in." She struggled to her feet again and waddled over to the window. "Oh, great, and now it's snowing! I shall probably end up giving birth in a snowdrift half way to the clinic." She slumped down on the window seat with a groan.

Judy concealed a smile. Abi really did look very funny, but she had completely lost her sense of humour ever since her due date had passed. She was extremely stressed because she was well aware her mother was still going to try and make her give her baby away, and she was banking on the support of Dr. Slater at the clinic on that score. She stood up again, and with her hands pressed into the small of her back she leaned backwards and groaned again.

"I am *never* doing this again!" she vowed,

scowling at Judy.

Judy laughed. "Don't have a go at me," she said. "This is all your own doing."

Abi moved over to the bed and sat down on the edge in an attempt to find a more comfortable position. As she squirmed around, the girls heard footsteps coming up the stairs, and Abi stiffened. The door flew open and Joan Thomson surveyed her daughter with a blank expression.

"Get your bag, Abigail. We're going to the clinic now." She turned to leave the room.

Abi struggled to her feet and held up her hand.

"Hang on," she said. "I'm not in labour yet. What's the idea?"

"They're going to start you off," said Joan with distaste. "Because you're a week late, they think it's for the best." She closed the door and disappeared downstairs again.

Abi looked at Judy and raised her eyebrows.

"Can they do that?" she asked in surprise.

Judy nodded. "Oh, yes, I've heard Mum mention it. They do it so the baby doesn't get too big to come out."

Abi stared at her.

"Can that happen?" she asked, panic sounding in her voice.

Judy shrugged. "Well...I guess so, but you're only a week late. You'll be fine," she said, a tinge of doubt in her voice. "Now, come on, let's get your stuff together. I'll help."

She began to gather up some things she felt Abi would like to take with her.

Abi watched her in amazement.

"I'm having a baby," she said firmly. "When am I

going to have time to play Connect 4?"

Judy stopped and looked down at the game in her hand.

She grinned. "Afterwards?" she suggested, then tossed the game onto the bed and looked around for something more suitable. "Sometimes it takes a long time to have a baby," she said, picking up items and then discarding them. "You may get bored."

Abi picked up a CD from her bedside table.

"I want to take this," she said quietly, holding it out to Judy. "I want to be listening to it when the baby's born."

Judy took it silently and put it into Abi's bag. She knew without looking that it was NightHawk's album, and that "Storm Rising" was the track Abi would listen to. She had started to zip the bag up when Abi thrust a notebook into her hand.

"Put that in, too," she said. "That's where I've written down my birth plan and what I want to call her. We'll take it in case anything happens to me, and then I'll know she has the right name," she added rather dramatically.

Judy opened the notebook and saw the front page was covered with scribbled-out names, finally ending at the bottom with the name Natasha underlined in red and the name Storm with a question mark beside it.

"I knew about Natasha," she said, in surprise. "What's Storm for?"

Abi shrugged. "Well, I suppose it could be a boy," she admitted. "So I thought that would do."

Judy smiled, popped the notebook in the bag, and zipped it up.

"Come on, then, let's go and get this over with.

And don't worry. No one can make you give the baby up." She paused and squeezed Abi's hand. "Anyway, I'll be there, and I won't let them." The two girls smiled at each other and made their way downstairs. Abi's parents were standing in the hall waiting for them, and her father reached out and took her bag from Judy.

"Thank you for your help, Judith," said Joan with a tight smile. "You get off home, now, and we'll take it from here." She nodded to the girl and opened the front door.

Judy stared at her in horror.

"But I'm her birth partner!" she exclaimed, her voice wobbling. "She wants me with her."

Abi nodded violently and clutched at Judy's arm. Joan shook her head.

"I'm afraid things have changed a bit," she said. "The clinic will only allow relatives in for the birth. We'll call you when it's all over." She held the door wide open and indicated that Judy should leave.

Tears were pouring down Abi's face as she tried to get her father on side.

"Dad, please tell her Judy must be there. I really need her!" she implored desperately. Arthur glanced at his wife, then shook his head firmly.

"Sorry, Abi, we have to go with what the clinic says. No friends." He paused, and his voice softened a little. "I'll call Judy the moment you've had the baby, and she can come over then."

Reluctantly Judy allowed herself to be ushered out of the house, and on the doorstep she turned and called back to Abi, "Stay strong, Abs. Don't let anyone bully you. I love you," and she blew a kiss to her friend.

Sobbing uncontrollably, Abi watched her go and

sank down on the stairs in despair. Judy had been her one source of strength throughout the whole pregnancy, and now she had left her at the final moment. She stared at her mother with hatred.

"I'm not going without her!" she shouted. "I need her there. I can't do it alone."

Joan walked over and pulled her to her feet.

"You should have thought of that nine months ago," she said cruelly, and marched her daughter out of the house and into the car. As her father reversed out into the road, Abi saw Judy standing on the pavement watching them. She waved a desperate hand at her friend, and Judy took a hesitant step towards the car. Then it sped off down the road, leaving her standing forlorn and worried.

Abi sank back in her seat and tried to compose herself. She was now missing her most important supporter, so she needed to rely on the good nature of Dr. Slater even more. She was fairly confident the doctor wouldn't allow her mother to take the baby away from her, but she realised she would need to be on her guard for when they tried to wear her down. She stared out the window as they turned out onto the dual-carriageway and headed off towards Reading. She frowned and leant forward to tap her father on the shoulder.

"You're going the wrong way, Dad," she said. "The clinic's in the other direction."

Her mother spoke without turning her head.

"There's been a change of plan," she said. "We're not going to the Merrilees Clinic any more. I've booked you into a small private clinic run by a friend of mine. It's very exclusive; you're a lucky girl."

Abi's whole body tensed, and she felt the baby kick. She swallowed hard.

"But I want to go to the Merrilees," she shrilled. "I want Dr. Slater to deliver my baby."

Joan turned her head a little. "The doctor doesn't do the deliveries. That's the midwife's job. And Dr. Slater proved somewhat of a disappointment." She paused. "No, you'll be much better off at the Birch Clinic with Dr. Munro. He and his wife have been friends of mine for years. She's the midwife. They'll take care of everything."

Abi sank back in her seat. She was petrified. Without the support of either Judy or Dr. Slater, she was entirely in the hands of her mother, and that was terrifying. Abi knew without a doubt she would be put under huge pressure to give up her baby, and she also knew just how much of a bully her mother could be. She desperately needed to tell Judy what had happened, but she could see no way she would be able to manage that. She leant her head against the window of the car and closed her eyes. She was so tired. The overlong pregnancy had taken its toll on her young body, and she felt ready to drop. She was seriously worried she might find it hard to withstand the pressures of her domineering mother. But there was no way she was going to let anyone take this baby away from her.

****

When Judy arrived back home, her mother met her on the doorstep. She knew instantly that something was wrong.

"Judy? What is it?" she asked in concern, noting the unshed tears in her daughter's eyes. "Is it Abi?"

Judy nodded and burst into tears. "Ye-es," she

215

sobbed onto her mother's shoulder. "They won't…let …me go…with her!" and she hiccupped violently.

Mary stroked her daughter's head and made soothing noises.

"Is she in labour now?" she asked gently.

Judy shook her head and rubbed a hand across her nose.

"No. But she's late, and they're going to start her off." She looked at her mother. "That's okay, isn't it?"

Mary nodded. "Yes, that's fairly normal," she replied. "But why can't you go? You're her birth partner."

Judy hiccupped again and sniffed loudly.

"Dunno. Mrs. Thomson said there'd been a change of plan, and that only family could be there for the birth. But Abi needs me, Mum," she wailed, grabbing her mother's arm and shaking it. "If she's on her own, they may make her give the baby up!"

Mary patted her hand reassuringly.

"Dr. Slater will never allow that. But maybe I could run you to the clinic in a wee while, and I'll see if I can persuade them to change their minds."

"Oh, Mum, would you?" breathed Judy with the glimmer of a smile. "That would be brill. You're the best mum in the world." She leaned forward and planted a kiss on her mother's cheek. Mary hugged her and smiled.

"You're a good friend, Judy," she said quietly. "I'm very proud of you."

As they drove to the Merrilees Clinic a short time later, Judy couldn't shake off the feeling of doom hanging over her. Abi's face at the car window as she was driven away still haunted her, and she was desperate to see that her friend was all right. When they turned into the clinic's car park, Judy scanned it quickly for the Saab.

"Their car's not here." She continued to peer around. "Mum, their car's not here!"

Mary slid her car into a vacant space and switched off the engine.

"I expect Arthur dropped them off and then went home," she said calmly, adding with a slight smile, "Can you really see him hanging around to watch his daughter give birth?"

Judy nodded and took a deep breath. "Come on, then, come and work your magic, Mum," she said, and got out of the car.

The receptionist at the desk greeted them with a wide smile. "Welcome to the Merrilees Clinic," she said in a sing-song voice. "Do you have an appointment?"

Mary smiled back and walked up to the desk.

"No," she said in a friendly tone, "we've come to see Abigail Thomson. I believe she arrived about half an hour ago." The receptionist looked blankly at her. "She's come to have her baby," Mary explained patiently. "My daughter is her birth partner."

The receptionist looked in her appointment book with a puzzled expression, then picked up the phone and punched a button.

"Hello, yes, it's Carrie. Some people are here to see Abigail Thomson. They say she's come in to have a baby." She paused and picked at her nail polish while she listened. "Well, I didn't think so. What shall I tell them?...Oh, okay." She replaced the receiver, gave Mary an automatic smile, and indicated that they should sit down. "Someone'll be out to see you soon."

Judy clutched at Mary's arm.

"Mum, something's happened!" she wailed. "She's dead, isn't she? Why can't I see her?" Tears began to trickle down her cheeks.

Mary led her over to the seating area and forced her to sit down.

"Calm down, Judy," she said firmly. "Of course she's not dead. She's a perfectly healthy girl having a perfectly healthy baby. They're probably going to tell us we can't go in. Leave it to me." She put her arm around Judy's shoulders and gave her a squeeze.

Judy fished in her pocket, pulled out a crumpled tissue, and blew her nose. Of course she was overreacting. She needed to calm down. She was just having a good look around the waiting area when a door in the corner opened and someone came over to them.

"Good lord! Mary Cromwell! I haven't seen you for years." Dr. Slater held out her hand to Mary. Mary smiled and stood up.

"Hello, Janet," she said, shaking the proffered hand. "Nice to see you. I believe you have my daughter's friend Abigail Thomson here to have her baby. We were wondering if we could see her?"

Dr. Slater frowned and sat down opposite them.

"Certainly Abigail came here for her antenatal care," she said, "but last week I had a call from her mother saying they were going to go elsewhere for the birth. I was rather shocked, and truth to tell a little worried, but there was nothing I could do to stop them."

Judy sat forward. "So Abi's not here?" she said quietly. "Where's she gone, then?"

Dr. Slater looked at her sympathetically.

"I'm afraid I don't know. Mrs. Thomson wouldn't tell me." She paused and thought for a moment. "I am a little worried because…" She looked at Judy doubtfully and then at Mary, who gave a slight nod. "Well, Mrs. Thomson was very set on Abigail giving the baby up for adoption, and I know that Abigail really doesn't want to. I would have made sure she didn't force her into anything, but now I have no control over the situation, and there are some rather less…savoury, shall we say…clinics, where the staff may not be so caring."

Mary pursed her lips and sighed. "This makes things very difficult," she agreed. "Abi must not be forced into giving up her baby if she doesn't want to, but Joan Thomson is a very forceful woman. We need to find out where they've gone." She glanced around her. "Do you have a directory of clinics in this area?" she asked.

Dr. Slater nodded and moved over to the desk, returning a moment later with a large volume.

"This has a list of all the registered clinics in the South," she said, handing it to Mary. "There are a lot, mind you, and there are also some that won't appear in that book. It's somewhere to start, though, I suppose." She sat down next to them, and they began to search.

An hour later they had come up with a list of eight possible clinics within reasonable reach of Newbury, and Mary suggested that they go back home and phone them all in turn until they found her.

Dr. Slater stood up and shook their hands again. "Good luck," she said sincerely. "I really hope you find her. I know it sounds dreadful to say, but I really don't trust her mother to do what's best for her."

As they drove back home, Judy glanced at her mother.

"D'you think we'll find them?" she asked miserably.

Mary sighed. "I don't know," she admitted. "Even if she's at one of the eight we've found, they may not tell us. And they may have taken her to some unregistered one."

Judy looked scared. "Would that mean they didn't know what they were doing? Might they hurt her?" she asked, her eyes wide.

Mary shook her head. "No, it would still need to be run by properly qualified people." She paused. "But they may not be adhering totally to the rules that govern clinics." She glanced at Judy and smiled slightly. "Don't worry. If she's possible to find, we'll do it, if it takes all night."

\*\*\*\*

Abi was sitting bolt upright in bed in a private room at the Birch Clinic. They had arrived about an hour before, and her father had gone straight back home, leaving her to her mother's tender mercies. She had been booked in and examined by a rather dour midwife, then been instructed to put on her nightdress and get into bed. She stared around the room. It was a fair size and contained a large hospital bed, in which she was now installed, a couple of easy chairs, a chest of drawers, a bean bag, and various machines that Abi realised she would probably be hooked up to. She shivered and slid down under the covers. She had never felt more alone or more terrified in her life. Her mother had gone off to speak to the doctor, who was apparently a friend of hers, and the midwife had left her to get undressed. She sat up again and pulled her bag towards her. She delved inside and pulled out the small grey stuffed rabbit she had bought to give to the baby, and cuddled it tightly. Her heart was pounding with fear, and she wanted Gideon so much it hurt. This was so not how she had imagined giving birth to his baby. They should have been together, in a meadow, or on a beach, or somewhere pretty, and there should have been music playing, and everyone would be happy and smiling and pleased she was having the baby. This was all wrong. Here everything was dark and scary. No one seemed to care about her, everyone was cross she was having the baby, and everyone seemed to want to take it away from her. She really needed Judy, and suddenly she wondered if she would be able to get to a phone without anyone seeing her. If she could at least let Judy know where she was, then maybe… She quietly got out of bed and grabbed a handful of ten-pence coins from her purse. Then she carefully opened the door of her room a crack and looked out into the corridor. There was no one in sight, and all she could hear was the faint murmur of voices coming from behind a closed door off to her left. Cautiously she tiptoed out into the corridor and turned to the right, away from the voices. Hopefully she would be able to find a phone somewhere. Hospitals usually had telephones on trolleys they could take to people's bedsides. Surely a posh clinic would have something similar? She walked on down the carpeted corridor until she reached a junction. She peered to the left and saw that the passage ended just round the corner. She looked to the right and her heart missed a beat when she saw a payphone attached to the wall about twenty feet away. Clutching her coins tightly in her hand, Abi waddled as fast as she could towards the phone. She had just lifted the receiver and begun to dial when she experienced an enormous cramp-like pain in her stomach. She cried out and doubled over, dropping the receiver and leaving it suspended and banging gently against the wall. She gasped and, breathing rapidly, tried to straighten up, but another wave of pain overcame her, and she cried out again and sank to her knees on the carpet. She heard a voice coming nearer, the words indistinguishable, and suddenly a pair of hands were under her armpits and someone was helping her up.

"It's okay, love," said a kindly voice. "It's only contractions. Doesn't look like we need to start you off after all."

Abi straightened up and found herself being supported by a different, younger midwife, who was smiling encouragingly at her. She opened her mouth to speak, but just then there came a sudden rush of liquid pouring down her legs and soaking into the carpet. Abi cried out in alarm.

"Oh, my god! I've wet myself," she gasped in horror, staring down at her soaked nightdress. The midwife chuckled and squeezed her arm.

"It's only your waters breaking," she soothed. "Perfectly normal. Come on, let's get you back to your room. What were you doing out here anyway?" she asked as she helped her along the corridor.

Abi stopped walking. Judy! She needed to call her. She turned to the midwife.

"I've got to call my friend," she said urgently. "She needs to be here, right now." Then she screamed as another contraction caught her unawares.

"Breathe," instructed the midwife, "like you were taught in antenatal classes. That's right. Breathe in, breathe out... That's good. Now, come on back to the room, and then you can tell me about your friend."

Awkwardly Abi staggered back to her room, and the midwife helped her change into a dry nightdress and get back into bed. Then she took her blood pressure and hooked her up to a machine that monitored her heartbeat and the baby's. Abi lay back against the pillows and watched as the changing figures were displayed on the screen and listened to the strange sound the heartbeat made.

"Sounds like a horse running," she said with a little smile.

The midwife grinned at her. "Wait till it speeds up a bit!" she said with a laugh. "My name's Sally. I'm here to help you, and anything you want or are worried about, please tell me. I'll do what I can to help you." She gently brushed Abi's straying hair off her face.

Abi smiled back. "Thank you," she said. "I've been really scared. My best friend is meant to be here, but my mum wouldn't let her come"—her voice wavered—"and she doesn't know where I am 'cause Mum and Dad brought me to a different clinic than we'd planned. I've never been here before." Her eyes filled with tears, and Sally stroked her hand gently.

"Don't worry. I'll look after you," she said. "Maybe your mum thought it would be too much for your friend to watch the birth?"

Abi shook her head violently. "No, no, you don't understand!" she gasped. "Mum wants me to have the baby adopted, and I don't want to. I need Judy here to make sure she doesn't take her away from me."

Sally frowned slightly. "No one can make you give up the baby if you don't want to," she said firmly. "Not even your mother. I'll take care of that," and she patted Abi's hand again.

Suddenly another contraction took hold, and Abi shrieked in pain and clutched Sally's hand.

"Time for a little pain relief, I think," said Sally with a look at Abi's face, and disentangled her hand in order to fetch the gas-and-air dispenser. She handed it to Abi. "Just put this to your mouth and press this button when the pain is too much," she explained. "It'll make you feel a bit woozy, but it helps a lot."

Abi looked doubtfully at it. "I wanted a natural birth," she began, but then as another contraction started she put the contraption to her mouth and breathed deeply. Immediately she felt slightly euphoric and the pain became less important. She breathed it in again and began to relax. The contractions were beginning to get closer together and even stronger, and Sally told Abi she was going to get the doctor to have a quick look at her to make sure everything was all right.

Abi was feeling slightly spaced out because of the gas and air, and she smiled sleepily and said, "Wish Gideon was here. And Judy. That'd be much nicer."

Sally smiled back at her. "Who's Gideon?" she asked.

"He's the father," slurred Abi proudly. "He's famous."

Sally raised her eyebrows. "Famous?" she asked in surprise, smiling slightly.

Abi nodded. "Yeah...he's famous...he's in America. With NightHawk." Her eyes closed as she felt the room begin to spin.

Sally stared at her. "NightHawk?" she repeated. "Gideon Hawk is the father of your baby?"

Abi nodded, her eyes still closed. "Yeah…but he do'n' want me any more," she muttered blearily, taking another breath of the gas and air.

"I think you've had enough of that for now," said Sally briskly, trying to remove it from Abi's hand. The younger girl clung tightly and opened her eyes.

"Still need it," she said thickly. "Haven't had baby yet."

Sally hesitated for a moment, then shrugged and let her keep it.

"Just going to get Doctor now," she was saying when the door opened and Abi's mother entered, followed by a short, stocky, greying man and the midwife Abi had met when she'd first arrived.

Abi opened her eyes again. "Get her out of here," she said distinctly, pointing at her mother. "Don't want her here. Want Judy."

The man walked over to the bed and smiled tightly at Abi.

"Hello, Abigail," he said. "I'm Dr. Munro. I think you've already met my wife." He indicated the older midwife. "We're here to help you through this. I see you've already had pain relief."

Abi fixed him with a baleful stare and gripped the gas-and-air dispenser even tighter.

"Yes, and you can't have it," she said menacingly.

Dr. Munro pursed his lips together and stiffened.

"That's all right," he said. "You may keep it. Now, I'm just going to check everything is going okay."

He bent down and gave her a quick examination, then turned to Abi's mother.

"Everything's fine so far. Do you want to stay in here with her?"

Abi struggled to sit up. "No!" she shouted. "I don't want her here! She wants to take my baby!" Then she fell back against the pillows as another wave of contractions began. Sally ran to her side and held her hand to help her through them, murmuring words of encouragement. When the contractions had passed, Sally turned to the group at the door.

"I think it might be best if I stay with Abi. She seems to be rather upset by your presence at the moment," she said to Joan. "She's been asking for her friend Judy. Is it possible we could get her to come in?"

Joan looked at her with dislike. "I decided it would be inappropriate for a young girl to witness the birth," she said firmly. "I shall wait in the waiting room, if that's what Abigail prefers." She turned and left the room without even a glance at her daughter.

Dr Munro took Sally to one side and spoke quietly. "Keep an eye on her," he instructed. "Apparently she's rather delusional, according to her mother."

Sally looked surprised. "Delusional?" she asked with a frown. "In what way? She seems okay to me."

The doctor bristled slightly. "I'm sure her mother knows best," he said sharply. "Apparently she thinks the father is some rock star or other. Obviously a story she made up to cover the shame of a quick shag behind the bike sheds. Watch her." With that, he turned and left the room, followed by his wife.

Sally looked at Abi. She was lying back on the pillows looking totally exhausted, her face wet with tears, the gas-and-air dispenser still gripped in her hand, but she opened her eyes and smiled wanly at Sally.

"This is hard," she said with a sigh. "When will it be over?"

Sally felt Abi's stomach, then checked to see how dilated she was.

"Bit longer yet, I'm afraid," she said with an apologetic smile. "You need to be ten centimetres dilated, and so far you're only about six." She glanced at the clock. It was eight o'clock. "May manage it before midnight, but somehow I doubt it."

Abi rolled her eyes. "Seriously?" she said. "I don't like this. It hurts." She took another burst of gas and air. "Wish Judy was here," she said as the room began to swim again.

Sally smiled at her. "How did you meet Gideon Hawk?" she asked casually.

Abi closed her eyes. "He used to go to school near me," she said. "Then his band played at our school dance, and we fell in love." Another contraction came and she sucked in the gas and air in quiet desperation, falling back on the pillows again as it subsided. "Then...he went...on tour...to America. He didn't write." She paused, breathing heavily. "I was going to go and stay with him, but he never wrote." She turned anguished eyes to Sally. "I love him so much. We were going to get married."

Sally had watched Abi closely during this speech and was pretty convinced the girl was telling the truth. She hadn't liked the look of the mother and was now beginning to worry that Abi's fears about having the baby taken away might be genuine. If her mother was saying she was delusional, it would be easier to get the doctor to pronounce her unfit to look after a child.

Sally touched Abi gently on the arm. "Abi, have

you got Judy's phone number?" she asked urgently. "I'll call her for you and see if we can get her here."

Abi's eyes opened and she stared woozily at Sally. "That'd be nice," she muttered sleepily. "Gi' me a pen an' paper an' I'll write it down."

Sally pulled a small pad and pen out of her pocket and handed them to Abi. The girl carefully wrote the number down and handed it back to her.

"Be careful," she whispered. "They don't want me to have her here."

Sally nodded and winked at her, then turned and opened the door. As she stepped out into the corridor and closed the door quietly behind her, Sally became aware of someone watching her. She spun around and found Sister Munro, the senior midwife, standing in the shadows.

"Oh, you made me jump!" she said with a nervous laugh.

Sister Munro held out her hand.

"What's that you've got there, Nurse Robins?" she asked without smiling.

Sally clutched the paper tighter. "Just…a phone number," she said, her heart sinking. The older woman stepped nearer and snatched the paper out of Sally's hand.

"And this is the phone number for…?" she asked, watching Sally closely.

"Just a friend." she said hesitantly. "I promised to call her."

Sister Munro spun around. "Follow me," she ordered, and marched off down the corridor into the waiting room. Abi's mother was sitting in a chair having a cup of tea and chatting to the doctor. Sister

Munro walked over and handed her the paper. "Do you recognise this phone number?" she demanded.

Joan peered at it for a moment. "Yes," she said. This is Judy Cromwell's number. Where did you get it?"

All eyes turned to Sally, and she felt her face flush.

"Ummm...Abi gave it to me," she faltered. "She's really scared and would love to have her friend with her. I..." She paused. "I offered to phone her." She raised her head and put her shoulders back. "I really think it would do her good."

Dr. Munro sighed. "Nurse Robins, this is very disappointing," he said, shaking his head. "I'm sure you're aware Mrs. Thomson said the girl was not to be here, and yet you were deliberately going to go against her wishes?"

Sally suddenly got her confidence back.

"But surely the wishes of the patient are of more importance?" she said bravely. "She's the one having to go through this, and she's only a child. Surely there's no harm in letting her have a friend to hold her hand, is there?"

Joan Thomson regarded her over the top of her glasses.

"Young lady, you have much to learn about life," she said bleakly. "I do not wish my daughter to have her friend here, and that's an end to it." She glanced at Dr. Munro. "I should also prefer it if this person were not attending to Abigail. I should like your wife to take over."

Dr. Munro nodded briefly and addressed Sally. "You heard Mrs. Thomson," he said shortly. "Your shift is now over. When you're next on duty we shall need to have a little chat," and he dismissed her with a wave of his hand.

Sally's mouth dropped open. "No…please, Abi needs me. She's terrified, and I've gained her confidence. Please let me stay until she delivers."

Her pleas fell on deaf ears, and within minutes Sally found herself outside the clinic, bag in hand, staring back at the window of Abi's room, her heart reaching out to the terrified girl. She knew she couldn't go against the wishes of the Munros without losing her job, and if she did lose her job she would be even less use to Abi. At least this way she would be able to return to the clinic the next day to check she was still all right. With a heavy heart, she made her way to her car and set off home, vowing to return first thing in the morning.

****

"Mum, this is impossible!" wailed Judy, as she put the phone down from the eighth clinic. So far five had denied all knowledge of Abi, one refused to give out any information about their patients, and the other two had gone straight to answerphone. "Can we go and drive to these three, just in case?" she pleaded.

Mary shook her head sorrowfully. "Sorry, Judy, they're miles apart. We'd be out all night and then probably not find her." She paused and glanced at the clock. "Look, it's nearly ten thirty now. We'll try the last two one more time, and then I think we're going to have to call it a day."

Judy jumped up and paced impatiently around the room.

"Mum, Abi's relying on me! If they take her baby away, it'll be my fault. I should be there." She picked up her coat and ran to the door. "I'm going to see if Mr.

Thomson is back yet—he *must* tell us."

Mary started to go after her, then shrugged and let her go. She needed to keep trying. She sighed and picked up the phone, dialling the seventh number again. Straight to answerphone. Same result with the eighth. She was just racking her brains for anything else they could try when Judy came back. She looked dejected, her shoulders slumped, and her face crumpled.

"He's still not there," she said. "Maybe he stayed at the clinic after all."

Mary seriously doubted he had and thought it was more likely he'd gone to ground at a friend's house for the evening rather than risk being bombarded by her daughter. She walked over and put her arm around Judy's shoulders.

"I'm sorry, love. I really don't know what else we can do, apart from trying these other two in the morning." She kissed the top of her daughter's head. "Now go to bed and get some rest. You'll be no use to Abi tomorrow otherwise. We'll call first thing in the morning." She smiled encouragingly at Judy. "And don't worry. They really can't force her to give it up, and they certainly can't do anything before the morning. Go to bed."

\*\*\*\*

At just after midnight, Abi gave the final push and her baby slid out into the hands of Dr. Munro. He lifted it up by its feet.

"It's a girl," he remarked, then handed her to his wife.

"Can I hold her?" An exhausted Abi reached out her arms as the baby was carried briskly past her.

"No," came the short reply from Sister Munro.

"She's not breathing yet. I need to clear her airways. You rest now." She disappeared rapidly out of the room carrying the baby.

"But…I want to hold my baby…" whispered Abi, sweat dripping down her face. "Please let me."

Dr. Munro came round to the head of the bed and looked down at her.

"Sometimes babies need a little help when they're first born," he said, not unkindly. "And that's what Sister's doing now. Sometimes they need a bit of help to get them breathing properly. No need to worry. You rest now. You can see her later."

"She's called Natasha," Abi murmured as her eyes closed and she allowed the longed for sleep to engulf her.

Dr. Munro watched over her for a moment, and then, when he was sure she was asleep, he opened the door and stepped out into the corridor. He nodded to Joan Thomson, who was standing just outside the door, a questioning look on her face, before he walked down the corridor and into the room at the far end, closing the door behind him. Joan opened the door to Abi's room, entered, and went to stand by her daughter. She stared down at her, pain in her eyes, hardly recognising the child she had brought up, the young body exhausted both physically and mentally by the ordeal she had just been through. As she stood there, Joan's eyes fell on the small notebook next to Abi's bed. She picked it up, and it fell open on the page of baby names. She scanned to the bottom, paused for a moment, then closed the book and replaced it where she'd found it. She briefly touched Abi's hand, her lips moving soundlessly, then turned and left the room.

\*\*\*\*

When Abi awoke the next morning, she lay for a moment wondering where on earth she was. Then she remembered, and immediately struggled to sit up. Every part of her seemed to be sore in some way or another, and she winced as she moved. She needed to see Natasha. Glancing at the clock, she was shocked to see it was nearly ten o'clock. She had slept for more than nine hours. Surely she should have been woken to feed her baby? She fancied she had heard her crying in her dreams and hoped the nurses had been looking after her all right. She reached out and pressed the bell by the side of the bed. Within moments the door opened and a nurse that Abi had not seen before entered carrying a bowl of water and a towel.

"Good morning," she said to Abi. "I hope you slept well. I've come to give you a bit of a wash."

Abi let her pull back the covers and begin to remove her stained and crumpled nightdress. The nurse began to sponge Abi's legs gently with the warm water and patted them dry with the soft towel.

Abi smiled at her. "When can I see my baby?" she asked.

The nurse avoided her gaze and carried on with the washing.

"The doctor'll be in to see you shortly," she said evasively. "You need some more rest. Would you like a cup of tea?"

Abi was slightly taken aback. "No, I want my baby," she said firmly. "I've been asleep for nearly ten hours, so how much rest do you think I need? Now, please, fetch me my baby."

The nurse finished her drying and folded the towel.

Then she gathered up her things and headed towards the door.

"The doctor will be in shortly," she repeated without looking at Abi, and left the room, closing the door behind her.

Abi lay back on the pillows, her mind in a whirl. Had her worst nightmares actually come true? Had her mother already taken her baby away? Could she have done that? Urgently Abi pressed the bell by the bed and kept her finger on it, until the door opened again and Dr. Munro walked in.

"There's no need to press it continuously," he remarked in a mild tone as he drew a chair up at the side of the bed.

"Where's my baby?" asked Abi shrilly. "What have you done with her? You can't take her away from me. She's mine!" She started to get out of bed. Dr. Munro put out a hand to stop her.

"Abigail, no one has taken your baby," he said calmly. "However I'm afraid I do have some bad news for you." He paused, and Abi felt the room sway around her as she turned to stare at him.

"What bad news?" she whispered. The doctor gently pushed her back so she was resting on the pillows once more.

"You remember that I told you babies sometimes need help to breathe when they're first born?" Abi nodded silently, her throat constricting. "Well, I'm sorry to say that your baby didn't manage to breathe. We tried all we could, but I'm afraid she couldn't do it." He watched her intently as she took in the information, her face turning as white as the sheets. "I'm afraid your baby is dead, Abigail."

Abi lay back on the pillows and didn't dare to move. If she moved, then she'd have to admit she was awake and what she'd just heard was true. If she stayed still, maybe she was still asleep. Maybe she would awake in a minute and find her baby next to her. Her Natasha. Gideon's baby.

"Abigail?" the doctor put his hand on her wrist to check her pulse. She snatched it away and pulled the covers up to her chin.

"Go away," she croaked, staring at him with wild eyes. "Go away. Go away. *Go away!*" This last was screamed at the top of her voice and followed by heart-rending sobs as she realised the news was true. She pulled her pillow out from behind her and threw it violently at the doctor, then reached to pick up things from the top of her locker and hurl them across the room. Dr. Munro got to his feet and walked quickly to the door.

"Nurse," he called urgently. "Come in here, please."

The nurse who had washed Abi reappeared and hurried to the bed. She caught Abi's wrists and pushed her back down onto the remaining pillow. "You must calm down," she said firmly, holding her still. "Now, stay calm, and everything'll be all right."

Abi stared at her wildly, tears streaming down her face.

"Nothing is all right!" she screamed. "My baby is dead. How can things ever be all right?" She closed her eyes tightly and kicked her legs against the covers. While the nurse still held her wrists, Sister Munro appeared and gave Abi a quick injection in her arm. Abi's eyes snapped open and she stared at the nurse.

"Are you trying to kill me now?" she demanded savagely. "What was that for?"

"Just something to calm you down," was the reply.

As she gazed at the sea of faces standing around her bed, Abi felt suddenly powerless, and she flopped back and closed her eyes again. They had beaten her. They had won. Maybe they hadn't actually stolen her baby, but it was the same effect. Her shoulders sagged, and she swallowed hard.

"Can I see her?" she asked in a whisper. The nurse glanced over at the doctor.

He shook his head and moved nearer to the bed. "I'm afraid not, Abi," he said gently. "It would only upset you further. In these circumstances, we deem it wise to deal with everything for you and leave you to begin to recover."

Abi opened her eyes and stared at him in puzzlement.

"But she's my baby," she persisted. "I want to see her, even if she is dead."

"Well, you can't, Abigail," said another voice from the doorway, and Abi looked up to see that her mother had entered. "The doctor's right. It wouldn't do any good. The clinic will dispose of the body, and we'll go home and get on with our lives."

Abi tried to sit up and found the room spinning wildly.

"What's happening?" she muttered, falling back onto the pillows again.

"The injection is kicking in," replied the nurse gently. "Just go with it. You'll feel better after another sleep."

Abi gave in and closed her eyes. Nothing mattered

anymore anyway. No one could help her now. As she drifted off to sleep again, she fancied she could hear her baby crying for her.

Chapter 18

*2005*

Abi poured two large glasses of Pinot Grigio and handed one to Gideon. He hadn't spoken since she'd finished telling him about the baby, and to judge by his face, he had a lot of questions to ask her. She sat down on the hearth rug again and sipped her wine. Eventually Gideon spoke without looking at her.

"So you never held her?" he said, so softly she had to strain to catch the words.

She shook her head. "No. They wouldn't even let me see her. Looking back, that seems very wrong, but I was so young and so distraught I didn't know any better."

"Does she have a grave?" he asked next, still not looking at her. She didn't reply, and eventually he glanced up at her. She was staring into the fire, her hair falling across her face. "Abi? Does she have a grave?" he repeated gently.

Abi shook her head. "No. The clinic 'dealt' with everything. I was so shocked I never even thought of that until ages later." She paused, and her voice broke as she continued, "I asked my mother, and she told me they don't bury babies that young, they just…dispose of them there." With a sob, she rested her head on her knees. "And I believed her. I was so stupid!"

Gideon put down his wine and knelt on the floor beside her.

"Don't blame yourself. You weren't stupid. You were young. Much too young for all that." He paused, and his face grew dark. "It seems everyone took advantage of that. Oh, that must have suited your mother just fine. It meant she didn't need to force you to give up the baby."

Abi raised her head and looked directly at him.

"Don't think it didn't cross my mind that she killed her," she said bleakly. "But I guess even she would stop short of murder."

"What happened next?"

She shrugged. "Judy and her mother turned up at the clinic just as we were leaving. They'd finally managed to track me down." She gave a tiny smile. "I think Judy was almost as upset as I was. She blamed herself for not being there. Stupid, of course. Then my parents took me home and made me get on with life as though nothing had happened." She gave a short mirthless laugh. "I went back to school the next week and stayed there until I passed my A levels. Then in September of '97 I went to Art College in Bath and never went back to my parents' house again. Until last week, for her funeral." She glanced up at him. "Same day you quit the band."

Gideon leaned back against the sofa and stretched his long legs out towards the fire. He gave a heavy sigh and took a long swig of his wine.

"Hell of a week," he said with a lopsided grin. "If I'd known it would end like this, I'd have thought twice about quitting the band." He glanced over at Abi and was shocked at the expression on her face. "Not because of the baby," he added hastily, reaching over and touching her on the arm. "Sorry, very bad joke. I haven't been able to stop thinking about you for months. I even dream about you."

Abi reached over, picked up the wine, and topped up her glass before she held the bottle out to Gideon.

He shook his head. "Better not," he said with a grimace. "I've got to drive back to Hampshire."

Abi frowned at him. "Not tonight, surely?" she said in surprise. "You can sleep on the sofa, if you like. It's quite comfortable."

In answer, he held out his glass, and she topped it up.

"Okay, if you're sure," he said tentatively, watching her.

"Well, I guess we've got a lot more to talk about," she said calmly, adding another log to the fire. "So it does seem more sensible. D'you need to call your parents?"

He grinned at her. "We're not teenagers now, you know," he said with a laugh. "They'll be fine."

Abi grinned back. "I suppose they will. How are they? I liked your parents," she remembered fondly.

"Same as ever," Gideon replied. "Loving the New Forest."

Abi was silent for a moment. "D'you want something to eat? I was going to snack, but if you're hungry I'm sure I can find something."

Gideon smiled at her. "Snacking is fine," he said, his voice quiet. "Crisps, chocolate, and alcohol. That's what rock stars live on. At least according to my mother."

"And marijuana." Abi raised an eyebrow. "You

stink of it. Did you have one in the car?"

Gideon had the grace to look slightly embarrassed. "Erm…yes, I did. Sorry. D'you mind?"

Abi laughed. "'Course not! Haven't had a joint for years. Almost forgotten what they smelled like," she said, getting to her feet. "I'll get some junk out to eat, shall I? We can picnic by the fire." She disappeared into the kitchen.

Gideon stared into the fire and sipped his wine. He had taken in so much life-changing information over the last couple of hours that he really felt he'd lost complete control of his life. He could still hardly take in what Abi had just told him. He'd been a father, albeit for a very short time, and he'd known nothing about it. A tiny part of him wanted to get up, leave, and just keep running, but another much stronger part was curious to stay. Although Abi had changed dramatically over the last ten years, he had seen enough hints of the girl he fell in love with for him to want to talk more. He had to admit he was scared, and he hadn't felt quite like that since the day back in '96 when he finally believed he'd lost her.

In the kitchen Abi was noisily unwrapping crisps and dips and arranging them all on a tray. She was unnerved to see her hands were shaking, and she stopped for a moment and leant against the worktop, closing her eyes and taking a deep breath. It had really taken it out of her, retelling the story of the baby's birth, and she was also trying hard to come to terms with the fact that Gideon was actually sitting in her living room, drinking her wine. She had dreamt of this day for so long, yet now it was here she was terrified. He seemed so much older and darker. His piercing eyes held a look of deep sadness, and his whole demeanour was one of mild despair. She accepted that her stories hadn't helped, but she also realised they still had a lot to talk about. She took a deep breath, picked up the tray, and carried it through to the living room.

"Here we go," she said with forced cheerfulness, placing the tray on the floor in front of Gideon. "Get stuck in. I'll see if there's some more wine."

She slipped back into the kitchen, returning moments later with a new bottle. She sat down cross-legged on the floor opposite Gideon and picked up her glass and raised it to him.

"To…old times," she said quietly. He hesitated for a moment, then raised his glass and gently touched it to hers. He finished the wine in one gulp and placed the glass on the floor beside him.

For the next twenty minutes they ate and drank in silence, sleepily watching the fire burn down and listening to the dogs whimpering in their sleep. Then Abi stood up and stretched.

"Wow, I'm stuffed," she announced with a yawn. "Think I could do with a coffee, too, to soak up some of that wine. D'you want one?"

Gideon nodded briefly and gave her a slight smile. She smiled shyly back and disappeared off to the kitchen. There was so much she wanted to ask him, but she didn't know how to do it. Having talked so much about what had happened to her, she felt she should be asking what had happened to him in the intervening years, but there was only one thing she actually wanted to know. She poured the milk on the coffees, added the boiling water, then carried them out to the living room. Gideon had got off the floor and was stretched out on the sofa with his eyes closed. Abi thought for a moment he had fallen asleep, but as she quietly placed his coffee on the table his eyes opened, and he stared at her. She sat down on the floor again and looked up at him, cradling her mug in her hands.

"Gid," she said, using her old pet name for him. "I have to know something." He sat up and nodded to her. "In August '95, when I hadn't heard from you and was beginning to get desperate, I saw you on the news…" She paused, and he looked at her questioningly. "You were with a girl. You were in Seattle, I think, and you got into a limo with some tart hanging on your arm. That destroyed me. Who was she? And did you really find someone that quickly?"

Gideon looked shocked. He sat forward and caught hold of Abi's hand.

"Christ, Abi, what d'you think I am?" he said. "I didn't look at another woman for years after we parted. I was still in love with you." He paused and frowned for a moment. "I think I remember the time you mean. We got followed everywhere by groupies, and they used to hang on me, and try and get me into bed, but I told them all I wasn't interested. That one was a real pest." He grinned. "If you could've seen what happened in the car, you would've been happier. I told her where to go, and Simon took over. He loved all the attention. I think he liked being with me 'cause I attracted them all but passed them on to him, and since all they cared about was sleeping with someone famous, he had a ball."

Abi shivered. That scene on the news had haunted her for years. She had honestly thought he had abandoned her, his head turned by the fame and attention. Now she felt so ashamed. She hung her head and her hair swung forward over her face.

Gideon laughed. "You're doing the hair thing again," he said. "I always loved that."

There was a slightly awkward silence for a moment before Abi looked up.

"I'm sorry, Gideon," she said quietly. "I actually thought you were being unfaithful to me. I thought you had had my letter telling you I was pregnant, and that you didn't want us any more. I'm so sorry."

Gideon slumped back against the cushions. "I can see why you might have thought that. I would have done. I thought you'd abandoned me, after all. I didn't receive any of your letters either. Where did you send them?"

"The record company. I guess they never passed them on." Abi's eyes reflected her pain.

Gideon frowned and shook his head. "No, they forwarded mail to us regularly," he said, his voice puzzled. "I wonder if you had the wrong address?"

Abi shook her head. "No. I thought of that, so I went and asked Simon's mum, and she had the same address. She said she often wrote to him that way."

"Yes, she did. Simon never told her where he was, so she had to." Gideon paused thoughtfully. "He certainly got plenty of letters from her that way."

Abi frowned. "Well, my mother hid your letters to me, but I can't imagine why anyone would hide my letters to you, can you?" Gideon was silent for so long she wondered if he'd heard her. She looked up at him. "Gid? Can you?" she repeated.

Slowly realisation dawned on Gideon's face, and his eyes glinted dangerously.

"Yes, I can," he said sharply. "Simon."

Abi gasped and stared at him in amazement.

"Simon?" she repeated. "But he's your best friend. Why would he…?" She shook her head in disbelief.

Gideon sat forward urgently. "Remember what he was like when you came to gigs? He used to hate it. He had this thing about girlfriends ruining the band. Like they had with other bands. But I never thought he'd go to such lengths to keep us apart." His face hardened as he thought back over the years. He began to see how Simon's behaviour had been the cause of a lot of trouble. In recent years they had not been nearly as close as in the past, and Gideon realised, sad though it might be, he could actually believe that Simon had kept the letters from him. His head snapped up and he stared at Abi, "Did your mother read the letters?" he asked abruptly.

Abi shook her head. "Only the first one. Oh, and possibly the postcards. Why?"

"Just wondering if Simon read yours," he said tightly.

Abi gasped, immediately realising the implications.

"Then he would have known about…all these years?" she stumbled over the words. "How could he not tell you?"

They stared at each other in silence. Then Gideon shook his head.

"No, even Simon couldn't be that cruel," he stated firmly. "He couldn't have read them. He must have just destroyed them." He stared at Abi with a dangerous look on his face. "And I'm going to fucking kill him."

Abi scrambled to her feet and perched on the end of the sofa.

"Why was everyone so against us?" she asked

softly. "We didn't hurt them."

Gideon's shoulders slumped, and he reached out and gently touched her arm. "Dunno. It's like they set out to ruin our lives."

"I thought they'd succeeded," said Abi slowly. "But maybe we can put some of it right, now."

Gideon gave her a small smile. "Maybe we can," he agreed.

They sat in silence for a minute, and then Abi glanced at the clock.

"Hell, it's nearly one," she said in surprise. "How on earth did it get that late? I think I'll turn in now. I'll get you a quilt and a pillow for the sofa." She jumped to her feet and ran upstairs to fetch the bedding.

Gideon bent down and began to clear away the food and drinks, piling everything onto the tray and carrying it into the kitchen. When Abi returned, he had kicked off his shoes and was rearranging the cushions on the sofa.

Abi dumped a pile of bedding on the chair and grinned at him. "Okay? I'll see you in the morning, then. Sleep tight," and with a wave she disappeared upstairs again.

Gideon stared after her, an inscrutable look on his face, before he bent down, closed the fire up, and began to make up his bed.

Chapter 19

*Wednesday, 23$^{rd}$ November 2005*

Abi awoke the next morning to a sound like a helicopter that seemed to be just outside her window. With a muttered oath she sprang out of bed and peered outside. A helicopter was indeed hovering at the end of her garden, and she found a camera pointing directly at her window.

"What the fuck!" she swore under her breath, wrenched open the door, and ran downstairs. "Gideon! Gideon, there's a sodding helicopter outside, taking pictures through my bedroom window. Where are you?" She stared around the apparently empty room. The sofa was still made up like a bed, and Gideon's clothes were scattered around the floor. She peered into the kitchen, then found herself looking in cupboards. She shook her head impatiently. "Where are you?" she shouted again.

"In the bathroom," came a distant reply, and Abi scampered up the stairs again. She tapped on the door and received permission to enter.

"Why are you in here?" she demanded, finding him sitting cross-legged in the empty bath, wearing only a T-shirt and boxers.

Gideon looked sheepish. "It's the only room they can't see into," he said apologetically. "Apparently they've found me."

Abi sat on the edge of the bath and surveyed him severely.

"Clearly," she said dryly. "So what do we do now?"

Gideon looked up at her, his eyes gleaming. She was dressed in checked pyjama pants and a white T-shirt, her hair was messed up, and her makeup had smudged.

He grinned cheekily at her. "You look good first thing in the morning."

Abi scowled at him. "That's as may be," she said, slightly self-conscious. "What are we going to do about the press? I looked out the front, and there are cars and vans out there, too. The garden is full of paparazzi. How am I going to get to work?" she demanded. "I'm a prisoner in my own home."

Gideon sighed and stood up in the bath.

"Sorry. Happens to me all the time," he said, stepping out onto the bathmat. "I had hoped they wouldn't have followed me here, though." He looked down at Abi. "D'you really have to go to work? I thought we could spend the day together."

"Well, it looks like we might have to, now," Abi replied sharply, raising an eyebrow at him. "Come on. We can't stay in here all day. If we're careful, we should be able to get to the kitchen and make a cuppa. We'll keep the curtains drawn."

She made her way out of the bathroom and back downstairs. The sound of the helicopter was still throbbing through the house, and Abi could also hear the engines of vehicles both arriving and departing. Someone hammered on the front door.

"Go away!" she shouted. "There's nothing here for you."

She went into the small kitchen and put the kettle on, glancing out the window as she did so. There was a bright flash, followed by the sight of a head ducking down below the windowsill. Abi swore loudly, flung open the window, and emptied a cold cup of coffee over the offending photographer.

"Fuck off and leave me alone," she snapped, slamming the window shut again. She grabbed a packet of biscuits, the kettle, some cups, and some tea bags and carried them back upstairs to the bathroom. Gideon was sitting on the edge of the bath, grinning. Abi dumped the stuff on the floor and plugged the kettle in on the landing.

"What?" she demanded of Gideon's amused face.

He chuckled. "Dreadful, isn't it?" he said. "See what I get all the time, everywhere I go? It's no fun being famous."

Abi snorted. "I'm sure it has its compensations," she said, attempting to make tea at the top of the stairs. "How can you stay so calm? I want to machine gun the lot of 'em!"

Gideon laughed out loud. "You haven't changed a bit!" he said in delight, taking the proffered cup of tea. "No milk?"

Abi gave him a look. "Get it yourself," she retorted. "I'm not going back down there."

"Are you really supposed to be at work?" he asked after a minute.

Abi shrugged. "Well, it is something I could re-schedule," she said eventually. "But I'll need to make some calls. Hang on." She disappeared into the bedroom to fetch her mobile, ducking down as she passed the window, in case the helicopter was still hovering, then ran back to the bathroom.

She made a couple of quick calls, then leaned back against the door and looked at Gideon. He looked really hot in his T-shirt and boxers, and she couldn't help thinking he had matured very nicely. He was rather too thin, and his face looked haggard, but when he smiled she could still see the teenager she'd fallen in love with. His hair was messy, and he badly needed a shave, but that only enhanced his good looks. Abi looked away, aware she'd been staring at him. She felt her face flush and bent her head to allow her hair to fall over it.

Gideon chuckled. "That hair thing again," he teased. "Bet you'll never grow out of that."

"So what are we going to do now?" She chose to ignore his comment. "We're pretty much stuck here today. Do these people usually stay long?"

Gideon shrugged. "Well, they are pretty keen to see me. I rather disappeared off the face of the earth, and they're all desperate for the story of why I quit the band." He paused rather too long, and Abi glanced up at him. "I suspect they want to see you, too. Someone will have got hold of the story about us from somewhere. Probably want to know if I quit the band for you."

Abi looked appalled. "How could they know about us?" she asked in surprise. "That was more than years ago."

Gideon sighed. "Someone must have told them. Simon or Chas, possibly."

Abi kicked the side of the bath in frustration.

"Hasn't Simon done enough?" she said angrily. "You don't wanna go and talk to them, do you?

Wouldn't that get rid of them?"

"It'll take more than that." Gideon shook his head. "I don't want to, anyway. I want to be left alone for a while, and I don't want them hassling you."

Abi gave him a look. "A little late for that, I think," she said dryly. "I've never been forced to make tea in my bathroom before." She thought for a minute. "What we need is to be able to go somewhere they couldn't possibly find out about. Any ideas?"

Gideon watched her as she spoke, more interested in her use of "we" than in anything else she was saying. He smiled to himself.

****

Judy flicked on the television as she passed by to fetch the children for breakfast. As she re-entered the room and popped Sabrina into her highchair, a picture flashed up onto the screen, and she froze. It was Abi's house, surrounded by vans from all the news channels, and with a helicopter hovering over the garden. She turned the sound up and moved closer.

"The whereabouts of elusive rock star Gideon Hawk was discovered late last night. It appears he's staying at the house of former girlfriend Abigail Thomson, in the little village of Sennen in Cornwall. Abigail and Gideon are known to have…" Judy muted the sound and stood quite still. This was all her fault. She needed to sort it, fast. The best way would be to get them out of there and to a secret location. She finished strapping Sabrina in, then snatched up the phone.

"Hi, Mum? Yeah, it's me…Have you seen the news?" She waited a moment. "Yeah, I feel awful. I sent him there, but it never occurred to me this would happen." She listened again as her mother spoke.

251

"Well, that's what I was thinking. Would that be okay?...Oh, thanks, Mum, you're a star. Could you have the kids, then?...Great! I'll be over in half an hour." Judy replaced the receiver and untied Sabrina from the highchair. "Sorry, pet, no time for brekkies. Grandma will feed you. Mummy's on a mission! Tommy, come and get dressed." She hurried out of the room and upstairs to get ready.

****

"Don't think you'll be getting your car back anytime soon," called Roger Hawk to his wife. Caroline appeared at the door, wiping her hands on a tea towel.

"What d'you mean?" she asked with a frown.

Roger pointed at the television. "The press have found Gideon. They have them besieged at Abi's cottage. Helicopters and all."

Caroline moved closer to the television and popped her glasses on the end of her nose.

"Oh, poor Abi," she said at once, perching on the edge of a chair. "She could have done without this." She looked at her husband and raised her eyebrows. "If he stayed there the night, that must mean they're talking?"

Roger looked over his glasses at her. "Or doing something else," he said with a grin.

Caroline flicked him with the tea towel. "Roger! Don't be coarse," she chided. "They haven't seen each other for years. They have a lot of talking to do. I hope they can get some peace."

****

Simon had been awake for hours, but he couldn't find a good reason to get up. He had done virtually nothing since he'd arrived home, and he was beginning to think he really should get his act together to try and find Gideon before he got together with Abi. He rolled onto his back and pulled the duvet up to his chin. His mother's house was very cold. She would only allow the heating on in the evening, and he'd grown used to a much more opulent lifestyle. He glanced at his mobile. It was nearly eleven o'clock. If he didn't get up soon, his mother would come banging on the door offering him tea. He hated tea. He rolled out of bed and dragged the previous day's clothes back on. Then he ran his fingers through his hair and made his way downstairs. Josephine was hoovering the living room, and Simon wandered into the kitchen and poured himself a large glass of orange juice. He sat down at the kitchen table and waited for her to finish. He quite fancied some scrambled eggs this morning. After a couple of minutes the hoovering stopped, and Josephine came in to join him.

"Morning, son," she said cheerfully. "Sleep well?"

Simon grimaced. "Not really," he said. "That bed's too small. And it's always so cold."

His mother's smile vanished, and she pursed her lips.

"Well, don't let me keep you here," she said sharply. "Shouldn't you be out looking for Gideon anyway?" Simon snorted. She went on. "Actually, I know something about that."

His head shot up. "What?" he demanded, staring at her.

"It was on the news. They found him last night. Apparently he stayed in a little village in Cornwall…" She racked her brains for a moment. "Yes, Sennen, that was it. I think it's near Land's End…" She tailed off as

Simon leapt up from the table and ran out of the room. She heard him thundering upstairs, only to return a moment later carrying his jacket and a holdall.

He pulled open the front door and ran out, calling, "Don't wait up," before slamming it behind him and racing out into the cold November day.

Josephine sighed and finished her sentence. "Apparently it's Abi's house he's staying at," she said, shaking her head. "And I suspect you needed to know that, you silly boy."

She put Simon's glass of undrunk orange juice back into the fridge and got on with her day.

\*\*\*\*

"So how long does it take to drive down here from Judy's place?" asked Gideon impatiently. Judy had texted Abi at eight o'clock to say she was on her way to rescue them. She gave no details but instructed them to have bags packed for a few days' stay and make sure they didn't get seen packing them.

"Four, four and a half hours," said Abi vaguely. "She should be here soon. I wonder what she has planned? I really can't see how she thinks she can get us out of here unnoticed."

Abi had dressed in jeans and a stripy polo-neck jumper, and had tied her hair into a high ponytail. Gideon thought she looked like a teenager again. He was dressed in the same clothes as the day before because he'd left his overnight bag in the car. He'd managed to tidy his hair, and Abi had lent him a spare toothbrush.

They were both quite on edge and had come very close to snapping at each other, so it was with great relief that they heard a tap at the door and Judy's voice calling, "It's okay, it's only me."

Abi opened the door just enough to let Judy in, then locked it behind her. Judy gave them both a quick hug before dumping a large holdall on the sofa.

"Right," she said efficiently, looking from one to the other of them. "You'll need to do exactly as I say if this is going to work."

Gideon and Abi nodded, and the three of them went and sat on the stairs, where there was less chance of them being seen from outside.

Judy grinned at them. "Well, isn't this fun," she said with a giggle.

Abi raised an eyebrow at her. "You try it for a morning," she retorted. "I had to make tea in the bathroom!"

Gideon grinned at Judy. "She's a lightweight," he said. "I have to put up with this all the time."

Abi gave him a look and turned to Judy. "So what's the plan?"

Judy smiled smugly. "Well," she said, "d'you remember my mum and dad's caravan, Abs?"

Abi nodded. "The one in Wales?"

Judy nodded. "Yeah, well, they've said you can borrow it for a few days to hide in. If we can get you out of here unseen, then no one can possibly know about the caravan, and you should be safe there." She paused and smiled at them. "You can only stay a week, at most, because the caravan park closes for the winter at the end of November, but that should be enough. Someone else'll be in the news by then. You'll be old hat," she added to Gideon with a grin.

Gideon and Abi looked doubtful.

"Judy, have you seen the people outside?" asked

Abi. "How on earth can we get out without being seen?"

Judy grinned again. "Ah, now that's the clever bit," she said proudly. "But we do need the help of another man. Is your neighbour Chris at home?"

Abi shrugged. "Dunno. I can call him, if you like."

Judy nodded, and Abi quickly dialled Chris's number from her mobile. He answered almost immediately and agreed to come round.

Judy looked pleased. "Excellent. Now, hopefully we can make this work. Is Chris a good sport?"

Abi grinned. "Oh, yes," she assured her friend. "He's game for anything."

Gideon looked at her suspiciously.

Judy saw the look and laughed. "Haven't you told him?" she asked Abi with a grin.

Abi shook her head. "More fun if he meets him," she replied with a glint in her eye, adding provocatively, "None of his business anyway."

Judy shook her head and laughed again. "Oh, right," she said. "Okay, let's get this show on the road. The idea is that Chris and I will pretend to be you two and will leave driving Gideon's car. I take it the Range Rover is yours?" she added, looking at Gideon.

He nodded. "My mother's, actually," he said.

Judy continued, "Then after we've drawn the paparazzi after us, you two can leave in my car and go to the caravan." She paused and frowned. "Actually, on second thoughts, it'll probably work better if you two leave first, disguised as me and Chris, and then we'll leave later, after dark, when you'd be more likely to slip away. What d'you think?"

Gideon looked dubious. "Might work," he said

slowly. "But these guys are pretty on the ball. They'll be expecting us to try something, I'm sure."

Abi rolled her eyes. "It sounds brilliant to me," she said. "Stop worrying so much. It's bound to work. Judy's plans always work." Gideon looked at her and grinned. "What?" she demanded. He shook his head and said nothing.

There was a sudden tap at the door, and Abi ran over.

"Hello?" she said.

"It's me, Abs," came a voice, and she quickly unbolted the door and let Chris in. He stood in the living room and looked around him with interest. "Wow, isn't this exciting?" he said. "What're we doing?"

Gideon regarded the newcomer with a raised eyebrow and then looked at Abi.

She grinned at him. "Gid, this is my neighbour and friend, Chris. Chris, this is Gideon Hawk." The two men shook hands briefly, while Abi went on, "And this is my bestest friend in the whole world, Judy."

Chris grinned at Judy. "Hello. I've heard so much about you, I feel I already know you." He gave her a hug.

Judy laughed. "Likewise," she said, eyeing him up and down critically. "Yes, this should work, you and Gideon are about the same height and build, and so are Abi and I. Right!" She clapped her hands. "Let's get down to business."

Half an hour later, Abi and Gideon were dressed and made up to look very closely like Judy and Chris. Judy had brought suitable clothes for Abi, and Chris popped back home to fetch something of his for Gideon to wear. The plan was that the real Judy and Chris would be seen by the reporters to be packing stuff into Judy's car, and then the fake Judy and Chris would appear and drive off, leaving the fake Abi and Gideon to wait a few more hours before effecting a highly noticeable get-away in the Range Rover.

"Okay, you both look great," said Judy, standing back and admiring her handiwork. "Don't you think so, Chris?"

Chris nodded, a devious grin on his face.

"Absolutely darling. Gideon could be my twin!"

Abi snorted and stared at herself in the mirror. Judy had packed the car with everything Abi thought they would need for the next few days, and when she came in Abi had changed clothes with her. All she needed now was to add Judy's thick winter coat and the woollen knitted hat she'd been careful to be seen wearing, and they would be set. Gideon was feeling extremely uncomfortable in a jumper and jacket of Chris's. He was wearing his own jeans because they discovered the younger man was slightly thinner, but Judy thought they looked near enough the same to fool the press. When Chris had returned to the house with the extra clothes, he'd taken care to wear the baseball cap and dark glasses Gideon was now sporting.

"Sunglasses in November?" he asked doubtfully. "I tried that the other day, and I couldn't see a thing."

Judy laughed. "Well, there is a bit of sun today, at least, and anyway, Abi'll be driving, so don't worry."

"Why does Abi have to drive?" he objected.

Abi rolled her eyes. "Keep up," she said impatiently. "They saw Judy arrive in the car, so it would look weird if she wasn't driving when they left.

It's meant to look like she arrived to pick up a friend."

Judy nodded vigorously. "That's it. You've got it. Now don't look directly at any of the reporters, and certainly make sure you don't speak. Just get in the car and drive off."

Abi looked at Gideon and took a deep breath.

"Are you ready for this?" she asked.

He shrugged. "As ready as I ever will be, I guess," he said with a lopsided grin.

Suddenly Abi clapped a hand over her mouth.

"Oh, my god!" she shrieked. "The dogs! I forgot the dogs!"

Judy held up her hand.

"Calm down!" she laughed. "I didn't forget the dogs. They'll come with us. That'll make it look even more authentic. I hope your mother doesn't mind dogs in her car, Gideon?"

Gideon grinned. "She loves dogs," he said. "They have a Labrador."

"Excellent. We'll take them with us, 'cause Chris will eventually be coming back here anyway, and he can look after them." She raised her eyebrows at Chris. "That okay with you?"

He nodded. "Of course it is," he said. "So where're we going to go, then?" he asked curiously.

Judy shrugged and laughed. "No idea," she said cheerfully. "Just take them on a wild goose chase all over Cornwall, I expect. You'll have to drive, of course."

He nodded and grinned. "Cool. Never driven a Range Rover before."

Judy looked at Gideon. "One more thing—Is there plenty of fuel in the Range Rover? We can't risk having to stop to refuel."

Gideon nodded. "Loads," he said. "I filled up on my way through Penzance, in case there weren't any more after that."

Abi stared at him. "This is not the back of beyond, you know," she said crossly. "We are in the twenty-first century down here."

Judy sighed. "Okay, you two, not now, eh? You've got a whole week to bicker in the caravan if you want to, so let's keep to the matter in hand. I also filled up in Penzance, so you should have enough to get you all the way to Llangennith." She paused and looked at them both. "Right. Are you ready? Is everything in the car that you want?"

Gideon nodded, but Abi suddenly darted towards the stairs and pulled out the tin box her father had given her.

"I want to take this," she said, holding it out to Judy. Judy looked curiously at it, then put on her coat, pulled her hat down as low as she could, and carried the box out to the car. When she came back in, she handed the coat and hat to Abi and frowned at her.

"What's in the box?" she asked.

Abi bit her lip. "Dunno," she admitted. "Dad gave it to me to bring home. He insisted I take it, but it's locked and has no key. I think he knows what's in it."

Judy looked slightly worried. "Don't open it yet," she said slowly. "Not till I say you can."

Abi looked surprised. "What? D'you know what it is?"

Judy shook her head. "No, but I have an idea. Please just wait until I ring you. Promise?"

Abi shrugged. "I guess so. I've waited this long.

Did you put the cardboard boxes in?" Judy nodded. "Okay, so long as I've got those, I'll wait. Don't take too long, though. I'm getting curious, now."

Judy nodded, then clapped her hands together.

"Right, people, let's get this show on the road. Abi, do your coat up and pull the hat down so your hair doesn't show. Gideon, collar up, hat and shades on. Tuck your hair into your collar. That's right. Now walk casually. Don't rush, and don't drive off like you're being chased." She handed Abi the car keys. "The key for the caravan is on here, too. You remember which one it is?" Abi nodded. "Right. Off we go, then. Good luck, guys. Call me when you get there."

She gave them each a quick hug, then opened the door just enough to let them out.

As the door closed behind them, Abi and Gideon both took deep breaths and walked casually over to Judy's car. Gideon folded his long legs into the passenger seat while Abi climbed into the driving seat. She thanked heavens she didn't need to adjust its position—that would have given the game away—and she started the engine with no problem. The cameras began to flash as they drove slowly up the track and back onto the road, Abi looking straight ahead, and Gideon pretending to look for something in the glove compartment. A couple of reporters called out to them as they drove off:

"Is Gideon staying here tonight?"

"Is he back together with his girlfriend?"

"Is it true he left the band for her?"

"We heard a rumour they have a child. Is it true?"

When she heard the last question, it took all Abi's self-control not to stop the car and punch the questioner, but she held her breath and kept driving slowly.

"Keep going," muttered Gideon under his breath. "Ignore them. They don't matter. Just keep driving. You're doing great."

Abi drove on, out onto the road, and indicated left onto the A30, in the direction of Penzance. As they gained speed, Gideon chanced a look behind them and saw to his relief that no one had followed them.

"I think it actually worked!" he said in mild surprise. "Well done Judy. And well done you, too," he added with a grin.

Abi glanced sideways at him.

"I don't think I'll really relax until we get there," she admitted. "And since we have a good five-hour drive ahead of us, we'd better get a move on."

Chapter 20

*Thursday, 24th November 2005*

Abi opened her eyes and lay for a moment wondering where on earth she was. The sound of the sea was far stronger than it was at home, and her bed was very hard. Slowly it came back to her, and she pushed herself up onto one elbow and looked around her. She was in one of the tiny bedrooms in the Cromwells' static caravan. She had been to the caravan often in her childhood, but now, returning as an adult, it seemed very much smaller and more cramped. She remembered she and Judy had shared this room on many an occasion, but she was beginning to find it claustrophobic even with just her in it. She slid out of bed and shivered. Looking around, she picked up a thick woollen jumper she had packed at the last minute. She pulled it on over her pyjamas and padded out into the main part of the caravan. She and Gideon had arrived at the caravan site late the night before and had pretty much just fallen into bed without even investigating their accommodation. They had had no problems with the press, and having heard from Judy, it appeared they had been successfully lured away from her house, as well. Judy and Chris had taken them on a long trek around the coast of Cornwall and finally lost the last of them as they crossed the Tamar into Devon, up near Morwenstow. Judy reported that the dogs were tucked up safe at home and she was on her way back home in Gideon's car. She was planning to drive to Wales later in the week, to swap the cars over.

Abi had a little hunt in the small kitchen and put the kettle on. Then she rummaged through the box of food Judy had thoughtfully provided for them and pulled out a jar of coffee and a packet of tea bags. She smiled to herself. That's the essentials sorted, she thought, as she searched for some mugs. She made herself a mug of strong coffee and carried it to the living room end of the caravan. They had a prime position on the site, right on the edge of the sand dunes overlooking the long sweep of Rhossili Bay. The day was overcast, and the waves were thrashing onto the shore, sending spray and foam all the way over to the caravans. Abi sat down on one of the window seats, curled her feet under her, and watched the world go by.

She was lost in thought when Gideon emerged from the other bedroom, hair on end, unshaven, and very bleary-eyed. He was wearing a T-shirt and boxers again and shivered as he joined her in the living area.

"Morning," he said with a yawn.

Abi looked round. "Morning. Kettle's just boiled." She nodded towards it.

Gideon wandered over, made himself a coffee, then joined her at the window.

"Bloody cold in here," he remarked, looking around. "Is there any heating?"

Abi nodded towards a fireplace behind him. "Yeah, there's a gas heater there, and I think some others dotted around. Remember, we turned the gas bottle on last night when we arrived? Hope it's full."

She watched as Gideon dropped to his knees in front of the heater and attempted to light it. His long bare legs were very tanned and muscular, and Abi gave a little shiver of excitement as she remembered how they used to feel, rubbing against her own. She felt her face begin to get hot, and bent forward to let her hair fall over it.

Gideon turned round. "I can't do this, Abi. Any ideas?" he began, then raised his eyebrows at her. "The hair again? Why this time?"

Abi flushed even more and turned to look out the window.

"No reason," she murmured awkwardly, studiously watching the flight path of a herring gull as it wheeled above the incoming tide.

Gideon chuckled. "Okay, then," he said. "But I still can't light this thing."

Abi rolled her eyes and crawled across the floor to join him. She felt around the side of the fire and pressed a button. Immediately a pilot light appeared, closely followed by a row of flames across the bottom of the fire. She sat back on her heels.

"How d'you get through the day?" she asked him, shaking her head in mock disgust. Gideon looked at her and raised one eyebrow.

"Pretty well," he stated. "I just use electricity." He pushed her gently on the shoulder so she wobbled and sat back down on her bottom. "I can rewire a plug in under three minutes," he added proudly.

Abi stared at him in amazement. "Three minutes?" she exclaimed. "Three minutes? You amateur. Anything more than two and you're a loser."

He narrowed his eyes at her. "Competition?" he

queried.

She nodded. "You're on. You do that light, and I'll do the kettle," and she leapt to her feet and carried the kettle into the living area. They looked at each other.

"Screwdriver?" asked Gideon cautiously. "Or am I supposed to do it with my teeth?"

"You can use a screwdriver," conceded Abi, and after rummaging in her handbag for a moment, produced a small silver one.

Gideon looked impressed. "You carry a screwdriver?"

Abi nodded. "Of course. Doesn't everyone?" she replied calmly. "We'll have to do this one at a time and time each other. You go first." She delved into her bag again and brought out a stopwatch. Gideon's eyes widened, but he said nothing. "Okay, start now!" and she pressed the button and sat cross-legged on the floor, watching him.

Five minutes later he finally fitted the plug back together and held it aloft triumphantly. Abi pressed the button on the stopwatch and laughed.

"Well, I wouldn't tell anyone about that effort," she said smugly. "Now I'll show you how it should be done." She picked up the screwdriver and grinned at him. "Ready?"

Gideon started the stopwatch, then leaned back against a chair and watched her work. He couldn't quite get his head around the fact that here he was, sitting on the floor of a caravan in Wales, with the girl he'd fallen in love with more than ten years before but hadn't seen since—and until the day before had always thought had abandoned him. Just over a week ago he'd been on stage in Central Park, the object of desire for thousands of fans. Now here he was, in his underwear, timing a girl in her pyjamas as she changed a plug. He grinned to himself. Then he started to chuckle. By the time Abi finally finished the plug—four and a half minutes, to his chagrin—he had tears of laughter pouring down his cheeks and couldn't speak. Abi stared at him in surprise. She started to grin, then leaned forward and snatched the stopwatch off him.

"I won!" she cried jumping to her feet and doing a victory dance around the small room. She ended up standing in front of Gideon, her bare feet planted firmly apart and her hands on her hips. "I'm better than you!" she said childishly and grinned down at him, her long hair swinging in front of her face. Gideon got to his feet and towered above her. She looked up at him, and he reached out a hand and brushed her hair back from her face.

"That's better," he murmured, smiling down at her. She stared back, suddenly insecure, and chewed on her bottom lip. She tried to move her head forward to release her hair, but Gideon was holding it behind her ears. She swallowed nervously, realising that for once she wasn't in control. Gideon let go of her hair and gently touched her cheek with his finger, then he grinned at her and said, "Yep, you won. Were you always this competitive? I don't remember."

Abi took a step away, and the tension was broken.

"Oh, yes, always," she said, slightly breathless, wrapping her arms around her body and walking towards the window. "Don't you remember the hula hoops?" she added cryptically.

Gideon laughed and moved off towards his bedroom.

"I'm going to get dressed. Too cold to sit around in underwear any longer," he observed, and he ducked into the tiny room and shut the door behind him.

Abi watched him go, then slumped down on the window seat with a shuddering sigh. What on earth was going on this morning? Had she really challenged Gideon Hawk to a plug-changing race? She shook her head in despair. Slowly she got to her feet and shuffled back to her room to get dressed. Maybe life would make more sense if she was wearing clothes.

****

"Just seen your car on the news, Caroline," called Roger, rubbing his hands in delight. "This really is rather exciting! It's being followed all over Cornwall."

Caroline sighed and sat down in front of the television. There was a close-up shot of her Range Rover with two people in it, driving along the A30 near Penzance. She peered closely at it.

"That's not Gideon," she said firmly. "So I doubt if that's Abi, either. They must be decoys!" she added with a smug smile.

Roger looked at her in surprise. "Very clever," he said admiringly. "So where's our boy, then? And who's that in the car?"

Caroline shrugged. "Only one way to find out," she said and reached for her mobile. She very quickly sent a text, then smiled at her husband. "If the press are following my car, then the decoy must have worked. I wonder where they've gone?"

"I wonder when you'll get your car back?" remarked Roger with a grin.

Caroline's mobile bleeped and she picked it up and peered at the screen.

268

"Wales," she said in satisfaction. "They're holed up in Wales."

Roger stared at her. "Holed up?" he repeated, chuckling. "Good heavens, Caroline, where do you hear these things?"

Caroline tutted. "Holed up, in hiding, under cover…call it what you like, but they've escaped the paparazzi for now," she said with a satisfied nod.

"But we still don't know who has your car," added Roger with a gleam in his eye.

\*\*\*\*

Simon sat nursing a cup of lukewarm coffee and staring down at a half-eaten full English breakfast. He wished he'd got a burger instead as he pushed the plate away in disgust. He'd spent the previous afternoon racing down to Sennen to catch Gideon, only to find he was too late and the birds had flown the nest. He had also discovered it was actually Abi's house Gideon had been staying in, so his trip was in vain anyway. He cursed his mother for not telling him the whole story the morning before. She could have saved him a lot of trouble.

He downed the rest of his coffee and sat back in his chair. He hated motorway service stations, and this one was no exception. He had attempted to get some sleep in the car in a lay-by just before Exeter, but it had not been very successful, and he was now wondering if he was going to manage the drive back to Newbury without a proper nap. Now he knew Gideon and Abi had reconnected, he really had no idea what he should do. It was only a matter of time before Gideon found out about, or at least suspected, his deception, and he really didn't want to be around when that happened. He wondered if he should just cut his losses and go back to the States. Maybe travel for a while. He had plenty of money; might as well use it.

He pushed back his chair and left the café, pausing to buy a newspaper as he passed the shop. As expected, the front page was covered in pictures of Abi's cottage, and of a Range Rover driving away from the house in the dark. Simon peered at the grainy photograph and shook his head. That didn't look like Gideon to him. A small picture at the bottom of the page showed another smaller car leaving the cottage earlier in the afternoon, and on closer examination, Simon surmised Gideon and Abi were in that one. Clever, he thought to himself. Someone hatched a decoy plan. Seemed a bit too clever for Gideon, and Simon reckoned he saw Judy's hand in it. Still meddling, he thought to himself as he got back into his hired car and set off up the M5 towards Bristol. Leaving the country was beginning to seem like the most attractive option.

****

"We're going to need to do some shopping," said Abi after unpacking the box of food Judy had sent with them. "Unless we can survive entirely on tea, coffee, wine, and chocolate biscuits," she added with a grin.

"Sounds all right to me," came the reply, from where Gideon was attempting to tune in the television. "What else do we need?"

Abi stuck her head round the corner and made a face at him.

"You say that now," she said, "but you wait until this evening. You'll be starving after our long walk."

Gideon looked up and frowned at her.

"Long walk?" he asked suspiciously. "You never

said anything about a walk. We're in hiding, you know."

"We're on the edge of a three-mile-long beach, one of the most beautiful in Britain," she said severely. "We're going to walk along it. From one end to the other."

Gideon got to his feet and walked to the window.

"We're right in the middle of it," he objected. "If we go from one end to the other we'll have to walk one and a half miles one way to that end, then turn round and come back…" Abi picked up a cushion and threw it at him. "All right, we'll go for a walk. Is there a pub at the end of it?" he added hopefully.

Abi grinned. "Actually, yes," she said. "But we can't go. We're in hiding, remember?"

Gideon swore under his breath. "Okay, we'd better go shopping, then. How do we do that without being seen?"

"Well, there's a shop on the site," said Abi. "But I'm not sure if it's open, 'cause the campsite bit is closed now, and it mostly serves that. Shall we go and look?"

Gideon shrugged. "Okay, may as well," he said, and squeezed into his bedroom to find his jacket.

Ten minutes later the two of them were wandering through the ranks of deserted caravans towards the entrance to the site where the small shop was situated. From what Abi could remember, it sold most essentials, and hopefully they would be able to get a couple of meals' worth without leaving the caravan site.

"Some of these caravans are massive!" marvelled Gideon, peering into them as they walked by. "Pity ours isn't that big."

"We're lucky to have it," chided Abi. "Imagine if we were still besieged in my cottage?"

Gideon grinned at her. "That was fun, too," he said. "Specially making tea in the bathroom."

Abi grinned back. "I guess so," she conceded. "But this is more relaxing."

Gideon wrinkled his nose. "I'm not really used to relaxing," he said. "I've pretty much been on tour for the last ten years. No time to call my own. This is a rare treat."

Abi glanced at him. "Hope you don't get too bored," she said with a little smile.

He reached over, pulled her hand out of her pocket, and held it in his.

"Not a chance," he said decisively without looking at her.

Self-consciously, Abi bent her head and let her hair conceal her face. His large hand was gripping her hand very tightly, and she was wishing she hadn't worn her gloves. The thought of feeling his skin on hers was tantalising, and she wriggled her fingers and squeezed his hand. He looked down at her.

"Okay?" he asked with a gleam in his eye. She nodded and gave a small smile.

The little shop luckily proved to be open, although only for a couple of hours a day, and Abi and Gideon quickly stocked up on a variety of tins, as much bread as they could, cheese, milk, bacon, eggs, wine, and lager. They were just about to pay when Gideon added half a dozen packets of crisps and a large bar of chocolate.

"Rock star food," he said winking at her. Abi grinned and delved into her bag for her purse. She suddenly became aware that the teenage boy behind the counter was staring at them.

"Gid," she whispered, "I think we've been rumbled."

Gideon smiled at the boy, who swallowed and managed to croak, "Oh, my god, you're Gideon Hawk! You're all over the papers this morning." He turned to Abi. "And you're Abigail Thomson. Wow, what're you doing here?"

Abi's face fell as she realised that she too was now going to be recognised, but Gideon smiled at the boy.

"We're staying here to escape the press," he explained with a conspiratorial wink. "Any chance you could keep our presence a secret?"

The boy nodded eagerly. "'Course I can. I'm a real fan. Please, can I get your autograph?" he asked, turning bright red as his feet shuffled awkwardly.

Gideon grinned. "Of course." He scribbled his name on the proffered piece of paper. "Just remember—we're not really here." He smiled again as the boy nodded.

Abi handed over the money for the provisions, and they thanked the boy for his discretion and made their way back to the caravan.

"This box is incredibly heavy," complained Gideon. "What did we buy?"

Abi grinned. "I think that one is mostly booze," she admitted with a laugh. "I've got the healthy stuff here."

"Not sure tinned chilli is very healthy," commented Gideon, puffing slightly as they finally approached their caravan.

Abi eyed him curiously. "You're a bit out of condition. Would have thought your concerts would have kept you fit."

"Sure, the concerts are fine, it's what gets eaten, drunk, and smoked afterwards that does you in," he replied with a guilty grin, attempting to open the caravan door with his elbow. Once inside, they unpacked all the shopping, and Abi made a couple of cheese sandwiches to keep them going on their walk.

A watery sun was just beginning to peep out from behind the clouds as they ran down the sand dunes and onto the beach. The tide was more than half way out, and there was plenty of sand available to walk on. Abi stopped at the bottom of the dunes and considered.

"If we go that way"—she pointed to the left— "we'll get to Rhossili. That's where the pub is and where you can walk to Worm's Head from. And if we go the other way, we can explore Burry Holms." She nodded to the right. "That's the little island. It's accessible at low tide, which should be in about an hour. Which do you prefer?" she asked, looking up at Gideon.

He looked from one to the other. "Let's go to the island," he said. "We can't go to the pub, and it's probably a bit late to walk all the way to Worm's Head now, isn't it?"

Abi nodded. "Yes. You have to be really careful with the tides there, too. You only have a small window to cross the causeway and get back before the tide comes back in. If we tried today, it would be getting dark before we got back, and that'd be dangerous." She turned to him, the wind whipping her hair across her face. "Maybe we could try that tomorrow, if the tide times are right."

Gideon reached out and pushed her hair back.

"Maybe," he agreed cautiously. "Let's see how tiring this is first."

Abi laughed. "You wimp," she said, her eyes glinting. "This is nothing. I walk the dogs along Sennen beach every day, and that's pretty big. Now, come on, let's go and explore." She set off across the sand in the direction of the little island at the far end of the beach.

Gideon grinned and ran to catch up with her, wondering whether it would be appropriate for him to hold her hand again. He fell into step alongside her and watched as she drew in the sharp salty air, and lifted her face to the chilly breeze. Tentatively he reached out and took her hand in his. She was not wearing gloves this time, and it felt soft and cold in his large hand. She glanced over at him and smiled slightly.

"You'll have to walk at my pace, then," she said. "I don't hang around."

Gideon grinned at her and picked up his pace to keep alongside her. They strode briskly along the beach, stopping every now and then to examine the various shells and bits of flotsam that had been washed ashore with the last high tide. Abi pointed out the different types of crabs they came across, and identified all the sea birds wheeling above them. As they approached Burry Holms, she told Gideon all about its history, and he found himself getting caught up in the romance of the tales of Iron Age forts and mediaeval monasteries. He looked at Abi with respect.

"You really know your stuff, don't you?"

Abi shrugged. "Spent a lot of holidays here. Judy's dad would take us everywhere and give us a history lesson or a nature lesson. I guess some of it stuck," she said with a grin. "Those were lovely holidays. I miss those days."

Gideon squeezed her hand and smiled down at her.

"Well, we're here now. Let's enjoy it."

She smiled back and nodded. "Look, the tide's nearly out far enough for us to get onto Burry Holms." She pointed to the narrow strip of rocks between the beach and the island, water still rushing across it. She turned to Gideon. "You should never cross until it's really clear," she said severely. "People have got swept away trying to go across when the tide's coming in. It rushes round much faster than you'd expect."

They stood together on the shore and watched as the sea slowly receded, until it was safe to clamber across onto the little island. Abi led the way, and Gideon found himself paying far more attention to her figure in front of him than to where he was walking. After a few minutes of scrambling, they found themselves on the grassy top of the small island and stood together gazing out across the wide expanse of sea, over towards the distant coast of Devon. To their left was the long promontory of Worms Head, stretching out from Rhossili at the other end of the bay, and the three-mile stretch of sand between them appeared completely deserted.

Abi glanced around. "Unusual not to see some fishermen out here at low tide," she said. "Some of them strand themselves and stay on here to fish until the next tide. Maybe it's the wrong season for fishing. I'm used to being here in August." She laughed and pulled her jacket more tightly around her against the cold November wind.

"Hope the weather was better then," remarked Gideon, moving slightly closer to her so their arms were touching.

"Usually," said Abi with a grin. "But I remember a couple of dreadfully cold Augusts."

They walked all the way around the island, and Abi pointed out a number of things of archaeological interest before they finally succumbed to the chill of the wind and decided to make their way back. Once down on the sand, Gideon took Abi's hand in his again and set off at a smart pace. She laughed, running to keep up with his long legs.

"Hey, wait up! Where'd this energy come from?" she demanded, attempting to slow him down by pulling on his arm.

Gideon chuckled. "I don't know about you," he said, puffing slightly, "but I'm freezing, and the thought of that nice gas fire and a can of lager is becoming ever more attractive." He grinned down at her. "Even the tinned chilli seems rather appealing."

Abi grinned back, and together they made it back to the caravan in record time. Even without the fire lit, it felt cosy and safe, and while Gideon went round putting on all the gas fires, Abi poured a glass of wine for herself and opened a can of lager for Gideon. She carried the drinks into the living area, put them down on the coffee table, and then curled up on the window seat. Gideon came in rubbing his hands together.

"Right. That's all the heaters on. It should be really warm in a minute," he said, picking up the lager and taking a long swig. "Ahh, that's better. Feel civilised now." He sat down at the other end of the window seat.

Abi pushed her hair behind her ears and looked at him seriously.

"I had a lovely time today," she said. "We never

really did anything like that before, did we? When we were young."

There was a moment's silence, and then Gideon grinned.

"No, I guess not. It was more a case of sneaking around trying to avoid your mother, and pretending we were at the cinema," he said. "We didn't really go places and just enjoy it. Too much stress."

Abi nodded in agreement and took a long swig of her wine.

"Shall we walk to Worm's Head tomorrow?" she asked with a gleam in her eye.

Gideon looked doubtful. "Maybe," he said cautiously. "Looks a long way on a cold day."

Abi snorted. "Wimp," she retorted. "It'll warm you up walking. Maybe we could risk the pub afterwards. If we go in disguise."

Gideon grinned. "Maybe. We'll see."

Chapter 21

*Friday, 25ᵗʰ November 2005*

Abi awoke the next morning feeling very relaxed and much warmer. They had kept the gas heaters on until they went to bed, and the caravan seemed to have retained its heat fairly well during the night. She lay on her back and stared up at the white melamine ceiling, the quilt pulled up to her chin. They had spent the evening very quietly, watching television, playing Scrabble, and chatting about innocuous subjects. Both of them had avoided talking about anything to do with their previous relationship or the recent revelations that had come to light, but Abi had felt her whole body tingle just at the thought of Gideon's touch. Even when he'd held her hand on the beach she'd felt ready to burst. She had no idea if he felt the same, and she certainly wasn't ready to ask him.

She threw back the covers and jumped quickly out of bed, pulling her thick jumper over her head as she did so. As she emerged into the main part of the caravan, she became aware of a delicious smell of coffee and bacon. Gideon was standing at the stove, wearing only a T-shirt and boxers again—Abi wished he wouldn't keep doing that. He was busy making breakfast. Two steaming cups of coffee were sitting on the worktop, and the kitchen area was full of smoke.

Abi grinned and coughed.

"You're gonna set the fire alarm off in a minute," she said with a laugh, picking up a coffee and taking a sip. "Mmmmm, nice coffee. Thanks."

She carried it into the living area away from the tantalising sight of his near-naked body, curled up on her favourite seat, and stared out the window at the wheeling gulls and pounding surf. The day was very overcast, clearly threatening rain, and Abi wrinkled her nose with distaste.

"Hmm, maybe no walk to Worm's Head today," she said sadly. "I think it's going to pour in a minute."

Gideon appeared around the corner, carrying two large plates of bacon and eggs. He deposited one on Abi's lap.

"There you go. See? I'm not totally useless," he said proudly, sitting down with his own plate on the floor next to the fire.

"If you're cold, why don't you put more clothes on?" said Abi with a sniff. Gideon grinned at her, and got stuck into his breakfast.

"Shall we just stay in and play games and stuff today?" he asked between mouthfuls.

Abi shrugged. "May as well. Don't really fancy braving the weather. Nice to watch it from here, though." She scraped the last of her egg off the plate and put it to one side. "We can always go to Worms Head tomorrow."

Gideon watched her as she sipped her coffee and gazed out the window. Her sleep-tangled hair fell around her shoulders, and her bare feet with their blue-painted toenails were tucked underneath her. Gideon had always liked her feet. Even as a teenager she had painted her toenails. Never her fingernails, just the toes. He liked that. He got to his feet with a grunt. Abi turned and gave a little giggle.

"You getting old?" she asked. "Getting out of breath carrying the shopping, and now grunting when you stand up—you sound like an old man." She paused, and her eyes glinted. "I suppose you are nearly thirty. Middle age approaches!" Then she squeaked as he bent down, picked her up in his arms, and carried her to the caravan door. He kicked it open with his foot and held her just outside in the misty air.

"One more comment from you, young lady," he said, " and you go outside, bare feet and all, and I lock the door."

Abi squeaked again and buried her face in his chest, all the while clinging round his neck as tightly as she could.

"Okay, okay! I'm sorry! I didn't mean it. Please put me down."

He began to lower her down outside the caravan.

"Inside, inside!" she yelled into his chest.

Gideon laughed and backed into the caravan, hooking the door shut with his foot. He dumped her unceremoniously back on the floor and stood looking down at her.

"Getting old, my foot!" he said in disgust. "You're looking at a man in his prime. A perfect specimen of manhood." He squatted down next to her. "I get followed by hordes of screaming girls, everywhere I go."

Abi leaned towards him and grinned.

"Yes, but why are they screaming?" she asked cheekily, then scrambled to her feet and ran into her bedroom before he could catch her.

She threw herself down on the bed and buried her face in the pillow. Gideon's proximity was beginning to drive her mad. She had to admit to herself she had never stopped loving him, and it was becoming clearer to her every minute she had never stopped desiring him, either. She rolled onto her side and propped her head up with her hand. She really hoped he felt the same, but they'd been apart for so long she felt they needed to get to know each other from scratch. Holding hands on the beach the day before had been nice, and she had to admit that when he'd picked her up to throw her outside she had experienced a real thrill of desire.

She sat up and hugged her knees, resting her chin on them. They really ought to talk more about the last ten years before they allowed themselves to get any closer. She nodded to herself, then jumped up and pulled on her clothes. Since they were planning on staying in for the day, she chose a bright red jumper, a short black denim skirt, and black woolly tights. She accessorised with a glittery red-and-silver scarf and a collection of bangles on her wrist before she brushed her hair and fastened it behind her ears with a couple of hair grips. Then she took a deep breath and returned to the living area.

Gideon had also got dressed, in ripped jeans and a faded navy NightHawk T-shirt, but his feet were still bare. He was sitting cross-legged on the floor in front of the fire, setting up a game of Connect 4. Abi gasped when she saw it.

"Where on earth did you find that?" she demanded, her face paling slightly.

Gideon frowned at her. "In the cupboard where you

found the Scrabble," he said. "Why? What's wrong?"

Abi stared down at the game, her stomach doing somersaults.

"Erm…nothing." She shook her head and turned to go and stand looking out over the bay, her arms wrapped tightly around her body. After a moment she became aware of Gideon's hot breath on her neck. She sat down on the seat abruptly, still looking out the window.

"Abi, what is it? You've gone really pale." Gideon sounded concerned, and Abi forced herself to look up at him.

"It's really silly…" She hesitated, then took a deep breath. "When I was packing to go to the clinic to have the baby, Judy put Connect 4 in my bag. She thought I could play it after the birth. We had a laugh about it, and she took it out. But now whenever I see the game I'm reminded of that day." She bent her head forward but her hair could not escape from its clips and her face remained visible. Gideon dropped to his knees in front of her and took her hands in his.

"Oh, Abi, I'm sorry," he murmured softly.

Abi shook her head. "It's not your fault…" she began, but he squeezed her hands to stop her.

"No, not sorry for that. Sorry I wasn't there for you. Sorry I never got your letters. Sorry you didn't get mine. Sorry about everything that happened back then." He put his hand under her chin and turned her face to him. "Abi, when did you find out you were pregnant? Was it before I left?"

Abi looked at him sadly. "I thought I was," she admitted, "but I didn't do the test till the next day."

"Why the hell didn't you tell me?" he demanded.

"Then maybe none of this would've happened!"

Abi's eyes filled with tears, and she pulled her hand away from his.

"I know," she whispered. "I know. I've thought of that nearly every day since. But I was terrified it'd scare you off." She stopped for a moment as she saw his face. "I know, that was probably the most stupid thing I've ever done. I was pretty good at doing stupid things in those days. I never thought before I acted, don't you remember?"

Gideon got to his feet and pulled Abi to hers, then guided her over to where the gas fire was flickering merrily, and made her sit on the floor. He sat opposite her and took her hands again.

"I'm sure you know I would have stood by you," he said gently. "And at least you did tell me in the letters. No wonder you thought I'd been scared off when I didn't seem to reply." He put up a hand and brushed a strand of hair off her face. "You must've gone through hell, and with no one to support you."

She looked up at him and sniffed. "I had Judy."

Gideon nodded. "Well, thank goodness for that, at least. But she was a sixteen-year-old girl. She didn't really know any more than you." He was silent for a moment. Then he looked her directly in the eyes. "Abi, didn't it strike you as odd that they wouldn't let you see the baby?"

Abi sighed. "Yes," she said simply. "But at the time I was so upset, and so tired, that I just gave in to whatever they said. I'd lost my fight. Then it wasn't until much, much later—years, in fact—that I was really able to sit down and think through what happened, and I realised it was all rather strange. By then, though, I'd severed all contact with my parents and didn't want to stir up all the old pain by going back to confront my mother." She sighed again. "I was a coward."

Gideon frowned. "You were a child," he said firmly. "I'm not surprised you gave up. But what did Judy or her mum say about the baby?"

Abi looked uncomfortable. "I didn't tell them I never held her. Not for years, but then I eventually told Judy. They assumed I'd said goodbye to her properly, and I just let them think that. I was ashamed I hadn't, but I didn't know what I could do about it." She looked at him, a tear trickling down her cheek. "I didn't talk about any of it for ages, even to Judy."

Gideon let go of her hands and sat back on his heels.

"They took advantage of you," he said at last. "They took advantage of your youth and the fact you thought you'd been abandoned..." He stopped and frowned. "And all the time your mother was hiding my letters. She knew I hadn't abandoned you, yet she let you suffer like that." He leaned forward again and wiped the tears from her cheeks with his finger. "I'm amazed she managed to keep you from finding the post when it arrived."

Abi frowned. "I've been wondering about that, too," she said slowly. "During the week it must have been fairly easy, 'cause I was at school, and the post comes around midday, but weekends were harder. In the summer holidays, I had a job for quite a lot of the time, but still, some of them must have arrived when I was home." She stretched out her legs and wiggled her feet in front of the fire. "Maybe she—" She clapped her hand over her mouth. "Oh, my god! I know how she did it. Aunty Margaret worked at the post office in town. She could have asked her to keep our mail to one side and then give it directly to her! Could she have done that?" She turned burning eyes on him.

Gideon looked doubtful. "That sounds a bit illegal," he said, "but I suppose it's technically possible. Would your aunt have gone along with it?"

Abi nodded. "Oh, yes, she's a dreadful woman. Mum would've told her I was getting mail from some undesirable person, and Aunty Margaret would have done what she said. My mother was a bully," she added darkly. "It wasn't just me she was nasty to. She didn't really like anyone. She seemed to be able to manipulate people to do what she wanted."

"She certainly must have had some control over that clinic you went to," Gideon said thoughtfully. "What you've told me doesn't sound like normal behaviour after a baby dies. How did she get all the nurses to go along with it?"

Abi sighed. "Well, the doctor and the senior nurse were a married couple and owned the clinic. My mother seemed to know them already. There was a lovely nurse called Sally who looked after me to begin with, but she suddenly disappeared before I had the baby. They told me her shift had ended and she had gone home. She never said goodbye. She was going to ring Judy for me," she added sadly. "Apart from them, there was no one else there that night. There was another nurse in the morning, but not at the time I gave birth." She stared at him in despair. "I think I was really stupid. I let them walk all over me. I should have demanded to see the baby and not stopped until they let me."

Gideon put his hands on her shoulders and shook her slightly.

"You mustn't blame yourself," he said firmly. "The state you must have been in afterwards... They were very much in the wrong." He looked serious. "I wonder why they wouldn't let you see her?"

"They said it would make it harder for me. I guess I believed them at the time. I felt so bad I just wanted to die anyway. Nothing seemed to matter any more. Looking back, it might have made it easier."

Gideon stared intently at her and frowned.

"I doubt anything could have made it easier," he said darkly. "God, I wish I'd been there. To think of you going through all that on your own..." He grasped her hands tightly in his and pulled her close. "It wouldn't have made the outcome any better, but at least we'd have been able to face it together."

Abi raised her head and nodded.

"I wouldn't have felt so alone," she whispered. "With you there, I could have coped better. You wouldn't have let them bully me." A solitary tear rolled down her cheek, and Gideon raised a finger and gently wiped it away.

"I certainly wouldn't," he agreed grimly, staring over her head, his eyes dark with emotion. "Things would have been very different had I been there."

Abi leaned forward and gently rested her head against his shoulder.

"I wish we could turn the clock back," she whispered. "Get rid of the last ten years. Make everything better."

Gideon put his hands on her shoulders and gently pushed her upright.

"Nice idea," he said with a wry grin, looking down at her. "But at least we're together now. Better than nothing, isn't it?"

"Yeah." Abi sniffed and rubbed a hand across her face. "Yeah, it's definitely better than nothing."

An awkward silence fell, and Abi shifted her position, pulling back from Gideon and smoothing her hair with her hands.

"I'll make some tea, shall I?" she suggested, moving rapidly across the room to the kitchen area. "And we could have biscuits too…or cake? Do you want cake?"

Gideon gave a low chuckle. "I don't actually want tea," he said in amusement, watching her hurried movements. "But if you insist, cake would be nice." He sat back on the window seat and glanced out at the driving rain. "Glad we didn't go for a walk."

Abi flicked the kettle on, noisily got some mugs out of the cupboard, and delved into a box to find some cake. She kept her back to Gideon while she worked, her mind a complete mess of emotions. With slightly shaky hands, she managed to pour the tea and cut two pieces of cake, then carried them over to the window seat. Gideon turned to her and smiled.

"Come on, sit down, and let's talk of other things," he suggested, taking a cup from her. "Tell me about your jobs."

Abi gave a shaky laugh. "Oh, sure, you want to hear about my boring jobs, when you've spent the last ten years touring the world as a rock star? You'd be asleep in seconds," she said, sitting down beside him. "D'you fancy looking at some of the old photos I found of us? Remember Judy's New Year's Eve party?

There's some from then."

She dropped to her knees on the floor and pulled one of the cardboard boxes out from under the table. Suddenly a vision of the tin box her father had given her popped into her mind. She sat back on her heels and spoke to Gideon over her shoulder.

"The tin box. The tin box Dad gave me. Maybe we should open that? I'm sure there's something important in it. Why else would he have given it to me?"

"What did he say about it?"

"Nothing, but he was very insistent that I take it and keep it. He said he'd lost the key but that I should be able to get into it." She paused to think a moment. "I think he knows what's in it. Shall we open it now?"

Gideon made a face. "Is this the one Judy said not to open?"

"Yes, but Judy can't possibly know what's in it. I don't know why she said that. Shall we?"

"Maybe you should text Judy first?" Gideon said cautiously.

Abi shook her head. "No, there's no way Judy could know what's in it," she said firmly, sounding very much like the Abi that Gideon remembered from ten years before. "It's my box, and I want to open it."

He took a deep breath and then gave a slight nod.

"Okay, then, let's do it. Where is it?" he asked, looking around.

"In my room." Abi got to her feet and went to fetch it.

Gideon got up from the floor and walked to the window. The tide was half way out, and the beach was full of gulls, some wheeling above and some picking amongst the shells on the sand. He closed his eyes briefly, then turned back into the room and watched as Abi carried the tin box in and put it in the middle of the floor. They both looked at it.

"Now what do we do?" asked Abi.

"I think your little screwdriver would be a good place to start," he said with a raise of his eyebrows. Abi nodded and delved into her bag to find it. Just as she triumphantly held it aloft, there came a tentative knock at the caravan door. They looked at each other.

"Are you expecting anyone?" asked Abi in surprise.

Gideon stared at her. "Expecting anyone?" he said in amazement. "We're supposed to be in hiding. Of course I'm not expecting anyone."

They both looked at the door as a light tap sounded again. Abi hesitated a moment, then walked over to the door and opened it a crack. The teenaged boy who had served them in the shop the day before was standing there. She opened the door wider and smiled at him.

"Hello. Can I help you?" she said pleasantly. The boy swallowed noisily, then reached out to his right and pulled a girl with dark brown wavy hair into view. She was about fifteen, very pretty and wearing jeans, a puffy anorak, and a bobble hat. She smiled shyly at Abi.

"Do you... I mean this is... Um, can we..." The boy was miserably unable to formulate a complete sentence but stared beseechingly at Abi.

She grinned in comprehension. "This is your, sister...girlfriend...cousin?" she hazarded, "and you're wondering if she could possibly meet Gideon, even though you said you wouldn't tell anyone we're here?" The boy looked about to speak, then nodded mutely.

Abi laughed and held the door open for them to enter. "So long as she's the only one you've told?" she added, frowning.

He nodded again and, taking the girl by the hand, led her into the caravan. Gideon had heard the exchange and had arranged himself on the window seat looking suitably moody and rock star-ish. Abi pressed her lips tightly together to stop herself from laughing.

"This is…?"

"Gareth," the boy managed to say. "And Caitlin, my girlfriend."

"There you are, then. This is Gareth and Caitlin, and they want to meet you," said Abi, pushing the two youngsters into the living area in front of her.

Gideon nodded at them. "Hi," he said. "Come and sit down."

The two teenagers dutifully sat on the floor at his feet and stared up at him. At this point, Abi could no longer contain herself and burst out laughing.

"Gideon, you horror! Be nice." To the visitors, she said, "Would you like a drink?"

Caitlin looked up at her and smiled. "Yes, please. D'you have any Coke?" she asked in a lilting Welsh accent. Abi nodded and fetched a couple of cans from the fridge. She sat down on the floor next to Caitlin and smiled at her.

"So you're a fan of NightHawk too, are you?" she asked.

The girl nodded brightly, causing the bobble on her hat to wobble.

"I love them," she said in a soft, shy voice. "I was really sad when Gideon said he was leaving." She glanced at him and blushed slightly. "But when I found out about you, I understood."

Abi looked at her in surprise. "What d'you mean?" she asked, glancing quickly at Gideon.

"Well, all the papers are telling the story of you two when you were teenagers," Caitlin said enthusiastically. "How Gideon went on tour, and you were separated for years and years… It was so romantic! And then he left the band to look for you."

Abi took a deep breath. "It wasn't quite like that," she said carefully. "We were together as teenagers, certainly, and when Gideon went on tour we…we lost touch through no fault of our own, as it turns out. But"—she looked severely at the two teenagers—"it was not romantic. There is nothing romantic about being separated from the person you love. Don't get the wrong idea about that." She paused and then grinned slightly. "And I don't think Gideon left the band to look for me."

There was a moment's silence while Gareth and Caitlin turned their attention to Gideon.

He shrugged. "Well, actually, I did, really," he said apologetically. "That was certainly my main motivation."

Caitlin grinned and clapped her hands. "I knew it!" she said in delight. "Now you've found each other again, and you can be happy for ever after."

Abi coughed. "It's not quite that simple—"

The girl interrupted her. "Why not?" she asked. "It's obvious you're still in love. Where's the problem?"

"How d'you mean, it's obvious we're still in love?" asked Abi faintly, her mouth going dry.

Caitlin rolled her eyes. "It said so in the papers,"

she said patiently. "They said that Gideon"—she blushed slightly as she said his name—"left the band to find you, and that you were in love. And you look like you are, too."

Gareth nudged her and frowned. "Shut up, Cait," he murmured. "You can't say things like that."

Caitlin shrugged. "Don't see why not," she said. "It's true, isn't it?"

Gideon looked over at Abi and raised an eyebrow. She gave a self-conscious grin and leant forward so her hair would fall over her face. She heard Gideon give a little chuckle.

"You're probably right," he admitted, smiling at Caitlin. "But when you get to our age, things are always a bit more complicated. Enjoy yourselves while you're young."

Caitlin stared at him, wide-eyed. "Well, if you're both in love, I don't see a problem. There's nothing stopping you being together, so just get on with it."

At that point Abi laughed out loud. "Wise words," she said shaking her head.

Gareth got up and pulled Caitlin to her feet.

"We must go now," he said. "Thanks for letting us in, and I promise not to tell anyone else you're here."

Gideon stood up and held out his hand to Gareth.

"Nice to meet you both," he said shaking hands firmly and then offering his hand also to Caitlin. She grabbed it enthusiastically and squeezed.

"Thank you so much," she said. "I shall keep watching the papers to make sure you two sort yourselves out." Then with a wave the two teenagers left the caravan and started up the path. As she closed the door behind them, Abi heard Caitlin saying, "I never got the chance to ask—" and Gareth interrupting with a muffled reply as they disappeared off towards the shop. Abi closed the door quietly and walked back into the living area. Gideon was standing looking out the window, and he turned as she came back in. He smiled at her.

"Well, that was interesting," he said, holding out a hand to her. "Apparently we're still in love. How d'you feel about that?"

Abi hesitated, then took his outstretched hand. She looked up at him.

"Well, I can only speak for me…" She suddenly frowned as she looked down at the hand she was holding. She reached out and gently touched the leather wrist band that adorned it. "You're wearing the wrist band I gave you," she whispered. "When did you put that on?"

Gideon looked down at her. "When I got dressed. I didn't think you'd noticed." He grinned at her. "I wore it until long after I stopped writing the letters. And ever since, I've always had it with me, and today I felt it was right to wear it." He looked very vulnerable for a moment and swallowed nervously. "Umm…do you…" He stopped as Abi let go of his hand and reached down inside her jumper. She pulled out a thin silver chain on which hung the ring he had given her on her sixteenth birthday. She held it up to show him.

"I've worn it on this chain ever since you went," she said. "Well, no, I wore it on my finger until the baby was born. After that it's been round my neck." She grinned a bit lopsidedly. "Not sure it fits any more, actually. I've grown."

"Oh, god, Abi, I've missed you so much!" breathed

Gideon, catching her hands again and pulling her close. "Caitlin was right. I did leave the band to find you, even though I still thought you'd abandoned me." He tilted her face up to his. "I've always loved you, Abigail Thomson, and I know I always will," and he bent his head and kissed her gently on the lips. Abi responded by sliding her arms around his neck and pulling him closer to her. As their bodies touched, she shuddered with desire, and her tongue slipped into his waiting mouth. He moved his hands down to cup her buttocks, and they pressed their bodies hard against each other.

Gently Abi pulled her mouth away from Gideon's and whispered, "I love you too, Gid. I never stopped loving you." Then their mouths met again, as they sank to their knees on the floor, their bodies entwined in an overture to their passion.

Chapter 22

*2005*

Abi lay on the floor in front of the fire, her head cradled on Gideon's chest and her legs entwined with his. Their lovemaking had been intense and passionate, almost desperate at first, and they were now both exhausted and euphoric. She wriggled to get more comfortable, and ran her fingers through his chest hair. Their clothes lay abandoned on the floor beside them, and neither of them had noticed the cold. Gideon raised a hand and gently stroked Abi's hair.

"Happy?" he asked softly, his mouth against the top of her head. She nodded, and moved her head to look up at him and smile. With a sudden movement Gideon flipped over and hovered above her, his dark hair falling forward and his piercing eyes boring into her. He pressed his lips hard against hers and slid a hand under her head.

"I love you," he murmured. "I will love you for ever."

Abi wound her arms around his neck and stared back into his eyes.

"I love you too," she said seriously. "Forever is a very long time. Do you really mean that?"

Gideon brushed her hair back from her face and ran a finger down her cheek.

"Yes, I do. I love you, and I want to spend the rest of my life with you. My only regret is how much time we've wasted."

Abi rolled him off her and sat up, hugging her knees.

"But you don't know me now. I'm not who I was ten years ago. I've really changed, and so have you. How do we know it'll work?"

Gideon sat up beside her.

"Because it feels right," he said immediately. "Surely you can feel the bond between us. Why, when we each thought the other one had abandoned us, did we both keep on loving each other? Why did I start dreaming about you again after all these years? Why did I have to look for you?" He caught her hands in his and made her look at him. "Abi, we're made for each other. Can't you see it?"

Slowly she started to smile as she gently nodded her head.

"I know," she said. "Had to make sure you really felt the same, though. We have changed a lot, but that's maybe no bad thing. I don't think I was very nice back then."

Gideon grinned. "You were always nice to me. But you were a bit cocky and full of yourself." He ducked as she threw a cushion at him. "And now you're more…grown-up, I s'pose."

Abi snorted. "Well, I should think so. I'm twenty-six!" she said with a grin. "So do you think we can make this work, then?"

"We'll never know if we don't try," said Gideon firmly. "So, Abigail Thomson, will you go out with me?"

Abi giggled. "Yes, Gideon Hawk, I would like that very much," she said primly. She leaned towards him and kissed him gently on the lips, then shivered suddenly as the cold caught up with her. She reached over and pulled her jumper over her head, then searched around for her pants and tights. Gideon got to his feet and was beginning to collect his own clothes when he suddenly stopped.

"We never opened the box," he said, staring at Abi.

She stopped, in her crawl across the floor to retrieve her skirt from the table, and peered round at him.

"I think we had other things on our minds."

Gideon picked up the tin box, where it had ended up following their passionate scuffle on the floor, and placed it on the window seat, while Abi scrambled to her feet and wriggled into her skirt.

She stared at the box. "You know, it's silly," she said quietly. "But I'm nervous about opening this. Don't know why… I've just got a strange feeling about it…"

Gideon gave her a quick hug. "Well, all the more reason to open it," he said with a shrug. "It may not be anything interesting at all. Let's open it and find out." He sat down on the window seat beside the box.

Abi hesitated, then also shrugged, picked up her little screwdriver from the coffee table, and sat down with him. She tentatively inserted it into the lock and started to jiggle it around. Nothing happened. Gideon sighed and took the screwdriver out of her hand.

"I thought we could unscrew the hinges," he said, raising an eyebrow at her, "not pick the lock." He applied himself to the two hinges at the back of the lid, and after a couple of minutes he had managed to loosen the first one enough to make the lid rattle.

Abi nodded encouragingly. "Keep going, and then maybe I can find something stronger to prise the lid off." She stood and went to look in the kitchen drawers. She eventually decided on a fairly solid-looking spatula and a short but sturdy knife.

"Maybe these will help," she said, returning to the living area and brandishing them at Gideon. He had managed to remove the first hinge completely, but the second one was causing him some problems.

"These screws are completely rusted in," he complained, trying to force them to turn.

Abi handed him the knife. "Try this," she said hopefully.

Gideon took it, and by inserting it under the lid on the side where he had removed the hinge, he was able to raise it enough for them to be able to see inside. The box was nearly empty, with just a few documents and envelopes at the bottom. Abi squeezed her hand through the gap and managed to grab hold of most of the papers. She pulled them out, then put her hand in again to get the rest. Gideon set the box on the floor, and they sat with the papers between them on the window seat. Abi stared at them, not daring to look. Gideon touched her briefly on the hand.

"Go on, Abs," he said gently. "It ought to be you that looks at it. There's nothing to be scared of. It can't be anything bad, can it? We already know your parents tried to keep us apart. Whatever's in here, we can deal with it together."

She flashed him a grateful smile and picked up the first paper. It was a birth certificate. An old birth certificate. A closer look proved it to be the birth certificate of Abi's maternal grandmother. Janet Emily St. Clair, born 1910 in Norwich, the daughter of a vicar and a housewife.

Abi looked up in surprise. "Never knew that," she remarked. "My grandma came from Norwich? No one ever told me that. Not that I ever met her." She picked up the next paper, another birth certificate, this time of her mother. Abi shuddered and put it aside.

"This is just going to be a lot of family history, isn't it?" She considered the stack. The next thing she picked up was a plain white envelope with her name written on it in her mother's handwriting.

"*To Abigail. To be opened after my death.*" Abi hesitated, then put it aside and picked up the next item. "Another birth certificate," she said. "Who this time? Uncle Fred? Auntie Margaret?" Her voice tailed off as she unfolded the paper and read it. Without a word she handed it to Gideon. He read it silently, then stared at Abi.

"It's her birth certificate." he managed at last. He looked at the paper and read aloud, "Natasha Storm Thomson, born 12$^{th}$ January, 1996 in Reading, Berkshire. Mother Abigail Thomson, Student…" His voice faltered. "No father recorded." He scanned down the page to the bottom. "Birth registered on… 14$^{th}$ January, 1996, by… by Joan Louise Thomson, Grandmother." He stared at Abi, his face suddenly pale. "Abi, your mother registered her birth. She named her Natasha. Why would she do that…unless…" He reached over and picked up the pile of papers. He quickly searched through them, then looked at Abi.

She swallowed. "What are you looking for?" she

whispered.

"Her death certificate." he said baldly. "It's not here."

Abi picked up the pile of papers and leafed through them. They were mostly envelopes, and she glanced at Gideon.

"Maybe it's in one of these envelopes?" she said doubtfully.

Gideon shook his head. "No, Abi, it's not here because it doesn't exist." He gazed directly at her. "Abi…Abi, I think Natasha might still be alive."

There was total silence as they stared at each other, neither daring to speak, not knowing what to say next. Abi had spent the last ten years believing her baby had died at birth. Suddenly there was the possibility she was still alive. The room spun dizzily around Abi—her world was out of control. She closed her eyes, and the room spun still more. She felt Gideon put his arm around her shoulders, and she let herself lean against him. He stroked her hair and muttered something soothing, but all the time her mind was whirring though the last ten years. Ten years of lies, of deceit, of heartache, of lost time. Not only had she been parted from Gideon at the whim of another person or persons, she had had her child taken away from her and had not been allowed to grieve. And now…maybe all for no reason. She opened her eyes and sat up, turning round to face Gideon.

"What do we do?" she asked, sounding lost.

Gideon nodded to the pile of papers. "We need to look at the rest of the documents," he said firmly. "There may be something there that sheds more light on this. Something that confirms my thoughts. Come on, open this one," and he handed her a plain white envelope. Abi peeled it open with her finger and pulled out a single sheet of paper. She read it slowly, her face draining of all colour, then handed it to Gideon, a strange look in her eyes.

"It's a letter to your mother, to confirm that Natasha has been taken to the Birtwhistle Children's Home in Kent," he read out. "It seems to be a private children's home, and your mother has requested they keep her updated on her progress." He lowered the letter and stared at Abi. He cleared his throat, and his voice cracked with emotion. "Abi...we have a daughter."

Abi's eyes filled with tears, and her face crumpled.

"All these years," she sobbed, "all these years she let me believe she was dead. And all the time..." She scrabbled around for a tissue to blow her nose. Gideon picked up another envelope and hurriedly opened it. His face paled.

"Abi...Abi, listen to this." He read, *"Thank you for returning the completed form signed by your daughter Abigail Thomson, Natasha's mother, giving permission for Natasha to be made available for fostering. We understand that adoption is not an option at this time."* Gideon looked at Abi and raised his eyebrows. She shook her head in bewilderment.

"I never signed anything," she gasped in horror. "I really didn't. She never asked me to. She couldn't, could she? She'd let me believe Natasha"—her voice shook as she said the name—"that Natasha was dead. I didn't sign anything."

Gideon shook his head. "I'm sorry, Abi, but your mother's duplicity knew no bounds. She must have forged your signature." He thought for a moment. "In fact, she must have done that in the first place, to get Natasha into the home. This letter is dated November '99. Let's see if there are any more." He picked up the pile of papers again.

Abi was in shock. What on earth had her mother been thinking? Why had she been so intent on not allowing Abi access to her own child? She must surely have been breaking the law.

Gideon was opening another envelope. "This one is dated in April 2000," he said. "Apparently Natasha was fostered to a couple in Tunbridge Wells for a few weeks, but it didn't go very well, and she went back to the home." He read on, then took a deep breath and looked at Abi, his eyes bewildered.

"What is it, Gid?" she asked apprehensively.

"Listen to this. *Natasha didn't settle in the foster home at all well, and after a few weeks she was returned to us. We feel she may not be suitable for fostering after all, and on your next visit maybe we can discuss some other options.*" He put down the letter, and they stared at each other.

"She visited her?" asked Abi in little more than a whisper. "My mother visited my daughter? It says, 'your next visit'? Gideon, she must have visited a lot. This is totally unbelievable." She picked up the rest of the letters. "Quick, we need to see if there are any more. They said discuss other options. D'you think that means adoption?" She turned terrified eyes on Gideon. "If she's been adopted, we can never get her back!"

Gideon was reading another letter.

"Abs, listen to this." he licked his lips and began to read. "*Since you haven't visited in a while, I thought I*

303

*should write to say Natasha has been asking for you. If you're not going to come again, I think it would be better if she knew this, rather than her continually wait for your arrival. Once again, I would urge that you try to get your daughter to sign the papers giving permission for her to be adopted. We feel this would be in Natasha's best interests."*

"Natasha had been asking for her!" Abi almost shouted the words in her disbelief. "My daughter liked my mother?"

Gideon was continuing to read, a frown on his face.

"That was dated earlier this year, back in June. Abi, I think she's still there. But why did your mother stop visiting?"

"She was ill. For months before she died. I doubt she could have visited anyone much in the last year, actually. Dad told me. She knew she was dying." She looked at Gideon, a mixture of hope and despair in her eyes. "D'you really think she's still there? Maybe my mother signed the adoption papers when she knew she was dying. Keep looking…" She reached out and picked up more papers.

None of them shed any more light until Gideon opened the final one.

"This is odd," he said with a frown. "Listen. *Dear Mrs. Thomson, I'm sorry to hear of your illness, but nonetheless your request is extremely irregular. Under the circumstances the trustees have instructed we concur, but the situation will need to be reviewed after a year.* That's dated July of this year. What d'you think it means?"

"It probably means we have got until July of next year to get our daughter back," said Abi, getting to her feet. "What shall we do?"

Gideon stared at her. "This is all too fantastic," he said, shaking his head. "It's beyond belief. Why would she..." He broke off as he noticed the envelope addressed to Abi that they'd found earlier. It remained unopened. He held it out to her.

"Here, read this. Maybe she tells you why."

Abi took the letter and ripped it open.

*"Dear Abigail,"* she read. *"I know you hate me already, and by now you'll know what really happened in January '96 and will hate me even more. I don't expect you to understand why I did what I did, but I did it for the right reasons—or so I thought—and maybe one day you'll know why. Natasha is a lovely child, and is safe. If you've found this letter, then you'll know what to do next."*

She lowered the sheet of paper. "And that's it. No explanation, no apology, not even a 'love from Mother' at the end." She looked at Gideon. "It's up to us now. We're on our own."

Gideon got to his feet and pulled her close to him.

"We're never on our own again," he said firmly. "We'll always have each other now, and together we can do anything, right?" He looked down at her and smiled. She nodded, her face serious. She had just opened her mouth to speak when her phone bleeped loudly. She jumped and stared over at it.

"That's a text," she said unnecessarily, picking it up. "I wonder who from? Oh, Judy... Oh, she's coming here tomorrow to swap the cars over. She says to make sure we're here all day and not to open the box till she gets here. She says she has something to tell us." Abi looked at Gideon and shrugged. "Think it's a bit late, don't you? How can Judy know something about this, anyway?" she added with a frown.

"No idea. Better text her and tell her we opened it already," Gideon suggested.

Abi bent over her phone and wrote a quick message back to Judy.

"*Already opened it. Bit of a shock. What do you know?*" She pressed send. Within thirty seconds she got a reply.

"*Told you to wait. What did you find?*"

"*Birth certificate. Lots of letters. She's alive.*"

"*Shit. Wanted to prepare you. Found something out and wanted to tell you. Don't go anywhere. I'm coming tomorrow morning.*"

"*Okay. We'll stay put.*"

"*Are you okay?*"

Abi paused before she answered that one, and looked at Gideon.

He shrugged. "Guess we are. Bit shell-shocked, but I think we're all right."

Abi nodded and texted. "*We're okay. Sort of.*" She added a smiley face.

When the last text was sent, she placed her phone on the table and sat back down on the window seat. Gideon sat beside her, and together they gazed out of the window at the darkening skies. After a moment or two, Gideon put his arm around Abi's shoulders. She leant back against him and rested her head on his shoulder.

"We have a daughter," she said softly. "She's nearly ten years old, and we've never met her."

Gideon's arm tightened around her shoulders, and he rested his chin on the top of her head.

"No. We haven't," he agreed, "but I think that maybe we're being given the chance to change that if we want." He looked down at her. "D'you want to?"

Abi sat up and looked at him. "Of course I do," she said at once. "But I'm very scared. What about you?"

"Same," he said with a slight smile. "And still rather bemused. Until three days ago I didn't even know she'd ever existed. It's all a bit much. First I find you again and discover nothing was as I'd thought it was, and then this…" He shook his head. "But of course I want to meet her."

Abi stood up and wrapped her arms around herself.

"What d'you think'll happen, Gid?" she asked, her voice shaking slightly. "D'you think we have a chance of getting her back?"

Gideon frowned. "Don't know. It's a very weird situation. She hasn't been adopted, though, so there's a chance." He paused to search Abi's face. "We must remember, though, that she knows nothing about us, and she may not like us. She may not want to leave the home."

Abi nodded. "I know. We'll have to wait and see." She smiled wearily at him. "God, I'm so tired! And we haven't done anything energetic." Gideon raised an eyebrow at her, and she blushed. "Well, nothing *very* energetic. Are you hungry?" she asked. He shook his head. "Neither am I. Shall we just go to bed? It'll make tomorrow come more quickly."

"Like kids at Christmas," said Gideon with a laugh. "Yeah, that sounds like a brilliant idea." He smiled at her and held out his hand. "Your room or mine?"

Abi blushed slightly again and took his hand. "Oh, yours. You have the double bed."

Chapter 23

*Saturday, 26<sup>th</sup> November 2005*

Abi woke to the sound of knocking at the door. She swore under her breath and nudged Gideon, who was snoring gently beside her.

"Gid, Gid, wake up! There's someone at the door!" she whispered urgently.

Gideon groaned and rolled over. "Answer it, then." His voice was slurred with sleep.

Abi tutted. "It might be the press!" she persisted, pulling the covers up to her chin.

Gideon sighed and turned over to face her. "Or it might be Judy," he said.

Abi leaned over and picked up her phone to see the time.

"At eight o'clock?" she said dubiously. "She'd have had to leave at five to get here by now." Reluctantly she climbed out of bed and pulled the quilt with her, wrapping it around her to cover her nakedness. Gideon protested loudly and tried to grab it back, but she slipped out of the room with a laugh.

At the door she called out, "Who is it?"

"It's me," came the muffled reply.

Abi opened the door a crack. "Judy?" she said in amazement. "It's only eight o'clock."

She opened the door fully and let her friend in, all

the time clutching the quilt around her. Judy gave her a quick hug and raised her eyebrows at the makeshift clothing.

"Still in bed, then?" she asked with a grin.

Abi frowned, and felt herself begin to blush. "As I said, Jude, it's only eight o'clock. Whatever time did you leave?"

She led the way into the living area, the quilt dragging behind her. Judy followed, sat down on the window seat, and looked around her.

"I haven't been here for ages," she said with a reminiscent smile. "I shall have to bring the kids next summer. D'you remember all those holidays we had here, Abs?"

Abi nodded and sat down next to her.

"'Course I do. They were magical." She bent forward and let her hair cover her face. "And these last two days have been…pretty good, too…mostly."

Judy looked around. "Is Gideon still asleep?" she asked.

Abi shook her head. "No, he was awake. Doubt he's gone back to sleep without…" She got to her feet. "Would you like a coffee?" Without waiting for the reply, she scuttled into the kitchen and put the kettle on.

Judy grinned to herself in satisfaction. Things seemed to be working out, then. At that moment, Gideon appeared from the bedroom, dressed in boxers and a T-shirt and rubbing his eyes.

"Hi, Judy. You're early," he said with a yawn.

Judy rolled her eyes. "Stop saying that, you two," she said. "I've got lots to tell you, and I think you have lots to tell me, so I thought we should have the whole day. I have to go back tonight."

"Am I still top news?" asked Gideon, crouching down and lighting the fire.

"Hmmm…about page four now, I think," Judy replied. "Some politician got caught with a prostitute, and he's taken top billing. You'll probably be safe to go back to your parents' house tomorrow. I'm sure your mum is missing her car."

Gideon ran a hand through his hair. "Yeah, she has texted me once or twice about it. Said Dad keeps seeing it on the news." He grinned.

Abi appeared just then with two cups of coffee, still attempting to keep the quilt wrapped around her.

"For God's sake, Abi, get dressed," said Judy in exasperation, relieving her of the cups. "I'm dying to know what was in your box, and I'm dying to tell you what I found out."

Abi turned and hobbled back into the bedroom in search of some clothes, and Judy turned to Gideon.

"Is she okay, Gid?" she asked with a slight frown.

He nodded slowly. "Well, sort of, I guess. This has all been a hell of a shock to us both." He gave her a lopsided grin. "Until Tuesday, I never even knew I'd had a child, and then I thought she was dead. Now I find she's alive and nearly ten years old. Bit much to take in, to be honest."

"I bet it is," Judy said sympathetically. "I was hoping to tell you what I'd found out before you opened that tin. I guessed what was in there was something to do with the baby, after Mum told me what she'd found out." She raised her eyebrows at Gideon. "And how about you and Abi? Are you okay together?"

Gideon grinned at her. "Yeah," he said. "I rather think we will be. Actually, she's not nearly so high maintenance as she was as a teenager."

Judy giggled. "That's true," she admitted. "Although I do still seem to have to get her out of scrapes."

"Get who out of scrapes?" asked Abi, suspiciously, as she emerged from the bedroom dressed in jeans and a bright green jumper.

"You, of course," said Judy, smiling. "That jumper's nice. It sets off your hair."

Abi sat down on the window seat next to her friend and looked at her expectantly.

"Well?" she asked. "What is it you've got to tell us, and how come you know something about this?"

Judy sighed. "Well, now you've opened the box, this isn't going to be much of a surprise, but it might explain a bit more about what happened when your baby was born."

"Natasha," chipped in Abi. "Her name is Natasha."

Judy's eyes widened slightly, but she went on. "A few weeks ago a new midwife came to work at the hospital with Mum, and they kind of hit it off. They started meeting up in their breaks and chatting a lot about their experiences. Anyway"—she took a deep breath—"this nurse told Mum a really weird story from her past. Apparently the thing that made her think of it was when Mum saw the announcement of your mother's death in the paper, Abi. She was reading it in the canteen at the hospital and happened to say what an unpleasant woman she'd been. The new nurse then said she wondered if it was the same Joan Thomson she'd come across many years ago, and proceeded to tell my mother your story. Apparently she'd worked in that clinic you went to, and she said she'd been worried about you, and tried to help you by phoning me…" She paused as Abi caught her breath. "But someone stopped her, and she was sent home, and denied any more access to you. She was told you were delusional and kept making things up about your pregnancy, about the father being famous." Judy glanced at Abi as she spoke, and saw that her face was very pale and had a set expression on it. "She had no choice but to go home, but she vowed to come back early the next day and check on you. However, she received a phone call the following morning terminating her contract. She was allowed to go in later in the day to collect her things, but then she had to leave. When she returned to the clinic she immediately asked what had happened to you, and was told the baby had died and that you and your mother had gone home. She was devastated and asked for your address so she could go and say how sorry she was, but she was refused access to the records. When she collected her belongings, she went to see what had happened to the baby's body but couldn't find it. However, just as she was leaving the clinic, she heard a baby crying. When she attempted to go and see it, she was told it belonged to someone who had come in that morning. She realised that might be true, that there was no way she could check up on it. The whole episode has haunted her ever since, and she had always worried that your mother had somehow taken the baby away from you."

Abi was silent for a long moment. "That was Sally," she said quietly. "I always wondered why she didn't come back. I just thought she'd let me down like everyone else."

"Mum thought the whole thing sounded very

strange, and when I told her you never got to hold the baby, she was most upset. She spoke to some of her contacts and managed to find out from one who'd also worked at that clinic at the time that a baby was born there in January '96 and was then sent to a children's home somewhere in Kent. I think that was your baby, and I suspect you might now have proof of that, from the things you found in the box?"

Judy sat back looking expectant, while Abi got up and went to sit by Gideon on the floor before she nodded and replied, "Yes. We found her birth certificate, and some letters from a children's home in Tunbridge Wells, written to my mother." She took a deep breath and glanced at Gideon. "Apparently my mother registered her birth and called her Natasha Storm Thomson." Judy gasped. "And …"—Abi paused to swallow hard—"she seems to have visited Natasha at the home on several occasions over the next few years."

Gideon reached up to the table and gathered the pile of documents they'd found in the box. He held them out to Judy.

"Here, have a look. The last letter from the home, dated in July, is most interesting."

Slowly Judy took the pile of papers and began to look through them. Once or twice she gasped, and by the end she had tears in her eyes. She stared at Abi and Gideon.

"She forged your signature," she whispered. "She knew she'd never get you to give up…Natasha, so she told you she was dead and forged your signature. But why did she do it? And why didn't she go the whole hog and have her adopted? And why the visits? None of it makes any sense."

Gideon shook his head. "No, it doesn't really, does it? That's why we need to visit the children's home and talk to them."

"And meet Natasha," said Abi.

Gideon reached out and squeezed her hand. "And meet Natasha," he agreed with a smile.

Judy looked worried. "Are you sure she's still there?" she asked anxiously. "There hasn't been a letter since July."

"But that one said they would reassess the situation after a year," said Gideon. "So she should still be there now. Unless she's been fostered. But she can't be adopted at the moment." He looked at Abi. "I think we should go down there on Monday. What d'you think?"

Abi looked up at him. "Seems a long way off," she said. "It's only Saturday."

Gideon grinned. "We've waited this long," he said. "We need to prepare for this. We must present a totally united and stable front if we want to have any chance of getting her back. That needs some work."

Judy nodded. "Yes, use the weekend to formulate your plan. You need to decide whether you want to tell her who you are or not. Maybe best not, until she gets to know you."

Abi got to her feet and walked over to the window. The day was overcast again, and the sea was crashing on the shore, sending spray all the way to the caravan. She turned and looked at the other two.

"I feel so strange," she said eventually. "I'm really having trouble with this. In the space of just over a week my whole life has changed. Absolutely nothing is as I thought it was. It's like I've been living someone else's life for the last ten years and now I've been given mine back. I need your help, big time, guys." She held out her hands to the other two. As one, Judy and Gideon got up and went to her, and the three of them clung together.

\*\*\*\*

"Gideon just texted me." Caroline came into the room holding her phone at arm's length in an attempt to read what was on the screen. "Have you seen my glasses anywhere, Roger?"

Roger lowered his paper and shook his head. "No, here, have mine," and he handed his reading glasses to his wife. She perched them on the end of her nose and peered at the screen.

"Oh, he says he's coming back tomorrow, with my car. About time. And he says can he bring Abi with him." She glanced at Roger. "That sounds promising, doesn't it? I'll say yes, of course." She carried on reading. "He says he's got some rather shocking news." Her eyes lit up. "D'you think they're getting married?"

Roger gave her a look. "That would scarcely be classed as shocking, surely?" he said. "Would you be shocked by that? I wouldn't. It must be something more interesting."

Caroline looked surprised. "That would be interesting! Our son arrives home for the first time in years, meets up with his girl friend of ten years ago, and then gets married. That seems pretty interesting to me."

"But not shocking, darling," said Roger patiently. "Trust me, it'll be something else. Now give me my glasses back, and go and make them a cake."

Caroline laughed and handed the glasses over.

"You know me so well," she said and left the room in the direction of the kitchen.

\*\*\*\*

When Simon arrived back at his mother's house late on Thursday, he had taken to his bed and not re-appeared until Saturday lunchtime. Josephine came back from shopping to find him slumped on the sofa watching the racing, a can of lager in one hand and a joint in the other.

"Simon," she snapped, dropping her shopping on the floor. "I told you I won't have that stuff in the house. Put it out *now*." Simon shrugged and stubbed it out in the ashtray without looking at her. She picked up the shopping again and carried it to the kitchen. As she put it away, she called to him, "And if you're going to stay here, you can pull your weight a bit more. You stayed in bed all day yesterday, and the house is a tip." She walked to the door and poked her head around it. "Did you find Gideon and Abi?"

Simon finally looked at her. "You should have told me he was at her house," he said in an accusatory manner. "That was a fucking wasted journey."

"I would have told you if you'd hung around to listen," said his mother mildly. "Why was it wasted? Had they gone?"

"Yes, of course they'd bloody gone," Simon snapped. "But that's not the point. If he'd already got to her, then there was no point in my finding him. It's too late now. He'll already know everything."

Josephine looked at her son suspiciously.

"Simon, what have you done? Were you trying to keep Abi and Gideon apart for some reason?"

"Yeah," said Simon, after a moment's hesitation.

His mother sighed and sat down on the sofa next to him.

316

"Okay. Tell me everything," she said wearily.

Simon looked at her with dislike and shook his head. "None of your business," he said rudely.

Josephine pursed her lips. "Well, if that's your attitude," she said sharply, "you can leave now. I will not be spoken to like that in my own home, by my own son."

Simon sighed and attempted to smile at her.

"Sorry, Mum," he said impatiently. "But you really wouldn't be interested."

"Try me. Maybe I can help," she said, attempting to keep her temper. "I know you never liked Gideon seeing Abi, but surely you've got over that by now."

Simon looked directly at her. "Okay," he said in exasperation. "You want to know what it is, I'll tell you. When we first went to America on tour in '95, Gideon was madly in love with her, and he wrote to her nearly every day. It was pathetic. She was only just sixteen, as if it was going to last anyway." He glanced slyly at his mother. "She wrote to him via the record company, you know, like you did, and I used to collect the mail they sent across to us. I didn't give Gideon the letters from her. I kept them all, so he thought she never wrote to him."

Josephine sat up and stared at him. "Simon Dean, how could you do something so wrong?" She gasped in horror. "You let that poor boy think his girl had deserted him? And what on earth would she have thought? She must have known he hadn't received her letters."

Simon was silent for a moment. "Actually, she didn't get his, either, but that wasn't my fault. I don't know why that was," he said defensively.

Josephine frowned at him. "How d'you know that?"

Simon shook his head. "Doesn't matter," he muttered, leaning back and staring at the television again. His mother picked up the remote control and turned it off.

"Simon, how *do* you know? Did you read her letters?" she demanded, her face like thunder.

Simon looked slightly nervous. "Not at the time," he said at once. "But when he said he was going to look her up again last week, I opened the first one." His mother gasped. "And then I had to open the last one, 'cause of what the first one said."

"What did the first one say, Simon?" Her voice was icy.

"She told him she was pregnant," he said bleakly.

There was a long silence. Josephine stood up.

"I have never been more ashamed of anyone in my entire life," she said coldly. "You realise you may have ruined two people's lives, their whole chance of happiness, with your meddling?" She paused. "So Abi and Gideon have a child?"

Simon shook his head. "No," he said slowly. "In the last letter, she said it died."

Josephine took a deep breath. "I remember some story about Abi way back then. Never did know what it was." She stared at her son. "So she went through that whole tragic time on her own, believing Gideon had left her?"

"Not my fault she didn't get his letters," whined Simon.

"But it was your fault Gideon didn't get hers. If he'd known about the baby, he would've been over here like a shot, if I know him," Josephine said firmly. "Now get out of my house at once. You're no son of mine." She turned her back on him, walked into the kitchen, and closed the door.

\*\*\*\*

"So you'll call me when you reach Gideon's parents' house, then?" Judy asked as she gave Abi a hug at the caravan door. "And let me know what you're planning to do on Monday?"

Abi nodded and grabbed Judy's hand. "Yeah, of course I will. And Judy, thank you. You've been marvellous. I couldn't have got through the last ten years without you."

Judy grinned. "Believe me, you couldn't have got through the previous ten years without me, either," she said with a chuckle. "I've spent my whole life getting you out of scrapes."

Abi laughed and nodded. "Yes, you have. I love you, Judy."

The two friends hugged again briefly, and then with a wave Judy disappeared down the steps and got into her car. Abi closed the door and wandered back into the living area. Gideon was sitting on the floor in front of the fire again, setting up a game of Connect 4.

Abi stared at him. "What are you doing?"

He looked up and grinned. "Got to break the curse of Connect 4," he said. "Come on, sit down."

Abi laughed and sat down cross-legged opposite him.

"Okay, then. Bring it on," she said beaming affectionately at him.

As they played, Abi watched Gideon. He had finally got dressed, in black jeans and a black T-shirt, and was looking dark and moody. His shoulder-length hair was clean and shiny, and the sight of his muscular brown arms reaching out towards the game made her tummy tingle. She dropped her counter in the top of the grid and smiled shyly at him.

"D'you realise," she said, "that last night was the first whole night we've spent together?"

Gideon dropped his counter in on top of hers.

"I win," he said with a self-satisfied smirk. "Yep, I had realised. Fun, wasn't it? Shall we do it again?"

Abi crawled round to the other side of the grid and kissed him on the lips.

"Yes," she said simply. "I think we should. And again…and again…"

She wound her arms around his neck and began gently nibbling his earlobe. His hand came up and brushed lightly across her breast before sliding round and cupping the back of her head. Their lips locked and they both moaned with pleasure as they sank to the floor to consummate their love.

Chapter 24

*Sunday, 27<sup>th</sup> November 2005*

As they sped along the A337 between Brockenhurst and Lymington, Abi glanced anxiously at Gideon.

"Won't your parents mind me coming?" she asked.

He smiled at her. "'Course not. They always liked you, and I think we've established that you're a lot nicer now than you were back then, so—" He broke off as she slapped his arm.

"Gideon! What a thing to say! I've always been nice." She paused. "Well, maybe I'm a bit more laid back these days…"

Gideon chuckled. "I love you," he said simply and flicked the indicator as they approached his parents' turning. "My mother's probably hoping we're going to announce our engagement, and my father will no doubt tease you mercilessly. However, when they discover what we actually have to tell them… I shall be very interested in their reaction."

Abi shivered a little and wrapped her arms around herself. Turning up at the house of someone you'd only met on a couple of occasions eleven years earlier, and announcing to them that you're the mother of their grandchild who is now nearly ten years old, seemed to Abi to be a little stressful, so she was dearly hoping that

Gideon would do all the talking. She was also hoping he was correct in his assumption that they liked her. She looked over at him.

"By the way," she asked with a frown, "how come the press never tracked you to your parents' house?"

Gideon shrugged. "Oh, Dad's got connections."

Abi looked puzzled. "What sort of connections?"

"Government, MI5," he said, as they bumped over a cattle grid.

"MI5?" gasped Abi. "Your father's a spy?"

"Not exactly. That's more MI6," he said. "MI5 is just internal security. They made sure Mum and Dad can live here without being bothered. Pretty useful, really."

Abi stared at him. "How on earth did he get into that?"

"Got recruited at Oxford, I think. He's worked for them on and off for years. Never really able to talk much about it, though… In fact, I'll probably have to kill you, now I've told you." He grinned again. "Here we are. This is it." He slowed down on the long gravel drive that led up to the front of the house.

Abi began to feel even more nervous. She was suddenly very aware of the differences between Gideon's background and her own, and felt extremely vulnerable. Neither of her parents had been to university. In fact, she was the first in her family to stay at school for Sixth Form. She tried to imagine her father having a conversation with Gideon's father, and failed miserably. The car came to a halt in front of the pillared front door, and Gideon switched off the engine. He looked at her and smiled.

"It's okay. They don't bite." Then he opened the

door and jumped out.

Abi followed suit, and they walked up to the front door together. As they approached, the door opened and Caroline stood there smiling at them. She held out her arms.

"Abi, how lovely to see you again," she said and gave the younger woman a peck on each cheek. She turned to Gideon. "So you finally bring my car back! It was most disconcerting to see it on the news." She grinned. "But quite fun, too. Now come on in, and have some tea. Or would you prefer coffee, Abi? We've got both."

"Tea would be lovely, thank you, Mrs. Hawk," said Abi shyly, following her hostess into the large hallway.

Caroline laughed. "Oh, call me Caroline, please," she said. "Mrs. Hawk always makes me feel old."

"You are old," came a voice from a doorway to the left, and Abi looked up to see Gideon's father smiling at them. He advanced and shook Gideon by the hand.

"Good to have you back, son. Glad you managed to escape those bloody media blokes. Would have got some of my friends onto them if you hadn't got away. Good time in Wales?" he asked, leaning forward and shaking Abi's hand as well.

"Yes, thanks, Dad, it was more relaxing, anyway." Gideon gave him a grin. "The escape from Sennen was actually quite fun, though."

Abi gave him a look, and Roger laughed.

"Okay, then, come on in to the drawing room. We've got the fire lit." He led the way into the huge wood-panelled room, where a welcoming log fire was roaring in the grate, a large chocolate Labrador asleep in front of it. "Don't mind Berwick. He thinks he owns the house," Roger said as he stepped over him and took his chair on the other side of the fire.

Abi smiled at the dog. "I love dogs," she admitted. "I've got two at home. Both Rough Collies."

Caroline, entering the room carrying a loaded tray of tea and cake, exclaimed, "Like Lassie! How lovely. They're so pretty. Now do sit down, Abi, and have some cake."

Gideon laughed. "You and your cakes, Mum," he teased. "Which one is it this time?"

"Chocolate fudge cake with Smarties on," she said serenely, smiling over at Gideon as she offered it to Abi. "Just the way you always liked."

Gideon flopped down in the chair opposite his father and sighed.

"This is nice," he said appreciatively. "Better than that gas fire, isn't it, Abi?"

Abi nodded from her perch on the edge of the sofa, balancing her cup of tea and her plate of cake.

"It's lovely," she agreed, wishing she could relax and enjoy it.

Caroline sat down beside her and smiled encouragingly.

"That's right, eat up," she said.

Abi took a bite of chocolate cake. "This is lovely," she managed with a nod.

"It was always Gideon's favourite when he was a little boy," said Caroline conspiratorially. "I'll give you the recipe."

Abi nearly choked on her cake, and Gideon burst out laughing.

"Mum, that's not really putting her at ease, now, is it? Talk about pressure!"

Caroline raised her eyebrows at him. "Well, we're still waiting to hear your 'shocking' news," she said.

Gideon glanced at Abi. She nodded to him.

"Well, firstly," he began, looking at his mother, "Abi and I have decided to try to resurrect our relationship. We discovered we both never stopped loving each other—sorry about the grammar—and although certain people were obviously trying to keep us apart—I'll explain who later—we're really glad to have found each other again and are going to give it another go." He smiled when he saw Caroline's delighted face, but raised his hand to prevent her from speaking. "There's more, Mum. You might want to hang on a minute." He reached out, took Abi's hand in his, and gave it a big squeeze. "This next part may sound a little strange, unbelievable, and hard to take in, but…when I left to go on tour back in '95, Abi was…expecting a baby…" He paused as he heard his mother gasp, and his father shifted in his chair. "She wrote to tell me, but I never received her letter, or the subsequent ones, and she never received any of mine. Consequently she thought I'd abandoned her because of the baby." He stopped for a moment as his mother reached out and took Abi's other hand.

"Abi, darling," she said. "You have a child?"

Abi looked at Gideon for help. He turned to his mother.

"Hang on, Mum, long story here. She went ahead with the pregnancy and planned to keep the baby, all the time hoping I'd write to her." He paused again and took a deep breath. "Then when the baby was born, Abi was told it had died."

Roger looked up and frowned. "*Was told* it had

died?" he repeated. "And that means…?"

Gideon nodded. "Yes, she was told it had died and has spent the last ten years believing that. Until Friday, the day before yesterday, when we discovered our little girl is still alive, and living in a children's home in Kent."

"Oh, Gideon," whispered Caroline, her hand over her mouth. "Oh, my poor things." She reached over and put her arm around Abi's shoulders. "You went through all that, believing you'd lost a child. Whoever is to blame for that must be…" She didn't know quite how to finish.

Abi cleared her throat. "It was my mother," she said distinctly. "The same person who hid Gideon's letters from me." Caroline stared at her in disbelief. "My mother wanted me to have the baby adopted, but I wouldn't agree, so apparently she hatched a plan to tell me she'd died, then forged my signature on some documents." She stopped for a moment and moistened her lips. "The really odd thing is, though…she'd been visiting our daughter over the years."

Roger leant forward towards Gideon. "What are you going to do now?" he asked with a frown.

"Hopefully, tomorrow we're going to go and find her," replied Gideon simply.

Caroline squeezed Abi's hand. "You poor thing," she said again. "What a dreadful experience! Gideon's right, it is almost unbelievable. You must go and find her immediately. Do you know she's still there?" she added, a worried look on her face.

Abi nodded. "It looks that way, from the letters we found. It really was a great shock. I still can't get my head around it."

Caroline smiled sympathetically. "I'm sure you can't," she agreed. "But how could your mother have behaved like that? To let a child—please excuse me, but you really were very young—think her baby has died... That's truly unforgivable." She shook her head sadly. "I hope you don't mind me saying that, but I know you didn't get on well with your mother, did you?"

Abi gave a short laugh. "That's an understatement," she said with a slight smile. "I left home as soon as I finished my A levels. I never saw her again until I went to her funeral last week. That was when all this started." She paused and took a deep breath. "I found the letters and realised Gideon hadn't abandoned me after all, and I also realised from reading them that he'd never received mine." She glanced over at Gideon. "We believe that Simon hid my letters to Gideon."

Caroline gasped. "Simon Dean?" she said in amazement. "Oh, Gideon, and he's supposed to be your friend. What was he thinking?"

Roger snorted. "He never liked Gideon to have a girlfriend. I always wondered if he wanted him for himself."

Caroline looked shocked. "Roger! Really! Surely not," she said doubtfully.

Gideon grinned. "You might think so," he said, "but no, Simon likes girls. He just has this thing about girlfriends and bands not going together."

His father nodded sagely. "Ah yes, I've heard of that syndrome," he said.

Caroline turned to Abi, a gleam in her eye. "So, what's she called?" she asked curiously.

Abi smiled shyly. "Natasha," she said.

Caroline nodded. "That's nice," she said. "Is it the name you chose?"

"Yes," said Abi. "Apparently my mother registered her, and used the names I picked."

"Names?" queried Caroline.

Gideon laughed. "Go on, tell her the middle name," he said.

Abi's hair fell over her face. "Storm," she muttered quietly.

"Storm?" echoed Caroline. "That's…unusual. Why Storm, dear?"

Abi blushed even more, so Gideon said, "Storm was really meant to be the baby's name if it was a boy, called after "Storm Rising," that track on my first album. But her mother just used both names."

Roger shrugged. "Well, nice to have an interesting name," he said, starting to get up. "Anyone want a proper drink? I know I could do with one." He walked over to the drinks cabinet and looked enquiringly round.

While Roger got them all drinks, Caroline pressed more cake onto Abi. She smiled at her again.

"So we have a new grandchild," she said with satisfaction, "and in this country." At Abi's inquisitive look, she explained, "Gideon's older sister Penny—I don't know if you remember her—is married, with three children, but she lives in New Zealand, and we don't get to see them very often. I do hope this works out for you," she continued, patting Abi's hand. "You and Gideon make a lovely couple."

Abi smiled shyly at her. "I was worried that you might think badly of me," she said. "I had a baby at sixteen, and my mother turned out to be truly evil. Not really the sort of person you'd want your son associated with, I would think."

Caroline shook her head. "I judge people on how I find them, not the mistakes they've made, and certainly not by their relatives," she said firmly. "I liked you ten years ago, Abi, and I still like you now. If you make my son happy, then you make me happy."

Abi blushed again and thanked her before accepting a glass of dry sherry from Roger.

"I'd like to make a toast," Roger said, raising his glass. "To Abi and Gideon and Natasha, and may they all be reunited soon." The others solemnly raised their glasses, and Abi and Gideon exchanged glances. He winked at her, and she gave a little smile in return. "And do you have a plan for tomorrow?" added Roger practically. "Are you going to call them first?"

Gideon shook his head. "No, we've decided we're just going to go directly to the children's home and take the letters we found in the box, along with Natasha's birth certificate. And some ID of our own, of course, and then see where we get."

Roger nodded. "Well, if you need any help, I have contacts in most government departments," he said. "I'm sure someone can be of assistance, maybe speed things up a bit... There's bound to be a lot of paperwork."

Gideon smiled. "Thanks, Dad, we'll bear that in mind." He squeezed Abi's hand again.

Caroline stood up. "I think I'd better go and check on dinner," she said. "I rather forgot about it. You children bring your things in and get settled. We'll eat in about an hour." She disappeared off towards the kitchen. Suddenly her head reappeared in the doorway. "I've put Abi in the blue guest room," she said. "Hope that's okay?"

Abi nodded. "Thank you. I'm sure it's fine," she assured her hostess and then followed Gideon back out to the car. They emptied the boot in silence, neither daring to look at the other, until Gideon started to chuckle.

"If only she knew!" he said, grinning down at Abi.

Abi frowned at him. "Of course she knows, Gideon," she said reprovingly. "But she wouldn't want to assume. We've only just got back together, after all. I shall manage fine in the guest room. I'm sure you know where it is?" she added, giving him a coquettish look.

He raised his eyebrows at her and handed her a couple of bags.

"Here, make yourself useful and take these in. Top of the stairs, turn left, first door. That's my room. I'll follow and show you to yours," and he continued to heft more luggage out of the car.

Abi went back into the house and started up the wide staircase that led out of the hallway. At the top she followed Gideon's instructions and found herself in a high-ceilinged, almost square room with a large sash window overlooking the forest. There was nothing in it to indicate the room belonged to Gideon, with the possible exception of a large, rather old teddy bear sitting on the bed, but Abi remembered his parents had not actually moved to the house until after he'd gone to America.

She walked over to the window and stared out onto the open expanse of forest, and the grazing ponies in the foreground. The light was beginning to fade, and everything was visible only in shades of grey. She rested her forehead against the cold glass and sighed. Gideon's parents had been so nice about everything. Maybe they really did like her. She heard Gideon enter the room behind her, and turned to face him. He heaved the bags onto the bed and came to join her, putting his arms around her and holding her close, burying his face in her hair.

"Mmmm, your hair smells nice," he murmured. Abi snuggled closer into him and smiled to herself. "Tell you what," Gideon went on, "I could really do with a fag. Fancy a walk? Dad doesn't smoke any more, so I'm trying not to smoke in the house."

Abi pulled back and looked up at him. "Okay," she said with a smile. "We can go and see the horses."

"Ponies," corrected Gideon absently, hunting through his pockets for his cigarettes and lighter.

Abi chuckled, and followed him out of the room and back down the stairs.

"I couldn't really share your room," she said. "You have a single bed."

Gideon grinned at her over his shoulder.

"Same bed I had in Newbury," he said. "It worked okay then, if you remember."

Abi felt herself starting to blush and let her hair fall over her face again. The memory of the evening of her sixteenth birthday would be with her forever. By her calculations, that was the day they had conceived Natasha, although how it had happened she was still not sure. They had used protection. Gideon had made sure of that. Abi frowned and touched Gideon on the arm. He turned as they reached the bottom of the stairs.

"What?" he asked, picking up his jacket from the

coat stand and shrugging it on. Abi retrieved her jacket but continued to look at him.

"Gid, how did we get pregnant?" she asked. "We used protection each time. And there weren't many times anyway. By my reckoning, we must have conceived her the very first time. But we used a condom."

Gideon nodded and, taking her hand, led the way out of the house and down the drive.

"Yeah, I was concerned about that," he said slowly, as they approached the road. "The only thing I can think is that we used an out-of-date condom that first time."

Abi looked at him in surprise. "Out-of-date?" she echoed. "I didn't know they could be. Wouldn't you have to have it for a very long time for that to happen?"

Gideon looked embarrassed. "Yeah, probably," he admitted and then went silent.

Abi waited for a moment. "Gideon?" she asked, the hint of a laugh in her voice. "How long had you had that condom?" The silence stretched on, and Abi squeezed his hand.

Finally, "About four years," he muttered, almost inaudibly.

"Four years?" Abi stopped walking and gaped at him. "You had a condom for four years and didn't use it?"

Gideon glanced sideways at her. "I got it when I was fourteen," he said. "Just in case. Simon bought a packet and gave one to me."

Abi grinned in the fading light. "Okay," she said. "I get that. I think a lot of boys do that. But why did you still have it?" He was silent again, and Abi peered at him. "Gideon, was it your first time too?" she asked in surprise.

He looked at her and nodded. "Yes," he said. "I didn't tell you 'cause you thought I was experienced, and I kinda liked that you thought that. But yes, you were my first."

Abi stared at him in the gathering gloom and then suddenly stood on tiptoe and reached up to kiss him. She put her arms around his neck.

"I'm so glad," she said simply. "But I wish I'd known. All these years I thought you'd done it with Angela McCauley in Sixth Form." She glanced up at him. "That was the rumour. Maybe she started it."

Gideon shrugged. "May have done. She wanted to, certainly, but I did have some standards," he said with a grin. "She did do it with Simon."

Abi gasped. "Really? Wow, she wanted you but settled for Simon." She giggled. "So he was having your castoffs even back then? No wonder he resented you." She looked away from him and watched the silhouette of a pony on the skyline. "But you did have girlfriends when you were on tour, didn't you?" she asked eventually.

"Yes, I did. A long time after I stopped writing to you, though. I was so angry for a while that I nearly followed Simon's lead and slept with anyone who asked me, but I resisted, and it was well over a year before I started a relationship." He stopped to catch her hand and pull her closer to him. "But it never felt right. There were several girls, over the years, but none of them felt right. None of them was you." He stared off into the darkness. "I don't think I treated them very well. I was still angry and hurt, and I resented them. I'm not proud of that time of my life." He put his arm around her and held her tight. "What about you? Was there anyone else?"

Abi sighed. "Unfortunately, yes," she said sadly. "After the baby was born, I was just too heartbroken to think of anything else, and I still wanted you, but when I went away to college I…well, I suppose I went a bit wild for a while. I was rebelling against everything and everyone, and especially you," she said with a short laugh. "I thought you'd abandoned me, and I was determined to show the world I didn't care, that I didn't need you… It didn't work. I just ended up hating myself, and missing you even more. So, when I finished college, I moved to Cornwall and have lived a single life ever since." She grinned in the dark, and he caught a flash of white teeth. "Until now, that is."

Chapter 25

*Monday, 28th November 2005*

Monday morning dawned wet and miserable, and as Gideon and Abi joined the heavy traffic on the M25 their moods reflected the weather. They had set off for Kent straight after breakfast and had barely spoken for the whole journey. They were both lost in thought and extremely tense about the day ahead of them. They had attempted to discuss their plan of action for when they arrived at the children's home, but neither of them seemed capable of formulating anything remotely sensible. In the end they decided to see what happened when they arrived and take it from there.

As they finally turned off the M25 and headed south towards Tunbridge Wells, Abi glanced at Gideon. He was driving in a very determined manner, both hands on the wheel and a cigarette hanging out of his mouth. Abi calculated he'd smoked at least seven during the two-hour journey—more than she'd seen him smoke in a whole day over the last week. She was even considering having one herself. She tentatively laid her hand on his leg, and he flashed her a quick smile.

"Okay?" he asked, returning his attention to the road.

Abi shrugged. "Not really. Hopefully will be later."

Gideon nodded, opened his window, and threw out his cigarette end.

The Birtwhistle Children's Home was situated about five miles north of Tunbridge Wells—a large Georgian house set in extensive and secluded grounds. It housed a maximum of eight children, and Gideon had discovered from their website that at present there were only six in residence. The closer Abi and Gideon got, the more nervous and edgy they both became. Abi found herself picking at the stitching on the cuff of her jacket, and by the time they turned off the road and through the gates to the home, she was trailing a very long piece of thread. She snapped it off in annoyance and flipped down the sun visor to look in the mirror. Her very pale face stared back at her, eyes dark rimmed and haunted. The events of the last two weeks had really begun to take their toll on her, and she wished she was feeling better for the possible first meeting with her daughter. Gideon pulled the car up in a small car park a few yards from the main door. He ran a hand through his hair and looked at Abi.

"How do I look?" he asked.

She nodded. "Not bad, a bit harassed, but okay." She thrust her hand into her bag and pulled out a packet of mints. "Have one of these, though. You stink of smoke."

He took one and popped it in his mouth.

"C'mon, then. Let's do this," he said, taking a deep breath and getting out of the car. Abi followed suit, and hand in hand they walked to the main entrance.

The door was securely locked, so Gideon pressed the button on the intercom, and they waited. Eventually a voice crackled out. "Can I help you?"

"Yes, please. We'd like to see the...the person in charge, please," Abi said. The intercom crackled again, and then there was a loud buzz and the door clicked open. Gideon pushed it, and they entered a large, relatively bare entrance hall with a black-and-white vinyl tiled floor. As they closed the door behind them, a woman in jeans and a thick woolly jumper emerged from a door to their right.

"Good morning, I'm Cathy Masters. How can I help you?" She advanced towards them with her hand outstretched and a pleasant smile on her face.

Abi and Gideon shook her hand, and Abi gave a small cough before asking, "Erm...well, are you the person in charge?"

The woman shrugged. "One of them," she said with a chuckle. "I should be able to help you. Would you like to come into my office?" She indicated they should follow her. The room was large, high-ceilinged, and furnished with heavy Victorian office furniture, including the huge leather-topped desk Cathy Masters settled behind while she waved Abi and Gideon onto a green Chesterfield.

Abi glanced at Gideon.

He squeezed her hand and smiled at Cathy, saying, "We believe you have a little girl here...called Natasha Thomson?"

The woman's eyebrows rose. "Yes, we do. You're not here about fostering, are you?"

Gideon hesitated a moment, then shook his head. "No, not really." He paused, unsure how to approach the subject.

Abi interjected. "We believe that she used to get visits from a Joan Thomson?" she said in a rush.

Cathy Masters leant her elbows on the desk and surveyed them closely.

"Yes," she said cautiously, frowning slightly.

Abi caught her breath. "Does…does Natasha know who she was, what their relationship was?" she asked quietly.

Cathy shook her head. "No. Mrs. Thomson asked that she shouldn't be told…" She paused and got to her feet. "I'm sorry, but I'm not sure I should be talking about this to you. May I ask what business it is of yours? Did you know Mrs. Thomson?"

There was a long silence, then Abi whispered, "Joan Thomson was my mother."

Cathy sat down again, her face showing a sudden understanding.

"Then you're Natasha's mother?" she said with a sigh. She glanced at Gideon. "And father?" He nodded. "Your mother wrote to me when she was dying," Cathy went on. "She said you might arrive, and that we were not to allow Natasha to be fostered or adopted until you did. We couldn't agree to that indefinitely, but although it was a very unusual request, the trustees insisted we were to wait for a year before re-assessing the situation." She looked from one to the other of them. "That was last July."

Gideon nodded and produced the pile of documents.

"Yes, we have a copy of your letter here. It was given to Abi after her mother died, along with other letters from you to Mrs. Thomson, and a copy of Natasha's birth certificate." He held them out to Cathy.

She took them from him and scanned quickly through them. Then she glanced up at Abi and Gideon over the top of her glasses.

"And do you have any identification for yourselves?" she asked. They both produced their passports and handed them over. "These seem to be in order," she said, handing them back. "Now what exactly is the situation? I understood you had Natasha when you were very young, too young to look after a child, and that you both agreed for her to go into care but not to be adopted." She frowned at Abi. "To be honest, I don't think that was necessarily in the best interests of your child."

Abi's eyes filled with tears, and she would have jumped to her feet to protest had Gideon not put a restraining hand on her arm.

"No!" She was almost shouting. "It wasn't like that at all. I thought she was dead!" She paused as she registered the shock in Cathy Masters' eyes. "I was told she was dead. I never signed anything. Neither of us did. For nearly ten years I've thought my daughter was dead." Tears poured down her cheeks, and Gideon slipped his arm around her shoulders and pulled her close.

He looked at Cathy and continued the story. "For some reason of her own, Abigail's mother decided it would be better for her if she thought her baby was dead. She knew that Abi would never agree to give her up, so she did it the only way she thought possible. What we don't understand is why she didn't forge Abi's signature on the adoption papers, as well, and why she continued to visit Natasha."

Cathy Masters sat back in her seat and shook her head in amazement.

"I'm finding this all rather hard to take in," she

admitted. "For nearly ten years we've been caring for Natasha in good faith, and all the time she was being kept from a mother who wanted her."

Abi nodded vigorously at this, wiping her eyes with a tissue.

Cathy continued, "In her last letter, your mother said that if you did come to find Natasha, we were to allow you access to her and allow you to take her away if it was what Natasha herself wanted. I realise that in all probability we haven't now, and never did have, any legal control over her at all, but since Natasha has lived here almost all her life, I would ask that you respect her wishes."

Gideon nodded. "Of course," he said at once, glancing at Abi, who sniffed loudly but reluctantly nodded her head.

Cathy Masters got to her feet. "Obviously Natasha is at school just now, but would you like to see around the home? See where your daughter has been living?"

Abi got to her feet with alacrity. "Yes, please," she said, blowing her nose again. "That would be lovely."

They followed Cathy out of the office and through another door marked Private. This led into a large living room with huge floor-to-ceiling windows that looked out over the well landscaped grounds. Gideon looked around appreciatively.

"This looks very nice," he commented. "I'm sure the children are very happy here."

Cathy flashed him a smile. "We do our best," she said. "Of course, nothing compares with a proper home environment, but for some of our children that's just not possible, and they're much better off here."

She led the way through the large room and into a

series of smaller rooms, each dedicated to some activity or other. A small smile began on Abi's face as she saw the art facilities, and Gideon nudged her when they passed through the music room.

"Where does she go to school?" Abi asked.

"There's a nice primary school in the village, about a mile away," Cathy replied. "Then the older ones go into Tunbridge on the bus for the senior school. Natasha's in Year 5. She's a bright child," she added, smiling at them both. She led them along a corridor and then up a long flight of stairs. "All the bedrooms are on this floor," she explained. "Luckily, we're small enough to be able to give each child his or her own room. Would Natasha be able to have her own room if she decided to live with you?"

Abi's mind flew to her tiny cottage and she had a moment of panic. There was barely room for her, let alone Gideon and Natasha. She turned wide eyes to Gideon. He nodded to Cathy.

"Oh, yes," he said smoothly. "That's no problem. We have a very small cottage at present but are in the process of buying a much larger family home," and he smiled engagingly at her. As they followed Cathy along the corridor, Abi stared at Gideon and raised her eyebrows. He grinned at her and squeezed her hand.

Cathy had stopped outside a red door with the name Natasha painted on it in yellow and blue, surrounded by stars and moons. She laughed and explained, "We let the children decorate their own rooms as far as is practical. Natasha's very artistic."

Abi glanced at Gideon and grinned. As they followed Cathy into the bedroom, he asked, "And is she musical at all? Does she play an instrument?"

Cathy raised one shoulder in a shrug. "Well, she plays the recorder," she said doubtfully, "but other than that she's not shown much interest in learning anything else." She turned to look at Gideon more closely. "I thought you looked familiar," she said suddenly, with a smile. "You were all over the papers last week. I remember now. One of our older girls is rather fond of your band—NightHawk, isn't it?"

Gideon smiled and nodded. "Yes. Sorry, maybe we should have said. We've spent the last week trying to avoid the press."

Cathy nodded. "I saw on the news. You seemed to be besieged at some cottage somewhere," she said with a grin.

"That was my cottage," said Abi. "It's a very long story, but we've been parted since before Natasha was born, and have only found each other again very recently. It's all been very traumatic." She found to her horror that she was about to cry again. She fumbled in her pocket for another tissue and blew her nose hurriedly. Cathy touched her arm sympathetically.

"Don't worry," she said kindly. "I can imagine this is a difficult time. It's not every day you discover you have a child! Now, this is her room. Feel free to look around, but please don't touch anything. She's very protective about all her things and will know if they've been touched."

Abi walked into the middle of the room and stared around her, trying to get some idea of the character of the little girl who inhabited it. The little girl she had given birth to. The little girl who had been kept from her for so long. She caught her breath and struggled to fight down the feeling of panic threatening to engulf her. This was her daughter's room. Yet it was the room of a stranger. She spun round and clutched tightly onto Gideon's arm.

"I can't do this, Gid," she murmured, her voice shaking. "I can't do this. I don't know my own daughter."

Gideon put his arm round her and held her close.

"Yes, you can, Abs. Yes, you can. Look around you." He gently turned her round to face back into the room again. "You don't know her yet. But now you have the chance to get to know her. Can you imagine what fun that'll be? She's part you and part me. What a combination! Let's start by seeing what we can find out about her from her room."

Abi cautiously let her eyes roam around the room. It was medium sized, furnished with a wood-framed single bed, a single wardrobe, and a chest of drawers, both painted in rainbow colours, a white bookcase crammed with books of all shapes and sizes, and a large basket in the corner spilling out with stuffed toys. The walls were covered with posters, mostly of animals—dogs, cats, horses, and—rather strangely—rats.

Abi slowly let go of Gideon to walk over to the bed and gaze down on it, trying to imagine her daughter asleep in it. The quilt was patterned with a geometric design in red, yellow, and green, and sitting on the pillow was a small grey stuffed rabbit with one very bedraggled ear. Abi caught her breath and stretched out her hand to pick it up.

"No touching, remember." Gideon's quiet voice behind her made her jump, and she withdrew her hand. She turned and looked up at him.

"The rabbit…" she managed. "I bought that rabbit

to give her when she was born. It disappeared in the clinic. I always wondered what happened to it."

Cathy Masters overheard the exchange and stepped forward.

"That was the only toy that arrived with Natasha when she came to us," she said gently. "It was in her carrycot, and she's remained very attached to it. As you can see, she used to suck its ear when she went to sleep."

Abi stared at the little rabbit, and her mind whirled as she tried to visualise her mother placing it in the carrycot with Natasha. Her eyes filled with tears again, and angrily she turned away and walked over to the window. Behind her she could hear Gideon questioning Cathy on one or two trivial matters, and she mentally blocked her ears and stared out into the garden. A watery sun was attempting to break through the clouds, and a trickle of water was running off the roof and dripping down onto the windowsill outside the bedroom window. Abi wrapped her arms around her body and sniffed. She had never been reduced to tears so much in her life—except of course back when Natasha had been born—and she was finding it very disconcerting. She heard someone say her name and turned round.

"Abi? Shall we go for a bit and come back when she gets back from school?" Gideon was asking her. She nodded and went slowly to join him.

"What time is that?" she asked Cathy, trying to make her voice as normal as possible.

"She gets home about four, and then the younger ones have tea at five. It would probably be best if you came after that. Her bedtime's not until seven thirty. Maybe come around five forty-five?" Cathy suggested.

"I would recommend you don't tell her who you are at first. Just spend this visit getting to know her a bit. Try to gain her confidence."

Gideon frowned. "You think that'll be hard?" he asked, glancing at Abi as he spoke.

Cathy hesitated for a moment. "She's…she's very strong willed," she said at last. "Knows her own mind. She won't be fooled by any nonsense. And she'll let you know if she likes you or not. Don't get put off," she added kindly, seeing their faces. "I'm sure it'll go all right. Now how about you go and get some lunch, and we'll see you back here later?" She ushered them out of the bedroom and back downstairs to the entrance hall. "I'll have her ready to meet you by a quarter to six," she promised as she showed them out, and with a cheerful wave watched them walk across the gravel path towards the car park.

They sat in the car in silence for a few minutes, neither of them knowing quite where to start. Eventually Gideon glanced at Abi and reached out to squeeze her hand. She looked up at him solemnly.

"Gideon, she's real," was all she said. He leaned over and took her in his arms, burying his face in her hair and deeply breathing in her scent. She returned his embrace, clinging tightly to him, her eyes screwed shut.

"I know," he murmured softly. "She really is." He gently released her and tilted her face up to his. "And in a few hours she'll be even realer!" he said with a crooked smile.

Abi sniffed and scrubbed at her eyes with a tissue.

"This is so weird," she said with a shake of her head. "Let's go and be normal for a bit." She fastened her seatbelt and looked expectantly at Gideon. He grinned at her, then started the engine and drove slowly down the drive back onto the road.

"Where to, madam?" he asked, glancing over at her.

Abi considered. "A nice country pub for lunch," she decided. "But nowhere you'll be recognised."

Gideon raised an eyebrow at her. "Can't guarantee that," he said. "It happens all the time. We'll give it a go, somewhere out in the country in November should be okay."

He turned out onto the main road, and they drove around for about half an hour before discovering, on the edge of a nearby village, a secluded pub advertising a special deal on lunches.

"This looks okay," said Abi, peering out of the window. "They've got a fire—I can see the chimney smoking."

Gideon parked in the empty car park, and the two of them made their way into the dimly lit pub. They ordered their food and drinks, then retired to a cosy corner just to the left of the roaring fire. Abi leaned forward and warmed her hands. Gideon grinned at her.

"Your hands are always cold," he said. "I remember warming them up on our very first date."

"Cold hands, warm heart," she replied serenely.

Gideon leaned back in his seat and sighed. "What a morning," he said. "And what an afternoon to come." He looked around appreciatively. "This is really quite nice, isn't it. D'you think they do bed and breakfast?"

Abi glanced over at him. "You think we should stay here?"

Gideon nodded. "We don't want to drive back tonight, do we? I'm sure we'll want to see Natasha again tomorrow. This is nice and warm, and nearly empty. Hopefully no one'll recognise me." He got to his feet and wandered over to the bar. A short conversation later, he returned to their table with a grin on his face.

"Turns out they have recognised me," he said, slightly smug, "but have agreed not to spread it about. I've booked their best room for the next two nights."

Abi frowned. "How much is it? These places can be very expensive, you know."

Gideon stared at her. "Abi," he said with a smile, "I'm loaded. Please stop worrying about money." Abi felt herself flush, and she let her hair fall over her face. Gideon laughed and sat down next to her. "Love you, Abs," he said affectionately. "Now let's have a nice relaxing lunch and then find some way to spend the afternoon until half five. Think we can?" he asked with a twinkle in his eye.

Chapter 26

*2005*

Half past five found Abi and Gideon speeding back along the road towards the Birtwhistle Children's Home, both lost in thought about the ordeal to come. They turned in through the gates at exactly five forty, and Gideon parked in the same place as last time, taking great care to make sure the car was straight. Abi sat patiently while he manoeuvred backwards and forwards, and eventually she put her hand on his arm.

"It's fine, Gid, let's get out now," she said gently, with a smile.

He grinned. "Sorry, just putting it off…" They got out of the car together, and Abi held his hand as they made their way up to the front door again. Cathy let them in at the first buzz on the intercom and welcomed them with a conspiratorial smile.

"Hello again," she said. "Natasha's in the games room. You come with me to the small living room, and I'll go and fetch her."

She opened another door marked Private and ushered them in. The small living room was actually fairly large, and furnished in a friendly and comfortable way, obviously designed to put people at their ease. Gideon walked to the fireplace and squatted down to warm his hands, while Abi perched on the edge of a large blue armchair. The silence in the room was broken only by the crackling of the fire, and when the door suddenly opened, they both jumped. Cathy appeared, ushering a small girl in front of her.

"Here she is," she said brightly. "This is Natasha. Tasha, these are the people who wanted to meet you, Abigail and Gideon. I'll leave you to get acquainted, if that's okay with you?" Natasha nodded solemnly. "And I'll just be in the next room, if you need me. I'll leave the door open."

She gently pushed the child further into the room, then slipped through a door opposite the fireplace, leaving it ajar. Gideon and Abi stood up and smiled at the child. She stared at them, then went to the fireplace and sat down on the hearth rug. She stared into the flames for a moment.

"We're not allowed fires in our rooms," she said without turning round.

Abi couldn't take her eyes off her. This was the child she'd been mourning for nearly ten years. This skinny little girl with curly shoulder-length dark brown hair and her father's piercing blue eyes. This beautiful child, dressed in jeans and a jumper, who had turned around and was now staring at them with a very guarded expression in her eyes. Abi sat down again.

"Hello, Natasha," she said with a smile. "I'm Abi, and this is Gideon."

Natasha stared at her. "I know. Aunty Cathy said." She said it with a scornful look. "Why're you here? You don't want to foster me, do you?"

Gideon sat down on the floor opposite Natasha and shook his head. "No, we don't want to foster you."

Natasha nodded. "Good. You wouldn't like it," she

said flatly. "I'm difficult."

Abi exchanged a brief look with Gideon, then joined the other two on the floor. She sat cross-legged and grinned at Natasha. "Why are you difficult?"

Natasha looked at her doubtfully. "Dunno. Just am," she said shortly, picking up the poker and jabbing at a log with it.

Gently Gideon relieved her of the poker. "Don't think we want to set the house on fire, do we?" he said with a chuckle. "Have you been fostered before, then? Didn't you like it?"

Natasha considered. "I've been fostered twice," she said slowly. "They were stupid people. They didn't get me. They said I was difficult." She scowled. "I could show them what difficult is, if I really wanted to."

Abi bit her lip, and let her hair fall over her face. She didn't doubt that this child could be difficult if she wanted to be, and realised this was not going to be an easy ride. She flicked her hair back and looked up to see Gideon smiling at her.

He turned to Natasha again. "D'you like it here?" he asked.

The child shrugged. "S'okay," she said dismissively. "It's my home." Suddenly she got to her feet and began to wander around the room, inspecting the decorations. She stopped in front of a painting of a horse and studied it, her head on one side. "That's all out of proportion," she said, shaking her curly head. "I could do it better." Then she continued around the room, touching each object that she looked at. Eventually she bounced onto the sofa and stared at them. "You're still here," she said.

Gideon looked at her with a frown.

"Of course we're still here," he said. "We've come to see you. We'd like to get to know you."

Natasha continued to bounce on the sofa. "Why?" she asked, breathlessly.

Abi glanced at Gideon helplessly, then she looked at Natasha.

"You like painting?" she asked, indicating the horse picture the child had objected to.

Natasha shook her head and stopped bouncing. "I like drawing," she corrected. "I'm very good."

Abi smiled. "What do you like to draw?"

"Animals, of course," said Natasha, doing a roly-poly on the sofa.

Gideon took a deep breath. "Abi can draw," he said to her. "She's an artist."

Natasha sat up and looked suspiciously at Abi.

"Are you any good?" she asked, raising her eyebrows.

Abi fixed her stare. "Of course I am," she said with confidence. "I like drawing people best. And I paint landscapes, too. Can we see some of your drawings?"

Natasha narrowed her eyes. "Maybe," she said cautiously. "They're in my room."

They were all silent for a moment, and then Gideon asked, "D'you like music?"

Natasha considered the question.

"Some," she said at last. "If I can dance to it. Some of the modern stuff is rubbish, though. That's what Nan used to say."

Abi glanced at Gideon. "Who's Nan?" she asked quietly.

Natasha bent forward and her curls swung over her face.

"No one," she said flatly.

"Is she one of the other girls here?" persisted Abi gently.

Natasha shook her head. "No, she's no one." She looked up at Abi. "She's dead."

Abi swallowed nervously, not wanting to let it go.

"Did she used to visit you?" she asked at last.

Natasha looked at her with a frown. "Yes. How d'you know?" she asked suspiciously.

Gideon smiled at her. "Cathy told us you used to get visits from an older lady. Was that Nan?"

Natasha jumped up again. "You ask a lot of questions," she said crossly. "D'you want to see my drawings or not?"

Abi nodded and got to her feet.

"Are we allowed to go to your room?" she asked as Natasha headed for the door.

The little girl stopped with her hand on the doorknob and called over her shoulder. "Aunty Cathy! I'm taking them to my room to see my pictures," and then she pulled the door open and skipped out ahead of them. Cathy appeared at the other doorway and raised her eyebrows at them.

"Have fun," she said. "And good luck. I'll follow you up there in a minute, in case you need me."

Abi and Gideon hurried out into the hallway and managed to catch up with Natasha just as she was getting to the top of the stairs.

"Come *on*," she chided. "My room's up here." She ran along the corridor and pushed open the door. Abi and Gideon followed her in and watched as she pulled a box out from under her bed and produced a large sketch pad. She laid it on the floor and opened it to the first page. She looked up at Abi and patted the floor beside her.

"Sit down," she invited impatiently. "Are these better than yours?"

Abi sat down beside her, and Gideon hovered behind them. The book was filled with pencil drawings of animals. Horses, dogs, rabbits, even tigers, and they were all extremely good. Abi reached out and flicked carefully through the pages.

"These are brilliant, Natasha," she said admiringly. "Do you do them from real life, or from photos?"

Natasha pointed to the first picture, of a shire horse.

"That was a photo," she said, " but this one"—she thumbed through the book until she found the one she wanted—"this one I drew from the actual animal," and she pointed to a very neatly drawn portrait of a Rough Collie.

Abi caught her breath. "That's wonderful," she said, her eyes shining. "D'you like Rough Collies? I've got two at home."

Natasha nodded. "I like all dogs," she said. "I'd love to have one, but we're not allowed to, here." She pouted slightly, then perked up a bit. "I've got a rat, though. Would you like to see her?"

She jumped to her feet again and ran to the end of her bed. She beckoned them over, and for the first time they noticed the cage hidden in the corner of the room. It housed a large brown rat, who stared at them balefully. Gideon bent down and had a closer look.

"She's lovely," he said politely.

Natasha giggled for the first time. "She's a rat," she said. "She's not s'posed to be lovely. Most people are scared of her."

Abi was looking around the room. "You've got a lot of teddies," she remarked indicating the basket in the corner.

Natasha nodded. "Yeah. People give them to me. Nan gave me most of them." She walked over and picked up a large stuffed lion from the top of the collection.

"Do you have a favourite?" asked Gideon. Natasha tossed the lion back into the basket and picked up the little grey rabbit with the chewed ear. She held him out.

"This one," she said. "I've had him longest. He's called Thunder."

Abi smiled. "That's an interesting name for a bunny," she said watching Natasha's face.

The little girl shrugged. "It goes with my middle name," she said.

Gideon raised an eyebrow. "And what's that?" he asked, already knowing the answer.

She looked at him under her long lashes. "Storm," she said at last, daring them to laugh.

Abi nodded. "That's a nice name," she said. "It's different. Who wants to be called Alice, or Sally, or Elizabeth, when they can have a cool name like Storm?"

Natasha considered for a moment, then nodded her head.

"I guess," she said at last. "At least it's not too girly."

Gideon saw a toy guitar leaning against the wall and moved over to pick it up. "D'you play the guitar?" he asked casually.

In a flash Natasha had snatched it from him and

replaced it exactly where it had been resting.

"Don't touch my things!" she shouted at him, stamping her foot.

Gideon backed away. "I'm sorry," he said contritely. "I'm sorry. It's just that I play the guitar, and I wondered if you did too."

Natasha scowled at him and sat down on the bed with her arms folded. After a moment she looked up at him.

"No, I don't. Are you in a band?" she asked curiously.

Gideon nodded. "Yes. Well, I was until two weeks ago, anyway."

"Are you famous?" she asked, staring at him. He smiled at her and nodded. "I'm going to be famous one day," she said firmly.

Rather sooner than you might have imagined, thought Gideon to himself as he watched her swinging her legs.

"What's your band called?" she asked, still staring at him.

"NightHawk," he said.

"Why?"

"Why what?" Gideon frowned at her.

"Why's it called NightHawk?" she said patiently. "It's a weird name."

"Well, my surname is Hawk," Gideon explained, "and it just seemed like a good name."

Natasha considered this for a moment, then nodded. "I s'pose so," she conceded. "If my surname was Hawk, my name would be Natasha Storm Hawk. Storm Hawk sounds cool." She said the name several times to see how it sounded.

Abi and Gideon exchanged glances, and Abi sat down on the bed beside Natasha and smiled at her. "D'you like the sea?" she asked.

Natasha nodded. "Yes. They take us to Hastings lots in the summer. I'm a good swimmer," she said proudly.

"I live by the sea," said Abi, "in Cornwall. D'you know where that is?"

Natasha looked at her as if she was mad.

"'Course I do," she said. "It's that thin bit where Land's End is. King Arthur was born in Cornwall." She frowned. "D'you live near Land's End?"

Abi nodded. "Yes, very near. It's very beautiful there. I have a cottage right by the sea. And I have two dogs, too."

Natasha jumped up and began to hop around the room.

"You told me about the dogs already," she said. "Why're you telling me all this stuff, anyway?"

Abi swallowed. "Just being friendly," she said faintly. "Thought you might be interested."

"Nan lived near London," said Natasha suddenly, continuing to hop.

"Was she nice to you?" asked Abi carefully.

"'Course she was," said Natasha in surprise. "Why would she come and visit me if she was going to be nasty? You're weird!" She hopped around Gideon, then collapsed on the floor in a heap. "She used to bring me toys. I think she didn't have much family, 'cause she used to pretend I was her granddaughter. I didn't mind," she said. "That's why I called her Nan. Don't know what her name was, really. Then she died and stopped coming." She looked sad for a moment, then looked from Abi to Gideon and said. "Have you brought me any toys?"

Gideon squatted down beside her. "Not this time, Natasha," he said, "but if you like, we can visit again and bring you something then?"

Natasha considered for a moment, then nodded.

"If you like," she said, nonchalantly picking at a loose thread on her jumper. "Nan used to talk to me about weird stuff," she went on seriously. "I think she was sad about something. Once she said to me that sometimes people do stuff that's wrong, but they can't put it right 'cause it's too late. I think she did something wrong, but she didn't tell me what." She looked up at them with wide eyes. "D'you think she murdered someone?"

Abi forced a smile. "I don't expect so," she said quietly. "There are lots of other bad things people can be sorry about, though. Maybe she upset someone."

Natasha shrugged and rolled onto her back. She stared up at Gideon as he hovered over her.

"Your eyes are like mine," she said suddenly, "really, really blue. I like my eyes." A bell rang in the distance, and Natasha jumped up again. "That's the supper bell," she announced. "I have to go and have my hot chocolate now, before bed." She headed towards the door, then turned and stared at them again. "You can come again…if you like." Then she ran out of the room, and they heard her clattering down the stairs.

Abi stared after her, her head spinning. Gideon sat down on the bed beside her and gave a chuckle.

"Well, and that's our daughter. We're gonna have our hands full with her," he said, putting his arm around Abi's shoulders.

She leaned her head against him and sighed. "Oh, Gid, what d'you think she'll say when we tell her? Should we have told her today?" she said, panicking slightly.

Gideon shook his head. "No, we just needed to let her meet us today. Next time, maybe." He paused and glanced down at her. "Funny about your mother, isn't it? Has she been feeling guilty all this time but couldn't admit what she'd done, d'you s'pose?"

Abi was silent for a moment. "I didn't think she was capable of guilt. I didn't think she had a heart. Maybe she did." She stood up and held out her hand to Gideon. "Come on. Let's go back to the pub. We can see her again tomorrow. I want to phone Judy and tell her how it went." She looked at him anxiously. "It went well, didn't it? D'you think it did?"

Gideon stood up and took her hand. "Yes it did," he said quietly. "Stop worrying."

They left the room, carefully shutting the door behind them, and made their way back down to the entrance hall. Half way down the stairs, they met Cathy Masters coming up to look for them.

"There you are," she said with a smile. "Sorry, Natasha just abandoned you, I believe. She likes supper time. I think she must have liked you—I gather she said you could come again?"

Gideon nodded. "Yes, we thought the same time tomorrow, maybe, if that's all right?"

Cathy nodded. "That's fine. See how it goes, but that may be the time to tell her who you are. Can't leave it too long—and she's a very bright child. She's probably already wondering why you're here." They had reached the bottom of the stairs, and Cathy let them out the front door and waved them off. "See you tomorrow, then, and have a good evening."

\*\*\*\*

Abi was woken the next morning by the sound of her mobile ringing. She reached out and groped around until she found it. She pressed the button and put it to her ear.

"Hello," she said rather groggily.

"Is that Abi?" asked a female voice.

"Yes…yes, it is. Who's this?" She struggled to sit up, and pushed her hair out of her eyes. She peered at her watch; it was seven thirty. Who on earth was calling her at that time?

"It's Cathy Masters," came the voice at the other end.

Abi was instantly alert, and she nudged Gideon with her foot.

"Hello," she said, "is everything all right?"

"Everything's fine," replied Cathy, "but I do have one little problem you may be able to help with."

Abi cleared her throat and kicked Gideon again.

"What is it?"

"Natasha's refusing to go to school until she's seen you and Gideon again," Cathy said. "So I was wondering how you'd feel about coming over now instead of this evening?"

By the time she had finished speaking, Abi was out of bed and pulling the covers off the still sleeping Gideon.

"Of course we will," she said at once. "Give us half an hour, and we'll be there." She disconnected the call and flung her phone onto the bed. "Gideon, Gideon! Wake up! We've got to go and see Natasha."

She ripped off her pyjamas and began searching for clothes. When they'd got back to the pub the previous evening, Abi and Gideon had celebrated the events of the day with a bottle of Champagne, and, in Abi's case, a lot of chocolate, and consequently they were both feeling a little the worse for wear. Gideon sat up and rubbed his eyes.

"What? Why? Now?" he muttered, trying to focus on Abi.

She nodded vigorously. "Yes. Apparently she won't go to school unless she sees us first. Come on!"

Gideon grunted and got out of bed. "I could see she was going to be trouble," he muttered with a grin, as he slipped into the ensuite for a quick wash. By the time he emerged, Abi was fully dressed and attempting to make her hair look acceptable without the use of straighteners.

"Abs, you look fine," said Gideon as he pulled on his jeans. "Natasha isn't going to notice your hair."

Abi looked at him in horror. "That goes to show how little you know about girls," she retorted. "She noticed the colour of your eyes. Of course she notices hair."

Five minutes later, they were in the car and on their way back to the Birtwhistle Home once more. As they drove, Abi speculated about the little girl's actions.

"Why would she want to see us this morning?" she asked. "She didn't seem that keen on us, did she?"

Gideon frowned. "Hmmm…she's a strange one. Difficult to see what she was thinking at all. She's very close with her feelings." He grinned at Abi. "Just be patient. We'll find out in a minute or two."

Abi managed to stay silent for the rest of the

journey, and when they arrived at the home, they found Cathy waiting for them on the doorstep.

"Good morning," she called. "Thank you so much for coming. Natasha's barricaded herself in her room and refuses to come out until she's seen you."

Gideon stared at her. "You don't seem very fazed by this," he remarked.

Cathy grimaced. "You get used to all sorts of behaviour here," she said. "I'm not surprised by anything nowadays. I told you Natasha was strong-willed, didn't I?"

She led the way upstairs to the little girl's room and tapped on the door.

"Tasha, Abi and Gideon are here. Let me in, please." There was silence from the other side of the door. Cathy knocked again, this time more sharply.

"Natasha, open the door, please."

"How do I know they're there?" came a suspicious voice.

Abi stepped forward. "We are here, Natasha. Open the door, please."

There was the sound of boxes and furniture being dragged across the floor, and then the door opened and Natasha stared at them. She was dressed for school in black trousers, a white polo top, and a blue sweatshirt, and her shoulder-length curls were tied up in a ponytail. She stood back to let them in, then closed the door before Cathy could join them.

"I want to be private with them," she said firmly.

Abi and Gideon stood in the middle of the room and waited, wondering how this child could have so much of a hold over them. Natasha indicated that they should sit on the bed, while she stood in front of them

361

with her hands on her hips.

"I need to ask you something," she said, frowning at them. "Why did you come to see me? How d'you know about me?" Abi moistened her lips. How could she find the words to tell this child that she was her mother? Natasha saved her the trouble. Without waiting for them to reply, she went on. "I thought about it last night. *All* night," she said impressively. "And…I think you two might be my mum and dad." She blushed bright red as she said the words, and bent her head forward. Unfortunately, her hair was tied back and nothing happened. Gideon grinned to himself. Natasha turned her back on them. "Well?" she said, after a moment, in a very small voice.

Abi glanced at Gideon, a lump forming in her throat, and they both got to their feet.

"Natasha?" she said, putting her hands on the child's shoulders and turning her round to face them. "You're right. We are."

There was a very long silence while they all three looked at each other. Then Natasha scowled at them.

"Where have you been, then?" she demanded, stamping her foot. "I've wanted a mum and dad for ages. Where *were* you?"

Gideon knelt down in front of her.

"We didn't know about you until last week," he said gently. "If we had, we would have come to find you much, much sooner."

Natasha digested this piece of information, and then looked at Abi, whose eyes were swimming with tears.

"Did you come to get me, then?" she asked. "D'you want me to live with you?"

Abi nodded. "We'd love that, Tasha," she said, tentatively trying out the pet name. "But only if you want to."

Natasha thought for a moment, then looked at Gideon.

"Can I be called Natasha Storm Hawk, then?" she asked.

Gideon smiled at her. "Of course you can," he said, taking her hand and squeezing it. "We'll explain everything to you as we go along. It's a very strange story."

Natasha turned and walked to the other side of the room. She looked all around her for a moment, then back at Abi and Gideon.

"Can I have a nice bedroom?" she asked.

Abi bit her lip. "Well, to start with—"

Gideon interrupted her. "Yes, of course you can. And to make it even more exciting, we're buying a new house, and you can help us choose it." He raised his eyebrows at her. "Would you like that?"

Natasha stared at him, and her face broke into a huge grin.

"I'd like that very much," she said happily.

Epilogue

*Saturday, 10th June 2006*

"So, how're things going then?" asked Judy, leaning back in her deck chair and stretching out her legs to catch the sun. "Tasha looks very settled. Does she like the school?"

They were sitting in the garden of Abi and Gideon's new house, on the top of the cliff overlooking Sennen Cove. They had been very lucky to find exactly the house they wanted in exactly the place they wanted, and had moved in at the end of February. Natasha had been spending weekends with them until they moved and had then joined them permanently, once she was able to have her own bedroom. Abi stretched out on the grass beside her friend.

"She loves it, as much as any child likes school," she said with a grin. "Although I'm not sure she likes having me teaching her art. She actually thinks she's better than me, so she doesn't really pay attention."

Judy laughed, but then her face became more serious. "How about your dad? Any progress there?"

Abi shook her head. "No. I went to talk to him. He did know all about what happened with Natasha, and he says he went along with her plan because he thought Gideon had abandoned me. He said I couldn't have coped with a baby on my own. He claims he didn't know she visited Natasha, but to be honest, I don't know if I can believe him or not. There's still a lot I don't understand. I really can't forgive him, Judy. Not yet, anyway. Maybe never." She stared out to sea, her face inscrutable.

Judy watched her for a moment. "And have you told her about 'Nan'?" she asked. "Told her who she really was?"

Abi turned haunted eyes to her. "How can we? To find out that the one person she thought was her friend had in fact been the person who took her away from her mother and put her in the home? I can't do that. Not now."

A sudden noise behind them made them turn just in time to see Natasha explode out of the french windows and come running over to them.

"Abi, Abi, Chris is here, and he's brought cake!" she cried, running over and turning a cartwheel in front of them. "It's a birthday cake for Gideon, an' it's got candles an' everything." She landed back upright and ran back into the house.

"Still not calling you Mum and Dad, then?" asked Judy, raising her eyebrows.

"No, not yet." Abi paused. "She refuses to until we're married. She's rather judgemental," she added with a grimace.

Judy laughed. "She's just like you, you know," she said. "At least you haven't got long to wait, only two weeks now."

Abi and Gideon were getting married on Midsummer's Day, and they had chosen to have the ceremony at the caravan site in Wales where they'd first learned of Natasha's existence. Abi grinned and held out her left hand, now sporting a large emerald-and-diamond engagement ring. She let it glint in the sunlight, then rolled onto her back and stared up at the clear blue sky.

"Won't it be lovely if the weather's like this," she said, wriggling with pleasure. "I'm so excited, Judy!"

Judy lifted her sunglasses and looked under them to get a better view of Abi.

"Me too," she admitted. "Wasn't it lucky the caravan site have a wedding licence? It's not every one that does, is it? And I love the idea of being a maid of honour at my age! Are you sure Natasha doesn't mind me doing it?"

Abi sat up and shook her head. "No, she's cool about it. Believe me, if she wasn't, you wouldn't be doing it!" She grimaced. "Not that our daughter rules us or anything. She's the flower girl, and gets to lead the dogs, as well." Abi stood up and smoothed her short flowery dress with her hands. "Good job it's only two weeks away," she added casually. "I might not be able to do my dress up if we had to wait any longer."

Judy stared at her. "Abigail Thomson!" she gasped. "Are you pregnant?"

Abi grinned and nodded, but put a finger to her lips.

"Yes, but not a word about it," she said, "if Tasha finds out, she'll give us hell for not waiting until after the wedding. I've only just found out myself. We'll tell her on the honeymoon. Only you, me, and Gideon know, and I'd like to keep it that way until we're married." She sat down on the grass at Judy's feet and caught her friend's hands. "Oh, Judy, it's going to be so different this time! Everything will be perfect."

Judy reached out and gave her a hug.

"You deserve it," she said simply, smiling at her friend. "One thing, though—What are you going to do about Simon? You can't let him get away with what he did, can you?"

Abi shook her head, and pulled away from Judy.

"We don't want to," she said with a frown. "But to be honest, we can't be totally sure that he did hide the letters. We decided not to do anything immediately, 'cause we wanted to concentrate all our energies on bonding with Tasha, so we're going to wait until after the wedding, and then Gideon'll try to contact him." She scowled into the distance. "I'm sure it was him, but Gid says we mustn't go public with it until we can prove it. Said he could sue us, or something…" She shrugged in annoyance.

At that moment, Gideon and Chris came out into the garden carrying a crate of Champagne and a tray of glasses. They put them down on the picnic table, and Gideon called back into the house. "Come on, everyone, drinks are outside."

Judy's husband Robert appeared, closely followed by Roger and Caroline Hawk, who were swinging their newly found granddaughter between them. Judy's two small ones were playing just inside the conservatory, out of the blazing sun.

Abi got to her feet again and ran over to Gideon, reaching up to kiss him on the cheek. Then, taking a bottle of Champagne and a glass, she called, "Let's drink a toast to the birthday boy!"

She expertly popped the cork out, catching the frothing liquid in the glass. She filled the other glasses, and when everyone had one, Abi raised hers towards

Gideon and said, "Happy thirtieth birthday, darling!" and took a sip of Champagne.

The others followed suit, and Judy watched with a grin as Abi surreptitiously emptied the rest of her glass into a large flowerpot.

Gideon raised his glass. "Thanks, guys," he said. "Now I feel really old." He put his arm around Abi and pulled her to him. "And I would like to make a toast, to my lovely wife-to-be and our beautiful daughter." He smiled at them both. "And in two weeks' time, we can do all this again at the wedding!"

Natasha hopped forward, pulled Gideon's arm down, took a quick swig of his Champagne and ran off down the garden laughing.

****

Two weeks later Abi and Gideon stood on the top of a large sand dune and gazed out over the huge sweep of Rhossili Bay and out towards Worm's Head. The bottom of Abi's ivory satin wedding dress was slightly damp and very sandy, and she had abandoned her shoes at the bottom of the sand dune. Gideon had discarded his jacket, and his tie hung untied around the unbuttoned collar of his starched white dress shirt. He put his arm around her and held her close, dropping a light kiss on the top of her flower-entwined hair.

She looked up at him and smiled. "We did it," she whispered. "We finally did it."

A slight puffing sound behind them made them both turn in time to see a dark curly head appear as a little girl in an ivory bridesmaid dress struggled up the sandy path. She was followed by two Rough Collies.

"Here you are!" puffed Natasha, stopping on the top and breathing heavily. "Everyone's looking for you.

We're ready for the cake." She looked at them severely. "Mum, Dad, come now. You're needed." She wriggled between them, took their hands, and the three of them ran back down the sand dune together.

**Watch for the next book in The NightHawk Series,**
***RHYTHM OF DECEIT,***
**soon to be available from The Wild Rose Press, Inc.**
**Here's a sample:**

*Friday 18<sup>th</sup> July, 2008*

"Tasha! Catch Ollie, can you? He's trying to go up the stairs again." Abigail Hawk's hand covered the receiver as she called to her daughter.

In a flurry of flowered skirt and long legs, Natasha shot past her mother and caught her eighteen-month-old brother just as he reached the third step. Grabbing him round the tummy, she swung him up in the air and around to face her. He chuckled his chubby baby laugh and grabbed a handful of her dark curls. Natasha grinned and, tucking him securely under her arm, carried him out into the garden, where she had been helping her father prepare the barbeque. Abi smiled to herself and uncovered the receiver.

"You still there, Judy?" she asked. "…Oh, just Oliver trying to go upstairs again. He's getting far too adventurous." She paused. "Oh, I know they do…You must have had that all the time with your two…I was just wondering if there's any chance you could have the kids for a couple of days next week?" She listened again and grinned. "Oh, thanks, Jude. You're a gem. We're going to London to talk to the record company… Yes, it is about time, isn't it? He's been planning on releasing a solo album for the last year. Maybe it'll finally happen." She listened again and laughed. "Yeah, well, I don't think that'll ever happen, do you? Not after what Simon did. No, I think he'll be going solo from now on. Anyway, see you on Tuesday, if that's okay?…Bye for now."

Abi smiled as she replaced the receiver. Things had been going pretty well for them during the last two years, and she had to admit to being extremely happy. Wandering over to the French windows, she stared out into the garden, where her husband Gideon was attempting to light the barbeque, hindered by the attentions of twelve-year-old Natasha and baby Oliver. She looked fondly at them, marvelling to think that less than three years earlier none of them had been together. She closed her eyes for a moment and gave thanks for the life they now all had, then stepped outside and ran to join them.

Gideon looked round and grimaced at her, his eyes harassed. "This bloody thing just won't light," he muttered, pushing his long dark hair back with a charcoal-blackened hand.

Natasha jumped in front of him. "Can I get the petrol, Dad?" she asked, her blue eyes dancing with mischief.

"No, you can't." Abi laughed, ruffling her daughter's hair. "Remember what happened last time?"

Natasha giggled and danced around the barbeque, blowing at it, trying to help it light. Abi sighed and took the matches out of Gideon's hand.

"Here, let me do it," she said and, leaning forward, rearranged the charcoal and the firelighters, then struck a match and pushed it in amongst them. Within seconds the firelighter caught and the flames began to lick around the charcoal. Abi stood back and surveyed her work with her hands on her hips. "You and fire are not good together, are you, Gid?" she said with a smirk.

"Remember the gas fire in the caravan?"

Gideon reached over and took the matches out of her hand. "I'd warmed it up for you," he said, trying to keep a straight face.

Abi stood on tiptoe and kissed his smutty cheek. "'Course you had," she said, then wandered over to the stone wall that bordered the garden, gazing out over the long sweep of Sennen Cove. She sighed and smiled; life couldn't be better.

****

Simon was hung over again. He lay on his bed with the curtains closed against the strong morning sun. Manhattan in July was far too hot for his liking, and he was beginning to regret not leaving the city the day before, to take up the offer of a bed at the house of a friend in Vermont. He'd spent the last two and a half years travelling around America and making significant inroads into the fortune he'd amassed during his years with NightHawk. Such significant inroads, he'd recently realised, that he'd need to start earning again in the very near future if he was to be able to maintain his current standard of living. Even his fairly substantial royalties from their albums weren't keeping up with his expenditure. His dearest wish was to get the band back together and for everything to be as it had been before Gideon left. Simon formed his hand into a fist and pounded it hard into the bed beside him. He would never forgive Gideon for that. Or, more accurately, he would never forgive Abi. Quite irrationally Simon blamed Abi for the fact that Gideon had left the band so precipitously, even though she'd had no contact with him over the ten years prior to that. That they were now married, had discovered their lost child, and had

3

another baby really rankled with Simon, and he had even managed, in his own mind, to conveniently play down his part in their original separation. The letters from Abi that he'd concealed from Gideon all those years ago still languished in his bag, and he was well aware that by now they would almost certainly know what he'd done. For that reason he appreciated that persuading Gideon to reform NightHawk was a lost cause. Simon realised he would need to launch his solo career or join another band if he were to get his finances back on track.

He knew that Charles Bond, the erstwhile bass player of NightHawk, was in New York with his current band, Velvet Shackles, and he'd arranged to meet up with him later in the day. He was hoping to be able to persuade Charles to form a band with him and then maybe rise to fame riding on the back of the previous success of NightHawk. If he was perfectly honest with himself, Simon realised that NightHawk without Gideon Hawk was a non-starter, but he was determined to get back out there and was relying heavily on the hope that Charles would help him.

With a grunt Simon swung his legs over the side of the bed and stood up. He closed his eyes for a moment until the room stopped spinning, then made his way unsteadily into the shower. The cool water did a fairly good job of waking him up, and ten minutes later he was dried, dressed, and staring at himself in the mirror. The face that looked back at him was not a pretty sight. His curly blond hair was straggly and unkempt, and his ruddy face showed the ravages of time and hard living. He leaned forward and peered more closely at his image. It was hardly the face of a rock star. He was thirty-two, no longer the fresh-faced teenager who'd first arrived in America with NightHawk thirteen years earlier. He found it hard to imagine the groupies thronging around him now. He stood back and looked down at his overweight body. Time to hit the gym and sort himself out. He doubted his ability to survive the rigours of one concert, let alone a whole tour.

With a sigh he turned back to the bed, hastily threw the covers over, picked up his jacket—despite the heat—and room key, and slammed out into the corridor. He was staying in the Western International Hotel on Central Park West, the same hotel the band had been staying in the day Gideon announced his departure in November of '05. It was the first time Simon had returned there since then, and he felt the old resentment again. He rode the elevator down to the first floor and strode out into the stifling heat of a Manhattan summer day. The last time he'd stayed there, he'd been mobbed by reporters and unable to leave his room without being approached. This time no one even registered his departure, and he crossed the busy street and entered Central Park without turning a single head.

Before meeting with Charles, Simon had an appointment with a tour manager the band had used back in their heyday. He was hoping to get some positive response to his idea of starting a new band with Charles.

As he crossed the park, he passed a newsstand and paused briefly to buy one of the English tabloid papers they had on sale. He carried it over to a shady bench and sat down to have a quick read. He grinned to himself when he saw the pictures of the dreadful weather most of Britain was experiencing and decided his decision to remain in the U.S. was a sound one. He flicked over to the next page and froze. A grainy black-and-white photo of Gideon, Abi, and the children arriving at some airport on their way back from holiday jumped out and gave him a mental slap across the face. Gideon was carrying the baby, and Abi had her arm protectively around the older child's shoulders. They all looked happy, healthy, and to Simon's mind smug, and he was tempted to tear the paper to shreds. He resisted and glanced at the caption beneath the photo.

*Former NightHawk guitarist and front man Gideon Hawk and his family arriving home from their holiday in Greece on Wednesday. It's rumoured Hawk is due to start recording a solo album later this month. When asked about the possibility of re-forming the band, Hawk immediately dismissed the idea.*

Simon closed the paper and tossed it into the nearest bin, then got to his feet and set off across the park towards the office of Seth Cotterill, the former tour manager. Simon had had no contact with Seth since shortly after the band split, and he was a little unsure of his reception. As he rode up to the third floor he rehearsed what he was going to say, and when the elevator doors opened he ran a hand through his hair, took a deep breath, and marched up to the door. He tapped sharply and after a moment received permission to enter. Seth Cotterill, a solidly built dark-haired man in his late forties, got to his feet as Simon entered.

"Simon," he said in his East Coast drawl, extending his hand. "Good to see ya. Take a seat." The two men shook hands briefly, and then Simon took the seat opposite Seth's desk and crossed his legs. "What can I do for you, man?" the tour manager asked, narrowing his eyes at Simon's rather dishevelled appearance.

Simon wiped the sweat off his brow with the back of his hand and sat forward in his seat.

"I need to get back into the business, Seth," he said. "I want to get a band going again with Charles Bond. Maybe get another guitarist and follow on from NightHawk. What d'you reckon? Will you help us?"

Seth leaned back in his chair and pursed his lips. "Nice idea, Si," he said, "but NightHawk is nothing without the Hawk."

"It won't *be* NightHawk," interrupted Simon, "but we could ride on the back of our earlier success. Bill us as former NightHawk members. That's gotta stand for something, surely?"

Seth got to his feet and walked over to the window, keeping his back to Simon.

"The thing is, Simon," he began, "no one's interested in you or Charles." Simon flinched. "If you could get Gideon to rejoin you and actually get NightHawk back, then I'd give you all the help you need." He turned round and grinned. "Not that you'd really need any help, if that happened." He saw Simon's face and sighed. "Look, man, you and I both know that Gideon *was* NightHawk. Without him, no one's even going to remember who you and Charles are. Get him on board, and we can talk again." After a pause he continued, "I heard he's about to do some solo work, so he's clearly ready to get back in the saddle. Maybe now's the time to ask him?" Simon was silent, and Seth looked at him inquiringly. "Simon? Is that possible? Or did you two fall out? I never really talked to any of you after the break up."

Simon got to his feet. "Thanks, Seth," he said with a wry grin, "that makes me feel much better." He held up his hand as Seth started to speak. "No, don't worry, not your fault. I'll talk to Charles and see what he thinks. Maybe enough time has passed and we can find a way to get Gideon back. I'll call you." With a wave he left the room, slamming the door behind him.

**She really fancied a night to herself.**

She made a cup of tea, cut herself a slice of cake, carried them both over to the fire, and sat down on the hearth rug. A basket of logs stood to one side of the wood burner, and Abi opened the doors and tossed another log onto the already roaring fire. She gave a little shiver of pleasure. She really liked to be warm. She was going to enjoy the evening.

She leant back against the sofa, extended her legs in front of her, and took a large bite of cake. No sooner had she done that than the doorbell rang. Abi rolled her eyes and tried to swallow her cake.

"Come in, Chris, the door's open!" she called, spraying crumbs in all directions.

After a moment the door slowly opened and a deep voice said, "I'm not Chris. Can I still come in?"

## Praise for Rachael Richey

"A real page turner with sympathetic characters. I liked how the plot was revealed with flashbacks to the past. A good read."

*~Jill Rudge*

~*~

"Storm Rising is an excellent first novel for Rachael Richey, cleverly written and well researched. I loved the suspense and the development of the characters, and I still feel a sense of excitement when I think about the way the plot develops. I was so glad to find there would be sequels, as I can't get enough of this kind of writing."

*~Julie Reeves*

~*~

"I love this! Was hooked from the beginning. I really loved the relationships developing between the characters and the mystery between them, as well. The story is full of brilliant twists and quickly becomes a real page turner."

*~Sophie MacKenzie*

~*~

"Rachael Richey has perfectly captured the vitality, excitement (and awkwardness!) of youth in her novel *STORM RISING*. What initially appears to be a straightforward love story quickly turns into something much more involved. The clever use of flashbacks adds an extra dimension, and there are hints of unfinished business surrounding some of the characters, which is intriguing."

*~Alison Coote*

**A word about the author...**

Rachael Richey writes Women's Fiction. She lives in Cornwall, England, with her husband and children. You can visit Rachael's website at: http://rachaelricheybooks.weebly.com/